PRAISE FOR STEVEN KONKOLY

Wide Awake

"[T]he pacing is brisk and the bloodshed cinematic enough that a first-timer can wolf down this entry without having knowledge of the first two. This sends the series out with a bang."

—*Publishers Weekly*

Coming Dawn

"A deft cat-and-mouse novel that keeps the action moving and the reader guessing."

—*Kirkus Reviews*

Deep Sleep

"Techno-thriller fans will delight in military vet Konkoly's obvious expertise when it comes to the authenticity and intensity of the numerous action sequences."

—*Publishers Weekly*

"A lively, roller-coaster thriller that moves like lightning."

—*Kirkus Reviews*

"Nobody's better at spy craft, action, and intrigue than Steven Konkoly. Thrilling entertainment from the first to the last written word."

—Robert Dugoni, *New York Times* and #1 Amazon bestselling author of *The Eighth Sister*

"Steven Konkoly has blown my mind! *Deep Sleep* is an intelligent, intense, and completely unpredictable high-concept spy thriller. I'm hooked!"

—T.R. Ragan, *New York Times* bestselling author of *Her Last Day*

"Fast paced, suspenseful, and wildly creative. A modern-day masterpiece of spy fiction."

—Andrew Watts, *USA Today* bestselling author of the Firewall Spies series

"A pulse-pounding conspiracy tale in the finest traditions of Vince Flynn and Nelson DeMille . . . *Deep Sleep* is a must-read roller coaster of a thriller."

—Jason Kasper, *USA Today* bestselling author of the Shadow Strike series

"Devin Gray is the hero we need in our corner. Relentless in pursuit of truth, vindication, and saving his homeland, he is the perfect protagonist for Konkoly's newest dive into the techno-thriller world. Again, Konkoly proves his mastery of the genre, drawing from real-rowed events to create a plausible and frightening glimpse into what's happening underneath our feet and behind the walls of power."

—Tom Abrahams, Emmy Award–winning journalist and author of *Sedition*

"Steven Konkoly delivers a conspiracy thriller unlike any other and proves he's at the top of his game. With a deft hand and an eye for plot intricacies, Konkoly will take you into a web of deceit that will shake you to your core and keep you turning until the very last page. The Lost Directorate has set a new bar in the world of thrillers, and Konkoly has taken his seat at the head of the table."

—Brian Shea, *Wall Street Journal* bestselling author of the Boston Crime series and coauthor of the Rachel Hatch series

"A master of action-adventure, Steven Konkoly has done it again, weaving a tale of high-stakes espionage that's ripped from today's international headlines. Plan to stay up very late reading *Deep Sleep*, as he keeps the pages turning!"

—Joseph Reid, bestselling author of the Seth Walker series

"I love a great conspiracy thriller, and Steven Konkoly has conjured one that's utterly chilling with *Deep Sleep*. From the high-stakes setup to the explosive finale, there's barely time to take a breath. Crack this one open and buckle in for one hell of a ride."

—Joe Hart, *Wall Street Journal* bestselling author of the Dominion Trilogy and *Or Else*

Previous Praise for Steven Konkoly

"Explosive action, a breakneck pace, and zippy dialogue."

—*Kirkus Reviews*

"Readers seeking a well-constructed action thriller need look no further."

—*Publishers Weekly*

"If you enjoy action thrillers that have both strong male and female characters, then this may be the series for you."

—*Mystery & Suspense Magazine*

"Exciting action scenes help propel this tale of murderous greed and corruption toward a satisfying conclusion. Readers will look forward to Decker and company's next adventure."

—*Publishers Weekly*

"Steven Konkoly's new Ryan Decker series is a triumph—an action-thriller master class in spy craft, tension, and suspense. An absolute must-read for fans of Tom Clancy, Vince Flynn, and Brad Thor."

—Blake Crouch, *New York Times* bestselling author

A TRUE KILL

OTHER TITLES BY STEVEN KONKOLY

Garrett Mann Series

A Clean Kill

A Hired Kill

Devin Gray Series

Deep Sleep

Coming Dawn

Wide Awake

Ryan Decker Series

The Rescue

The Raid

The Mountain

Skystorm

The Fractured State Series

Fractured State

Rogue State

The Perseid Collapse Series

The Jakarta Pandemic

The Perseid Collapse

Event Horizon

Point of Crisis

Dispatches

The Black Flagged Series

Alpha

Redux

Apex

Vektor

Omega

Vindicta

The Zulu Virus Chronicles

Hot Zone

Kill Box

Fire Storm

A TRUE KILL

STEVEN KONKOLY

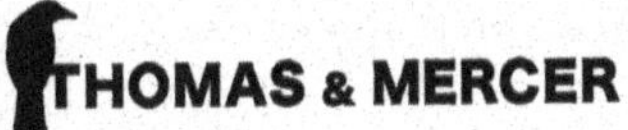

This is a work of fiction. Names, characters, organizations, places, events, and incidents are either products of the author's imagination or are used fictitiously. Otherwise, any resemblance to actual persons, living or dead, is purely coincidental.

Published by Thomas & Mercer, Seattle

www.apub.com

EU product safety contact:
Amazon Media EU S. à r.l.
38, avenue John F. Kennedy, L-1855 Luxembourg
amazonpublishing-gpsr@amazon.com

ISBN-13: 9781662524486 (paperback)
ISBN-13: 9781662524479 (digital)

Cover design by David Drummond
Cover image: © Liufuyu, © George Doyle / Getty

Printed in the United States of America

To Kosia, Matthew, and Sophia—
the heart and soul of my writing

PART I

CHAPTER 1

MONTANA. Garrett Mann muttered the word over and over, staring at the satellite image displayed on a wide-screen monitor in one of the smaller Critical Incident Response Group (CIRG) conference rooms. He'd commandeered the space for ARTEMIS's follow-up investigation, after the AXIOM raid. The rest of the task force basically camped out here during working hours or—like tonight—long after, sipping reheated coffee. He'd have to kick them out at some point this evening, so they could function tomorrow morning.

None of them had real offices or workspaces, including Mann, who had recently sacrificed his spartan, rarely used office to one of CIRG's Deputy Tactical Section heads. This conference room served as their home away from whatever cheap DC-area apartment or run-down motel room most of them now called home. Nobody showed much interest in leaving here at the end of the day.

He zoomed in on the rural compound. It couldn't be that easy. Right? Overhead surveillance suggested the answer—a hard fucking NO. But they couldn't know for sure unless his task force searched the property on foot, and he needed more than a theory based on a fragment of a conversation overheard by an AXIOM employee with a traumatic brain injury. The bullet that had struck her head and miraculously glanced off her skull in the final moments of the station's existence hadn't been fired by Mann's crew. AXIOM security officers had executed the entire ten-person operations-center team, before rushing to the rooftop where karma caught up with them.

The sole surviving operations-center tech at the Georgetown station, after waking up from a two-week bullet-induced coma, shared what she knew, or could remember, about the AXIOM operation. Unfortunately, she didn't know anywhere near as much as Mann had hoped. Her specific job had been to babysit the SATCHEL data upload. To ensure that the DOMINION data transferred from AXIOM's Tysons Corner headquarters properly migrated, and that AXIOM could assume full control of the DOMINION program from Georgetown. She and two others had been assigned this task without knowing the program's purpose. The more involved side of the operations team had presumably known additional details that could have proven useful, but accurate bullet placement had permanently erased that information.

All Mann's task force understood at this point was that the SATCHEL, which had been hand-carried by Gerald McCall from Tysons Corner to Georgetown, contained the data required to operate and coordinate DOMINION—AXIOM's private army of cartel sleepers. AXIOM had attempted to send the DOMINION data to MONTANA via sophisticated satellite arrays mounted to the rooftops of both the Tysons Corner headquarters and the Georgetown station, but Mann's team managed to destroy both arrays before the data could be transmitted.

As much as Mann would like to claim that he'd purposefully stopped DOMINION in its tracks by taking out the arrays, the destruction of the communications gear had essentially been a wider gamble to panic AXIOM. Cut off secure communications. Prevent the upload and subsequent destruction of evidence. He'd been on the right track with the latter, but to be entirely honest, he had no idea how consequential the destruction of those arrays had ultimately been. It had forced AXIOM and their client to take one desperate measure after another to keep DOMINION alive without the ability to send it to MONTANA.

MONTANA made sense to him based on what one of the AXIOM employees had described. The sole survivor said that one of their highest-priority emergency protocols for DOMINION was to send it to MONTANA. She'd overheard one of the user-end operation techs say something about MONTANA being their last hope if everything had gone wrong.

They never got to execute the MONTANA plan, because Mann's task force melted the Georgetown array before they could plug the SATCHEL into the station's mainframe and transmit it. McCall and the rest of AXIOM's higher-ups then tried to carry it away on a helicopter, which clearly hadn't been arranged with AXIOM's survival in mind. Harrison Greely murdered McCall with the help of the helicopter's crew and stole SATCHEL, before attempting to escape.

That worked out about as well as McCall's attempt to escape. Mann's team forced the helicopter to crash a few blocks away, presumably killing everyone on board. Though Mann wasn't exactly convinced that everything and everyone had burned up in the helicopter crash, specifically Harrison Greely and SATCHEL. It was nearly impossible to say due to the intensity of the fire that had consumed the helicopter and everything on board. And a slowly escalating string of Mexican immigrant– and cartel-blamed violence in the United States had emerged over the past few weeks.

Forensics teams started to scour the wreckage once the blaze had been extinguished a few hours later but were unable to assure his task force that Greely had perished and the duffel bag containing the SATCHEL data device had been destroyed. Body parts had been scattered everywhere, many of them fused to the helicopter's metal frame. They found four skulls in the charred wreckage, two of them attached to deeply scorched skeletons, which gave them a rough count of who had been on board when the helicopter went down—but nobody knew exactly how many people had been on the helicopter when it departed the rooftop of AXIOM's Georgetown station.

Reports from his teams had varied. The FBI surveillance-sniper team, consisting of Jax and Javier positioned across the street, had snapped off several bullets at the helicopter—and Jax insisted they'd hit one of the pilots. A hole in one of the skull's foreheads supported their report. Unfortunately, the helicopter door gunners drove them off the rooftop, keeping them from witnessing the rest of the engagement.

Before someone inside the helicopter had pounded her with rifle-caliber bullets, Serrano claimed to have knocked one of the door gunners out of it, which was later confirmed. A mangled, bullet-riddled body was found in the alley next to the AXIOM building, a short-barreled automatic rifle in a dumpster a few feet away. She reported a second gunner in the helicopter, which made sense.

Four bodies appeared to be the magic number. Two pilots. The remaining door gunner. And Harrison Greely. But something kept gnawing at Mann.

"You're still here?" asked a familiar voice, startling him.

He'd been so absorbed in his own thoughts—trying to make sense of the data beaming from the numerous computer screens, wall maps, and thick data reports littering the conference room—that he hadn't noticed how much time had passed. A quick glance at his watch solved the mystery. 8:26 p.m. Jesus.

Mann looked over his shoulder. "You ditched the wheelchair?"

"It's still in my office," said O'Reilly, director of the FBI's Critical Incident Response Group and Mann's boss, before adjusting her posture on two crutches. "Figured I'd give these a try while nobody was around. So much for that."

"You look uncomfortable," said Mann.

"I am. Everything hurts like hell. But I was getting a little too comfortable in that wheelchair," she said, before taking a few clearly painful steps into the conference room. "Speaking of uncomfortable. You look like someone pissed in your coffee. Right in front of you. After you told them not to."

Mann stifled a laugh. O'Reilly had a way with words.

"I just can't let go of the gut feeling that this SATCHEL thing somehow survived the crash," he said. "And the DOMINION plan has been activated."

"I can authorize you to take a look at McCall's estate."

"It's too obvious," said Mann. "And I've already taken a long-distance look."

"That's news to me," said O'Reilly.

"Well. You just got back."

"So, James knows about this?"

"The overflights of McCall's Montana property were paid for by a private entity," said Mann. "That entity generously provided the task force with the results—which indicated zero activity. Day or night."

"Wow. Sounds like some south-of-the-border generosity," O'Reilly said.

"Impossible to say," said Mann. "This stuff arrives anonymously. We do our best to vet the information."

O'Reilly shook her head, before making her way farther into the room—each step drawing a painful grimace.

"How are they doing?" she asked.

"Who?"

"Cata," said O'Reilly. "Everyone else down south."

"Recovering," Mann said. "Shaking it off."

"But spending money on reconnaissance we can't authorize?"

"Among other things."

"We still owe them more than a few bags of money," said O'Reilly.

"A handshake and a pat on the shoulder in a private ceremony attended by three medium-ish-ranking US officials?" said Mann. "Trust me. They're good. Not that they were doing this for money. But the money will help them in ways we can't imagine. And they're already giving some of it back."

"So. Nothing at McCall's ranch?" asked O'Reilly.

"Not that we can tell," he said. "The MONTANA reference from the sole survivor in Georgetown hasn't been backed up by any of the employees in Tysons Corner."

"Compartmentalization," said O'Reilly. "The operations techs left in Virginia during the evacuation of AXIOM's Tysons Corner operation didn't know about Georgetown. Most of the techs sent to Georgetown didn't know about MONTANA, the final possible location for SATCHEL. The sole survivor only overheard a mention of it. She obviously wasn't read into the final plan. Anyone that knew more than a broad reference to the final location was executed."

"They tried to kill her," said Mann.

"They tried to kill everyone."

"Good point."

"So, the ranch in Montana?" said O'Reilly.

"Are you suggesting we take a closer look?" asked Mann.

"Is there a downside?"

"Not really," said Mann. "But the aerial surveillance was extensive—and very expensive. No signs of activity."

"It took our interrogation team nearly a week to uncover the Montana reference and your team a few more days to connect the dots. When did the surveillance take place?" O'Reilly said.

"Three days after that," said Mann.

"Nearly two weeks," said O'Reilly. "If the SATCHEL somehow survived the Georgetown raid, whoever stole it could have reached McCall's ranch within several hours of the helicopter crash. It's not hard to maintain a zero profile in an isolated location like that; you know that better than anyone. You took your team off the grid, and even I couldn't find you. And I have extensive experience finding people that don't want to be found."

"Another good point," Mann said. "I'll start working up a plan to hit McCall's ranch. We'll obviously need warrants, local agency cooperation—all the kind of stuff we'll need you to arrange."

"Since when has any of that stopped you?"

He shrugged. "With the task force on the brink of dismissal, I figured I should get back in the habit of embracing the red tape and following official procedure. But . . ."

"But what?"

"Just for the record—"

"There is no record, unless you're recording us," said O'Reilly.

"Sorry. It's a phrase I can't shake," said Mann. "But for the record—"

O'Reilly rolled her eyes while shaking her head.

"McCall's ranch in Montana is too easy. Too obvious."

"Back to my original question. Is there any downside to checking it out?"

"An ambush?" Mann said. "My official task force is down to four out of the original nine. Not to mention the half dozen or more Mexicans that gave their lives. If the Sacramento field office hadn't abruptly stopped us from raiding Raul's house, the task force might be down to zero."

"I can arrange a hard-hitting raid, if that's what you'd prefer," said O'Reilly. "James is on board. She doesn't give a fuck. Like me."

"Sounds like you might have rubbed off on her a bit," said Mann.

"No. *You* rubbed off on her," said O'Reilly. "She may be a high-top, but she knows how to get shit done. You've demonstrated that perfectly. She's a Mann acolyte."

"Not exactly career enhancing."

"I think she's happy where she is."

"Sounds like someone else I know."

"Birds of a feather," she said. "I would have retired a few years ago if I didn't think otherwise."

"One of these days, I want to know the full story," said Mann.

"Which story?"

"The one that gives you access to the strangest assortment of black ops professionals."

"I don't know what you're talking about."

"Of course you don't," said Mann. "Full raid package on the ranch. It's an isolated location, so I'm thinking helicopter insertion. FBI SWAT. A sniper team providing overwatch—possibly arriving a day in advance? Whatever you can arrange. No reason to take any chances."

"I'll get this rolling," said O'Reilly. "Is it okay if the sniper team isn't FBI?"

"As long as they don't shoot at us, I don't care who you arrange."

"You've worked with them already," said O'Reilly.

"Rico and Emily?"

"M and M. Yep," she said. "And I have three new candidates for the task force. Two SWAT. One Special Surveillance Group. I can set up interviews."

"Interviews? Is there anything wrong with them?" Mann asked.

O'Reilly broke out into a low-key laugh, the agonized look on her face betraying the pain still radiating from the stab wound she'd taken to the abdomen.

"Sorry," said Mann. "Laughter isn't the best medicine in this case."

"I'm fine. Been through worse," she said between a few deep breaths. "Nothing terribly wrong with any of them. The usual bullshit. No longer on the fast track—or any track—because they took a bolt-cutter to the barbed-wire fence of bureaucracy one too many times."

"Team players?"

"Aside from not having any problem with the collateral damage that comes from breaking the rules in the field."

"I can live with that," said Mann. "Are they aware of the ARTEMIS attrition rate?"

"They are," said O'Reilly.

"How soon can we get them here?"

"They're in town," said O'Reilly. "Ready to get to work. Their bosses were eager to move them along. They're staying with investigative specialist Kelsey Cook, one of the ARTEMIS candidates. She has a three-bedroom town house in Georgetown."

"Family money?" said Mann.

"A philandering, rapey Greek diplomat's money," said O'Reilly. "Cook's team had been watching the head of the Greek embassy's Office for Economic and Commercial Affairs for several months because he'd been meeting covertly with a Belarussian diplomat—a known Russian proxy. A briefcase was handed to the Greek diplomat during one of their last meetings. Audio surveillance was spotty at best during the handoff, but the conversation suggested that the briefcase contained a significant amount of cash."

"Payoff money?" said Mann.

"Bingo. Presumably payoff money for the diplomat's growing list of victims and mistresses. The Russians really didn't want to lose this contact. Long story short, phone taps and various surveillance tapes confirmed that the briefcase vanished a few days after the transfer. Lots of panicked phone calls from the Greek to the Belarussian contact, who never picked up. The Greek diplomat's wife called 911 a few days after that. She'd found him floating in their terrace hot tub. Two empty bottles of ouzo nearby."

"He passed out and drowned?" said Mann.

"The first EMT group on the scene took the right steps when confronted with a suspected drowning. Thirty chest compressions, followed by two rescue breaths after checking for obvious airway obstructions. They couldn't inflate his lungs."

"What?"

"They dug farther down his throat and found several green olives lodged in his larynx. The autopsy found more olives jammed as far down as his upper trachea."

"Jesus. Someone had a grudge," said Mann. "Obviously, she had nothing to do with that?"

"Obviously," said O'Reilly. "The only reason I brought this up is to let you know that Cook is the punchiest of this new group. There's no doubt in my mind that she snuck in and stole that briefcase. Several months later, she's the beneficiary of a four-million-dollar life insurance policy and the proud owner of a Georgetown brownstone. Her mother took out the policy, which must have cost twenty-plus-thousand dollars a month. She fell off a cliff during a hike outside of Santa Fe, New Mexico."

"Sounds like a suicide. The life insurance company didn't investigate?"

"They did. But she'd been hiking with the same group of women for a few years," said O'Reilly. "Just lost her balance at the worst possible moment, and that was that. Two-hundred-and-thirty-foot rocky plunge. Plus, the autopsy showed she had terminal pancreatic cancer. Maybe a month or two to live."

"Insurance investigators didn't find that odd?"

"She was more of the holistic type," O'Reilly said. "Nothing documented in any database."

"Damn. That's probably the cleverest way to launder money I've ever heard of," said Mann. "Or—a mom taking care of her daughter outside of the system."

"Or both," said O'Reilly. "Just letting you know who you're dealing with."

"She sounds like a perfect fit," said Mann.

"That's what I thought."

"And the other two?"

"Jeff Miles," she said. "Had a little trouble explaining why he blasted a bedroom closet door with every shell in his shotgun during a counterterrorism raid—without issuing a warning to the closet's occupant."

"I assume he didn't kill anyone who didn't need killing?" said Mann.

"No. The guy inside had just racked the slide of a fully automatic Uzi. Nobody else heard it."

"Can't blame him for good hearing."

"Wasn't the first time Miles shot first and assessed the situation later. His SAC contacted me about a week ago to recommend him for ARTEMIS."

Mann laughed. "We seem to be a dumping ground for career risks. Who's the third?"

"Shana Bilyk," said O'Reilly, not adding any more.

"That's it?"

"Shane Bilyk transitioned a few months ago. Spotless record. Ten years of SWAT experience," said O'Reilly. "Things haven't gone smoothly with her colleagues since the transition."

"As long as she's a little flexible with the rules—our arms are open," said Mann, before turning to the team. "Right?"

They all agreed without the slightest hint of bias. No eye rolling. No hesitation. Just immediate acceptance. Even Turner didn't make a joke—which Mann had fully expected. Not because he was biased. Because he was an eternal smart-ass. His quick nod represented everything the task force had come to represent over the past few years. A tight-knit group of "misfits." Everyone here had been *kicked out of the club* for whatever reason. Nobody cared why, as long as everyone did their job and did everything humanly possible to keep their teammates alive. A tall order, given what ARTEMIS faced. O'Reilly grimaced slightly. Barely noticeable—but noticeable to him.

"What?" said Mann.

She let out a sigh. "I almost declined the transfer. Bilyk wasn't exactly happy about being dumped here. I assured her she was working with the best and that her transfer was a blessing in disguise. She didn't look convinced. She goes by the book. Not a rule bender by any stretch. You might have your work cut out for you with her."

"I'm not worried," Mann said. "This group could use a little balance. A little leveling out isn't a bad idea."

"That's kind of what I was thinking," said O'Reilly.

"*Bilyk* is a Ukrainian name," said Chad Lianez, looking up from his phone.

"How would you—" Mann started.

"Simple Google search," said Lianez.

"Yes. She's not very fond of Russians," said O'Reilly. "Which—to be entirely honest—is why I'm willing to take a chance with her."

"Let's set up breakfast with our new recruits. Somewhere other than here. I'd like to meet with all of them at the same time. See how they interact. The sooner, the better. Then we'll get to business."

"Do you want me there?" O'Reilly asked.

"Hell no," he said. "You need to maintain at least some level of plausible deniability going forward. They're either going to get up and walk out the door immediately or keep shoveling Denny's down their throats after I tell them exactly what we plan on doing going forward."

"Denny's? Are you trying to make a bad first impression?"

"That's the first test," said Mann. "If any of them decline breakfast, they're off the team. I have standards."

CHAPTER 2

Cata Serrano jolted awake at her kitchen table, one of her hands knocking an empty water bottle to the floor. The other barely missing the empty tinfoil-lined Styrofoam container she'd pushed away after a late dinner. She'd had the same nightmare again: the rooftop in Georgetown. The dream changed a little every time, but the outcome remained the same—no matter how hard she tried to alter it. Tonight, she'd gone back to one of the earliest versions.

She bursts onto the rooftop and empties her rifle into the escaping helicopter, sending it into an uncontrolled spin. The helicopter disappears below the edge of the rooftop, a fireball shooting skyward moments later. Now she's lying on her back. She's not sure if she's wounded or just resting. The dream never gives her time to make that evaluation. Harrison Greely appears, standing over her with a pistol—laughing. She reaches for her rifle, which is inexplicably gone, while screaming, "I killed you!" Greely shakes his head and laughs, before pulling the trigger.

Some nights, he knifed her. Others, he stomped on her head. Some nights, the helicopter rose out of the flames and he gunned her down a moment later. The one thing that remained constant: She lost every time. And she had no intention of losing, which was why she was taking an outrageous risk to put an end to whatever remained of Greely's legacy.

Maybe he was dead. Maybe he wasn't. Dreams were dreams; she wasn't superstitious. But the evidence of his death, surrounding the helicopter crash, hadn't been conclusive enough for her. If Mann's task force could shut down DOMINION, at least Greely's current ambitions would be temporarily halted, giving them time to find and terminate him.

She reached across the table and grabbed a half-filled pack of Delicados cigarettes before crumpling and tossing them to the floor. She was done with them; she'd been done with them since she left the United States. But the gravity of this morning's meeting had reignited the urge, and she'd gladly obliged. The first few had tasted like a sweet, chemical-laced bag of burned popcorn, but they gradually eased up—until she was back in the tobacco company's sweet embrace.

But why had she quit them prior to an hour ago? Bad for her health? No shit. Distracting from the job and life? Sure. The reason went far deeper. Garrett Mann deep. She felt close to him on too many levels, even though they were nearly two thousand miles apart. But he'd never given her any indication that more existed between them, even though he had promised to take her on a trip to Spain at some point soon. She'd sensed something different in him when he said that. A different air between the two of them. A possible future.

But what kind of future? A future where Garrett Mann takes her on a pity trip to Europe—or a sincere attempt at a relationship together outside of the task force business? Even Cata wasn't sure if that was what she wanted right now. The only thing she knew for sure was that she had no real future here in Mexico. She had been marked by the cartel and her former police force. If this meeting didn't go well, it was time to go. Farther south into Central America, or back into Mann's protection, if the offer was still on the table.

She glanced at the bottle of tequila on her dresser. A few hits would take the edge off this meeting. Or maybe she needed that edge. First contact with the cartel went one of two ways: They either scheduled you for another meeting, or they sent you home. Most people never made it home. She obviously hoped for the former—but even if they set up another meeting, she had to be cautious.

They knew she wasn't some rookie cop or street sweeper bringing them information overheard in a bodega. She was the real deal, had been on their asses for more than a few years before disappearing. If they didn't like what she had to say, she might not make it out of the meeting room alive. Actually—she'd probably get out alive. The low-level soldados sent to interview her wouldn't, but she'd be marked for death and unlikely to get out of the city. Or maybe she would. She hadn't gotten this far by accident.

Either way, she was taking a big chance by insisting on this meeting. A chance she didn't have to take. Cata could walk away with her share of the money Mann had bestowed upon her and the rest of her Mexican colleagues. But it made sense to her to take this chance, and it made sense to Garrett, even though he'd begged her to back off. He had a way of doing that—warning you against a course of action while at the same time agreeing it held merit.

He wasn't being duplicitous. Garrett had run his task force the same way. He'd broken more rules than she could count, most of them in the last few months. He not only talked the talk, but walked the walk—another reason why she had taken an incredible risk setting up this meeting. At his demand, Deputy Director Dana O'Reilly had arranged private medical care for her Mexican colleagues—through her two CIA contacts. Mann and O'Reilly had managed to keep her friends out of the spotlight and safely return them to Mexico once they'd stabilized.

Cata had kept in close touch with Mann ever since they'd parted on a private runway outside DC. He was her only hope of truly ending the journey she'd started years ago. If he cracked the MONTANA code and recovered the SATCHEL, his task force could identify every DOMINION operative in the United States. And instead of cutting through miles of red tape at the US Department of Justice to shut DOMINION down, they could lean on Juárez Cartel operatives in the United States to remove the disease.

And she was likely his only hope of making sure the DOMINION network posed no threat to the election. The last thing the Juárez Cartel wanted was a US administration seriously committed to shutting down the border and spending billions on a new "war on drugs." The new Mexican president hadn't exactly taken a hard-line stance against the cartels, but she'd signaled that she'd be in favor of a more aggressive approach—with US support. Cata hoped her offer would bring the cartel into the fold. Not too far in, but far enough to keep AXIOM's client, True America, from pulling DOMINION's strings and possibly winning the election.

Screw it. She grabbed the bottle of tequila and twisted the cap. A few swigs later, she felt a little more emboldened. This wasn't her first rodeo. She could handle this.

CHAPTER 3

Mann decided to walk back to the hotel tonight. He could count the number of minutes he'd spent outside in the last week on one hand, and he needed some fresh air—even if it hit his nose as a mix of exhaust, restaurant food, and occasionally urine.

The walk wasn't the best idea, given that Jessica Mayer had positively spotted a still-unidentified surveillance team three nights ago, which had followed her Uber from FBI headquarters to her apartment in Silver Spring—and even tried to track her on foot after she walked past her apartment.

Mayer had ditched them within minutes, using a nearby DC Metro station and her two decades of countersurveillance experience. What had those idiots been thinking? They were lucky she hadn't doubled back on them and expertly inserted a knife into each of their mid-cervical vertebrae. Instead, she'd made her way back to FBI Headquarters and CIRG Division, where Mann and a few other members of the team were still struggling to make sense of the scant evidence on hand.

A few phone calls later, Deputy Director O'Reilly, with Director James's approval, had secured Mann's team rooms on the same floor of the Conrad Hotel, along with armed and armored FBI transportation to and from the hotel. There was no real need to post FBI SWAT on the floor, due to the heavy Secret Service and State Department security presence in the hotel, but Luke Turner collaborated with Chad Lianez and Callie Jackson, their surveillance experts, to create an early-warning system in case someone took a swipe at them.

Actually, Lianez and Jackson had done most of the work, setting up cameras and motion sensors. Turner surreptitiously delivered the unauthorized weapons they might need to shoot their way out of the situation. Mann's task force hadn't surrendered every surprise they'd unearthed at AXIOM's LABYRINTH facility in New Mexico. They were as safe as possible for now from that "someone," who they suspected was True America.

Harrison Greely had boarded that helicopter—that much they knew. They just couldn't confirm that he'd burned up in the helicopter wreckage. Same with the SATCHEL. Recent crime patterns across the US suggested that the SATCHEL had somehow survived, but it was entirely possible that a few AXIOM field operatives working directly with the DOMINION army had avoided apprehension and were working with True America to do their best to implement fragments of the original plan. But this felt like more than fragments. Mann just couldn't prove it. Yet.

A strong hand grabbed his right shoulder. He tried to spin to the left and draw his service pistol, but the hand kept him in place while another yanked his weapon out of the cross-draw holster on his left hip.

"Jesus, Garrett. That was pathetic," said Jessica Mayer, releasing her grip. "Are you trying to get yourself killed?"

He turned to face her. "I was deep in thought."

"Deep in thought on the street will get you killed."

"Apparently," said Mann. "What are you doing out on the mean streets?"

"I was having a drink with Ray and Luke at the hotel bar when I got a text that you left on foot. Figured I'd teach you a lesson."

"Lesson acknowledged and appreciated," said Mann. "Are you guys at the rooftop bar?"

"Where else?"

"Sounds nice."

"You're obviously welcome to join us," she said. "At some point you'll have to sign off on the tab. May as well enjoy a drink with a view of the city."

"O'Reilly's going to regret putting us up in the Conrad," said Mann.

"Nah. We've mostly behaved," Mayer said. "DoorDashing Chipotle or Panera. Nothing excessive."

Mann glanced around. "Do you think they're still watching us?"

She patted his shoulder and urged him along. "I highly doubt it. I'm not the only agent on the streets watching over you. My Special Surveillance Group colleagues are on the job. And if they spot a potential hostile, the FBI SWAT team sitting in an SUV less than a block away will pounce on them."

"Good to know," said Mann.

"You already knew that."

"True. But you managed to evade all of them."

"That's what I got paid for, before joining ARTEMIS," she said.

"Looks like you're still getting paid for good work."

"This is pro bono work," said Mayer. "To keep you alive."

"Very appreciated work."

"We'd appreciate it if you didn't make it hard on us," she said.

"Message received," said Mann. "Seriously."

And he meant it. The task force had suffered severe losses. More than half of the original ARTEMIS crew was gone at this point. Nobody could have predicted that they'd unearth a network of hundreds of cartel assassins trained by a Washington, DC, defense-contractor corporation to be turned loose on the US population to influence the upcoming election. Discoveries like that tended to come with messy repercussions—for everyone.

The two of them walked a few more blocks, toward New York Avenue, before Mayer broke the silence.

"What's the endgame for us with this DOMINION business?"

He really didn't have an answer. At least, not one he thought would satisfy her. But he couldn't exactly ignore her, either. She understood the stakes for all of them, both professionally and realistically.

"MONTANA. Sounds like it's where they wanted to send the database," said Mann. "So they could run the army they created."

"But where's MONTANA?"

"In Montana," said Mann.

"You don't believe that," she said. "Or we'd already have hit that place."

"Feels too obvious. And the recon confirms it."

"Are we absolutely certain?" Mayer asked. "If I were them, I'd have that place stocked with supplies and locked down tight. No signs of life. It's their last refuge—if we believe the few AXIOM employees that supposedly overheard classified conversations. All they have to do is lay low for another two months. Three, if they wanted to push it up to the election. A small price for the potential payoff."

She was right. If True America made efficient use of the DOMINION network for the next few months, without going overboard, they could tip the scales and win the election. Still kind of a long shot, given their baggage. But America's collective memory was short these days, with social media platforms fully defining a vast percentage of the population's "beliefs."

"I guess we'll never know unless we hit the place," said Mann.

"Full FBI task force team," said Mayer. "Explosive Ordnance Team. Electronics Exploitation Team. SWAT. Aerial surveillance during the raid. A full package. We won't be alone to do our 'thing,' but if they're buried underground running DOMINION, we'll shut it down."

"When did you gain all of this wisdom?" asked Mann.

"Been watching."

"Not me."

"We've all been watching you. Learning from your successes and mistakes," Mayer said. "Mostly mistakes."

"Funny," said Mann. "But probably true."

"It's not as bad as you think," said Mayer, before gently grabbing his shoulder. "New York Avenue. The Conrad is to our right."

"One drink," said Mann.

"That's what they always say."

CHAPTER 4

Cata traded the phone for the tequila on her nightstand. A few swigs later, she slammed the bottle down mere centimeters from her phone. *Where the fuck is he?* She'd called him more times than she could count—or remember, after draining most of the bottle. She squinted at her watch. Ten-ish p.m. her time? Midnight his time. Fair enough . . . but where the fuck was he?

She stared at the ceiling, starting to fade away. Maybe it was better this way. She'd taken detailed notes when she returned from her meeting. Nothing good could come from a call at this hour. They could hash this out later.

Her phone buzzed. Cata knocked it behind the nightstand. *Shit.* A minute later, she'd recovered it and navigated to the missed calls—the last being from Mann's number. Her better judgment told her to go to bed and call him in the morning. The tequila said otherwise. She hit his number. Mann answered immediately.

"I'm drunk," she told him.

"That makes two of us," said Mann. "Sort of. I only had a few drinks, but—"

"You're a lightweight," she said.

"That I am," he said. "How did your meeting go? I didn't want to call. Figured they were all over you."

"It went well. I'm still alive."

"That's a good sign," said Mann. "Nobody followed you home?"

"Not that I could tell," said Cata.

"Wish I could say the same here," Mann said. "We're basically in lockdown."

"They're actively looking for you?"

"Yes, but we're safe. As safe as it gets here in DC. What did you learn today?"

Cata rubbed her temples, the last few nips of tequila kicking in.

"Not much. But the fact that I made it back to my apartment alive indicates they have some interest in my proposal. And the fact that they haven't broken into my apartment to shoot or abduct me says that they did some research into my proposal—and they're interested in another conversation."

"You're back at your apartment?" asked Mann. "You have the money to stay in a hotel for now. I assume it would be a little safer?"

"I'm not a threat to the cartel. How many times do we have to go over this?" Cata said.

"You don't know what they're thinking about this," said Mann. "Nobody does. Just Enrique Mendoza."

Mann wasn't wrong. As the head of the Juárez Cartel, Mendoza would have the final say in something this big.

"I know, I know. But they were receptive to what I had to say, or we wouldn't be talking right now. Trust me. The next meeting will be different. If I walk out of that one alive, we're in business on some level," said Cata. "Then it all falls on you. How are things looking?"

"Hard to say," said Mann, which was one of several code phrases they'd memorized.

Hard to say meant that pieces were still missing.

"I need to clean up for bed," she said. "It's been a long day."

"Rest up," said Mann. "Talk to you later."

She turned off the light on her nightstand before opening her bedroom window several more inches and poking her head outside. Nothing hovered above the antenna. Had to be sure. Cata communicated with Mann using the encrypted satellite phone he'd given her prior to her return to Mexico. She'd connected the phone to an antenna Velcroed to the frame of her bedroom window, when she was trying to reach him while in her apartment.

The only way the Juárez Cartel could intercept their call was to climb on the apartment rooftop and lower a radio frequency receiver into position above the portable antenna. She checked for a receiver every time she placed or received a call, then checked again every few minutes during the conversation.

Cata undressed and stepped into the shower with the phone. Once she got the shower running, she called Mann. He answered before her phone registered a ring.

"We're no closer to grabbing the DOMINION software than we were when we hit the Georgetown annex."

"Jesús Cristo," she said. "That puts me in an awkward situation down here."

"I understand," said Mann. "We're leaning toward investigating the most obvious lead."

"It's a false lead," said Cata. "Or worse. Like the bombing at Raul's house in Sacramento. The whole place could be rigged with explosives, just waiting for you."

"We're well aware of that possibility," he said. "This won't just be the task force. We'll pull FBI SWAT agents from the nearest field offices, plus every regional FBI bomb technician we can muster. The works."

"Then what are you waiting for?" said Cata. "Hit the ranch."

"The wheels turn slow here in DC," said Mann.

"*Entiendo.* So why are you still there?"

"In DC?"

"Where else?" said Cata.

"We need the backup," said Mann.

"Since when?"

"Since we're taking on a national conspiracy instead of a few serial killers," he said. "And we can't just waltz into houses anymore."

"Fair enough," said Cata. "But mission accomplished on my end. *La Triada está muerta.*"

"Yet here you are, taking meetings with the Juárez Cartel."

"That's all for the task force. I don't want to live here anymore," she said. "What's my status, by the way? I haven't heard much from the State Department lately."

"Things are a little stuck here. Not a lot of Mexico love in the US right now," said Mann. "But you're fast-tracked for a green card. EB-2 National Interest Waiver. You should have all the paperwork you need right now to enter and stay in the US until the green card is official."

"I do. Thank you," said Cata.

"Then get on a plane or drive your car over the border. Tomorrow," said Mann. "You've done your duty. Done your job. Get out while you can."

"Why?" she asked.

"So I can take you on the trip I promised," said Mann. "You kind of bailed on me at the last minute."

"I didn't have a passport."

"Yeah. Well. Now you have a passport."

"For flying back and forth to the US," she said.

"It works for other countries, too," said Mann. "That's the point of a passport."

"I understand how it works," she said. "I'll keep working the cartel angle here—until it's time for me to head north."

"When's that?" asked Mann.

"I don't know. But when the time comes, I'll know."

"Don't wear out your welcome down there," he said. "They don't like loose ends, and you are most definitely the kind of loose end they'd eventually like to tie up. It's not a matter of *if*, it's a matter of *when*."

"I'm well aware of that," she said. "I'll be careful. Always have been."

"Be extra careful," said Mann. "AXIOM still has contacts in the cartel. And True America isn't opposed to throwing money around to solve problems."

"I know what I'm doing."

"I know you do," said Mann. "Just don't forget. You're always welcome up here. No way for you to wear out your welcome."

She didn't know how to interpret that and didn't have the mental bandwidth right now to try.

"I'll keep that in mind."

CHAPTER 5

Harrison Greely gently nudged the joystick forward, his wheelchair responding in kind. Slowly accelerating, he settled into a manageable pace he could easily control. It had taken him over a week to figure that out. Whiplash was real in this kind of high-end wheelchair if you weren't careful or if you were impatient. He'd discovered that the hard way during his first few days out of bed—after stubbornly refusing the headrest installation. He didn't want to look like Stephen Hawking with some kind of weird head brace.

But he didn't want to snap his neck, either, and lose the use of his arms, too. It was bad enough that he was paralyzed from the waist down. Something he'd never conceived possible. Nobody does, until it happens. Why would you? Life is safe when you examine the statistics. Airline travel is infinitely safer than driving the same route, and fatal car accidents are also nearly nonexistent, statistically, when you factor in the millions of hours a day Americans spend in vehicles.

He could go on and on about statistics, but what was the point? Jumping from an out-of-control helicopter and trying to land on an airbag that looked about as big as a grilled cheese sandwich from the sky had nothing to do with statistics. It had everything to do with luck. And depending on your perspective, the result of Harrison's jump was either lucky or unlucky. Lucky, from his perspective.

The fall from the helicopter should have killed him. He'd missed the airbag by a few feet, landing in a partially seated position on the asphalt rooftop—which pulverized his lower spine. If he'd landed flat on his back, or on his head, he'd either be dead or blowing into a tube to move his wheelchair—his body just a vessel to keep his brain alive.

Losing the use of his legs was bad enough. But stem cell research was closing in on therapies for paraplegia, and he had the money, resources, and connections to move himself to the front of that treatment line. All hope wasn't lost. Thankfully, the SATCHEL landed on the airbag. The Russians didn't hesitate for a second to exploit the situation. Within seconds, they were screaming at him, pistols aimed at his face, demanding that he identify the location of the last remaining operations center that could run the DOMINION program.

Insufferable people. Abysmally basic and entirely predictable. That's what happens when a fascist government murders or chases away anyone with an original thought. He knew what they were thinking the moment they raced onto the rooftop: steal the duffel bag, occupy the operations center with mercenaries—then renegotiate the terms of the original deal. That was the amusing part.

They actually thought they could take the SATCHEL and somehow "make it work" without his help? Harrison understood and spoke Russian fluently. He'd earned a master's degree in Sovietology at Boston University back when the Soviet Union existed, and had studied Russian language for six years. He very clearly understood their intentions, which were felonious and treacherous to say the least.

Ironically, they destroyed their only hope of somehow getting away with their plan. The fake cigarette pack that contained the stolen software download required to run the DOMINION database had spilled out of his pocket when his body hit the rooftop. When Harrison tried to retrieve it after regaining his senses, one of the Russians stomped on it, essentially eliminating any chance the Russians had of getting away with their plan. Not that they would have made it off the rooftop alive if they'd tried to leave with the duffel bag or the cigarette pack.

Harrison had his own ground teams working the area. They broke into the town house shortly after he jumped from the helicopter, guided by a GPS beacon sewn into his shoes. They accessed the rooftop within a few minutes of the helicopter crashing. His team "reasoned" with the Russians at gunpoint. Pistols in the hands of Russian embassy employees versus suppressed rifles in the hands of former Tier 1 operators. Hardly a negotiation. A single bullet to one of the more volatile Russian's foreheads set the tone for the rest of the interaction.

The SATCHEL was back in True America's hands, as originally agreed. The Russians would be rewarded later, despite their little stunt. They had played an amateur hand and had lost. Not a big problem in the grand scheme of things. But most definitely a warning sign that the Russian angle might be a little more volatile than expected. All this for policy shifts True America would have pursued vigorously, regardless of the role the Russians played in financially and logistically aiding them.

Maybe there had been more to the attempt to steal DOMINION than pure greed. Possibly a leverage play? It was conceivable, that the Russians had discovered he'd been pursuing alternative sources of funding—despite the painstaking effort Greely had invested in concealing those talks. Regardless of their motives, the Russians had been assured that as long as they continued to provide support, and didn't engage in any more backstabbing nonsense between now and the election, their interests would be well served should True America achieve their political goals.

He pressed a button on his chair, and a bulked-up mercenary in full body armor and weapons kit opened the door. Short-barreled rifle. Sidearm. The works. The other buttons summoned different groups: Medical, to address any residual pain or odd sensations; Butler, to dress him and take his meal orders; Nursing—he didn't want to think about it. Of all the buttons he despised, Nursing was at the top of the list, but it was the button he had to press the most. They helped with all the unsavory and mundane things he couldn't do on his own now. For now.

"Hendrick."

"Good morning, Mr. Greely."

"Nothing good about it."

"Never is," said his primary bodyguard, a former member of the South African 4th Special Forces Regiment.

"Is everyone in a good mood?" asked Greely.

"Hard to say," said Hendrick. "I don't think I've ever been in one."

Greely grinned. He liked Hendrick, which was more than he could say about everyone else he was about to meet. Bunch of snakes and hangers-on.

"Am I presentable?" said Greely.

Hendrick gave him a quick up and down. "You're good, sir."

"My fly isn't unzipped?" Greely asked, referring to an incident the other day when Nursing had left him flapping in the breeze after a bathroom call.

"All hatches are battened down for whatever storm awaits you."

"You think there's a storm brewing?"

The mercenary shook his head. "Nothing seemed out of the ordinary. A little impatience is all I sensed, sir."

"Well. They can fucking wait," said Greely. "Without my sacrifice, they'd be flying to Moscow right now or slithering back into the holes they've been living in for years."

The sacrifice that ultimately occurred certainly hadn't been his idea. He'd known he was taking a risk embedding himself in AXIOM, but he had no idea that Garrett Mann's task force was so close to stomping Gerald McCall's operation to pieces.

"Let's get you into the operations center," said Hendrick, before bracing himself against the wall.

Greely felt it, too. A not-so-slight tilt to the right, his wheelchair riding it out.

"Sorry, Mr. Greely. Someone obviously didn't get the word," said Hendrick.

"Well. Make sure they do."

"I'll make some calls," said Hendrick. "Ready?"

"I suppose."

"Do you want me to push you in?"

"Absolutely not. You'll enter before me," said Greely.

"Understood."

Then again—if he bumped into a wall or doorframe on the way in, they'd all chuckle inside and have every reason to doubt his ability to control the next few months. People tended to take trivial failures and magnify them. Especially when they had delusions of grandeur. And right now, at least two people sitting in that room would like to see him pushed into the drink strapped to his wheelchair. He hit the switch to disable the motor controls.

"Hendrick. I changed my mind," said Greely. "I'd like a smooth entry. I still have trouble with this ridiculous contraption."

"I'll have Rafe precede us," said Hendrick. "Give you the gravitas you deserve."

Rafe was one of at least a dozen mercenaries who had worked with True America for the past several years. Standing six foot two—nothing but muscle and sinew—he'd send a subtle message to the chameleons in the room looking to put Harrison out to pasture. Clara Furst and Gary Smith, relatively new members of True America, could hardly be trusted, even though they were talented and useful. Trent Summers, the potential True American presidential candidate, had been around for decades, traveling the circuit and spreading the good word. It was a complicated relationship, but one poised for greatness if everyone could keep their shit together for a few months.

CHAPTER 6

Clara Furst's initial thought when Harrison Greely entered the room in a motorized wheelchair was *Glad he's in a fucking wheelchair.* She wasn't proud of this instinctual reaction, but it took one of her biggest worries off the table. That Harrison Greely—son of True America's disgraced founder, Jackson Greely—would somehow try to step up and claim the reign originally sought by his father. Or, at the very least, play a public role in True America's administration—should they win the election.

No way he could steal the spotlight now. Or even appear in it. It wouldn't take Garrett Mann's task force more than a minute to put the pieces together. They'd no doubt identified him going back and forth from AXIOM's Tysons Corner headquarters and Georgetown station. Their surveillance of both locations and operational planning had clearly been exceptional. Remarkable enough to pull off perhaps the most audacious midday mid-city shoot-out and takedown in Washington, DC, history. They probably had Greely tagged by the end of the day, if they hadn't identified him prior to the multistage attack.

He had to stay out of public sight from this point forward, his role relegated to what had been originally agreed upon. His tragic and slightly miscalculated jump from the helicopter had been a saving grace for True America. The last thing their campaign or potential administration needed was Greely's name in the mix.

Everyone knew about their party's radical roots, but they didn't need to be reminded daily. The movement finally had a chance to write the future of the country; they didn't need Harrison Greely's face on the book.

"Look what the cat dragged in," said Furst. "Good to see you moving about."

She had to give him credit: He somehow managed to keep himself composed in the face of her admittedly snide greeting. It was no secret that the two of them didn't exactly get along.

"Good to be up and running the show again," said Greely. "The blow to AXIOM came as quite a surprise, but it appears that we're still in business—despite a few critical oversights."

Touché. There was the Greely she'd come to know and hate. She stifled a laugh.

"Yes. Mr. Dominguez has been very helpful, along with Kyle Stull, one of the senior DOMINION operations techs, who was home recovering from gall bladder surgery during the attack. He's helped train a new operations team in record time."

Dominguez had been in the field, talking with one of the LABYRINTH-created cell leaders in Pennsylvania, at the time of the ARTEMIS attack, subbing in for Marino, who Greely had murdered on the Georgetown station rooftop. Furst's first order of business after learning about the attack had been to bring Dominguez into the fold. He was their only physical nexus to the DOMINION field teams upon Marino's demise.

Furst hadn't held back when they met. She'd offered him an obscene amount of money and the promise that he would be melted in a drum of lye and poured down the same drain as his wife and three middle schoolers if he didn't cooperate. She still wasn't sure which of the two sides of the offer had compelled him to join their team.

Kyle Stull was a different story. He was just glad to be alive. When shown the fates of his colleagues at the Georgetown station, Stull didn't hesitate. He didn't even ask for money. All he wanted was the same salary, plus a new life insurance policy. Stull wasn't stupid. After the AXIOM raid, he understood his longevity situation, which could only be characterized as *not great*. With his 401(k) from AXIOM still intact, he wanted to make sure his family was cared for if this new, not-exactly-voluntary partnership went sideways.

"Are we ready to move to the next phase?" asked Greely. "Or do we need some more time to build up the pressure?"

Furst considered his question, which she felt didn't address some of the more pressing factors. Time to play diplomat. Greely had considerable influence over True America's bankroll, which she strongly suspected was filled and refilled with Russian money. And with AXIOM effectively out of the game, they were now paying one hundred percent of DOMINION's operating costs. A little over a month ago, they were essentially paying AXIOM a generous fee, with the promise that AXIOM would be brought into the lucrative government fold once True America took over the reins of power. A profitable but high-stakes gamble on AXIOM's part that kept True America's costs low—until AXIOM imploded.

They faced the same fate if they didn't use DOMINION cautiously and wisely. They also risked failing altogether if they didn't use DOMINION properly and leverage its full potential.

"I recommend that we build up a little more pressure while we assess the progress of Garrett Mann's task force. They've been quiet lately. If they still pose a serious threat, we design and implement a plan to diminish the task force to the point where it's no longer a threat."

"You mean, take it out?" asked Greely.

"If necessary," said Furst. "Unless we can identify a less chaotic and attention-attracting option."

"AXIOM has been down that road before, and it backfired spectacularly," said Greely. "Mann's people have their flaws, but they're clean as far as we can tell—and they're well alerted to any attempts to blackmail or intimidate after the bus ambush. All their immediate families and significant others are still under US Marshal protection. We need to lure Mann back out into the open, away from DC."

"We're working on it," said Furst, before turning to Anya Fiedrick, True America's envoy to the Russians.

"It's taking a little longer than we expected," said Fiedrick. "Or maybe they're being extremely cautious. Either way, all the pieces are in place. It's only a matter of time. Speeding up the process would draw suspicion."

"Or Mann is watching us right now," said Greely. "Taking his time."

"They can't get near this place without us knowing. We've made sure of that," said Furst. "And our surveillance assets are keeping a close eye on them. ARTEMIS hasn't left DC."

Greely shrugged. "We can't afford to let our guard down. Mann's task force has proven to be extremely resourceful over the past few months."

"We're counting on it," said Fiedrick. "And when he makes his move, that'll be the end of his task force."

"I wish I shared her optimism," Greely said. "The man has nine lives. One mistake on our end and all of this is sunk. We've all witnessed his wrath. One of us got to see it firsthand. It wasn't pretty."

"His luck can't last forever," said Furst.

"Have we considered taking out his people right now, before they hit the road again and essentially disappear?" asked Greely. "Once they leave DC, we'll be holding our collective breath again, waiting for their next move."

"May I?" said Hector Dominguez.

Furst nodded.

"By all means," said Greely.

"We've kept as close an eye on ARTEMIS as possible since the attack, using a combination of mercenaries and DOMINION assets—"

"At this rate, the world is going to run out of mercenaries," said Greely. "I assume you're going to tell me this group is better than the last few AXIOM hired?"

"I have no idea," said Dominguez. "I worked under Marino managing the DOMINION cells. They were en route to DC when the Georgetown annex was attacked."

"Someone at the Tysons headquarters summoned them the morning of the attack," said Furst. "Likely either Jeremy Powell or Gary Litman."

"A lot of good it did them," said Greely. "Anyway. Continue."

"One of the task force members, a Special Surveillance Group investigator, spotted their tail a few days ago. The entire task force has been moved to a hotel within walking distance of FBI headquarters."

"Doesn't sound like a hard target to me. Hit them while in transit," said Greely.

"In one of the most locked-down parts of Washington, DC?" asked Furst, before Dominguez responded.

"And we haven't identified any discernible pattern of travel. Just random sightings inside the hotel lobby."

"Then figure something out at the hotel," said Greely. "We're only talking . . . how many agents on the task force?"

"Eight," said Dominguez.

"Eight rooms. We pay off a member of the hotel staff to give us their room numbers, and hit them while they're sleeping," said Greely.

Dominguez turned his head toward Furst with a look that nearly screamed, *He has no fucking clue how this works, does he?*

"I assume the team is staying at the Sofitel or Conrad?" said Furst.

"The Conrad, ma'am," said Dominguez.

"Yeah. We're not getting into the Conrad without causing more trouble than it's worth," she said. "The Conrad regularly hosts dozens of foreign diplomats—which means it'll be swarming with Secret Service and Diplomatic Security Service agents. Not to mention a certain number of foreign security agents authorized to carry firearms. Plus whatever FBI security Mann managed to arrange. We're not hitting the Conrad."

"Then I guess we have no choice but to wait and hope he takes the bait," said Greely.

CHAPTER 7

Chad Lianez rapped on the frame of the open door, interrupting Mann's conversation with Deputy Director O'Reilly. They simultaneously turned their heads and kept neutral faces, until Lianez started to look seriously uncomfortable. In all reality, he had disturbed an inconsequential midmorning coffee break. But why make it easy on him.

"So sorry," said Lianez. "I just assumed because the door was open—"

"That we weren't having a serious conversation?" said O'Reilly.

"No, ma'am," said Lianez. "It just appeared—"

"Like we were having coffee and shooting the shit?" said Mann.

"I didn't mean to imply—"

"We're just messing with you," said O'Reilly. "What's up? You look a little too excited and alert for nine in the morning."

"I think we figured it out," said Lianez. "It's not conclusive, but it's pretty damn convincing."

Mann got up, a little more intrigued than the last several times Lianez had announced that they had solved the SATCHEL mystery. O'Reilly gripped the side of her desk and pulled herself upright. Mann started to move for her crutches.

"You touch those and you'll need your own pair," she said. "No coddling around here."

"My bad," said Mann. "See you in the conference room."

"Shouldn't we—" started Lianez.

Mann took his arm and led him out of the office, letting go and speaking once they'd moved well out of earshot.

"Coddling includes waiting for her," said Mann.

"I see."

"Do you really think you figured it out?"

"I do," said Lianez. "But I'm not sure it's going to help us with the search warrant. There's still no connection to the ranch in Montana."

"You might be surprised," Mann said. "Depending on what you uncovered and how."

Lianez stopped walking.

"The *how* part might be a bit of an issue," he said, lowering his voice.

"How big of an issue?"

"Gupta-level issue," said Lianez. "He won't say how he sourced the imagery."

"Sourced? That's Gupta-speak for *stole*," said Mann.

"Most likely," said Lianez.

"What kind of imagery?"

"Overhead. I'd say it was some kind of FBI or Metro Police Department surveillance drone operating in the area around the Russian embassy. Likely launched from a concealed location near the embassy the moment things started to go south on the streets. Possibly helicopter- or aircraft-based."

"How would he have known to look for something like that?" asked Mann.

O'Reilly, who had crept up on them, shed a little light on the question.

"Gupta and his people were instrumental in stopping the drone attack on the mall a few years ago," she said. "They have a unique and very comprehensive understanding of DC's surveillance systems and capabilities. I'm just surprised it took him so long to find it."

"He said the imagery hadn't been uploaded to a server," said Lianez.

"No wonder it took a while," said O'Reilly. "Sounds like one of the State Department's Crisis Response drones. They're used in diplomatically sensitive airspace, for real-time observation if a threat is identified. Replay of the feed is not accessible to the drone operator for obvious reasons, but the recording is preserved on a hard drive . . . somewhere. That's why it took this long for him to get the feed. And I don't want to know how he got his hands on it."

"Neither do I. All we need to do is confirm that something resembling the SATCHEL didn't burn up in the helicopter," said Mann. "That should be enough for us to move on the ranch in Montana. At least cross it off the list. I still think it's too obvious."

"It's all on the footage," said Lianez.

"What?" O'Reilly said. "Why didn't you lead with that?"

"Yeah, a little more information earlier in this conversation might have been nice," said Mann. "You could have started with that in the doorway."

"I thought you'd want to see it for yourself, rather than have me describe it," said Lianez.

"Good point," said Mann.

"I'll really need some convincing to go for a warrant," O'Reilly said.

"Ma'am, this is pretty convincing," said Lianez. "And that's not the only surprise. Watch this."

For the few minutes it took to play the entire feed Lianez had initiated, the task force remained dead silent—eyes fixed on the retractable wall-screen. The clarity wasn't the best, but the drone had caught the Russians red-handed. And not only the Russians—another crew had been poised and ready to grab the SATCHEL.

Luke Turner broke the silence.

"Is he dead?"

"Hard to say," said Lianez, adjusting the view. "His head doesn't look cracked open, but he missed the airbag. A forty-foot back-flop off a helicopter doesn't leave you with the best prognosis."

"The duffel bag looks fine," said Callie Jackson.

Turner stifled a laugh. "Can't say the same for Greely."

"Are we sure it's him?" said O'Reilly.

"Can't be one hundred percent sure," said Lianez. "But his outfit matches what our surveillance team in Tysons Corner observed, plus what Jax and Javier saw through their rifle scopes. It looks like he tossed the SATCHEL, which landed square in the middle of the airbag, before he jumped. But he should have jumped with the bag. The short delay between the two cost him. The helicopter was out of control."

"True America and Russians working together. Shocker," said Mann. "I guess the big question is, who took the SATCHEL? True America clearly intended to steal it with Russia's help. But the Russians are very opportunistic. If they grabbed it on the rooftop, they would have held on to it and used it as leverage against True America."

"Wait until you see the rest of the footage," said Ray Mills. "I don't think the Russians have it."

O'Reilly nodded at Lianez, who continued the show.

"The drone flies right over the rooftop in question but doesn't stop, which is a little odd, given the fact that an out-of-control helicopter just passed underneath it," said Lianez.

"Probably on autopilot, heading directly toward a location passed to it by MPD's gunshot detection system. The system's sensors can triangulate a gunshot to within a hundred feet, sometimes tighter. A live operator would have taken control of the drone when it reached the location identified by the system," said O'Reilly.

"Makes sense," said Lianez. "The drone stopped directly over AXIOM's Georgetown annex, then immediately sped back toward the helicopter crash site."

"That's where it gets interesting," said Mills.

"Very interesting," said Lianez, fast-forwarding the feed. "Check this out."

Mann studied the image. *What the fuck?*

"Same rooftop. No SATCHEL. Different body," said Mann. "Obvious pool of blood under the new body's head."

"That's a bingo," Mills said.

"And that's you quoting too many movies," said Mann. "How much time elapsed between the first images of that rooftop and the last?"

"Two minutes and twelve seconds," said Lianez.

"Something went down on that rooftop in the two minutes that elapsed," said Mann. "The big question is—"

"What went down?" said Jax.

"Funny," said Mann. "But yes."

"Interior security camera footage from an antique shop across the street from the town house sheds some light on the subject. *Some* being the operative term," said Lianez.

Two sedans pulled up to the town house, double parking on the street. Six people got out of the vehicles, including the drivers, and piled into the brownstone's ground-floor entrance. They didn't ring the doorbell or mess with keys. Someone had obviously left the door open for them. None of them appeared armed.

"Russians?" said Mann.

"They clearly had prearranged authorization to enter the building. We're still looking for these cars," said Lianez. "Video quality is poor, as you can see—but we did pull a partial from one of the plates. If we find it, we might be able to link it to the Russian embassy. But that's a long shot."

"Who's 'we'?" asked O'Reilly. "Members of the task force?"

Mann met Lianez's nervous glance and nodded. No reason to keep secrets.

"Gupta and his friends," said Lianez.

When O'Reilly didn't immediately protest, he guessed they were in the clear. She knew everything there was to know about the mercenaries Lianez had just referenced.

"Fair enough," said O'Reilly. "Continue."

Three Suburban-size SUVs pulled up a few seconds later, two arriving from the east, the other from the west. A team of nine entered the apartment building, the drivers remaining with the vehicles.

"As you can see, this group is different. Kitted up and heavily armed. They return to the SUVs three minutes later and leave," Lianez said.

"Did they leave with Greely?" asked O'Reilly.

"I know I sound like a broken record," said Lianez, "but it's impossible to say, given the video quality. The same number exited the building. We can count bodies coming out. Two of them looked like they might have been carrying something heavy between them, but we've zoomed in as close as possible and can't confirm."

"In terms of who went in and out of the building," said Callie Jackson, "all we can say is that only five of the original six people who entered the brownstone—presumably Russians—returned to the sedans. The sixth Russian is likely the one who appeared on the rooftop in a different position from Greely."

"True America hit the building, accessed the rooftop—and got into a bit of a scuffle with the Russians," said O'Reilly. "Leaving one of the Russians behind."

"Sounds about right," said Lianez.

"Then we have to assume True America possesses the SATCHEL. And that they're somewhat in bed with the Russians—which is seriously bad news for the upcoming election," said Mann. "Unless I'm missing something."

"I think you hit the nail on the head," said Lianez. "And here's something else to back up your theory. Surveillance drone footage identified at least seven more airbags in the vicinity of the AXIOM Georgetown annex. Each airbag is located on the rooftop of a property owned or leased by the Russian embassy."

"Greely always planned to jump onto one of those rooftops with the SATCHEL. Brilliant," said Luke Turner.

"Yeah. He just didn't think he'd make the jump from an out-of-control helicopter," said Jackson.

Mann rubbed his chin. That helicopter couldn't have been arranged at the last moment. It had been ready and waiting. Damn. Greely had planned to steal the SATCHEL all along. This changed everything.

He wouldn't have grabbed the SATCHEL without a plan to operate DOMINION. He'd need the software to do that.

"Any chance we could secure interviews with the tenants of those buildings?" asked Mann.

"Is that a rhetorical question?" O'Reilly said. "Mayer, Mendoza, care to weigh in?"

Jessica Mayer stepped up. Her years of experience as a Special Surveillance Group investigator tailing foreign diplomats yielded a quick answer. "If the residences are leased by the Russian embassy and the occupants were part of the scheme to deliver SATCHEL into True America's hands, we'll never secure an interview."

"Agree," said Frank Vincenzo, another one of their Special Surveillance Group investigators. "The Russians aren't very big on cooperating with the FBI, even under the most innocuous of circumstances. No way they'll talk with us after getting their hand caught in the cookie jar. And don't even ask about the possibility of a surveillance warrant."

Mayer continued, "The scant evidence in our possession wouldn't come close to convincing a FISA judge to issue a warrant to enter one of these residences and plant devices. And even if we could pull off a miracle warrant, it's unlikely that the tenants would produce information pertinent to furthering an investigation. To be honest, I would be surprised if the tenants haven't been moved into the embassy or sent back to Russia."

"Wonderful," said Mann. "I guess the big question is whether True America has the second part of the equation. The ability to use the SATCHEL database."

"MONTANA," said O'Reilly.

"Presumably," said Mann. "Whatever that actually means."

"The ranch?" O'Reilly suggested.

Mann shook his head and grumbled. "Too damn obvious. But what other choice do we have? Is there enough here for a warrant to hit the ranch? I don't think we'll find their secret lair there, but assuming the whole place doesn't blow sky high prior to or during our entry, we should be able to find something to point us in the right direction."

"The sky-high thing is kind of my boundary," said Luke Turner. "Sacramento was a fucking disaster."

"I can get a warrant for this. James is on board," said O'Reilly. "And we'll take every precaution to make sure this isn't a repeat of Sacramento."

"What does that mean?" asked Ray Mills.

"Bomb technicians searching the house. Some extremely sophisticated explosive device detection equipment deployed prior to the bomb techs entering the house. Electronic countermeasures to prevent detonation signals. Not to mention some stuff I'm not cleared to share with you," said O'Reilly.

"Sounds reasonable," said Mills.

"There's no downside that I can see, other than possibly tipping our hand with the MONTANA connection," said O'Reilly. "If we're wrong about the ranch, they could move the real site. Make it even harder to find."

"My guess is, they only have one more backup location that can handle DOMINION. We just need to find and disable their operation well before the election," Mann said. "As far as tipping our hand is concerned, I think we'll be fine. Searching all of McCall's properties is a logical investigative progression—which is why we should probably hit all his higher-profile properties in the US at roughly the same time. Maybe even hit up law enforcement agencies overseas to take a look at his foreign real estate. To discourage speculation."

"That'll take time," said O'Reilly. "Could be weeks until the first international raid goes down."

"Agreed," said Mann. "But at least it'll be in the works if True America has contacts in the Department of Justice or State Department. The Montana ranch has been his second home outside of Maryland, so it shouldn't look odd if ARTEMIS takes the lead on that raid. His house on the Chesapeake would be the last place he'd stash sensitive information. A waste of time for a specialized team like mine."

"Don't push it," said O'Reilly. "ARTEMIS is still on very shaky ground."

"Skating on thin ice," said Luke Turner.

"Walking a tightrope," said Jackson.

"Without a net," added Mills.

"Out on a limb," said Jessica Mayer.

"On a knife's edge," said Kerri Wallace.

Frank Vincenzo started to say something, but O'Reilly cut him off.

"Please. I'm about to vomit in my mouth," she said. "I'll get you the warrant. But we'll hit the ranch my way. SWAT and the bomb techs first. I can't afford to lose the legendary ARTEMIS task force. Might look a little too suspicious and convenient on my part if you all went up in smoke before the Congressional hearings."

They all shared a quick laugh.

"Odds are high that the ranch will be a nothingburger," said Mann. "But you can never be too careful."

O'Reilly paused for a long moment, her eyes drifting downward. Her expression going deadpan. Clearly somewhere else. Somewhere in her vague past. Mann still hadn't gotten to the bottom of that. She resurfaced just as quickly as she had submerged.

"No. You can't," she said. "I know a little something about that."

"More than just a little—apparently," he muttered.

PART II

CHAPTER 8

The helicopter banked hard to the right, Mann's shoulder slamming into Callie Jackson, who had somehow anticipated the maneuver and remained upright in her seat. The sudden turn's g-forces kept him pressed against her until the pilot eased out of the turn a few moments later. Jax's insistent elbow helped him back into place before they suddenly gained altitude, the pit of his stomach dropping.

He hated helicopters. Disliked flying in general. But helicopters made no sense to him. Too many moving parts, and no leeway if any of those parts stopped moving. A 747 could lose all engine power and still land safely in the hands of a skilled pilot. If a helicopter lost any power to either of its rotors? He didn't want to think about it. They dropped a few seconds later, Mann not having any choice but to think about it.

When the helicopter steadied, he took a deep breath and released it. Since they hadn't crashed, the maneuver could mean only one thing: They'd just cleared the hill south of the target. The helicopters—four military-converted UH-60 Blackhawks and two military-upgraded Bell 407s—were on the final approach to McCall's ranch. It was the largest fleet Deputy Director O'Reilly could put together without flying helicopters out to Montana from the East Coast or Chicago.

One of the Blackhawks would hover a few feet over the flat, eight-vehicle-bay rooftop on the southside of the mansion, depositing the four HRT sniper teams who would spread out along the rest of the rooftop and establish positions watching every possible axis of approach.

Mann and the ARTEMIS surveillance team would drop with the snipers to provide another layer of protection watching over the FBI agents involved in the operation. Jax and Lianez would hand-launch two AeroVironment Wasp AE drones and scan the surrounding brush, woods, and structures for threats. They'd also set up a temporary radio frequency–disruption tower to spoof hostile radio signals that could be used to remotely detonate explosives.

The tower transmitted a signal that didn't impede FBI-encrypted communications devices but would scramble reception by any other devices within a few hundred feet. Hardwired bombs were the Special Agent Bomb Technician group's job—and they had two bomb squads in the first helicopter to hit the landing zone about fifty yards south of the mansion.

Once they cleared the LZ of potential explosive threats, the remaining four helicopters, two Blackhawks, and the two Bells would off-load a total of twenty-six FBI SWAT agents, who would secure the ground perimeter and accompany the bomb technicians into the house.

And that was just the first wave. Eight SUVs packed with forensics and IT specialists, along with special agents from nearby field offices, would depart from a staging area several miles away after the bomb techs declared the house safe. Barring any immediate threats, McCall's ranch was about thirty minutes away from being the busiest site outside these hills—temporary home to nearly seventy FBI agents and a few dozen more local law enforcement officers.

The helicopter's crew chief got up from her seat behind the pilots and proceeded to open the sliding doors on both sides of the helicopter. The sharp, almost citrusy smell of warm pine needles washed through the passenger compartment.

"Thirty seconds to target," said the crew chief over Mann's headphone.

The Hostage Rescue Team operators removed their headsets and donned their ballistic helmets. They left their weapons alone; the operators had checked and rechecked them before boarding the helicopter.

Mann resisted the urge to fidget with his rifle, his hand tapping the side of the handguard. Jax didn't react at all. She looked stone-cold ready to go, her rifle slung across her ballistic vest. He leaned over to check on Lianez, who looked like he might puke any second. Beads of sweat dripped down the sides of his face.

Mann focused on the interior of the helicopter. If he looked outside, he'd likely join Lianez.

"You good?" yelled the lead HRT operator over the whine of the helicopter's engine and pounding of its rotors.

He gave the guy a thumbs-up and feigned a thin smile. The operator glanced to Mann's left and raised an eyebrow. Was something wrong? Jax nudged him.

"You might want to take off your headphones," she yelled.

Shit. He already felt like a rookie hanging out with these hardened HRT operators. Now it was confirmed. All he could think about was not tripping and falling on his face when he hopped down from the helicopter—which was all but guaranteed. The Blackhawk flared and came to a stop before leveling out. The crew chief hustled from one side of the helicopter to the other, glancing down through each door, before emphatically signaling with both hands.

"Go! Go! Go!" she barked at them.

HRT went first, the eight operators out in the blink of an eye. Mann jumped next, dropping to a knee but not tumbling in embarrassment. He pushed himself up and turned to face the helicopter door, the rotor wash pushing against him. Lianez and Jax followed, quickly steadying themselves. The rest of the helicopter fleet split up and passed to the left and right of the house, before disappearing from sight beyond the trees to the north of the ranch. A small show of force meant to discourage any initial resistance.

The helicopter rose about twenty feet and steadied. The crew chief tossed a thick metal cable attached to an exterior winch to the rooftop, which struck with a heavy thud. She then attached three industrial-looking D rings to clips embedded in the cable, before sliding their gear out the door.

Two square, reinforced Pelican cases contained the drones and controllers, plus one rectangular case housing the RF disruption tower, transmitter, and battery packs. The three containers dangled in midair for a few moments, swinging back and forth from the rotor wash, before the crew chief carefully lowered them to the rooftop, where Mann, Lianez, and Jax immediately disconnected them and pulled them clear of the cable. They'd practiced detaching the D rings a few dozen times, until the crew chief felt confident that they wouldn't screw it up. HRT didn't like to linger in the open to unscrew mistakes.

The moment the D rings were detached, the cable retracted under the watchful eye of the crew chief. The helicopter roared away as she secured the end of the cable to the winch. Several seconds later, the rooftop went quiet, except for the distant thump of rotor blades and quick scrambling of feet as the HRT sniper teams moved across the mansion's roof to their positions.

Mann inserted the earpiece attached to his tactical radio. "HRT. This is Mann."

"All teams up," said the HRT leader, who was in communication with his operators through a separate net.

"Let me know when we can bring in the bomb techs," said Mann.

"Give us a minute to scan the area."

He didn't reply. The protocol for radio communications was a controversial subject of discussion across every agency. The military used a very formal radio protocol, to avoid any confusion. *Over* meant the conversation was still live. *Out* signified the end of the conversation. Pilots were a little less formal. You could talk to them in plain but abbreviated sentences. HRT operators basically grunted and spoke their mind. All good—until the shit hit the fan and everyone needed to know who was saying what.

Less than a minute later, Mann received a thumbs-up from the HRT commander, who was positioned on the northeast corner of the garage. He was serving as both the detachment's leader and a spotter for one of the snipers.

Mann turned to Jax and Lianez, who had unfolded and assembled the ten-foot-tall tower structure and were in the process of attaching the transmitter to the top. "How long until the tower is operational?" he asked.

He wouldn't call in the Blackhawk carrying the bomb technicians until the radio frequency–detonation threat had been neutralized. Landing zone options near the house were limited. Not exactly hard to guess where they'd land. A single, well-placed IED could have catastrophic results.

"Two minutes," said Jax. "We're about to raise and secure the tower. Then I need to run some diagnostics to verify we have a good signal."

"Sounds good," said Mann, before passing the word over a satellite push-to-talk phone to the bomb squad team leaders.

The phone had been a precaution suggested by Jax. The helicopter might be too far away for the tactical radios to reach them. While his surveillance team raised the tower, the two Bell 407s reappeared and overflew the ranch, before taking overwatch positions a few hundred feet above the trees to the east and west of the house.

Jax attached the transmitter's power cable to the battery pack, while Lianez studied a handheld radio frequency detector.

"We're good," said Lianez, before helping Jax open the cases containing their drones.

Mann let the pilot know, and the deep hammering of a Blackhawk's rotors cut through the clamor of the two Bell 407s flanking the ranch. The two bomb teams finished physically clearing the LZ several minutes later, timed almost perfectly with the launch of both drones. With the drones now providing overwatch, the Bell 407s departed to join the lineup of helicopters approaching the ranch.

Mann jogged over to the HRT sniper team watching the woods to the east.

"How does it look?" he asked.

The team leader put a hand on Mann's shoulder and gently pushed him down until he was crouched and his head sat below the lip of the wall that lined the garage rooftop.

"Anyone could be hiding out in those woods," he said. "And you're a high-value target. They don't need a bomb to derail your task force's investigation. Just a few well-placed bullets."

"You're right," said Mann. "But I feel like a self-important idiot sneaking around like this while everyone else is exposed."

The HRT sniper-spotter pairs didn't have the luxury of remaining out of sight, especially the three teams situated on the ranch's rooftop, which wasn't flat. Two of the teams were dangerously exposed. They lay at the apex of the rooftop, covering the north and south approaches—each on the opposite side of the ridge, their backs open to 180-degree gunfire behind them. The only thing standing between them and a bullet was the ballistic shield they each wore on their backs. The third team, which watched over the western approach, at least had a wide brick chimney to partially shield them.

"Better than being dead."

"True," said Mann, which was why he had requested sniper support.

The bomb at Raul's Sacramento house had clearly been meant for his task force. True America, or whoever was running the show now, had to know the FBI wouldn't fall for the same trick again. They'd look for an easier and far less messy way to cripple ARTEMIS. The first Blackhawk loaded with SWAT agents appeared to the southeast, flying at treetop level. Mann scooted over to Jax and Lianez, who were tucked away next to the main house rooftop—intently staring at the ground control–station screens sitting on their laps.

"All clear on electro, optical, and infrared," said Jax, preempting his question. "And yes, we'll keep the drones away from the LZ."

"Have I become that predictable?" asked Mann.

"You've always been this predictable," said Jax. "What's going on with the snipers?"

"Same. All clear—for now," said Mann. "I was kindly reminded by one of the HRT guys that I need to keep a lower profile."

"Yeah. I was going to mention that."

"But you didn't."

Lianez chuckled.

"Don't laugh. Turner is next in line to run ARTEMIS if I get clipped," asked Mann.

"Shit. I hadn't thought of that. Maybe you should crouch down a little further, or just crawl from now on," said Jax.

"Funny," said Mann.

"On a serious note, how are you going to take part in the raid if you have to hide up here?"

"I'll head down when SWAT and the bomb techs clear the house," said Mann. "They brought a few extendable ladders."

"You should probably head down while they're kicking up a bunch of dust," said Lianez. "Give you some cover."

"You guys really don't want Turner taking over, do you?" said Mann.

"Is it that obvious?"

Mann stifled a laugh before passing along the suggestion to the SWAT commander. He could lie low on the wide, wood-and-stone-encased porch until they cleared the house.

CHAPTER 9

Special Agent Luke Turner scooted forward as they approached the landing zone to make room for the SWAT agents, who took positions on the bench attached to the helicopter's skids. He sat cross-legged, elbows on knees, his FBI-issued rifle pointed toward the thick cluster of trees due east of the house. He missed the heavy-barrel HK416s taken from the LABYRINTH raid—exceptional rifles capable of burning through multiple sixty-round drum magazines without overheating—but they'd deep-sixed all the small-arms weapons used in the Georgetown raid in the Chesapeake Bay. Rifles, shotguns, and a few submachine guns. No reason to tempt the FBI's forensic gods.

That said, he'd convinced Mann to hold on to a few of the more exotic goodies found in New Mexico: the two remaining AT4 rocket launchers, several dozen 40mm high-explosive rifle grenades and two M320 grenade launchers that could be attached to rifles or fired independently, a crate of thirty M67 fragmentation grenades, and enough C4 plastic explosive bricks to take down the mansion his helicopter was approaching.

Out of the corner of his eye, he spotted one of the SWAT teams already on the ground extending a ladder to the top of the garage, presumably for Mann. Moments later, a thick cloud of dust kicked up from the helicopter landing just ahead of them, obscuring his view and presumably that of anyone who might be watching from a distance. Smart. They couldn't afford to lose Mann.

He scanned the trees through the magnified hybrid sight attached to his rifle, looking for anything out of place. Thermal sweeps of the acreage surrounding the target house hadn't identified anything worth investigating on foot or with a micro-drone. As far as they could tell, the ranch and its surrounding grounds were deserted. Like Mann had suspected. What had he called it? A nothingburger? Sounded about right. His earpiece crackled.

"We're up," said the pilot, moments before the helicopter dipped forward and accelerated toward the landing zone.

Turner grabbed the doorframe next to him, even though he was tightly affixed to the helicopter by a lanyard connected to a tight harness. The helicopter's skids never touched the ground when they reached the LZ. To say that the pilot knew her shit was an understatement. The four SWAT agents slid off the benches and hit the deck.

"We're clear," said the team leader, sprinting toward the house.

The pilot never responded. Just hit whatever combination of controls necessary to rise over the house and peel off to the east. He waited until she leveled off before detaching his lanyard and heading back inside the helicopter. The Bell 407 wasn't a workhorse like the Blackhawk. It only carried four passengers, which was why he rode the external bench on the way in. No crew chief. Just a copilot, who hadn't said a word since they took off from Bozeman International Airport.

He had the passenger compartment to himself now. No matter where the pilot positioned them around the target, Turner could move freely to cover the most probable threat axis. The pilot's voice boomed in his earpiece.

"Comfy back there?"

"Good to go," said Turner, slightly annoyed.

"See the case behind the rear seats?"

What the hell was she talking about? He grabbed the top of one of the seats and pulled himself up. A long Pelican case lay behind the seats.

"I see it," said Turner.

"You might like what you find in that case."

"We'll see," he said, pulling the case over the seats and dropping it on the deck.

He unsnapped the three tension locks and opened the case. *Oh. Wow.*

"Is this legal?" he asked.

"We're in the testing phase," said the pilot. "In desperate need of testing. Maybe it's not the weapon we need. Maybe it is."

"I'd be happy to help with the evaluation," said Turner.

"Do you need any help figuring it out?"

"Nope," he said, kind of lying.

The XM250 light machine gun was belt fed from an attached rigid pouch containing fifty to two hundred rounds, or a standard thirty-round magazine. From what he could tell, the four pouches inside the case carried a hundred rounds of 6.8mm ammunition. That was the kicker with the XM250. This light machine gun, which essentially resembled an oversize rifle, fired a far punchier bullet than any of the FBI's standard rifles.

"The sight has been zeroed for two hundred meters," said the pilot.

About two football fields. Right for this kind of job.

"I heard the sight is a little complicated," said Turner, knowing that was probably the understatement of the year.

The adjustable magnification XM157 fire-control system integrated a laser range finder with environmental sensors, aiming lasers, and a digital compass. The device basically took everything into account and gave you an aimpoint to hit your target—with automatic gunfire. Hard to argue with that, but he'd never used anything like this before. He'd relied on his instincts instead, which had served him well up to this point.

"Don't fuck with the sight," she said. "It has a bunch of bells and whistles that you don't have time to learn. Right now, it's configured to give you the range to any target you sight in on. You'll see that in the reticle. The rest is up to you."

"Perfect," said Turner. "What about my counterpart in the other Bell?"

Kerri Wallace had been in the helicopter that landed ahead of them, presumably headed south to cover the SUV convoy's approach. The two of them would provide close-in, armed overwatch. The Bell 407s had been chosen as their shooting platforms for their better maneuverability and smaller size than the Blackhawks—though, if worse came to worse, the crew chiefs on the Blackhawks could provide additional firepower.

"Ask her yourself!"

He triggered the tactical radio net. "Kerri. This is Turner. Have you seen the light? The XM250?"

"Oh yeah," she said. "And I think I'm in love."

CHAPTER 10

Mann slid down the ladder, using his gloves to slow his descent. When his feet hit the ground, he crouched and evaluated the situation. A thick cloud of dirt enveloped him as the second Bell 407 landed about twenty yards away. He peered through the haze and caught a glimpse of Turner, who waved emphatically. Not a friendly wave. More of a *get the fuck out of sight* wave. Message received. He headed toward the front porch, his earpiece coming alive halfway there.

"Garrett. This is Turner."

"Take it easy. I'm headed for cover," said Mann.

"Just wanted to check in. Saw you climbing down the ladder."

"Sorry," Mann said. "Everyone is either pushing my head down or lecturing me on the difference between cover and concealment. I'm not that important, by the way."

"Nobody wants your job," said Turner. "And while we're on the topic of how unimportant you are, do we need to go over the difference between cover and concealment?"

Mann reached the porch and hunkered down behind the stone wall before responding.

"The stone wall around the porch is cover. The dirt cloud is concealment," he said. "Unless the porch is rigged with explosives."

"I really hope it isn't," said Turner. "I don't want to take over the task force."

"How are things looking up there?" asked Mann.

"Got some new toys," Turner said. "We're going to fly a little higher. Let the drones do the low-altitude work."

"Must be some nice toys?"

"XM250s," said Turner.

"Christmas came early," said Mann. "Hopefully, we won't need those. It's been quiet down here. HRT hasn't spotted anything unusual. Same with Jax's drones."

"Kerri and I haven't identified anything, either," Turner said.

"Let's hope it stays that way," said Mann, some movement near the front door catching his eye. "I have to go. Looks like they're about to breach the house."

"You know where to find me."

Turner's helicopter, the last to hit the landing zone, lifted off and disappeared over the house.

"Mann. This is SWAT lead. We're ready to breach."

He shifted to face the front door, where two four-agent SWAT stacks lined up several feet away from the entry on both sides—and a distant huddle of bomb technicians waited for his signal.

"Do it," said Mann, too aware that he might be sending all of them to an instantaneous death.

"Breaching!" yelled one of the bomb techs, before turning the dual front doors into splinters.

They didn't go with the usual hinge-lock breach, followed by a portable battering ram. One of the bomb techs had recommended simply disintegrating the door, which accomplished two goals simultaneously. First. It would trigger any explosive devices rigged to the door. Second. It would provide immediate access to the house. Not for the humans involved. The FBI's Hazardous Device Operations Center had given them a few experimental devices to use during the raid. No secondary explosions rocked the porch or grand foyer.

"Sending the next wave," said one of the bomb tech team leaders.

Two of the techs crouched on the porch in front of the now-obliterated front doors set a pair of four-wheeled remote-controlled vehicles on the deck. A moment later, the vehicles sped inside. Several seconds after they disappeared from view, two explosions rocked the inside of the house. *Jesus!*

"All clear."

"All clear?" said Mann.

"Yes. The RPVs swept the foyer before we exploded them. Any trip wires, pressure devices, or motion sensors would have been detonated by the explosion or triggered by the RPVs," he said. "We're ready to send people inside."

"Send them in," said Mann.

The two teams, each accompanied by two uneasy-looking SWAT agents, entered the house. About thirty very long minutes later, one of the bomb techs' team leaders stepped through the blasted front doorway onto the porch and shook his head.

"We didn't find anything," he said over the tactical net.

"And my surveillance team hasn't detected any unusual RF activity," said Mann.

He started to get up, but the SWAT agent crouched next to him with his rifle pointed toward the nearby trees nudged him.

"Keep your head down, sir," said the agent.

The bomb tech held up a hand and motioned for him to stay in place.

"Give us another hour to pry this place apart. We really didn't see anything unusual on our first sweep. Doesn't look like anyone has been here in months, but better safe than sorry," said the bomb tech.

"That really should be your motto, instead of *Initial success or total failure*," said Mann.

"They basically mean the same thing," said the bomb tech. "One just sounds a little less like something you'd say while intentionally overcooking chicken."

"I'll have to remember that one," Mann said, grinning. "Is there any way you break up your teams into smaller groups to speed up the process?"

"I feel comfortable doing that after the initial sweep. Divide and conquer. This place is bigger than a ski lodge."

"I'll send in some more agents to escort them through," said the SWAT commander.

"And SWAT. Be on the lookout for any possible false walls or hidden doors. If AXIOM used this site as a DOMINION relay, it'll be well concealed."

"Got it. We'll keep our eyes peeled for anything suspicious," said the SWAT commander.

"Hopefully, this'll be a big nothingburger—like you said," said the bomb tech.

"We can only hope," Mann said.

It looked more and more like this was the dead end he'd predicted. Only time, and some deep forensics investigation, would tell.

CHAPTER 11

Dmitri Sokolov stifled the urge to puke. The rest of his small team did the same. The wind had shifted a few minutes ago, bathing them in the putrid stench of their own body waste. He balled up his fists and kept still. He was starting to lose it, and any movement could give away his position. Three days out here, doing nothing but pissing and shitting in a nearby pit—while keeping a specialized blanket suspended over them, about four feet above the ground. A covering that had kept his team from being detected by the FBI's infrared and thermal-imaging technology.

Wonderful from a safety and security standpoint, but that was about the only upside to the arrangement. The worst part being that they couldn't leave the overhead cover to do their business, so all he smelled at this point was three days of festering human stew. And it got far worse at night, when they had no choice but to pull the sides of the cover down.

They were far more vulnerable to detection after dark, when the temperatures outside dropped and their body heat would stand out like an emergency flare. The place turned into a hotbox of body odor and excrement, making it nearly impossible to sleep for more than a few minutes without gagging.

He'd suffered similar conditions before—in Chechnya, Georgia, and Syria. Especially in Syria, where sophisticated US military surveillance assets operated around the clock. He knew that the FBI's inventory of drones and surveillance aircraft paled in both quantity and quality compared to US military equipment, but he had no intention of taking any chances. The cost of failure was possibly his life. Almost certainly his freedom. And without a doubt—the five-million-dollar bounty. That was the big difference. He'd endured hell for weeks on end for several thousand dollars. For five million, he could deal with this for a few more hours, or however long it took for his target to poke his head out again.

Not that the bounty was guaranteed at this point. The size and scope of the raid cast doubt on his crew's ability to successfully execute the mission. They hadn't expected this many FBI agents. Certainly not so many helicopters. Or any helicopters, for that matter. The FBI's methodology was unorthodox, to say the least. And completely unexpected. That said, all he truly needed was a clear shot for one of his two sniper teams. This had been the plan all along. He'd brought the assault and heavy weapons teams to give everyone the best chance of escaping. His snipers weren't stupid. They knew that the moment Mann's head exploded, the hunt would be on—and they didn't stand a chance of escaping dozens of FBI SWAT agents.

Mann appeared again for a moment, but he didn't stay visible long enough for any of Sokolov's snipers to take a shot. *Fuck me!* This whole thing could have been done already if Mann had kept his head up for more than ten seconds. On the rooftop. On the porch. Anywhere!

"Dragon Actual. This is Dragon Four," said the spotter assigned to one of the sniper teams. "Primary target is now inside the house."

Son of a bitch! They were stuck here until he showed his face again. But would he? They'd had a chance to take him out when the first helicopter dropped the FBI snipers and drone team on the roof of the garage. Unfortunately, they hadn't expected Mann to land with the first helicopter, and missed the opportunity. He hated to think they'd missed their only chance.

The FBI task force that had swarmed the house had effectively kept him out of sight since one of the snipers on the rooftop had pushed his head down. Since then, Mann had appeared only a few times, for a few seconds. Not enough time for Sokolov's snipers to take a reasonable shot.

But at some point, the FBI would finish the search of the house and reemerge. Hopefully, Mann and the agents would let their guard down long enough for his snipers to take a shot. Patience. One well-placed bullet was all it would take. Regardless of the chaos that would ensue, he had enough firepower to keep the feds at bay and execute his escape and evasion plan. The plan wasn't guaranteed. Especially with six helicopters at the FBI's disposal, but he felt confident they could still get away. Some of them, at least.

His satellite phone buzzed. He checked the screen—one of the client's roadside lookouts just outside Bozeman. The same contact who had notified him of the helicopters headed up Montana Highway 86, toward McCall's ranch. A quick text that changed everything.

> 8 SUV convoy headed north. They're bringing four ATVs. ETA 22min

He acknowledged the message and took a few moments to consider the options. Eight SUVs. Thirty to forty more agents? Plus the means to pursue them off-road? The helicopters were bad enough, but Sokolov had mapped out routes that would make it difficult for aerial surveillance to track them. But with ATVs trailing them, their chances of getting out of this had just taken a serious nosedive. The smartest move would be to call off the attack. Explain the situation to his contact and hope for another chance.

A five-million-dollar contract only came around once in a lifetime, but therein lay the problem. You only get one lifetime. What was the point of fulfilling the contract and rotting in jail or a coffin? None. The challenge would be convincing his crew to throw away their potential windfalls. Not all of them would be keen on the idea of walking away from this kind of money. They weren't being paid anywhere close to as much as Sokolov, but some of them would kill their own mothers for a few thousand dollars. He dialed a number he'd memorized.

"I just heard the news," answered his contract broker. "The client really wants the target eliminated. They've doubled the contract amount. I've just sent the details."

"Holy mother. Did you see this?" said the mercenary next to him, holding up his push-to-talk satphone. "One point five million dollars. They must really want this guy dead."

"You sent the details to everyone?" asked Sokolov, instantly understanding the situation.

Barring the arrival of a platoon of armored personnel carriers and flight of Apache attack helicopters, at least half of Dragon Team would take their chances against close to eighty FBI agents. And not just investigative agents—seasoned SWAT and HRT operators. Fuck.

"The client is willing to go as high as two and a half times the original fee," said the contact.

"Three times the original amount," said Sokolov, having nothing to lose at this point.

If he refused to participate, someone would probably kill him, thinking they could get his share, or be ordered to kill him by the same man on the other end of this call.

"To be honest, your client will likely end up paying out far less than originally budgeted, given the arrival of those SUVs," said Sokolov. "Not many of us are likely to avoid capture or make it out of this alive."

"There's a reason the bounty was so high on this job," said his contact. "You knew that when you took the job."

"The number was definitely hard to resist," Sokolov said. "Three times?"

"Agreed. I just sent out another message to your people."

"The contract price just went up again," said the mercenary who had announced the original increase. "One million, eight hundred and seventy-five thousand. What's going on?"

"I need to let you go. If we're going to have any chance of pulling this off, we need to get moving."

"See you on the other side."

"Hopefully," said Sokolov.

The mercenary behind the team's light machine gun gave him a quick look. "Did you renegotiate?"

"Yes. This is no longer a sniper operation," said Sokolov.

"Then what is it?" asked the gunner.

"Basically, a suicide mission," said Sokolov. "Any problem with that?"

"For one point eight million? None at all," he replied.

"Everyone else good?"

The other three nodded eagerly.

"All Dragon teams, this is Dragon actual. The contract price went up for a reason," said Sokolov. "We have no choice but to do this the hard way."

CHAPTER 12

Mann stood in a cavernous hallway leading out of the mansion's vaulted-ceiling great room—huddled around an oversize digital tablet with the two bomb team leaders and the SWAT commander. Out of an abundance of caution, they'd chosen the spot because it was one of the few central locations in the ski lodge–size complex that wasn't exposed to massive windows and potential snipers. One of the bomb techs guided them through the schematics, using the tried-and-true finger-pointing method. With his gloves on, he wouldn't activate any of the features on the screen.

"We've mapped out all the obviously accessible spaces in the mansion, lodge, ranch, or whatever you want to call it. As you can see, it's quite extensive," he said.

"This technology is amazing," said Mann.

The bomb techs had basically mapped out the entire mansion just by walking through it, leaving icons with notes in each room, identifying points of interest for further investigation.

"It's a modified form of echolocation. The lead tech wears a transponder on their helmet, which constantly transmits and receives signals. Thousands per second. The software in their backpack does the magic and maps out the rooms, hallways—anywhere the tech goes. It constantly updates to link the spaces together. It even creates a fairly accurate three-dimensional image of each space. This is just the two-dimensional image."

"Can it detect hidden doors or false walls?"

"Not yet. But they're working on it," said the tech. "Speaking of doors. We've hit a few that were locked, but with SWAT's help, we've managed to enter them without using explosives. Nothing even remotely suspicious so far. I suggest we switch up roles at this point. More SWAT agents searching for concealed doors and stuff like that. One bomb technician per team. If SWAT finds a possible disguised entry, we'll divert some techs to help ensure we're not looking at an improvised explosive device on the other side."

"Sounds good. The rest of the crew is inbound," said Mann. "If we find anything remotely resembling a server relay or operations center, they'll work their magic on it. They can even trace security system signals back to the source. If anyone is watching us right now or has been alerted to our presence, they have the capability to trace the signals and feeds."

Mann's earpiece crackled. "This is HRT. We're taking sniper and light machine gun fire. Best guess is, it's coming from the south and southwest. I have one down on the south side of the house. They're crouched behind their shields. Shit. Two down now. One on the north side. Same situation. They're stuck in place. The third group is taking fire but hasn't identified any targets."

Mann turned to the SWAT commander.

"Get your people inside immediately. Same with the SWAT agents and bomb techs spread out around the house. This is the rally point. We need to come up with a plan to fortify the house against a concentrated assault."

The SWAT commander issued the order before grabbing Mann by the shoulder.

"The house is too big to fortify. Too many access points. They're gonna get in," he said. "We need to consolidate. Upstairs. High ground."

Automatic gunfire erupted outside the house.

"Heavy gunfire coming from the north," said the HRT commander. "They just ripped into the team positioned by the chimney, and we're effectively suppressed. I can't poke my head over the top for more than a second or two without taking fire. We're not going to be much help right now. They're focused on keeping their shields in place."

Mann had somehow walked right into another trap. But how? They'd been extensively and continuously watching the house and surrounding land for over forty-eight hours.

"Keep your people behind their shields and get together with my surveillance team—they know what they're doing. Work with them to pass along tactical information over the net," he said. "You're our eyes and ears now."

"Copy that," said the HRT commander. "Hey. I can hear ATVs out there. Or some kind of motors."

"This just keeps getting better," said one of the bomb techs. "How far out is the convoy?"

"At least another fifteen minutes," Mann said.

Automatic gunfire echoed from a different direction, bullets ricocheting through the great room next to them and ripping through the sturdy wood-framed furniture.

"Light machine gun fire coming from the east and west," said an agent over the net. "Tore right through us on the porch. We have one KIA. Three wounded. One of them life-threatening."

"Bring the wounded to the rally point. The rest of you stay at the front door for now and make sure they don't rush the house," said the SWAT commander.

"Jax. Notify the convoy. Tell them to pick up the pace—but to be careful on final approach," said Mann. "And I need you to trigger the full emergency medical response out of Bozeman. Let them know the situation. Mass casualty event. They'll probably expand the response package."

"I'm on it," Jackson said.

"This is gonna be a long fifteen minutes," said the SWAT commander.

"Maybe. Maybe not. We still have a few tricks up our sleeves," Mann said, before contacting Turner and Wallace.

CHAPTER 13

Turner charged the XM250 and flipped the selector switch to automatic before answering Mann's transmission.

"We're on the way," said Turner. "Switching to air support–coordination frequency to coordinate with Jax and Lianez. Sorry to cut you off, but we need to focus."

"Copy," said Mann. "You know where to reach me. I'll be monitoring the channel. Happy hunting."

"Kerri. You ready?" said Turner over the new radio channel.

"We're inbound. About ten seconds behind you," said Wallace. "Standing by for targeting information."

"Jax?" said Turner. "What are you seeing?"

"Two machine gun positions. One southeast of the house. The other southwest. We haven't been able to pin down their locations yet," Jax said.

"ANGEL ONE copies," said the pilot. "We'll approach from the east, which will give us good tree cover until we're almost right over the house."

"We'll keep looking for the—stand by. We have a new development," said Jax. "I have three groups of two ATVs racing toward the house. Approach directions are from . . . due north, due east, and southwest. The southwest group is headed for the front door. The rest for the back of the house."

"Composition?" asked Turner.

"Two riders per ATV," said Jax.

"SWAT can handle the group headed to the front door," Turner said. "Air assets will focus on the other two groups. Pass that along to Mann."

"Passing to Mann," said Jax.

"Left-side engagement," said the pilot matter-of-factly. "Ten seconds to get your shit together."

Turner didn't respond. No time for that. He grabbed the tether line attached to his harness and clipped in to the thick welded loop affixed to the helicopter near the left doorframe, before he dropped to the deck and scooted onto the bench extending a few feet beyond the helicopter door. He tightened the tether moments before the helicopter banked left, and gravity pulled so hard against his harness he could barely breathe. If he'd clipped in two seconds later, he'd be toppling through treetops. These HRT pilots weren't fucking around.

"Two ATVs pulling up to the center of the west wing of the house," said the pilot. "Two more heading for the far end."

Made sense. Easy access points. He'd studied the extensive imagery taken from aircraft and drones. It was all they had to make any deductions about the interior design. Even O'Reilly's black ops group couldn't dig up the architectural plans. The west wing, as they'd called it during the planning phase, faced north toward the mountains and featured six evenly spaced, well-furnished patios positioned in front of wide sliding doors below transom windows. Guest-wing was their best guess.

The east wing clearly had served as McCall's private enclave. A second, slightly smaller two-story vaulted-ceiling structure with a wide flagstone fireplace dominated the wing. A long stretch of one-story floor-to-ceiling windows opening to a sprawling stone patio with a hot tub sat a little farther east. Presumably the primary suite. Both spaces were harder to breach against a determined defense. Choosing the west wing allowed them to enter at multiple points, forcing defenders to spread thin. He hoped the agents below hadn't taken the bait.

"Engaging," said Turner, before sighting in on one of the ATVs.

The sight reticle read 642 meters, the distance closing fast. Still a little far away for accurate fire, but if he could slow them down, that would buy Mann some time.

His bullets hit about fifteen feet behind the vehicle, its two occupants immediately hopping out and taking cover behind it. He adjusted the sight picture to better account for the ATV's speed and fired again, the next burst ripping through the back of the four-wheeled vehicle and knocking one of the hostiles backward into plain view.

Turner pressed the trigger again, this time a longer burst. Dirt kicked up around the shooter, mostly obscuring him. When the dust started to settle a few moments later, the target lay motionless on the ground. Turner made quick work of the second hostile, the ATV's frame no match for a few dozen 6.8mm bullets.

A series of sharp thunks above his head immediately drew his attention to a small cluster of holes punched through the helicopter's metal fuselage—a few feet above the door. More bullets peppered the length of the tail boom a moment later. Had to be one of the machine guns to the south. Or both.

"Taking accurate automatic fire. Several along the tail boom. A few just below the rotor assembly," said Turner, squeezing off a less-focused burst toward the second ATV, which had already reached the house.

His bullets sparked off the ATV and shattered the sliding glass door in front of it, just as two heavily armed, body armor–clad figures disappeared inside. He had no idea if he'd hit any of them.

"Copy," said the pilot. "Taking extreme evasive maneuvers."

He didn't like the sound of that.

"Jax. Not sure if you caught this. Two hostiles made it inside the west wing. Sixth slider down from the great room. I nailed the two in the other ATV," Turner said, just before the helicopter banked left.

The helicopter rolled far enough for him to stare straight out and see only the top of the target house's dark-shingle rooftop. He let the XM250 dangle by its two-point sling and instinctively grabbed the nearest seat stanchion with both hands. Not that he could have kept himself from falling if his tether or harness failed. Just as he began to seriously question whether the thick strap attached to his harness was strong enough to withstand the strain, the helicopter leveled and dipped forward, rapidly accelerating.

The helicopter sped away from the house at a near-perfect perpendicular angle, taking no further hits on the way out despite the sound of intense gunfire. Turner leaned out as far as the tether allowed, both of his hands back on the light machine gun—but none of the remaining ATV clusters appeared in his field of view.

He was about to ask the pilot why she had turned toward the hostile machine gun fire instead of away from it, but figured out the answer before he could embarrass himself by asking. The only way the gunners could effectively aim their weapons at a helicopter flying at a fast closure rate—nearly overhead—was to rise and expose themselves to gunfire from the house or the other FBI helicopter. Turning away from the gunners would have allowed them to stay prone and continue to send bullets in their direction. His earpiece came to life.

"This is Jax. I just passed that along to Mann."

The helicopter started to ease into a left turn.

"Looks like we're heading in for another run," said Turner.

"Jax. This is Wallace. I got a few bursts off, but we had to break the engagement. Ground fire nearly took out our tail rotor. ANGEL TWO is out of the fight," she said. "At least four hostiles made it to the northeast corner of the house before we broke off. Two ATVs made it to the front of the house. I didn't get a good look at their numbers. I started to engage them when he had to abort the run."

"Lianez says you took down one of the hostiles. The others breached a window at the far end of the west wing," said Jax.

"Jax. This is ANGEL ONE. Any way you can mark the machine gunner locations for us?" said the pilot. "Our gun runs won't be very effective at full speed, and I can't slow down until I have a better sense of where they're located."

"Not without crashing the drones into them. Mann and the SWAT commander are the only two with tablets that can see our feeds," said Jax. "I can try and talk you onto your targets."

"That'll have to do," Turner said.

"Jax. This is Mann. Sorry to break onto the air-coordination net. Go ahead and crash the drones as close to the machine gunners as possible. Give ANGEL ONE and Turner some reference points to use to formulate the safest and most effective strategy to keep those gunners occupied and out of the house. The last thing we need in here are those machine guns. The Blackhawks are inbound. ETA two minutes. Use them to fill in the gaps in your coverage."

"ANGEL ONE copies. Jax. We're heading back in to make sure they don't run for the house after you crash the drones," said Turner's pilot.

"Copy," said Jax. "We'll have the drones down in less than fifteen seconds. And don't forget, they still have at least two snipers out there. One on each side of the southern road approach to the house. That's about all we know about them, other than they're good shots. Even if you take out the machine guns—don't linger."

Turner had forgotten about the snipers. Wonderful.

"We won't," the pilot said.

"Which side do you want me on?" asked Turner.

"Stay where you are," said the pilot. "I'm going to sweep down the eastern side of the approach."

Turner couldn't stop thinking about the snipers, and how he was basically just flapping in the breeze out here. Maybe he should get inside the helicopter. Belt into one of the forward-facing seats. He could still do his job from there. He reached up to unclip the tether clip from the frame anchor, but the helicopter dipped forward and rapidly picked up speed. The house appeared above the trees, and bullets started snapping by a few seconds later. Next time. *If there is a next time.*

CHAPTER 14

Sokolov didn't waste any time organizing the mercenaries who had made it into the house. If he hoped to pull this off, they had to move swiftly. No holds barred. His team was spread out and outnumbered, but his crew possessed an advantage that should even the odds, if not tip them in his favor—Russian-made RGN hand grenades. High explosive instead of fragmentation. Purposefully designed to maximize casualties in close-quarters fighting. Each mercenary carried six, plus one smoke grenade. The only grenades carried by the FBI would be flash-bangs. Barely a nuisance compared to the RGN.

He opened the door leading into the west wing hallway and led his team out. The two mercenaries who'd survived the helicopter gun run had already secured the only interior-access point to the wing. The FBI had wisely not rushed in to confront his men. But their decision to remain on the defensive would only delay the inevitable.

"Let's go."

He sprinted to the end of the long, wide hallway and knelt next to one of the two who had arrived first. His counterpart was busy placing explosive charges on the double door that separated the west wing of the house from the great room.

"Anything?" asked Sokolov.

"The door is locked. The team on the other side can expect the same for the east wing. The FBI wants us to knock before entering."

Sokolov chuckled. "They have drones up, so they know we're coming from both directions. They've likely retreated upstairs. There's a double staircase leading to the second level. Nothing but railings—all open lines of sight to the ground floor. We won't have an easy time getting up there."

"What about the east wing?" the mercenary asked.

"There's a spiral staircase leading up from the second great room, but I'm sure it will be covered. Same with the working kitchen. Tight quarters, death traps for anyone trying to climb them. They have close to thirty agents or EOD people up there. More than enough to allocate a few agents to each of those."

"We have grenades," said the mercenary.

"Ever try to throw a grenade up a spiral staircase?" said Sokolov. "Think about it for a moment."

"I see your point. Why don't we just burn the two wings down with our white phosphorus grenades and wait for them to emerge?"

"Not enough time. A large convoy of federal agents is headed our way," said Sokolov. "We'll blow the east and west doors open simultaneously and roll in two smoke grenades from each side. We'll be blind for a while, but it'll get us inside. They'll be blind, too. Once we get to covered positions, we'll toss a few RGN grenades upstairs to break up the initial resistance, followed by a few more through the doorways to each wing. We should be able to see them from the ground level. Then we rush the stairs. We've done work like this before. Those FBI agents have never fought like this. They won't know what hit them."

"For the money," said the mercenary, pointing a fist at Sokolov.

Sokolov fist-bumped him and the rest of the men.

"For the money," he repeated.

The only motto that mattered in their line of work at the end of the day. And loyalty. Most of the time.

CHAPTER 15

A quick exploration of the second-floor schematics on one of the bomb technicians' tablets had led to an obvious decision: Mann's crew would make their stand in the west wing, which was nearly a carbon copy of the level below them. Only two access points led directly into the west wing: the double door off the grand stairway's landing, and a spiral staircase that led to a second kitchen behind the kitchen that was visible to the great room. It offered no advantages, since it was feet away from the hallway entrance.

The east wing had a spiral staircase in the second great room and a regular staircase at the far end of the hallway. Three widely spread points of access to protect instead of two that may as well count as one.

The SWAT commander convinced Mann to leave the doors open on both sides of the spacious landing. Let their attackers decide which side to explore first, or possibly trick them into splitting up their forces. Nine heavily armed hostiles—based on Jax's last estimate. A number that twenty FBI SWAT agents and ten bomb techs should be able to handle, but they couldn't underestimate the desperation of their attackers.

The group tasked to ambush them clearly saw the odds they faced and decided to continue the attack. They were either True America fanatics or an obscenely well-paid mercenary force. His bet was on the latter. The group had skills that were hard to replicate outside of hardcore, special operations military veterans.

The more Mann thought about it, the less optimistic he became. The FBI SWAT agents dispersed throughout the rooms behind him didn't have the same training or rough edges. If enough of the mercenaries broke through into the west wing, the results could be catastrophic. Room-by-room close-quarters combat, ignoring well-drilled and strictly observed rules of engagement, wasn't on the FBI menu. Mann's hastily assembled plan could fall apart just as quickly as they'd put it together.

Automatic gunfire raged outside for a few seconds, immediately followed by the thunderous boom of heavy rotor blades that rattled the house. One of the Blackhawks, for sure. The Blackhawk thumps were immediately followed by a more rapid rotor tempo—and several short bursts of automatic gunfire. Turner was keeping the hostile machine gun teams busy. Buying Mann time.

The convoy was still eight minutes out. Not that the SUVs could approach until the machine guns and snipers were neutralized. The agents in the house were on their own for now. And it should be enough. Thirty FBI agents should be able to hold off nine mercenaries. The big question was, At what cost? How many more FBI agents would die? Not that he had any control over that answer at this point. The cake was baked inside the house. An attack was imminent.

Crouched just inside the opening to the west wing, Mann glanced at the SWAT commander.

"You sure about this?" asked Mann.

"There's no way to detonate the charges remotely," he said.

"Make sure they stay out of sight," said Mann. "No heroics."

"They understand the situation."

Another Blackhawk roared overhead, accompanied by a short gun battle.

"Jax. How are we doing out there?" asked Mann over the air-coordination net.

"Keeping the machine gun teams and snipers in place," she said. "That's about it. ANGEL ONE keeps pushing the envelope. Lingering a little too long."

Something about what she said got him thinking. *Shit!* How had he not thought of this earlier? Jax had the ladder he'd used to climb down from the garage roof. She didn't like the idea of being trapped up there. SWAT didn't argue, because they didn't need it at that point.

"Have any of the hostiles changed positions? Significantly?" Mann asked.

"Not from what I can tell. We still haven't nailed down the snipers, but they're southwest and southeast of the house. Same with the machine gunners."

"Have the helicopters taken any fire from positions behind the house?"

"No," said Jax. "Shit. We're clear to the north. Fuck. How didn't I see that?"

"I didn't see it, either," said Mann.

"ANGEL ONE confirms," said Turner's pilot. "We haven't taken any fire from the north. I could drop off Turner behind the house. The other FBI shooter is in one of the Blackhawks. They could drop her off."

"Negative. I need them up there suppressing the machine guns and snipers," said Mann. "The two HRT operators. They can climb down using the ladder and slip inside the back of the house—"

A rapid series of shattering explosions ripped through the house below them, cutting off his transmission.

"Here they come," said the SWAT commander, before taking off down the hallway.

Mann followed close behind. "Jax. Did you copy my last?" he asked, before ducking into the last of the doorways on the north side of the hallway.

The room served as their first aid station. Two agents lay side by side on one of two queen-size beds, an agent kneeling on the bed between them—digging through a backpack trauma kit. Both agents were out of the fight, but their injuries looked survivable. Extremity wounds. The agent lying on the other bed had two agents working frantically to keep her alive. They'd removed her tactical vest and looked like they were preparing for field surgery.

The agent hovering over her with a pair of surgical scissors gave Mann a quick glance—and shook his head. He wasn't sure what the gesture meant, but he didn't interrupt them. They knew what they were doing. His job was to keep the rest of the FBI agents out of this room, and away from those scissors.

"HRT is on the move," said Jax.

"Got it. HRT. Do you copy?"

"We're ready to attach the ladder," said the HRT commander. "Where do you need us?"

"I don't know yet," said Mann. "There's a stairway just outside the garage, at the end of the east wing's first-floor hallway. Use that to access the second level and wait inside the stairwell for instructions. There are no friendlies anywhere other than the second floor's west wing."

Mann peeked out of the doorway. Thick white smoke drifted through the landing, followed by grenades that clunked and skittered across the hardwood landing beyond the west wing entrance. They didn't look like flash-bangs, an observation confirmed a few moments later. Their explosive blasts popped his ears like a rapid, unexpected flight descent. He counted at least four explosions. Definitely not flash-bangs. High explosive, from what he could tell. Shit. They'd come prepared to clear rooms. This would undoubtedly get ugly if they got through.

"Stand by to detonate charges on my command," he said. "There will be no countdown."

"Copy," said one of the two SWAT agents closest to the doorway. "Standing by."

The SWAT agents carried enough flexible breaching strips to "collar" the west wing entrances with explosives. Working with the bomb technicians, they quickly connected the strips and affixed them to the outside of the doorframe casing—running detonation wire along the floor to the nearest agents.

The blast strips were designed to warp or disintegrate the hinge side of a door, depending on the door's composition. Placed correctly, it would pop the hinges so agents could rapidly pull or kick the door out of the way. Mann had no idea what kind of effect the thin strip of explosives would have on their attackers, other than it should severely disorient them. Maybe even knock them flat, like one of the bomb technicians had guessed. Either way, the blast should give the rest of the attackers pause, buying the agents more time.

Mann extended the compact tactical mirror attached to his ballistic helmet and positioned his head so he could see the entrance to the hallway without exposing himself to gunfire or fragments. Two grenades sailed into the hallway and bounced off the far wall. Instinctively, he pulled his head back a little farther.

Explosions rocked the hallway, followed immediately by automatic gunfire. Bullets snapped past the doorway as he readjusted his head to peek with the mirror. Two men emerged from the smoke at the entrance and dashed into the hallway.

"Detonate now!" he said.

The end of the hallway disappeared in a bright-orange flash, which was instantly replaced by a smoke-enshrouded shower of debris.

"Engage targets as they appear," said Mann, leaning far enough out of the doorway to see the entire entryway through his rifle's holographic sight.

Two bodies lay on the floor, one of them struggling to get up on one knee. Mann started to apply pressure to his trigger, but several agents beat him to the shot. Rapid semiautomatic fire rippled from the doorways, knocking the target backward into the grand staircase landing. At least three grenades flew through the opening, skidding along the hardwood floor and stopping at various points next to or just beyond the first set of doors.

The grenades exploded before he could pull back, the concussive blast slamming his back and head against the doorframe behind him. His helmet and the hard plates in his vest absorbed most of the impact, which allowed him to quickly recover and scramble into the room's vestibule before bullets started to splinter the white doorframe he'd just hit. The gunfire intensified. Automatic bursts from the mercenary team drowned out the underwhelming semiautomatic rifle and pistol fire from the agents.

He leaned out and snapped off a few hasty shots at a figure crouched along the wall, before a bullet skipped off the right side of his helmet. He backed up and dropped to his stomach, then crawled back to the door. No reason to keep appearing in the same place. Mann leaned his rifle out in time to see the hostile force toss grenades into the second set of doors from the end of the hallway—the first rooms where he'd positioned agents. Mann pressed the trigger repeatedly until he expended the rest of the rifle magazine, dropping at least one of the seven attackers to their knees.

Two near-simultaneous floor-shaking blasts ejected flaming wreckage into the hallway. Agonizing screams beckoned for help. When the initial explosion cleared, the hostiles divided into two groups and ducked into the rooms, leaving the mercenary Mann had just shot clawing at the wall to get back up. While Mann reloaded, a maelstrom of gunfire from the agents in the rooms closer to the action hit the wounded attacker like a hammer, pinning him against the wall as bullet after bullet pounded him.

Inside the two rooms, the screams were silenced by bursts of automatic gunfire. *Jesus.* He'd just lost four agents. They'd placed two in each room, starting with the second room in from the hallway, and one in the room across from him. Three in this room to keep the wounded agents alive. A bizarre stillness descended as the mercenaries no doubt prepared to repeat their room process. He had to slow this down.

"SWAT. Shut the next set of doors!" said Mann, moments before several grenades crisscrossed the hallway.

The door on the opposite side of the hallway slammed shut, deflecting two grenades and sending them deeper down the corridor. Panicked voices from the room on Mann's side left him with the distinct impression that his order had come just a fraction of a moment too late for them. All doubt was erased a second later when the door, which they must have managed to partially close, burst outward in a hail of large burning splinters.

The two deflected grenades exploded in the middle of the hallway, several feet from the next set of doors, momentarily sparing the two agents who had shut their door. Momentarily, because the explosions drove the rest of the agents back inside their rooms long enough for the mercenaries to regain the upper hand. One group crossed the hallway and entered the room that had just been destroyed, the last mercenary drawing fire from the agents farther down the hall.

"Shut the next set of doors," said the SWAT commander.

Smart. At least someone was thinking. No sooner had the FBI regained fire superiority in the hallway than two staggered sets of grenades sailed out of the enemy-occupied rooms. A single grenade rolled directly across the hallway and stopped at the foot of the closed door, and two others were sent farther down the hallway. The results? Too predictable.

The closed door was blasted to pieces, and the two high-explosive blasts in the center of the corridor forced the rest of the FBI agents to take cover long enough for the mercenaries to toss another grenade into the room they'd failed to secure just moments earlier. This time, they didn't rush into the hallway after the blast to finish off the agents. They knew they'd be waiting, and that half of them wouldn't make it.

"HRT. This is Mann. We're in a bad way here," he said.

"We decided to go a little off script. We're inside the main great room, next to the eastern staircase leading up to the landing," said the HRT commander. "Sounds like a fucking war up there."

"It's more like a slaughter. They're clearing rooms with high-explosive grenades," said Mann. "We've slowed them down for now, but this crew knows what they're doing. We're just waiting for the next shoe to drop."

"Did they leave anyone on the staircase landing?"

Mann did the math. Jax had reported that nine had breached the house. They'd taken out two with the blast strip and one outside the first set of FBI-occupied rooms. He'd counted seven in the hallway when they nailed that one. The mercenaries had thrown everyone into the fight.

"No. The landing should be clear," he said.

"We're on the way," said the HRT commander. "We'll toss flash-bangs and make some noise. Hopefully pop a few stupid enough to stick their heads out. With their attention divided, we should be able to contain and neutralize them."

"Music to my ears," said Mann.

CHAPTER 16

Sokolov crouched next to the open slider and peered outside. Unbelievable. An oversight—or maybe a ruse? Hard to say, but it had become clear over the past several minutes that the FBI wasn't very good at close-quarters combat. Or maybe they knew what they were doing, and Sokolov's twenty-plus years of clearing insurgents from their hives across the globe put him at a decisive advantage. Either way, it was time to change things up. They'd figured out how to stop his brute-force advance. He stepped back inside the room and wiped the sweat from his brow.

"Ready for phase two?" he asked the mercenary. He was so hopped up on adrenaline, he couldn't remember the man's name. And it didn't matter. Nothing mattered but killing Mann and escaping.

"We can't go back out there," said the mercenary.

"We're not all going back out," Sokolov said. "That would be suicide. But I do need the other group on this side of the hallway."

"What exactly are we doing?" asked the mercenary at the door.

"Bypassing their defenses," said Sokolov. "They've figured out our game."

"We can't go through the walls. We didn't bring breaching gear."

Festerov. He finally remembered the name. Not that it mattered.

"We're not going through the walls," said Sokolov. "But we are going to shoot through them. Then use the balcony to flank."

"They're not covering the balconies?" asked Festerov.

"Not that I can tell," said Sokolov. "The dividers are semiprivate, but I can see all the way to the end. There's nobody out there. We use the same tactic, but outside. All we have to do is shoot out the glass and toss grenades."

He struggled to remember the other mercenary's name. No need.

"Prep a grenade and signal for the other group to cross the hallway," said Sokolov. "Same procedure. Just get them across."

The mercenary nodded before pulling the pin on one of the high-explosive grenades. He inched toward the doorway and started a series of hand signals at chest level. All just barely out of sight of the FBI agents. If they only knew. Sokolov had extensively drilled his team in the use of hand signals, having learned the hard way—more than once—how even the most rudimentary radio jamming could stop an operation in its tracks.

Radio contact had been spotty from the moment they had entered the house. Deliberate interference, from what he could tell. Possibly intercepted. He'd switched them over to hand signals while he could still contact everyone over radio.

"Ready to go," said the other mercenary—Abelev, he remembered now.

The adrenaline was wearing off. Time to reboot!

"Do it," said Sokolov.

Abelev released the grenade lever and leaned a few inches forward to toss it down the hallway. His head slammed into the doorframe before he released the grenade, blood spraying the wall next to him. He slumped to the floor, both hands holding his neck. Neither hand holding the grenade. Fuck. Sokolov backpedaled out of sight of the doorway, tripping over one of the dead FBI agents and slamming into a nightstand and lamp next to the bed.

The grenade detonated, blasting most of the room apart. Festerov flew through the open slider, his body slamming into the thick wooden balcony railing and folding in the wrong direction—before he flipped out of sight. Time stood still for a while. Everything fuzzy. Sokolov faded in and out.

The team across the hallway finally reached him, after what felt like far too long. He shook his head, trying to break out of the haze.

"What the fuck just happened?" he asked, unable to put the pieces together.

"We're surrounded," said the mercenary. "They're on the staircase landing now."

"What about the balcony? That's our only way," said Sokolov, suddenly feeling very lucid. "How many grenades do we have left?"

The team didn't respond. They weren't reacting as quickly as before. Was this some kind of mutiny? Where were their weapons? He glanced at his chest, realizing that his rifle had been detached from its sling. Gone. His hand shot to his hip holster—the pistol missing. He patted the pouch attached to his vest.

"Where's my phone? What is this?" Sokolov demanded. "How long have I been out?"

"A few minutes," said one of the mercenaries who had crossed over from the other room. "It's over. We've surrendered. This is pointless. Volkov has your phone and is talking over the details with the FBI. This is done. The FBI is very interested in our client. They've offered us a deal. Witness protection if we cooperate."

"A deal?" said Sokolov, the sound of rotor blades reaching his ears. "Why aren't we all in handcuffs with guns to our heads?"

"They're guarding the room and covering the balcony," said the mercenary. "There was no other way, Dmitri."

None of this made sense.

"Where's Volkov?"

"Negotiating with the FBI."

The helicopter sounded closer. A lot closer. It was hard to tell through the ringing in his ears. It was hard enough to hear anything.

"What don't you understand about this?" said Sokolov. "We just killed more than a dozen FBI agents. We're not getting out of this alive."

"Volkov said—"

The helicopter sounded like it was in the room.

"You fucking idiots!" said Sokolov, before the room darkened. "Volkov is the only one getting out of this alive!"

He turned toward the balcony slider—a helicopter now blocked most of the view of the nearby trees and distant mountains. An FBI agent lay prone on the deck of the passenger compartment, aiming a light machine gun at the room. The agent shook his head.

CHAPTER 17

Luke Turner pressed the trigger and didn't let go until the entire one-hundred-round pouch ran dry. Smoking hot brass casings filled the passenger compartment as the 6.8mm bullets shredded the guest room—and everyone in it. With the XM250's bipod firmly resting on the steel deck, he placed every single bullet inside the room, sweeping back and forth at different heights. Chest. Waist. Knee. Floor. Nothing could survive that. And anyone who did wouldn't get the necessary first aid. Mann had made that clear.

Mann stood on the balcony of the room he'd defended for several grueling minutes and witnessed the execution he'd just ordered. Under the circumstances, it had to be done. He'd lost more than a dozen FBI agents today. Added to the Sacramento bombing and his own losses over the past few months, the people behind all this had killed over thirty FBI agents. The gloves had to come off at some point. Today was that day.

He gave Turner a thumbs-up as the helicopter flew by, weighed down by the thought of where it was headed. Mann stepped back into the room and glanced at the two medic-trained FBI agents, who had somehow kept their bullet-riddled colleague alive. They nodded at each other before he made his way into the room across the hallway, where two SWAT agents and a bomb technician pointed their weapons at a hog-tied man known as "Volkov," the sole survivor of the mercenary team.

Mann ignored his pleadings and made his way to the floor-to-ceiling window at the opposite side of the bedroom, where he pressed a button on the wall—which electronically changed the window tint from opaque to fully transparent.

Four mercenaries stood in the road, hands above their heads. Two in sniper ghillie suits. The others wore body armor, their helmets on the ground next to them. They'd left their weapons behind before making their way into the open to surrender. Volkov had convinced them to surrender, granting them the same safe harbor promised to the men who'd died with their leader—Sokolov. The Bell 407 helicopter appeared in his peripheral vision. High to the left.

"Gun. I see a gun," said Mann over the tactical net, before raising his rifle.

He fired at one of the snipers, who had taken off running, shattering the glass in front of him. Turner took care of the rest. The dirt kicked up around the four mercenaries long after their bodies had dropped to the ground and stopped moving.

"ANGEL ONE heading back to refuel," said Turner.

"We'll take it from here," said Mann, not wanting to say any more over the net.

He'd coordinated the last two "events" over satellite phone with Turner.

"The convoy just turned off Horse Creek Road," said Jax.

"Jax. Why don't you have the convoy hold at the road," said Mann. "Until we can confirm the route to the ranch is safe."

"Copy that," Jax said. "Same with the Blackhawks? They're holding about a minute away."

"Yes," said Mann. "No reason to risk one of our helicopters."

"No reason at all," said Jax.

He turned to leave the room, finding the doorway blocked by the SWAT commander, bomb technician leader, and HRT commander.

"We heard you might need some help flushing out the rest of the hostiles," said the SWAT commander.

"Let's step outside," said Mann.

Once they were in the hallway and out of earshot, Mann took a knee, the gravity of the morning pulling him down. If he could have lain on the floor and curled up into a ball without making a complete fool of himself, he would have. He just wanted to disappear right now, but he couldn't. He had one more job to do before he could stop and let it all sink in.

"This is on me," said Mann. "I'll clean it up myself."

"We'll clean this up together," said the bomb tech.

"Won't take as long that way," said the SWAT commander.

"Count us in," said the HRT commander. "No offense, but I'm not entirely sure you're capable of picking up one of those bodies and carrying it more than fifty feet. Let alone a few hundred feet uphill."

"Exactly," said the SWAT commander.

Mann stifled an exhausted laugh. Nothing was funny about anything that had just transpired.

"What?" the HRT commander asked.

"I wasn't planning on carrying them all back to their original positions. I was just going to grab a rifle from one of the dead mercenaries in the house and throw it in the middle of them. Say they pulled it out and fired at the helicopter. That's why I made sure to take part in the shooting," said Mann. "So I could testify that the shooting was justified, and your agents could testify that it was my call to open fire."

The HRT commander put a hand on Mann's shoulder. "I'll take care of the rifle. Grab a couple casings from the house and throw them on the ground. You've done enough today."

"I wish that were true," said Mann. "But the day isn't close to being over. Emergency medical flights are ten minutes out. Ambulances twenty to thirty. Let's get the wounded triaged and ready for transport."

Mann leaned against the wall and slid to the floor before removing the satellite phone from his vest. He wasn't sure how he'd explain this to O'Reilly—who was probably standing next to Director James in one of the situation rooms, waiting for an update. He pressed O'Reilly's speed dial button, morbidly thinking that fighting off another wave of Russian mercenaries would be easier than this phone call.

CHAPTER 18

Dana O'Reilly placed the handset in the cradle. She'd just been officially "called on the carpet." James wanted to see her in the FBI director's executive conference room. Well. She'd had a good run at the FBI. A healthy pension, nice investment portfolio, and stress-free life awaited her on the outside. If she could resist the multiple temptations her experience would summon. The moment she stepped outside her office, Kevin appeared. Her executive assistant looked perturbed.

"How bad?" he asked, having been the one to forward the call.

"If I don't return to my office—you know where to send my personal belongings."

"What personal belongings?"

"You know me all too well."

Her office was devoid of pictures, citations, diplomas, plaques, memorabilia—anything that suggested she existed. That was how she preferred it. When she was at work, which was most of the time, that was all that mattered. What she was doing now, in the present. That was what she told herself, anyway. The truth was that she just wasn't the sentimental type. Attachment wasn't in her blood anymore.

"You'll be back," he said. "They can't afford to get rid of you."

"I like your optimism, Kevin. But things went very sideways in Montana this morning."

"How sideways?"

She looked around before whispering, "A dozen KIA."

"I'm so sorry," he said.

"Nothing to be sorry about," she said. "It hasn't hit the news yet, so—"

"Please tell me you were not about to tell me to keep this to myself," said Kevin.

"The safe in my office?" she said, changing the subject.

"I doubt they'll let you keep your service-issued firearm," he said.

"There's a small notebook inside, in addition to my pistol," she said. "It's coded, so don't bother."

"Two irretractable insults in a row. I don't know if I can work with you anymore," he said jokingly.

"You probably won't have to," she said. "But I need you to hand-deliver that notebook to me if I don't return. The code is—"

"One. Two. Three. Four," he said.

"You do know me too well," said O'Reilly. "I might actually miss you."

"Well. That's the nicest thing you've said to me in the two years and five months I've worked for you."

"Open the safe as soon as I leave and grab the notebook. If they sack me, the safe will be their first priority," said O'Reilly. "And there's also an unopened bottle of Macallan thirty-year, double-cask Scotch in the safe, which is yours regardless of whether I do or do not return."

"Oh dear. That's a five-thousand-dollar bottle," said Kevin, whom she knew to be a connoisseur of Scotch whisky.

"Which is why I haven't touched it," she said. "And for the record, it was a gift, so don't let this go to your head."

"Whether you return or not, we shall share that bottle," Kevin said. "Deal?"

"Deal," said O'Reilly.

"Good luck," said Kevin. "See you in a few minutes."

"Fucking optimists," she said, heading out of the CIRG section.

It took her close to fifteen minutes to reach the reception desk in the director's wing. She didn't even have to introduce herself. The executive assistant team buzzed her in, one of them escorting her to the executive conference room. None of them said a word to her. Not a good sign of things to come. The nameless assistant opened the door and motioned her inside, closing the door behind her.

Executive Assistant Director Camilla James sat alone in the seat to the right of the head of the table, where the director would sit.

"Have a seat," said James, pointing at the chair across from her.

O'Reilly hadn't expected to be seated next to the director. She'd figured she'd have a bleacher seat at best, most of the table being occupied by lawyers from the Department of Justice's Office of the Inspector General. This really was going to be a one-on-one throat-slitting. She set herself down in the surprisingly plush chair. The closer you got to the top, the better the seat.

"How are you doing?" asked James.

O'Reilly cocked her head. "I'm sorry, ma'am. What?"

"How are you doing?" she repeated. "It's been a tough morning."

It took her a few moments to adjust and remember that James was a human being. Not just another cog in the machine set in motion to fire her.

"I still don't know what to think," said O'Reilly. "We took every precaution possible—even though nobody expected a problem."

"Good thing you didn't downplay the threat like Mann suggested, or it could have been worse," James said.

"I don't see how," said O'Reilly.

"I think you do," said James. "There's a reason you're in charge of CIRG. It's the least linear of all the FBI divisions. You command several highly specialized sections, ranging from behavior analysis desk jobs to hostage rescue operators. And you know how to mitigate risk."

"Doesn't feel like it right now."

"I know it doesn't," said James. "But you have to look at the bigger picture. Your due diligence kept the investigation alive. If you'd let Mann run that show, all of ARTEMIS's hard-earned knowledge and work would have been wasted. Bled right into the ground."

"Wait. So . . . the ARTEMIS investigation is still active? Even after this morning?" asked O'Reilly. "Or is that what you're going to propose to the director? Or am I going to propose it?"

"The director will not be joining us," James said. "I've already made the proposal, and she agreed—with terms."

"Then why are we here?"

"Because this is, without a shadow of a doubt, the only room in this building that cannot be bugged," said James. "And the director wanted this discussion to stay between you and me."

"Am I fired?" said O'Reilly. "Just want to get that question out of the way before we continue."

"You are not fired," said James. "But ARTEMIS is suspended, pending review."

"What does that mean?"

"It means that Director Ashford believes that this morning's ambush validated Mann's continued investigation—but she wants to put the brakes on the carnage that seems to inevitably follow this task force."

"Sounds like she's feeling some external pressure?" suggested O'Reilly. "From the attorney general's office, or maybe even the White House?"

"Maybe," said James, which meant *yes*.

"Has anyone walked the attorney general's office or the White House through the details? Explained exactly why Mann's investigation is so critical to national security? To election integrity? DOMINION could turn the tide of the election. Polls already indicate that DOMINION is having an effect. Immigration is now everyone's top concern. Not just a single party's bogeyman."

"That's above my pay grade," said James. "Until we prove it. You know how this works."

"Or doesn't work," said O'Reilly. "True America is gaining in the polls."

"True America isn't on the ballot," said James.

"They are if Harrison Greely is running DOMINION," said O'Reilly. "I guarantee he's sealed a deal that will give him the power to implement key tenets of the True America agenda if a new administration wins the election. Someone high up in the party signed a deal with the devil. Probably a lot of those contracts floating around Congress and statehouses nationwide."

"We need solid proof to raise that kind of alarm. Hard evidence," said James. "We need the DOMINION database, and the software used to coordinate the army of sicarios hidden across the country."

"What about the Russian connection to True America? All the rooftops with airbags waiting for Greely to jump down with the database needed to run DOMINION?" asked O'Reilly. "All properties owned by the Russian embassy or known proxies to Russian oligarchs. Can't be a coincidence."

"I need something far more definitive, since DOMINION didn't end up in Russian hands," said James. "Does Mann have any more tricks up his sleeve?"

O'Reilly shook her head. "I'm confused. You're telling me we need Mann to continue his investigation, but you're also telling me that his task force is suspended. The two sentiments are at odds."

James shrugged. "What I'm telling you is that Director Ashford understands the importance of the investigation. She also understands the optics of losing over thirty FBI agents, and the handcuffs that can be slapped on the Bureau if she doesn't appear to be cooling things down."

"So, what you're saying—"

"You know what I'm saying," said James. "And you know how to make it happen. We don't need to spell it out. Or do we? I know how much you love long, drawn-out conversations and briefings."

"I suppose we would be wasting words," said O'Reilly. "And if it blows up in my face?"

"Then it blows up in my face, too," said James. "If you haven't figured it out already, I have your back."

"Now I wish this was being recorded," said O'Reilly.

"Somehow, I knew you'd say that."

"I'm fairly predictable once you get to know me," said O'Reilly. "So. Resources?"

"ARTEMIS is suspended," James said. "They will have no access to any government resources."

"Outside help?"

"Same answer."

"But they're not under investigation. Right?"

"They will need to make themselves available to the OIG," said James. "I'm sure they'll start digging into the Montana raid sooner than later."

"They might have to go dark," muttered O'Reilly.

"I didn't hear that," said James. "Any other questions?"

"No. I think I can work with what I have," said O'Reilly. "How will I update you on my progress?"

"You don't," said James. "Until you absolutely must."

O'Reilly started to ask a follow-up question, but James cut her off.

"You'll know when," said James.

"I'm starting to become way too predictable," said O'Reilly, already plotting the way forward.

CHAPTER 19

Mann walked away from the cluster of forensics technicians collecting evidence from the road in front of the mansion to take O'Reilly's call. So far, the worst he'd heard from one of the techs was "Damn. He didn't hold back, did he." That, and Ray Mills had cast him a dubious look at one point, which he met with a slight shrug and raised eyebrow.

"Do you still have a job?" Mann asked.

"That's your new greeting?" said O'Reilly.

"The way things have been working out lately, it's not a bad idea," said Mann. "Sorry. How are things back at headquarters?"

"Weird," said O'Reilly.

"Okay. I was expecting to hear something like—*it's really bad* or *it's pretty much the end of the world*," said Mann.

"Oh, it's both of those," said O'Reilly. "But I still have a job, and you still have a job. Sort of."

"Sort of? Sounds like administrative leave. Can I book the next flight to Fiji? I really need a vacation."

"ARTEMIS is technically suspended—pending review," O'Reilly said. "So you're all still on active duty."

Interesting. They could still use their credentials in the field, access DOJ buildings, and log on to FBI systems. In other words, they were still in business—sort of, like O'Reilly said. She was being a little nebulous, which he suspected was intentional. Someone might be listening?

"Review of what?" he asked.

"I wasn't told."

"You said *technically*."

"I did?" said O'Reilly. "Sorry. ARTEMIS is suspended as of now."

He considered his next question.

"Do you need us back in DC?"

"I don't need you back right away. I can't reassign you, since the task force is suspended—pending review. But I can't have you hanging out in Fiji unless you take vacation time. Which I don't suggest," said O'Reilly. "OIG will probably have some questions for you and your team soon enough. Maybe stick around here and reconnect with old friends. Relax while headquarters sorts this out."

Old friends.

"Too bad I can't spend a few days at an all-inclusive resort in Mexico," said Mann.

"You could take a few vacation days, but given the task force's focus, Mexico might not be the best idea," O'Reilly said. "But you could bring Mexico to DC. There's a new restaurant in Silver Spring that's about as authentic as it gets."

Bring Mexico to DC. Message received. What else? Lianez hadn't heard from Anish Gupta, and they didn't have a number for O'Reilly's old friends.

"Any new Indian restaurants?" asked Mann. "The task force is kind of a Texas Roadhouse crowd. We're not on the same frequency when it comes to food."

"I do have some recommendations. Just got a Yelp alert. Great reviews so far. Worth checking out, from what I can tell," said O'Reilly. "A friend of mine also recommended it. I'll send you a link when I get a chance."

"Appreciate it," said Mann. "I guess I'll just have to make the best of my time in DC."

A long pause ensued, which was odd for O'Reilly. She didn't waste a second when it came to conversation.

"How are you doing?" she asked. "Sorry. I'm not very good at this. I was going to ask you that first, but you caught me off guard with the job question."

"I'm not very good at this, either, which is why I led with a joke. No way they'd get rid of you," Mann said.

"Thank you," said O'Reilly. "But back to the question."

"Not good. Not good at all."

"Yep. This feels all too familiar," said O'Reilly. "Let me get you that link. I think you'll like their menu."

"Can't wait," said Mann. "Any way you can send a plane to pick us up? I hate to check any baggage. Tends to get lost."

"I'll arrange a plane," said O'Reilly. "Eight a.m. departure from Bozeman?"

"Sounds good," Mann said. "Thank you."

"You're welcome. We wouldn't want any of your luggage to get lost."

"No. We wouldn't," said Mann. "I'm really attached to some of the items."

"I don't doubt it. Goodbye," said O'Reilly, before disconnecting the call.

How long would it take for the call to come in? He guessed it would be quick. His satellite phone buzzed. *UNKNOWN.*

"Special Agent Garrett Mann," he answered.

"I just got the news. Fuck. Sorry," said Anish Gupta.

"It is what it is," said Mann. "I think you know that better than I do."

"It never hits easier. It just gets easier—to accept. Part of the job," said Gupta. "I don't know if that makes any sense."

"Oddly, I think it does," said Mann. "Thank you."

"So. About that menu," Gupta said. "We're still working on it, but it looks promising. That's all I can say right now."

"You do know this is an encrypted satellite call, right?"

"Yes. Yes. I just get carried away sometimes. It's Dana's fault. She had to be all dodgy on the phone, and I got into the role. Sorry. Switching gears. Back to normal," said Gupta. "We're at Bozeman International Airport, dropping off Emily. Long story short. We identified a spotter team near the convoy departure point. Emily will follow them as long and far as possible."

"Can't you just grab them?"

"And risk dead-ending the search for DOMINION?" said Gupta.

"What about Jax's virus?"

"Garrett. We need to focus right now."

"What does that mean?"

"It means we're just as vested in tearing True America to fucking pieces as you are, but I don't have the time to explain our methodology right now," said Gupta. "Cool?"

"Did the virus work or not?"

"It worked," Gupta said. "But the signals went dark a few minutes ago. My guess is that they deep-sixed their devices."

"Shit," said Mann. "Text me a number I can use to reach you. We're headed back to DC tomorrow morning. I don't want to waste any time nailing these fuckers."

"Number inbound," said Gupta. "We'll touch base tomorrow. Dana made it clear that we'll be working together again. Kind of an ARTEMIS two-point-oh."

"I'll reach out after we arrive in DC," said Mann. "Thank you for helping again."

"Don't thank me. Thank Dana," said Gupta. "But—you're welcome."

"Looking forward to seeing you again."

"No, you're not."

"Actually. I am," said Mann. "There's not many like us out there."

"Bingo. Yes," said Gupta. "Will your Mexican friends be joining us? Dana sounded optimistic."

“Hopefully sooner than later,” said Mann, before nodding at one of the forensics technicians, who’d motioned for him to join them. “If I’m not in a federal penitentiary.”

“That doesn’t sound good.”

“It isn’t,” said Mann. “Time to put on my tap-dancing shoes.”

CHAPTER 20

Harrison Greely arrived nearly an hour before the meeting was scheduled to start, situating himself at the head of the conference table. He enjoyed a gourmet lunch and a glass of red wine while he waited. He was done playing games. This entire movement had been built on his father's back. It was his legacy. Not Clara Furst's or any of the other latecomers'. They'd all play critical roles in True America's ascendancy, serving as its public face, but Greely would pull the strings from the shadows. This hierarchy needed to be firmly established and maintained moving forward. Furst had done an incredible job getting this far, and would no doubt continue to serve admirably as one of the new administration's key advisers, but she wasn't running the show. Far from it.

A few others slated for high-level appointments in the new government could also benefit from a warm piece of humble pie, but he didn't want to push everyone at once. That was a recipe for mutiny. Especially when his leverage wasn't based on lifelong friendships and trust. More like a few handshake agreements over drinks promising power and obscene wealth in exchange for temporary financial support. The agreements all hinged on one premise: the distinct impression that he was in charge. Otherwise, his potential benefactors could shake someone else's hand—and he'd find himself wheeled over the side.

Furst's assistant arrived ahead of the rest of the attendees. He looked understandably troubled when he found Greely at the head of the table, but didn't bring up the seating change. He nodded politely, exchanged a few meaningless pleasantries, and arranged the other primary attendees' places. Digital tablets. Notepads and pens. Water glasses. Water pitchers. Napkins. Six places in total.

The waitstaff was in the process of clearing away lunch when Furst burst into the conference room.

"What is this?" she asked.

"What's what?" said Greely.

"You know exactly what I'm talking about," she said. "Now isn't the time to make changes."

"The seats?"

"Don't play dumb."

"I'm not. Your seat has always been here," he said, motioning to the seat directly to his right. "Time for a quick reminder that none of this would exist without me."

"I don't recall you being around when we won the election in 2008," said Furst.

"That's because you were one level above an intern at that point, and I was out wrangling every major donation made to the party," said Greely. "Behind the scenes, of course, because my father—the actual founder of this party—lost sight of the long game. It hasn't been easy remaining in the shadows."

She looked like she wanted to explode, but kept her cool. Time for some diplomacy.

"Clara. You're the new face of True America. There's no disputing that. Everyone respects you," Greely said. "And you've earned that. A few years from now, if things go according to plan, you'll be answering to one person, and one person only. Yourself. I'll be long gone, admiring my father's legacy from a distance. Probably still in a wheelchair."

She looked a little less defiant.

"You're our best hope. My best hope to see this through," said Greely, meaning it. "Summers. Smith. Hill. They'll serve the cause faithfully and effectively execute the agenda. But anyone can fulfill their roles. Your job in the new administration will require the very finesse that brought you from intern to the next chief of staff."

"Chief of staff might be a reach," said Furst.

"Can't hurt to ask," said Greely. "They'll owe us. But perhaps senior adviser to the chief of staff or White House deputy chief of staff might not rub too many members of their current campaign staff the wrong way. We'll already be making some considerable demands."

"Attorney general? Secretary of Defense? Secretary of State?" said Furst. "Yeah. I'd say they might feel a little arm-twisted at that point."

"They have zero chance of winning the election without us," said Greely. "Even with DOMINION, there's no guarantee they'll win. But if they do, this is the price they'll pay."

"And if they refuse to honor their commitments?"

"They won't, because things would get really ugly if they did," said Greely. "Impeachment, to start. Imprisonment to follow. Utter destruction of a major political party for all eternity. We have the leverage to bury them so deep, they'll never recover. Meticulous records of everything. Trust me. They'll be faced with permanent destruction. One-party rule for decades."

"ARTEMIS is the wild card," said Furst.

"It goes deeper than that," Greely said. "The FBI is aware that we're involved on some level, which is why we need to make damn sure DOMINION succeeds. If election day goes our way, there's nothing they can do to stop us."

"We're still a few months away," said Furst. "An eternity in politics."

"Exactly. Which is why we need to bury ARTEMIS sooner than later," said Greely. "Or keep them out of our business."

"I'm not sure which option will be easier," Furst said. "Montana didn't exactly go as planned."

"No. It didn't," said Greely. "Mann doesn't seem to be taking any outsized risks. The big question is, where does his investigation stand after Montana? The ambush clearly must have raised some serious eyebrows at headquarters—which is why I think we need to lay very low."

"Mann might not give us that option," said Furst. "His task force has proven very resourceful. He found LABYRINTH and somehow connected it to AXIOM. If they were watching AXIOM, they've obviously connected LABYRINTH to True America. And we have to assume they strongly suspect we're running DOMINION. They basically watched you pry the SATCHEL from McCall's dead fingers. Plus, Mann has some form of outside help that doesn't seem to be constrained by any rules at all. We have zero information on them. They're like ghosts."

"I'm very aware of them," said Greely. "In one form or another, they've stopped every iteration of True America from 2007 onward."

Furst shook her head. "2007?"

"2008 was a bit of a miracle, to be honest," said Greely. "We should have been deep-sixed a year earlier. But the beltway has a way of rewriting history. And nobody wanted to talk about the epic US intelligence and security failures that took place under that administration's watch. Ironically, sweeping it under the rug was what ultimately led to their ouster—and ushered in our era. Unfortunately, it was short lived."

"I know. I was there," said Furst. "Time to share the full story. What are we up against?"

"I don't know if it's a good idea," said Greely.

"Not a good idea? I've dedicated my entire life to True America, and I'm clearly not afraid to break a few eggs to move our national agenda forward," said Furst. "What happened in 2007, and how does it relate to 2009 and today?"

Greely glanced at his watch. "We don't have enough time. I'll bring you up to speed after the meeting."

Furst took out her phone and made a call. "We've pushed the meeting back an hour. There have been a few new developments that Mr. Greely and I need to analyze. Please make the recently arrived attendees comfortable until we're ready."

"We probably shouldn't make them wait," Greely said. "They're self-important people."

"They can sip fancy sparkling water and nibble on gourmet bites a little longer," said Furst. "I need to know who and what we're dealing with before we make any more decisions. Maybe it wasn't the best idea to kill another dozen FBI agents. Maybe, given whatever you're about to tell me, we should have called off the attack and let them find nothing."

Maybe the reason Greely disliked Furst had more to do with the fact that she tended to be right all the time, rather than her seemingly disrespectful and entitled attitude. He'd chosen her for the most important role in the silent coup for a reason. She was the best suited of everyone in the party to pull it off.

"The story actually goes back a little further," said Greely. "And it's not exactly a story I'm proud to tell."

When he'd finished giving Furst an abbreviated history of True America's previous failed plots and conspiracies, she remained silent—breathing slowly—for at least a minute.

"Frankly, I'm surprised you're still alive," said Furst.

"That's your response?"

"For starters."

"Well. The only reason I'm still alive is that I've kept an exceptionally low profile," said Greely. "The FBI turned my world upside down in 2009 but didn't find any link between me and any of True America's conspiracies. I stayed as far away as possible without becoming completely irrelevant. No financial links. No documented communications with leadership. For all practical purposes, it appeared that I was estranged from my father. All by design. That's the one thing he did right. One of his few truly strategic visions. Keeping the appearance that I had nothing to do with the movement. The Department of Justice's final investigative report specifically exonerated me. That's why I'm still alive. If I had been implicated on any level, I'm sure General Sanderson's people would have killed me."

"It definitely kept you invisible," she said. "To be honest, I was surprised to learn that you'd be playing such an active role in the revival."

Active role. She had a way with words.

"The revival wouldn't be possible without me," said Greely. "In addition to quietly building the trust of the Russians over the past decade and discovering AXIOM by keeping my ear to the ground in certain circles, I personally funded the AXIOM deal and everything you're looking at right now."

"We have strategic silent partners—"

"No. We don't. But we will, when we have something concrete to offer. I deemed it far too risky for the movement to solicit money or influence from the private-sector moguls who bankrolled True America in the past. It's not like I could go to them and say, *Third time's the charm.*"

"Then where did you get the money?" said Furst.

"My father and Lee Harding, his partner in crimes, so to speak, stashed away a sizable rainy-day fund in offshore accounts, which they agreed I would manage and grow. I had a finance degree and an MBA. Even more important, I could be trusted. He had more silent partners in the 2007 plot than the Department of Justice discovered. More than he needed to pull off his admittedly shortsighted stunt."

"But he still took their money," said Furst.

"My father and Lee Harding sincerely believed that by eliminating most of Congress and striking a symbolic blow to a few hostile mainstream media outlets, he could usher in the True America era. He thought he would need the money to finish the job. I saw where the next True America plot was headed and made the strategic decision to keep the funds in reserve. Plus, the conspirators weren't hurting for money. Hijacking the government to make people even wealthier and more influential seems to have a timeless appeal to the wealthy and influential."

"You were hedging your bets," said Furst.

"And keeping my distance. They never told me the plan, but I could read between the lines. And I had heard some things through my sources. True America was already losing steam. People were getting tired of the obstructionist politics in Congress and America's statehouses. The president and administration polled neutral, which wasn't a bad thing, but the excitement was fading. Reelection in 2012 felt like a long shot, and I knew some of the conspirators from my dad's days. They flew under the radar back then, but I remember them meeting regularly with my father and Harding. I kind of knew things would get ugly; I had no idea exactly how ugly. I'm glad I hedged my bets. Even if their plan had worked, you can't murder or maim millions of Americans and not expect to lose the full faith and trust of your supporters."

"DOMINION isn't exactly a soft touch," said Furst. "If the American people ever learned the truth, that would be the end of us—forever. Three strikes, right?"

"I would imagine so," said Greely.

"Which is why I think we—as in everyone remotely suspected of being part of the revival—need to lay as low as possible for the next few weeks. Maybe a month. Keep DOMINION running, and dial that up or down as required to influence voters, but give ARTEMIS nothing to work with. You said yourself that certain factions within the Department of Justice and White House had grown weary with the constant bad news and limited results. We lose nothing by laying low. We risk losing everything if one of our cabinet picks has already been identified and is grabbed by Mann or his unsavory friends. For all we know, they're already watching a few of them. They haven't exactly kept the lowest profile."

"We know the FBI isn't actively watching former True America political appointees," said Greely. "Everyone they've targeted has either been assassinated, jailed, or killed themselves."

"What about the CIA? What if there's a persons of interest list that a certain group of CIA operatives and black ops mercenaries likes to check in on from time to time—for old times' sake?" said Furst. "Or a former Mexican police officer with a dozen friends hell-bent on bringing anyone remotely involved with LABYRINTH to justice?"

"There's no nexus between us and the serial killers," said Greely. "AXIOM created LABYRINTH and DOMINION. We just leased DOMINION."

"Think about how that will sound with a gun in your mouth," said Furst. "And a very pissed-off woman's finger on the trigger."

She was right. As usual.

"They're not going to like the idea of being cooped up here for a month," Greely said. "It's quite maddening, and I haven't been here for very long."

"There's plenty of room, and the service is impeccable," said Furst. "Like an all-inclusive resort."

"They don't pay for anything out of pocket on the outside as it is. Life has been like an all-inclusive vacation since they got anointed."

"They need to stay out of sight until the temperature drops out there. Right now, it's hotter than the surface of the sun."

"And if they refuse?" asked Greely.

"Then we dump whoever refuses—literally," said Furst. "And find replacement cabinet picks."

"Then it's settled," Greely said. "Effective immediately, this is everyone's new home for a while."

"There's no guarantee that Mann won't find us. But this move will significantly cut down on our exposure," said Furst.

"Agreed."

"And do you mind moving over a seat?" she asked. "This isn't about a power dynamic. This is about managing anxiety levels. It will look odd to our soon-to-be sequestered friends if you're seated at the head of the table. The fewer perceived shake-ups, the better."

"I suppose you're right," said Greely.

"Thank you," said Furst. "I'm going to have a talk with security about the new arrangement. Make sure it's clear that nobody leaves. I could see Trent Summers getting up and simply walking out."

"Not a bad idea," said Greely. "If I wasn't confined to this wheelchair, I would have been long gone."

"Well. I'm not glad you're in a wheelchair, but I'm certainly glad you're already here," she said, headed for the door. "I have a feeling you might have been the hardest to convince to remain in lockdown."

"You know me a little too well," said Greely as she stepped outside.

But not as well as you think. He'd left a few details out of their conversation. Like the new capability that wasn't exactly low key—but he was itching to try out.

PART III

CHAPTER 21

Serrano barely slept, which wasn't a new development. Except now she had nothing and no one to blame but herself. Logically, she understood the chemical-biological process. She'd just gotten herself caught in a bit of a bad loop lately. Trying to negotiate with people who didn't like to negotiate took its toll. She felt wired all day, waiting to learn her fate. A shallow grave outside the city, no response at all, or maybe—just maybe—a deal of some sort. A deal that would likely be so lopsided, it would keep her awake for the rest of her life.

She'd watch TV late into the night, hoping to fall asleep. When sleep didn't come around twelve, she'd walk several blocks to the nearest 7-Eleven and buy a pack of cigarettes, a chicken salad sandwich, some chips, and a few miniature bottles of tequila if the store manager had stocked them behind the counter. If not, she'd just grab a normal-size bottle.

The illogic went like this: She'd smoke a few cigarettes to "calm her nerves" and down a few glasses of tequila to "put her to sleep." Predictably, the nicotine kept her in a light sleep once she managed to drift off, and the sugar in the cheap tequila woke her up a few hours later. Serrano had more or less broken her smoking habit, so she'd typically crumple the pack the next morning and toss it in a trash bin on her way to grab breakfast. If she'd been forced to purchase a large bottle of tequila, she'd pour it down the sink. Rinse. Repeat.

She should have taken Garrett up on the European-vacation option. Would it have killed her to take one week off? He'd suggested two, citing some scientific study about how it takes typical Americans a week to truly start relaxing—which she'd found both hilarious and misguided.

She didn't work a mindless desk job in the city. Her every living day for the past several years had been dedicated to avenging her mother's murder, working one shittier police assignment after another until she was finally fired. The scientists hadn't dug into that demographic yet. If they did, they'd probably find out it would take five years of vacation to just bring them down a few notches.

That said, she should have taken the opportunity. Mann was just trying to help. Show her how to give herself a break. Maybe it would have helped. Maybe she would have stayed longer. She had enough money to do pretty much whatever she wanted. But even the money stressed her out. Racked with guilt, she spent hours plotting how to use it to help the children who had lost their mothers to the cartels' killers. The parents who had lost their daughters.

There was literally no end to her misery, which was why she stood inside a fluorescent-lit, visibly dilapidated convenience store at half past midnight, shrugging in shame as the night cashier slid a pack of Delicados out of the plastic display case behind him. He'd given her the bad news about the small bottles when she entered a few minutes ago, so she slid the full bottle across the counter, along with a bag of spicy-hot Takis and her sandwich.

She got a half block away from the neon-fluorescent hell before the black Suburban she'd spotted a block down from the 7-Eleven pulled up next to her. Just a few feet away. The front and rear passenger doors opened before she could make the mistake of reaching for the compact pistol tucked into the small of her back. The man in the front passenger seat pointed a double-barrel shotgun at her midsection. The man who opened the rear passenger door slid into the third row between the two captain's chairs.

"Señorita Serrano?" said a man from the driver's-side captain's chair.

He held a pistol against his right thigh, barely visible in the dingy orange light cast by the nearest streetlight.

"*Sí,*" she said.

"Get in," said the man in the back seat.

"Where are we headed?" she asked.

"Someone would like to have a word with you."

"Is that someone in the back?" she said, nodding toward the third row.

"What do you think?" he said.

"Why didn't you just pick me up when I left my apartment?" she said. "I assume you're very familiar with my nightly routine."

"I like chicken salad, and I travel around the city a lot," he said. "But I wouldn't trust myself to grab a chicken salad sandwich from a random 7-Eleven. You looked like you knew what you were doing. Have you ever picked a bad one?"

"Never. I grab from the back of the row."

Was he making small talk, or did he seriously not know how perishable foods at a convenience store were stocked?

"See? No matter what happens tonight, you made the trip worth my time," he said.

Sounded like she had a chance of surviving the night.

"Are you getting in?"

"I don't suppose I have a choice?" said Serrano.

"You always have a choice," he said. "You could go for the pistol tucked into your jeans; that would be a choice. A bad choice. But a choice nonetheless."

"What do you want me to do with the pistol?" she said.

"Nothing. We'll take care of it," he said. "Turn around, please."

She did what he asked and was immediately relieved of the pistol. A breathable, opaque hood dropped over her head a few seconds later; her first instinct was to grab the hood.

"Drop your hands to your side!" said the voice from the back of the SUV. "This is standard procedure. You know this."

She nodded and put her hands behind her back, where they could be easily cuffed.

"No need for that," said the voice. "My associate is going to pat you down for any other weapons."

Serrano figured she could earn a little trust by making the man's job easier.

"I have a flip-out serrated knife in my right boot," she said. "And a switchblade tucked into my belt. Left, front side."

Someone, presumably the man in the front seat, confiscated both weapons almost instantly. Then he proceeded with one of the most thorough pat downs she'd either given or been given.

"She's good," said the man who had searched her.

"We're going for a ride. About an hour," said the man in the back seat. "If you fuck around at all during the drive, the man in the back row will shoot you through your seat. Understood?"

"Sí." She nodded.

"Bien," he said. "Get in. I'd like to check out this chicken salad sandwich."

They helped her into the back seat.

"Can I buckle my seat belt?"

"Safety first," said the man.

More like caution *first.* She lifted the 7-Eleven bag and placed it on the floor between them. Or so she thought. She couldn't see.

"Help yourself," she said.

She listened closely, waiting for the sharp cellophane rip. He hadn't torn into it right away.

"Still another three days left on the expiration date," she said. "My rule is two days or more."

"You sure you don't mind?" he asked.

"I might throw up if I eat right now. Or drink," she said.

"Understandable," said the man, pulling the rest of the cellophane off. "So. Explain to me exactly what you want and what we get in return."

"I have a list of friends and colleagues in the state who have lived in fear for their lives and the lives of their loved ones for far too long because they either had a hand in investigating or spoke out against the hundreds of women killed by La Triada," she said. "I seek your organization's sworn word that they are hereby safe from the Juárez Cartel. They pose no further threat. They just want to get on with their lives. Lives broken or shattered by La Triada, which the cartel tolerated and protected."

He didn't respond for several seconds.

"Not bad. A hint of dill, which is a nice touch. What else?"

"What?" she said. "Oh. Sorry. We'd also appreciate your help with a somewhat delicate matter inside the US."

"And you speak for who, again?"

"I've been asked to discreetly represent the interests of an FBI task force," she said. "I unofficially worked for them on a few important concerns related to La Triada."

"They must not like you very much," said the man. "Or this was your idea."

"Eighty-twenty," said Serrano. "The other way around."

"Interesting," he said. "What kind of matter in the US do you need our help with?"

"A few hundred of your former associates, mostly low-level sicarios or enforcers, who now work on behalf of an American organization," she said.

"The American government?"

"No. A private corporation using them to stoke anti-immigration sentiment," said Serrano. "Their goal is to sway the election in favor of a new administration. One that has promised to start a new war on drugs and illegal immigration—by locking down the US side of the border with soldiers and putting intense pressure on your new president to do the same on this side."

"Well. We can't have that, can we?" he said.

"Could be costly," said Serrano.

"Annoying," he said. "But we've yet to see a year-to-year decline in profit, despite the best efforts of both governments."

"This feels different," she said.

"Might be," he said. "So. You want us to remove this element and lay off your friends?"

"Yes."

"In exchange for what?"

"The hundreds of traitors to your organization," she said.

This was where she hoped they hadn't already found any of the LABYRINTH graduates and heard their side of the story. He'd know she was full of shit and that the graduates hadn't betrayed the Juárez Cartel. From what Raul had told them, the graduates truly thought they had been promoted and were still working for their cartel.

The man laughed. "I expected more from you, Señorita Serrano. I'm not sure how this benefits us. The element you refer to sounds like a US problem, not ours."

"I wouldn't be so sure about that," she said. "They represent a very unpleasant link to your organization. A link the new administration would be sure to exploit to start a real war against the cartels, not the phony one they've pursued for decades."

"Why would this new administration draw any attention to the hidden army that helped them win the election?" he asked. "What aren't you telling me?"

She knew this would be a tough sell. Time to shift strategy.

"They don't know who they're working for," said Serrano, taking a huge risk.

"Who doesn't?"

"The sicarios and enforcers your organization planted in the US to help facilitate the free flow of fentanyl and other drugs," said Serrano. "Alejandro and Raul defected, taking a lot of information with them. They helped a private company kidnap hundreds of your people and convince them that they had been chosen for a special operation by the Juárez Cartel in the US. This couldn't have gone unnoticed. Right?"

"It didn't," he said. "But this started a few years ago, and nothing abnormal or unpredicted has popped up on any level of our operations. We started replacing them slowly, watching very closely."

"And?"

"Nothing," he said. "We're slowly replacing our entire network."

"I'm surprised you would tell me this," said Serrano.

"What are you going to do? Tell the powers that be in the US that we're doing what we've always done?" he said. "Go ahead and walk that into DEA headquarters. You'll never be seen again. This dance we've been doing with the US government isn't new. The music may be different, but the moves are pretty much the same."

"I feel like it's going to be different this time," said Serrano. "The network is fully in the hands of the end user. They're not going to waste a single political opportunity to score points with the American people. They'll sacrifice the network, which believes they're doing your bidding. Imagine dozens of your former employees at Guantanamo Bay, giving up everything they know about the Juárez Cartel."

"If they still believe they're working for us, they'll die before they give up anything useful," he said.

"Seriously? They turned lifelong jihadists into spewing fountains of information—leading to hundreds of drone assassinations in the Middle East and a near-complete dismantling of al-Qaeda and ISIS. Imagine living under the constant threat of a drone strike."

"We have considerable influence in Mexico City," he said.

"But does the government have land-based missile batteries at their command? *Your* command?" said Serrano. "I know the answer."

"We have surface-to-air missiles," he said.

"MANPADs?"

"You know your business."

"You're not going to hit a Switchblade drone hovering over one of your boss's villas with a thirty-year-old Stinger missile or one of your new RBS-70 man-portable systems," she said, repeating what Melendez had told her.

He'd briefed her and then grilled her on the subject. Then she'd done her own digging on the internet to fill in the gaps. The man didn't respond right away, which was a change.

"Here's the deal . . ." she said.

"Okay. This should be good," he said.

"Everything we've talked about so far entirely depends on my friends back in the US . . . basically pulling off a miracle," she started.

"So. I'm wasting my time?"

"No. I'm offering you a one-time, low-investment opportunity to benefit from something that you have no influence over in the end," she said. "And avoid any backlash. It's kind of a no-brainer.

"If my friends pull this off, they'll be in a position to apprehend the entire network. Messy work. Agents and police officers will die. All fingers will point back at the Juárez Cartel eventually," she said. "But they're willing to give you the opportunity to wipe that slate clean. Put this whole mess in the past. We give you the network and you disappear it. Forever. Even if the election goes the wrong way, you'll be in a better position to weather that storm. And if it goes the right way, the gesture won't go unnoticed. I can't make any promises, obviously. I'm nobody. But some people very high in the US Department of Justice are watching this closely."

"I'm inclined to just let this ride," he said.

I'm inclined? She suddenly realized they hadn't left the city. They'd made too many turns.

"Look at you," he said. "A former Juárez traffic cop with some serious sway."

"I lucked into it," she said.

"No, you didn't," he said. "I don't believe in luck or fate. We make our way in the world. For better or worse. Fate and luck are lazy constructs. Soft landings for failures. You never hear successful people credit luck or fate for their achievements. In fact, they're the first to kick those concepts to the curb when they're suggested. Hard work and determination eclipse intelligence and intuition, which are viewed as randomly assigned traits. Luck did not seat you in this SUV."

"You can't write off intuition," Serrano said.

He laughed again. "Very true. I give intuition a bit of a pass. But I think it's born of hard work and determination. Meaningful experience."

"Señor Mendoza," she said.

The head of the Juárez Cartel.

"I like to vet my prospects in person," said Mendoza. "And I'm still not sold. I'm still inclined to let this ride. Let decades of experience guide my decision. Let the American politicians wring their hands in front of their constituents long enough to look good, before the entire issue slowly fades away. Time is on our side, Cata. Time is never on a politician's side."

Time to go for broke.

"I'll release a comprehensive media package implicating the Juárez Cartel and local politicians, many of whom still hold office, in covering up the decade-long femicide here in Ciudad Juárez," said Serrano. "On top of that, the package will spell out the cartel's connection to the network currently operating in the US. Blaming you for feeding sicarios into the system. My friends in the US have agreed to cooperate with that angle. It's all a bit of a long shot, but my guess is, there'll be three Switchblade drones circling over every property you own in Mexico, twenty-four hours a day, within a few months of all this information going wide. And killing me will trigger the package's immediate release. I've taken precautions, crafted by the best in the business. And I'm not talking about my FBI friends."

"Finally," he said.

"Finally, what?"

"A real negotiation," said Mendoza.

"I don't get it," said Serrano.

"A real negotiation usually involves a legitimate threat," Mendoza said. "I'm not sure yours has the teeth you think, but you have a deal—if we get that list."

"And if you don't?" she asked. "If we fail to acquire it?"

"Then life goes back to normal," said Mendoza.

"What's normal?"

"Whatever it was before you reached out to me."

"And my friends?"

"The same as it was before you reached out to me," he said, the SUV coming to a slow stop. "No threat implied."

Someone removed the hood, revealing that the SUV had stopped in front of the 7-Eleven in her neighborhood. The store's ridiculously bright lights forced her to squint.

"Thank you," she said.

"For what?"

"For not killing me," she said.

"I'm going to let you in on a little secret," said Mendoza. "You and your friends have never been in any baseline danger from my people. I preemptively and proactively neutralize real threats as they materialize, or I predict them. I do hold grudges, but only against people who have gone out of their way to fuck me over. Cops digging around for information about a decade-old murder investigation? Members of the military speaking out about the same murders? Not a danger to me. That has always been the baseline, and the only reason they are still alive. Stay at or below the baseline, and you don't attract my attention. That said . . ."

He stopped, letting his words sink in before continuing.

"You have now attracted my attention, Cata. This package of yours concerns me," he said. "It's not at the top of my list of concerns, but it has made the list. Do you understand what I'm saying?"

"I do," she said.

"I'm not convinced, so let me spell it out for you. This network of former cartel associates embedded in the United States? Given the opportunity, I'd love to close the book on them and mitigate any bad press they might generate for my organization. But I'm not going to lose any sleep about it if your mission fails," said Mendoza. "Now. This media package of yours is a different story. Walking the press and public through the entire history of La Triada to the conspiracy up north is the kind of negative attention that could interfere with my business. I suspect it won't, but why take the chance?"

"It's leverage to ensure you hold up your end of the bargain," said Serrano. "Whether we fail or succeed to shut down the sicario network and deliver it to you, the package will not be released unless you go back on your word."

"I very much understand the concept of leverage, and I'm good for my word," said Mendoza. "But I will kill every single one of your friends down here—after I torture and murder everyone they hold dear, right in front of their eyes—if you go back on yours. Understood?"

"Sí."

"If you don't survive whatever business you have planned up north, I'll need to speak with whoever has been entrusted with the package—so I can shake their hand on it. If not. Well. There's no need to recap what will happen."

"I'll make the necessary arrangements," said Serrano. "In case I don't return."

"I think we're on the same page now," said Mendoza. "You can unbuckle your seat belt."

The moment she released the seat belt, her door opened; a strong hand grabbed her arm and pulled her out of the SUV. The man with the shotgun returned her plastic shopping bag. She felt the weight of the tequila bottle. More like the pull of it.

"Thank you for the sandwich," said Mendoza, still a shadow inside the vehicle.

The three-SUV convoy sped away moments later, the other two oversize SUVs having joined them at some point during the short drive. Several minutes later, she climbed the stairs to her second-floor apartment, where she found a neatly folded paper bag containing her pistol, knives, keys, and cell phone lying in front of her door. She hadn't even noticed that her cell phone and keys had been taken and hadn't bothered to check. She was still in a state of shock.

Serrano set the bag on the kitchen counter, tempted to open the bottle or rip open the cigarette pack. Not tonight. Maybe never again. She grabbed her cell phone and dropped onto the couch, staring at the ceiling long enough to almost fall asleep. *No sleep for the wicked,* she thought, before dialing Mann's number.

CHAPTER 22

Mann was wide awake when Serrano's call came through. A few minutes before one in the morning her time. Almost three in the morning for him. To say he was relieved would have been an understatement. If she hadn't called, he would have been forced to wait until tomorrow morning to check in. An eternity to get her take on recent developments.

"Everything okay?" he asked.

"I'm alive. And I'm safe—for now," she said, a little shakily. "I met Enrique Mendoza tonight. They picked me up outside of the local 7-Eleven around twelve thirty and drove me around for about fifteen minutes, before dropping me off in the same place. I had no idea it might be him until he said something that tipped me off. He confirmed my intuition. Or someone very close to him did a convincing job of pretending to be Mendoza."

"You saw him?" said Mann. "We've heard he had some work done on his face recently."

"I've heard the same," said Serrano. "But no. I had a hood over my head most of the time. The rest of the time, he was in the shadows."

"Are you sure you're okay?"

"I'm alive. And we have a deal," she said. "So I'm about as okay as I can be, under the circumstances."

"Is there something you're not telling me? You don't sound good," he said, trying not to overstep.

"It's complicated. I'll explain later," she said. "But I'm fine. I promise. What are the next steps?"

Nothing about her situation was right. But he had to keep playing along.

"What's the catch?" asked Mann. "Are we still talking about the same deal?"

"We are. It's just that he didn't respond well to my threat."

What the hell had she been thinking?

"You threatened him?"

"He didn't leave me a choice," said Serrano. "I earned his respect, but it came at a price. Which doesn't have anything to do with the DOMINION mission. Please. Let's leave it there for now."

"Are you in danger?"

"I'm always in danger down here," she said. "Garrett. Please drop this for now. I'll explain later."

"As long as you're not in any immediate danger."

"I'm not," said Serrano. "So. What's the next step? Has anything changed?"

"Not really," said Mann. "The task force is still suspended, but we're meeting with some of our old friends tomorrow. Along with some new friends. We'll probably go dark from that point forward. How do things stand with your colleagues?"

"I have six, not including myself," said Serrano. "I'm trying to track down a few more."

"Six is more than enough," said Mann. "I have three new agents, and we've picked up a few more, compliments of Bauer and Berg. How soon can you be ready?"

"Give me a few days to discreetly pass the word and let everyone get their business and affairs in order," she said. "It might come as a surprise that we're heading back so soon. I should have a timeline for you by tomorrow afternoon."

"Sounds good," Mann said. "I'll get to work trying to arrange transportation. Unfortunately, I no longer have access to agency resources for investigative purposes. I'm basically suspended from fieldwork. You might have to book your own flights to DC, and I'll reimburse everyone with some of the funny money still in the task force's possession."

"That's fine. Once I get a firm departure timeline from everyone, I'll book the flights," said Serrano. "First class or business, of course."

"I suppose that's in our budget. And make sure to stagger the flights. Split up the group. I don't entirely understand the capabilities of who we're up against. If they've identified anyone on your team—even a single person—your flight would be a tempting target."

"You really think they'd take down an airliner?"

"They have no problem killing dozens of FBI agents," said Mann. "A regional jet carrying sixty or so civilians wouldn't give them pause."

"I suppose you're right," she said. "I'll split us up but get us into DC around the same time. Make it easier on your people."

"Don't worry about us," he said. "Worry about yourself until you get here. I'm guessing there will be no shortage of opportunities to get yourself killed after you've arrived safely. Sorry. Sounded kind of grim."

"Actually, I like the sound of that," Serrano said. "Not the getting-killed part. The making-a-difference part."

He paused a little too long. Not wanting to say the obvious.

"I know what you're thinking. *This isn't your fight anymore*," said Serrano. "I'm too tired to explain why you're wrong."

"And I'm too tired to hear why I'm wrong," said Mann. "But we're beyond grateful and very humbled that you insist on having our back. You and all your friends. Seriously. It's hard to explain."

"It's late," she said. "Save the explanation for later."

"I will," he said. "Sleep tight."

"Whatever," she said, ending the call.

He called Emily Miralles, one of the operatives sent to him by Audra Bauer at the CIA, via Karl Berg. She'd arrived in Ciudad Juárez ahead of Serrano's return and rented a room in an apartment within sight of Cata's apartment. A week after Serrano returned, she leased another apartment across from Cata's favorite 7-Eleven. And another halfway between the two.

Miralles hadn't bugged Serrano's apartment. Cata would have found the listening device by now. Instead, she'd used a laser microphone, which picked up the vibrations on the south-facing windows of Serrano's apartment. She'd also infected Serrano's phone with the same software Jax had used to track AXIOM from New Mexico to Virginia—with a slight tweak.

Anish Gupta had embedded additional code to the virus, which allowed them to turn the phone into an eavesdropping device without anyone knowing. Mendoza's people should have placed the phone in a signal-proof bag. Miralles had texted him shortly after they picked Cata up and drove off. Every device in Mendoza's SUV, plus the two escort vehicles, had been infected by the same virus within seconds. Given more devices to infect, the virus would spread like wildfire. Unless Mendoza's people had ditched every digital device in the convoy before reaching their destination, ARTEMIS now possessed a treasure trove of location data on the Juárez Cartel.

Emily answered immediately. "She's tucked in, safe and sound. I don't anticipate the cartel circling back. I'll send you the audio files. If you agree with my assessment about her safety, I'll head north very early tomorrow morning. All eyes and ears in this city report to the cartel. I'm already getting some looks. No need to overstay my welcome unless Cata needs my help."

"I'll go through the audio the moment I receive it," said Mann. "But it sounds like you can start packing up."

"I'll keep an eye on her until I leave."

"Thank you."

"The sooner she heads north, the better," she said. "Mendoza sounds all calm and well spoken on the recording, but he's a fucking animal at heart. A monster. She can never return here. Ever. That much is clear, from what I heard."

"What about her friends and their families?" said Mann.

"They're useless to him without her," said Miralles. "No Cata. No leverage. She needs to entirely disappear when this is done. She's the only link to her threat. He'll let sleeping dogs lie without her."

"I think I understand."

"You better understand. Because you're probably the only one who will be able to convince her that returning to Mexico will be the end of her—and all her friends, if they choose to return. Mendoza, like every other criminal boss of any consequence, hates loose ends. No matter how inconsequential they may seem. It's always the loose ends that take them down."

"This sounds like the end to an embittered former district attorney's TED Talk."

"Am I wrong?" asked Miralles.

"No. You're not," said Mann. "I need you to hold my feet to the fire on this. Their lives will depend on it."

"Deal," she said.

"I'll see you tomorrow evening?" said Mann.

"If nothing goes sideways tonight," she said.

"I appreciate what you're doing."

"Yep," said Miralles. "Have you been to the CITADEL?"

"The—what?" said Mann.

"That's the name of our new compound," said Miralles.

"I haven't."

"I haven't seen it in person, but Rico tells me it's a trip."

"As in a long trip out of DC?" said Mann.

"No. A trip—as in Gupta put it together."

"This doesn't sound good," said Mann.

"I agree. It'll be weird," she said. "But I trust him without reservation, so whatever you encounter tomorrow—keep an open mind."

"Message received," said Mann. "And thank you, again."

"Garrett. If you thank me one more time, I'm going to walk off the job. Understood?"

"Understood," he said, ending the call.

The audio files arrived on his computer a few minutes later. He listened to the entire thirteen-minute exchange, agreeing with Miralles's assessment. Cata wasn't in any immediate danger.

Sleep didn't come for at least another hour. Maybe longer. He spent the time thinking about how Cata would react if she discovered that Miralles had been watching over her since she had returned to Mexico, at his request, and that her phone had been turned into a bug. The imaginary conversations swirled in his head to no conclusion before he passed out.

CHAPTER 23

Mann understood the concept of a surveillance detection route. What he didn't understand was how maddening the SDR conducted by the three Special Surveillance Group operatives attached to ARTEMIS would be. Seven hours driving the rural roads of Maryland, Delaware, and Virginia to eventually arrive at a long-neglected corporate warehouse farm on the outskirts of Fredericksburg, Virginia. Brutal.

Not because of the time. He'd driven long distances before. That was all ARTEMIS had done for nearly two years. Drive eight hours to the next tip or lead, which often turned out to be a waste of time. His issue with the long drive today was that he felt like the task force was running out of time. That he needed to get to work, which meant he didn't have time to fuck around with a seven-hour SDR. Of course, that was exactly what was required to ensure that nobody followed the task force to the warehouse complex.

His SUV must have arrived last, but not long after the others. His task force stood in a cluster next to the other two SUVs, clapping when his vehicle pulled up.

"Jessica. Thank you for the ride," said Mann. "Is it safe to get out now, or should we drive around for a few more hours?"

"Funny," she said, before opening her door and hopping out.

Mann glanced over his shoulder at the two agents in the second row. "It's not too late to go back to your old jobs."

Shana Bilyk, a hardened SWAT-trained agent from Minnesota, smirked and shook her head before opening her door and getting out. "I'm good."

"Lunch isn't always that nice," said Mann.

Mayer had timed their SDR perfectly with a stop at an outrageously expensive oceanside restaurant just north of Ocean City. Not a coincidence.

"Nice try," she said.

"Miles?" said Mann.

"I think I'll stick around," Miles said. "There's a kind of brutal honesty here that you don't get in a field office. I find it refreshing."

"I don't know if *refreshing* is the best way to describe what we have going on here," said Mann. "But it definitely beats the day-in, day-out politics and infighting at the office. If you don't mind the occasional mercenary assassination team paying you a visit from time to time."

"O'Reilly didn't mince words," said Miles. "I understand the risks involved."

"I didn't mean to suggest either you or Bilyk didn't," Mann said. "But the task force has turned into something of a meat grinder lately."

"That's what happens when you piss off the wrong people," said Miles. "I'd rather be put through a physical meat grinder than an administrative one."

"I assume things got out of hand in Boston."

"Nobody likes their darkest secrets exposed to the light," Miles said.

"Well. If it's any consolation, everything is out in the open here," said Mann. "We illegally work with Mexican nationals, former–CIA black ops mercenaries, and whoever else is willing to lend a hand to take down the bad guys."

"My kind of crowd," said Miles.

"Everybody says that."

"Then . . . maybe you're doing something right?" said Miles, before taking off.

He'd like to think so. Hard to say, when you've killed off half your task force in less than six weeks. He followed Miles to the group, where Luke Turner greeted him.

"That little shit Gupta still hasn't answered any of our calls," said Turner. "We're not taking another step until he starts communicating with us."

Mann pulled out his phone and called Gupta, who answered immediately.

"Looks like everyone arrived safely—but more importantly, untraced."

"You're starting to piss everyone off," said Mann. "Me included. Where are we headed?"

"You tell me," said Gupta.

"Let me guess. The middle of the warehouse farm?"

"Do you think I'd pick a location that obvious?"

"Yes. I do. Because your first thought when choosing the headquarters location would be to go with something not so obvious. But anyone with half a lick of common sense and an IQ over eighty would think the same thing, too. So you'd start to think about going with your first instinct and putting the HQ in the center. It makes sense if your most likely threat is a lower-layer assault. *Lower layer* meaning any hostile force approaching on foot, in vehicles, or helicopters."

"Helicopters?" asked Gupta. "Lower layer?"

"Don't play stupid," Mann said. "You've been at this far too long for me to fall for that."

"Busted. Helicopters operate the same as a ground assault. They just enjoy the advantage of surprise, which can be a decisive factor."

"And if their intelligence sucks, they drop their assault team on a rooftop two blocks away after alerting every hostile within two miles. Without precise intel, they're far less useful than a convoy of armored vehicles or a rapidly moving platoon of soldiers."

"So, your mental gymnastics puts the HQ in the center of the warehouse complex?" said Gupta.

"No. Yours does," said Mann. "On the surface, your question is designed to make me doubt my assumption, but you know I'm not that easily duped. So your question is actually a ruse—hoping I will remain steadfast in my assumption."

"That the HQ is in the center."

"No. That it's not in the center," said Mann. "But it is."

"Now I'm confused," said Gupta.

"We'll see you in a few minutes. Unless I'm wrong."

"Dammit. You're not wrong," said Gupta. "But I don't follow your logic."

"You weren't supposed to. I could have gone back and forth for hours with the whole 'If you hinted at this, you must have meant that, but then that means you meant something else' routine," said Mann. "I'm just completely guessing."

"Well. You guessed right," Gupta said. "It's the most defendable location from your lower-layer assault, but the most likely target if someone is attacking from a higher altitude."

"If they're dropping laser-guided bombs, cruise missiles, or high-explosive drones on us, we have bigger problems than we ever anticipated," said Mann.

"I agree," said Gupta. "Hey. Do you mind doing me a favor?"

"Go for it."

"Can you guys spread out around the facility and approach the center from different directions? I want to test our perimeter sensors."

"It's been kind of a long day, but why not?" said Mann. "I assume you're not in the exact center of the complex?"

"Of course not," said Gupta. "I can show you where we're located so you can get everyone in position. Three-hundred-and-sixty-degree coverage."

"Perfect," said Mann.

"Ready?" said Gupta.

Something was off.

"Ready," he mumbled.

Three warehouses to Mann's right, Gupta stepped out of an open door and waved.

"Here we are," he said over the phone.

"You got me," said Mann.

"I quadruple-reversed the logic, if that makes any sense."

"It doesn't," Mann said. "But I can't deny the fact that you got me."

"Sort of. Full disclosure," said Gupta, "we're in the warehouse behind the one I just exited. And we do have a full array of sensors protecting us, along with some nasty stuff. If you pull the SUVs forward past the first row of warehouses and turn right, Rico will guide you into the warehouse serving as our garage."

"*Nasty* as in explosive?" said Mann.

"All will be revealed shortly," said Gupta. "But yeah. Mostly remotely triggered Claymores."

"Why does that make me feel like not driving into the complex?"

"Remotely *triggerable*," said Gupta. "Does that sound better?"

"Not really," said Mann, before disconnecting the call.

He gave Gupta a thumbs-up before addressing the task force.

"Everyone back in the vehicles. We have another eight hours ahead of us," he said.

"You're joking," said Turner.

"I am," said Mann. "We're supposed to drive past the first row of warehouses and turn right. Melendez will guide us the rest of the way."

"Good to hear Melendez is back," Turner said.

"Along with a few new additions to the team coming from their side," said Mann. "Miralles will arrive in a few hours."

"So. Things went okay down south?" said Turner.

Today's SDR had kept him from discussing the cartel situation with the entire team.

"We have a tentative deal with the Juárez Cartel," said Mann. "I'll explain in more detail when we assemble a little later."

"Is Cata okay?" asked Turner. "That's what I was asking."

"She's fine. According to her. But she didn't sound so good," said Mann. "The sooner we get her out of there—along with the rest of her crew—the better. I'm expecting a phone call from her soon, with details of their travel plans."

"They can't go back, can they?"

"Not unless we acquire the DOMINION database. And even then, I'm not entirely convinced they'll be safe. We'll hash this out with them when they arrive," said Mann.

"They've earned the right to stay here—under our nation's protection."

"I couldn't agree more. It's just a matter of convincing the right people," said Mann. "I think if we pull this off, the powers that be will help them."

"I hope so."

"If not, we'll do everything we can to make it right," Mann said.

"That right there is why I haven't disappeared and fled to some obscure island in the Pacific. See you inside," said Turner, before heading to his SUV.

"I'd find you and drag you back if you vanished," said Mann.

Turner glanced over his shoulder. "You couldn't outsmart Gupta, who gave himself away from the start. You ain't finding me if I don't want to be found."

"Probably true," said Mann, turning to Jessica Mayer, who was standing next to their SUV with an impatient look on her face.

"The door was open when we arrived," said Mayer.

"Which door?"

"The warehouse door where Gupta appeared?" Mayer said. "I didn't want to say anything."

"It was open when we drove up?" asked Mann.

"Yes," said Mayer. "But don't feel bad. Turner didn't see it, either, or he would have mentioned it."

"You saw that and just let me go on and on with Gupta?"

"It's been a long day," said Mayer. "I needed a little entertainment."

Mann laughed. "Well. I hope I delivered."

"Oh. You delivered all right," said Mayer, before getting in and shutting the door.

They followed the rest of the convoy past the first row of warehouses, where they spotted Melendez a few warehouses down. He directed them inside the empty, cavernous space, instructing the drivers of each SUV to park directly behind the three rows of a dozen or more vehicles. Sedans. SUVs. Jeeps. A few vans. Any type they might need for whatever job came up.

Melendez met them by their vehicles, pulling two metal platform trucks like the kind you find at Home Depot, except they didn't clang and rattle like the wheels were about to fall off.

"How much gear did you bring?" asked Melendez.

"Pretty much all of it," Mann told him.

"Only enough to fill up the back of three SUVs?"

"We've used up most of what we took from LABYRINTH over the last month or so," said Mann. "And I no longer have access to FBI field resources. We should probably rush-order some 5.56mm ammunition to one of the storage facilities we rented."

"We have plenty of ammunition," said Melendez. "And enough personal gear and weapons to equip a platoon."

"Good. Because Cata's crew has to travel commercial," said Mann.

"How many?"

"Nine, including Cata," said Mann. "Everyone is returning."

"Incredible."

"Truly," Mann said. "I gave them all a very liberal amount of cash taken from LABYRINTH. Enough to scoop up their families and vanish for good. Leave the Juárez Cartel behind. And they're coming back."

"We have plenty of gear to equip them," said Melendez. "Any AT4s left?"

"I don't know what you're talking about," said Mann. "But two would be a good guess."

"Claymores?"

"Thirty-two," said Mann.

"Good," said Melendez. "We're having trouble sourcing those."

"Gupta made it sound like he had plenty."

Melendez shrugged. "We have four."

"Four?" said Mann. "Where?"

"We haven't deployed them yet."

"Gupta said the entire complex was rigged with remotely detonated Claymores."

"He also convinced you that we'd occupied one of the warehouses in the center of this place," Melendez said.

"I wouldn't say he convinced me," said Mann. "But, yeah. I guessed wrong. I had a fifty-fifty chance."

"I'm not headed to Vegas with you anytime soon," said Melendez.

"Smart call," said Mann. "Is Miralles still on time?"

Melendez nodded. "Last I checked. Cata and her group?"

"I'm still waiting for the details," said Mann. "Sounded like a few days from now. Her people need some time to get their affairs in order. I don't think they expected this quick of a turnaround."

"It's a big ask. I have nothing but respect for them," said Melendez.

"Same with you and your crew."

"True America has to be stopped for good. We thought we put an end to them before, but they keep coming back. This time, I don't care what it takes," said Melendez. "I've been around from the start. I was there when they tried to poison Congress and several media outlets. And I was part of the crew that stopped them from killing tens of millions of Americans they deemed to be political enemies by infecting them with a rabies-grade virus that destroyed their brains—either killing them or leaving them needing intensive care for the rest of their lives. Whatever they're up to right now may not be as extreme, but the goal will be the same. Complete control of the nation."

"O'Reilly, Bauer, and Berg convinced me that True America's link to DOMINION was extremely problematic, but this is next-level shit," said Mann.

"And I just violated about a dozen NDAs drawn up by various US government agencies," said Melendez. "But I'd be happy to tell you the rest of the story—later. As in after we flush True America down the toilet."

"What if we fail?" said Mann.

"Even more reason to tell the story," said Melendez. "Because you'll be out of a job and there's only one group that will be hiring ex–FBI agents who worked for a task force that tried to take down True America."

"If any of us survive."

"Been at this for close to twenty years. This latest iteration of fascist fucks isn't going to punch my ticket," said Melendez. "See you inside. Gupta is eager to get things rolling. Dinner after his briefing."

"I'm glad you brought that up. The dinner part," said Mann. "How is this going to work from a logistical standpoint? We can't order food to an abandoned warehouse."

"Not sure we've worked that out yet," said Melendez. "But there's a stove, a refrigerator, and a freezer inside, along with shelving units stocked with nonperishable stuff. Lockers for all our gear. It's not as bad as it sounds. We've been working out of here off and on for a few years. Several levels of state-of-the-art security, starting with the road in and the woods surrounding it. Motion and sound sensors everywhere. Daytime and IR video. The closer you get to this warehouse or the primary space, the more robust the coverage. Drone radar. Counterdrone system. Encrypted burst-satellite communications. Air-gapped outside of that. We've worked safely and discreetly out of here for long enough to trust what Gupta created. And your team's SDRs worked flawlessly. I had three vehicles follow you from the Conrad. They broke contact before you reached the coast."

"Frank Vincenzo's team reported that something might be off," said Mann.

"And he pulled over to grab coffee in Greenwood, Delaware. Amity Coffee Roasters," said Melendez. "We knew we'd been made, so I told them to keep driving for about ten minutes, then make their way back to base."

"We started a series of switchbacks after that," said Mann.

"Which threw the other two teams off your scent," said Melendez. "They lost you within a half hour."

"So. You know about the storage facility," Mann said.

"The fake one in Annapolis?" said Melendez.

Mann laughed. "Was it that obvious?"

"Yes and no. I know more about your task force than the opposition. But yeah. The storage bins you loaded into the convoy looked a little devoid of contents. Where was the real storage facility?"

"Fredericksburg," said Mann. "Which is kind of weird since you chose Frederick, Maryland, for this place."

"Like minds," said Melendez.

"Really makes you wonder," said Mann. "So. You own this entire complex?"

"Since the pandemic," said Melendez. "The owners lost most of their tenants. You have to admit, it's not a bad place to go dark. Or as Gupta likes to say, *Go to the mattresses.* I think he's watched *The Godfather* one too many times."

"It's actually perfect," said Mann. "But regarding sleeping arrangements. How does that work in a warehouse?"

"We have thirty or so air mattresses," said Melendez. "I'm not going to lie. It's kind of a weird sleepover situation."

Turner appeared. "Couldn't help but overhear. Air mattresses? A stove in the middle of a warehouse? This sounds weird as fuck. *Squid Game* vibes."

"Wait until you see it," said Melendez. "It's not as bad as it sounds. And the whole place is about as secure as it gets. You know enough about Gupta and our crew to know I'm not exaggerating."

"Open mind," said Turner. "The story of my life lately."

"Seriously," said Mann.

CHAPTER 24

Gupta greeted Mann the moment he stepped into the adjacent warehouse, which appeared to be entirely empty.

"What do you think?" asked Gupta.

"I think you've either invented some kind of invisibility device, or this warehouse is empty."

"We're in the warehouse diagonal to the northeast," said Gupta, leading them to a door on the other side.

"I assume every warehouse in the complex is under some kind of surveillance?" said Mann.

"Seventy warehouses?" said Gupta, pausing long enough for Mann to guess the answer.

"So I'm right," said Mann.

"We obviously take a layered approach," said Gupta. "The closer you get to our HQ, the more robust the surveillance and security."

"I suppose some Claymore mines might help out?"

"I would never ask."

"You don't have to," said Mann. "What's mine is yours."

"Mi casa, tu casa," said Gupta.

"Something like that," Mann said. "How many of these do you operate? I don't see your crew growing deep roots anywhere."

"You're right. We don't keep a primary location," said Gupta. "But this is by far our most extensive. We own a few adjacent warehouses at a massive complex outside of Las Vegas, which gives us good reach out west. And four sites around the world with enough room to house vehicles and specialized gear that can be difficult to source rapidly in other countries or continents. Poland. Spain. Argentina. Colombia. Plus, we have safe houses that can serve as temporary operations centers sprinkled across the country. Along with some trusted arrangements and untraceable long-term rentals overseas."

"Sounds like you're trying to sell me on this," said Mann.

"Well. If we don't succeed in shutting down DOMINION, all of you are definitely going to be fired," said Gupta. "Probably get fired either way."

"You bring up a good point. Let's put a pin in that until later," said Mann. "What about Asia?"

"Asia is admittedly a complete blackout area for us," said Gupta. "Sanderson's original program originally focused on—"

"General Sanderson being the founder."

"Correct."

"And he's not part of the program anymore?"

"He consults and continues to develop relationships that help the organization," said Gupta. "But to get back to your original questions. One. We have no ground-level presence from the Middle East to Japan. Local contacts? Yes. But no organic ability to operate."

"Surprising, but not shocking. The FBI has a very hard time infiltrating Asian transnational criminal groups. Same with the Middle East. Just too many regional language and societal variations. All it takes is one minor mistake to blow the whole operation."

"Exactly," Gupta said. "As the child of two Indian immigrants from Chennai, I can attest to it. You serve roti or naan and claim to be from Chennai—it's like ordering a grinder in New Orleans. If you claim to be from New Delhi and serve beef for dinner, you may as well be ordering a pop in Florida. And there are variations. Beef is a traditional dish in Kerala and Goa, along the southwest coast of India. These aren't insurmountable challenges, but finding candidates willing to take them on has proven to be—"

"Insurmountable," said Mann.

"Basically," said Gupta. "And reason two is that Sanderson's original program focused almost exclusively on three threats. Mexican cartels, Colombian cartels, and Slobodan Milosevic's regime. Basically, the three largest thorns in the US's side from the mid-eighties through the late nineties."

"Why them?"

"Money. General Sanderson had a grander vision for the program, but funding was tight. The first batch of operatives who went undercover in each of those areas of operation were given two primary directives. First. To infiltrate and set into motion plans that would destabilize leadership and weaken the targeted organizations. The ultimate downfall of Pablo Escobar and Slobodan Milosevic can be directly attributed to those efforts. Mexico proved to be a little more problematic.

"The second directive related to money. Sanderson's operatives were given the green light to steal whatever they could get their hands on, without undermining the first directive. A few hundred million dollars was transferred over time to Sanderson's slush fund through various well-planned thefts from these criminal operations. Ultimately, that's what landed him in hot water. Obviously, the acquisition and unaccountability of these shadow funds was illegal by any definition, and a whistleblower within the organization couldn't resist the opportunity to walk away with close to thirty million dollars. The going rate for recovering fraudulently acquired money was around twenty percent in those days."

"Thirty million times five is a staggering figure," said Mann.

"We were well funded," said Gupta. "Unfortunately for the whistleblower, none of that money was ever recovered, so he took a comfy job in the Pentagon managing some of our nation's most guarded secrets—and was stabbed in the neck inside his office during what might be one of the most audacious Pentagon breaches in history."

"I don't want to know any more," said Mann.

"I do," said Turner, who had caught up to them at some point.

"Trust me. You don't," said Gupta, before opening the door at the opposite end of the warehouse.

He led them diagonally across a concrete pad to another warehouse. Once the entire group was inside, he shut the door behind them.

"Is this a rave?" asked Kerri Wallace.

"Be cool if it was," said Gupta. "That's our operations center."

LED lighting lined the roof edges, slowly transitioning through the entire color spectrum. A two-story shipping container structure, three containers wide, lay in the center of the warehouse, its windows and doors facing toward them. At least two dozen metal picnic tables sat in front of the structure, flanked by two propane-fueled grills on each side. Dozens of sleeping bag sacks and air mattress bags sat piled up against the opposite side of the warehouse. They were literally going to the mattresses here.

"This is impressive," said Mann. "If not a little odd. We're going to sleep in the open here?"

"We have sleeping room inside for six," said Gupta. "By my count, your crew plus your Mexican associates brings the entire count to twenty-seven. Not to mention our VIPs, who will be sleeping inside the containers—if they choose to stay overnight."

"VIPs?" asked Mann.

"They're here now, which is why I'm moving things along," Gupta said.

"Our CIA friends?" said Mann.

"Yes," said Gupta. "Maybe someone from the FBI, too."

"Dana?"

"She didn't tell you?" said Gupta.

"Of course not."

"Can't blame her," said Gupta. "Sorry to rush you guys inside, but your SDRs took longer than anticipated. Which is a good thing. Better safe than sorry."

"That's fine," Mann said. "Where do you want us to drop all of our stuff?"

"Leave it here for now," said Gupta. "We can organize it later."

Mann turned to his crew. "We're heading inside for a quick briefing."

"What's for dinner?" asked Callie Jackson.

"We have a bunch of freezers behind the containers," said Gupta. "Once we're done inside, you can grab whatever you want and fire up the grills."

"Does the next warehouse have sleeping quarters?" Frank Vincenzo asked.

Mann shook his head. "See that pile of sleeping bags and air mattresses?"

Vincenzo glanced in the direction Mann had indicated. "Wonderful."

"This is the ARTEMIS lifestyle," said Turner. "We went from sleeping in SUVs on the side of the road or in weed-filled parking lots at the very beginning to bedbugs at middle-of-nowhere Bates-style motels to a few weeks of luxury at the Conrad in DC—and now we're sleeping on air mattresses in a warehouse, baby! Next stop, tents at state parks."

"Yeah. For those of you who are new to the task force, it can get a little rustic," said Mills.

"What are you complaining about?" asked Turner. "You always got to sleep in the forensics van."

"With Dr. Torres? No disrespect meant to the dead, but he snored like a chain saw and emitted toxic fumes half the night," Mills said. "Still hard to believe he's gone. They're gone."

Gupta gave them a moment to honor their lost colleagues before ushering them to the makeshift operations center.

"This shouldn't take long. Just a quick orientation and update on where everything stands," said Gupta. "You can leave your equipment out here. Nobody can get near the warehouse complex undetected. And they certainly can't get anywhere near this warehouse or any of the adjacent buildings without triggering several sensors."

"I'll be recounting the Claymores when we're done with the briefing," said Mann.

"Fair enough," said Gupta, opening the door.

"Well, well," said Audra Bauer as Mann stepped inside after Gupta.

She sat next to Dana O'Reilly, his boss, and Karl Berg, a former CIA legend—whom they had met at the hospital after O'Reilly had been attacked. The three-counter-wide first floor of the two-story structure had been expanded to create a constricted but functional briefing room with a massive wide-screen television at one end and a few wide-screen monitors attached to the side walls. Instead of a table, which would've taken up too much room, the space was filled with folding chairs. A bare-bones operation, as Gupta had suggested.

"Look what the cat dragged in. Frankly, I'm surprised you're still alive. Looks like the Montana ambush had one goal: to kill . . . you," said Berg.

Mann still hadn't come to terms with that concept. But he couldn't argue with the overall assessment. The Russian mercenaries had oriented their two machine gun teams, snipers, and one assault group facing the front entrance. They could have effectively wiped out most of the FBI force dropped by helicopter in a matter of minutes, leaving an easy mop-up operation against any agents who somehow made it inside the house. But they'd hesitated when the FBI raid force was at its most vulnerable. That was what stood out the most to the agents who had been on the scene and had analyzed the data.

The reconstruction of the fateful thirty-nine minutes made one thing clear: Thanks to the HRT commander and the constant vigilance of the FBI SWAT officers, the snipers never had a clear shot at Mann. They'd kept him out of sight the entire time, and once the FBI convoy started its short journey to the ranch, the Russians faced a choice: Leave and report failure. Or go for broke before the convoy arrived. It was no coincidence that the assault on the house kicked off about a minute after the convoy had departed. Gupta's surveillance team confirmed that a satellite call had originated from a bluff overlooking the convoy's staging area.

"It still doesn't make sense," said Mann. "The task force doesn't just disappear without me. Turner could run ARTEMIS. Jax could run it. O'Reilly could run it." He was essentially expendable.

"You've gotten ARTEMIS this far against all odds. And you're not backing down, which puts you in True America's crosshairs," said Berg. "Who appears to be beholden to the Russians on some level. That said, if I were Harrison Greely, I'd be looking for a new source of funding and support. Nothing good comes from an alliance with the Russians."

"Russian mercenaries are nothing new," said Mann, taking a seat.

O'Reilly rose on her crutches. "We've identified Dmitri Sokolov as one of the dead mercenaries at the Montana mansion. He broke with Wagner before Prigozhin marched on Moscow. Sokolov is a Putin acolyte—or at least he was smart enough to see the writing on the wall and pretend to be one. If True America hired Sokolov for the Montana ambush, the contract was ultimately approved by Putin himself—which makes sense, given the dozen or so airbags arranged on Russian-owned rooftops near AXIOM's Georgetown annex, just blocks from the Russian embassy. The Russians knew that Harrison Greely planned on screwing over AXIOM. What they didn't count on was Greely taking precautions to prevent DOMINION from falling into Russian hands."

"True America swooped in very quickly to save Greely and recover the SATCHEL," said Bauer. "They had rapid-response teams ready to go at a moment's notice."

"But without the Georgetown annex or the operations center at their headquarters in Tysons Corner to run DOMINION, how are they still running the sicario network?" said Berg. "Answer that question and you win the game."

"MONTANA. Whatever that means," said Bauer, who had not been introduced.

Mann glanced over his shoulder. His team looked uneasy. He turned back to the front of the briefing room.

"We have some new task force members who don't know most of you," said Mann.

Bauer got up. "Sorry. We kind of jumped right into things. They have good instincts," she said. "For obvious reasons, we'll skip last names. I'm Audra, and I ran the National Clandestine Service for a few years. I worked for the CIA for just under thirty years and still consult at Langley. Karl?"

Karl Berg didn't get up. "I'm Karl. I was smart enough to retire before Audra, but I worked there for longer."

His brief statement generated some laughter.

"Much smarter," Bauer said.

O'Reilly sat down. "For the three FBI newcomers, all I can say is that I trust these two implicitly. I've worked with them officially and unofficially for a long time. You've met Rico, who helped you bring your gear in. I've known him for at least twenty years. Same with his counterpart, Emily, who is on her way back from Mexico. The two gentlemen—and I use that term loosely—sitting next to us are affiliates on loan from a trusted crew in Los Angeles. Garza and Ripley. Both are former Tier One operators."

"Their other associate, Brooklyn, a former Israeli commando, is tracking down a lead in Tampa," said Bauer. "That leaves the Mexican contingent, which I assume Mann has explained."

He had indeed read them into the situation involving Serrano's people, making sure they were okay "shooting and scooting" with Mexican nationals who had no authority to be engaged in law enforcement activity in the US. None of them indicated the slightest problem with it. Mann checked the text that had hit his phone a few minutes ago. He responded with Be cautious before addressing the group.

"I just received word that they will be arriving two days from now. Separate flights out of Mexico City with one stop each. Cata's team will layover in Dallas. Sofia's in Miami. If both flights are on time, they'll land about ten minutes apart at Dulles. The team split between the two aircraft. Nine in total. We'll have a full house tomorrow. Any questions?" said Mann, addressing the new FBI additions to the team. "I know that nothing about this arrangement feels right."

Kelsey Cook—an SSG investigator—raised a finger, but Melendez jumped in before Mann could take her question.

"Mexico City?" asked Melendez.

"Flights were limited out of Ciudad Juárez, multiple stops in the US or other international airports before arriving in DC—and Cata doesn't trust the local airport operators. The cartel owns everything in that city. She'd prefer not to be tracked too easily. She knows they'll try."

"Why didn't they drive to Phoenix or Albuquerque a few hours away?" said Melendez. "Mexico City is a full day's drive from Ciudad Juárez."

"She doesn't trust the Mexican border agents or our Customs and Border Patrol agents in that sector. Or any sector along the border," Mann said. "I don't really blame her."

"They know she's headed north," said Jessica Mayer, an expert in tracking people who didn't want to be followed. "One stop. Two stops. Does it really make a difference if they know what flight she boarded?"

"She wanted to coordinate a near-simultaneous arrival here in DC for obvious reasons," said Mann. "Among other concerns."

Mayer squinted slightly before nodding. "As long as they get here in one piece."

"That's the idea," said Mann. "What else?"

"Warrants?" asked Kelsey Cook.

"Since the task force is suspended . . ." started Mann, before deciding to be bluntly honest. "We're operating on our own. So . . . no. Nothing we do will be covered by a warrant or technically authorized and approved by the Department of Justice."

"But our boss—" started Special Agent Shana Bilyk.

"Is not here," said Mann, glancing from her to O'Reilly.

Bilyk didn't look comfortable with the arrangement.

"I'm here, and I'll be the first to go down if we're called to the carpet," said O'Reilly. "But we have my boss's tacit approval, and her boss has intentionally *turned a blind eye* to the situation. Her boss being the director of the FBI. I haven't spoken with her directly, but Assistant Director James said she's very eager to bring whoever has been responsible for the deaths of our agents to justice. Unfortunately, her hands are somewhat tied by the attorney general, who would rather cut the DOJ's losses here than risk more. And hope it all goes away."

"Which it won't," said Berg. "Not if DOMINION works. Odds are high that it'll get worse. True America tends to double down every time they rear their ugly heads. DOMINION is a means to an end for them. Maybe they won't try to murder tens of millions of Americans who are not aligned with their ideology—this time around. But I guarantee their endgame will have a similar result. A full reshaping of the country in their image, which Harrison Greely's father made clear was a very European image. And not the southern part of Europe, if you catch my drift."

O'Reilly got to her feet again, which looked like a bit of a struggle. She was pushing herself too hard, given the near life-ending injuries she had sustained at Raul's hands.

"I mean this in all seriousness: If you no longer want to be a part of ARTEMIS, I completely understand," she said. "You've all sacrificed and taken risks far beyond what was ever expected of you when the task force was formed. Not only will there be zero hard feelings, but I will go out of my way to get your careers back on track. For some of you, that might be a stretch. Sorry. Didn't mean to make a joke out of that, but you know what I mean. Think about it and let me or Mann know. I believe he feels the same way."

"Absolutely," said Mann, standing up. "To say things have gotten out of hand is an understatement. We've lost several members of a team originally formed to hunt down what we thought was a single serial killer. But that all changed, and we've paid the price. I do believe we're doing work critical to our national security—regardless of the legality moving forward. But if you want to get off the bus now and call it good, you have my utmost respect for having come this far. That includes our newcomers. I just ask that you lay low, and out of the Office of the Inspector General's sights, until we either win or lose this next gambit."

Nobody said a word, or even gave a visible hint that they might take them up on the offer.

"Special Agent Bilyk?" said Mann.

"What? I was just asking questions. You know. Exercising some on-the-spot due diligence," she said. "Everyone else here has had the luxury of months or years contemplating the shady dealings of the task force."

"I wouldn't exactly call our dealings—" started Mann.

"Shady? They're shady," said Bilyk. "And everyone here knows it, from the top on down. And I'm fine with that. That's why I signed up. I'm tired of following the rules. But I'd like to know when I'm breaking them."

"So far, you haven't broken any," Mann said.

"Except by showing up here," said Bilyk.

"I think you have a winner on your hands, Garrett," said Melendez.

"Same," said Mann. "Are we good?"

Bilyk shrugged. "I'm good. I can't speak for everyone else."

"Anyone else?" he asked.

When nobody objected to moving forward on their current trajectory, Mann nodded at Gupta.

"Let's bring everyone up to speed," said Mann.

"First of all. While this warehouse complex feels a little light on security, I can assure you that we have the place locked down. And not just this warehouse. The entire facility. Multiple layers of security. You may have noticed that your phones don't work here," Gupta said.

Half of the agents pulled out their phones to check.

"We're actively jamming cell signals. We'll issue you encrypted satellite phones shortly. Mann was given one a few days ago. Sorry for the secrecy, but this is one of our most important locations, and I didn't have time to configure a few dozen satellite phones prior to your arrival. This operations center is essentially air-gapped, except for the encrypted satellite feed that brings us the internet and will allow you to make untraceable calls. Impossible to intercept unless you're hovering directly above us . . . which would be detected and immediately neutralized by a rudimentary, but effective, anti-drone system. Questions?"

"In-and-out procedures?" said Turner.

"Three-hour SDR. Minimum," said Gupta. "Has to be worth it."

"Food and drink?" said Jackson.

"Fully stocked. You can make pad thai with shrimp if you have a recipe," said Gupta. "And wash it down with a pinot grigio."

"I don't think we'll be here long enough to get past the 'burgers and hot dog' phase," said Mann.

"That's how things are looking," said Gupta. "But you never know. Long story short. With Lianez's help, I planted radio frequency receivers on two of the vehicles in the FBI convoy staged at the Bridger Canyon Fire Hall on Route 86. Same with two of the FBI helicopters attached to the assault group. All disguised as communications pods. To be honest, I think the FBI needs to take a closer look at their immediate post-flight security procedures. Anyone attached to the task force could have planted bombs on all your vehicles or aircraft. Security was nonexistent. Same with preflight hull inspections."

"Point taken," Mann said.

"Anyway. I'm basically rehashing what some of us already know right now. We picked up some uncommon RF activity from the helicopters' receivers when they passed the Bridger Canyon Fire Hall. Satphone frequencies triangulated to a hill overlooking the site. Same when the convoy departed the site when Mann cleared them to approach the ranch."

"Where were you located?" Jackson asked.

"Just south of the staging area, in a school parking lot with Rico and Brooklyn," said Gupta. "Since I was tuned in to the frequency, I detected a long call placed minutes before the attack on Mann's task force, which I continuously monitor and triangulate."

"Were you able to listen to the call?" asked Jeff Miles, one of the new FBI members.

"Unfortunately, no. The encryption was top shelf, like ours," said Gupta. "Anyway. We're tracking the signal, and determine that they're on 86, headed in our direction. Signal triangulation of a moving source isn't exactly the most precise tracking method, but there's not much traffic on this road, so we were able to identify it with a high level of confidence."

"Visual and digital," said Melendez.

"Exactly. A Jeep Wrangler passed the school a few minutes later, the signal triangulation sitting right on top of it. And it's the only car on the road. So. We give it some room and follow it to Bozeman International Airport. We got close enough at one point to transmit Jax's daisy-chain virus to all their digital devices, but they destroyed those devices at the airport before returning the Jeep rental. They put them in airtight, acid-lined plastic pouches. Their phones were fried when I pulled them out of a trash bin in the rental-return lot. A very unorthodox procedure."

Mann cut in for a quick observation. "So unorthodox that we have to assume they somehow figured out how we tracked AXIOM's sole survivor from New Mexico to the Tysons Corner headquarters."

"The good news is that Brooklyn, one of our 'on loan' associates from Los Angeles, was waiting for them when they entered the departure terminal. She overheard where they were headed—Tampa through Atlanta—and booked tickets on the same flights. First class, so she could board at the last minute and slip into her seat without having to walk by them. Changing outfits and wigs in Atlanta for the final leg of the flight. She's a pro," said Gupta. "Unfortunately, Tampa presented a challenge. A town car whisked them away the moment they stepped outside of the terminal. She got the license plate but was unable to plant a tracker on the vehicle. I ran the plates—"

"How?" asked Jeff Miles.

"It's really better to just roll with it during his briefings," said Audra Bauer. "I've been dealing with this for the better part of two decades."

The group broke into an awkward laugh for a moment. Even Bilyk managed a chuckle this time.

"The license plate dead-ends with a car service that must be a word-of-mouth-only operation," Gupta went on. "I got nothing from the plate. Dead-end address—a storage locker in Tampa. All indications pointing toward a shell company. It would be incredible if we could access the resources of an organization that regularly monitors shell companies and overseas accounts for transnational criminal activity pointed at the United States."

Nice touch. Mann spoke up.

"Sounds like the kind of information that the Criminal Investigative Division might be able to procure."

"I need to get back to the office, before they start to miss me," said O'Reilly. "And in case you forgot, ARTEMIS is suspended."

"So I've been told," said Mann.

"I'll see what I can do with CID," she said.

"All we need is an address," Melendez said. "We'll daisy-chain from there."

"I didn't hear that," said O'Reilly.

"None of us heard any of this," said Mann.

CHAPTER 25

Cata Serrano casually scanned the passengers jammed into the gate area. Boarding for their flight to Dallas, the first part of their two-leg journey to Washington, DC, was about to begin, and people did what they always did—crowded the gate. Once the gate agent started announcing boarding groups, they'd push forward even more aggressively, like a mob trying get a seat on the last plane out. And for some of these people, possibly including herself, this *was* the last plane out.

She made eye contact with Javier, who stood in the human traffic jam. He shook his head ever so slightly. Bella, seated a few rows to Cata's left, took out her phone and pretended to snap a selfie. The picture hit Cata's phone a few seconds later. She studied it for a few seconds, before replying.

Cata: Definitely JC. Seen him before.

Tianna: Confirm. Known JC enforcer.

Cata: Curious if he'll board the plane.

Javier: Doubt he'd risk a US Customs check. Any more out there?

Maria: Everyone is starting to look the same at this point.

Cata: We were lucky to spot one of them before this gate rush. Tianna. You'll be the last of us to board since you're seated closest to the front. If this guy boards the plane, we need to know.

Tianna: Copy.

Thirty-nine minutes later, after the flight crew shut the door, Tianna texted her.

Tianna: He did not board the plane. Did not see him interact with anyone else near gate.

Cata: I'm not sure if that's a good or bad thing. I'd feel better if he were onboard.

Javier: The cartel is thorough. Wanted to confirm we're headed north? They have skin in this game.

Cata: True. Let me check back in with the other group. They board an hour later than us.

Serrano switched to the other text group to check in with Sofia.

Cata: Sofia. JC did not board the plane. Possible one we didn't ID slipped by. Anything on your end?

Sofia: Nobody is standing out. I think you got lucky with that ID.

Cata: Agree. Stay sharp.

Sofia: Why would they go to the trouble of sending someone thru the airport and to the gate? Did they think we'd drive all the way to MC to pretend to get on a flight?

Cata: No idea. Could be routine cartel paranoia.

Sofia: We'll let you know if we spot anyone suspicious.

Cata: Have Gloria board last. She's seen more pictures of these soldados than all of us combined. I'm very curious if they're tracking your flight too.

Sofia: Will do. See you in DC.

Cata: Vaya con Dios.

Serrano put the phone in her lap before taking a few deep breaths with her eyes closed.

"Feel better?" asked Javier, seated next to her in the middle seat.

"I was until you interrupted me," she said.

"I don't like that they followed us all the way from Ciudad Juárez to a gate in Mexico City," said Javier in a hushed voice.

"They didn't follow us. We added a few hours onto our trip down to make sure nobody followed us," she said. "They knew exactly where we were supposed to end up, down to the exact gate. This is a massive airport with hundreds of flights headed to the US every day. They'd need dozens of spotters spread out across the airport, which isn't practical. Especially since this isn't Juárez Cartel territory. They have a lot of influence down here, for obvious reasons, but no presence. An army of Juárez enforcers combing the airport would not be welcome without previous coordination, which would cost them a fortune on more than just a financial level."

"So. How did they find us?" Javier asked.

"You know the answer," said Serrano.

"They've been watching and listening to us very closely," said Javier.

She shrugged. "You can only be so cautious, right? For all I know, they have a camera installed in my apartment that read my computer screen when I booked my flight. I'm less concerned that they identified our flight, than the fact that they felt the need to make sure we got on board."

"Something to think about for a few hours," said Javier.

She sent a short text to both groups and one to Mann.

"Everyone needs to think about it more before we land in the US. Their presence at the airport feels off to me. If they wanted us to know they were there, they would have made their presence known. They didn't. We got lucky with Tianna."

"Well. We have about three hours until we land in Dallas," said Javier. "Let's run through the scenarios."

CHAPTER 26

A little over three hours into their four-hour layover in Dallas, Cata received a text from Sofia.

Sofia: We're under surveillance. Not cartel. But zero doubt. Did Mann send a crew to watch over us?

Cata: He did not.

Sofia: That's what I guessed. This crew sucks. And they do not know all of us. Neva was able to sit behind one of them and watched her send pictures of me and Patillo.

Cata: Calling.

She got up and walked to a less-crowded part of the terminal before dialing Sofia's number.

"I'm clear," said Sofia.

"Same," said Serrano. "I think. We haven't identified anyone suspicious, and we've been trying since we arrived at the gate. What did the woman look like?"

"White woman," said Sofia. "Well dressed. Looks like she's on a business trip."

"Are you sure they hadn't figured out you made them and were just fucking with you?"

"Certain. We've been watching this woman closely for about an hour. She's mediocre at best and thinks she's being discreet. I know the difference."

"Well. That leaves us with a decision that needs to be made very quickly. We're about to board," said Serrano.

"We're still an hour or so away," said Sofia.

"How's your tequila tolerance?" Serrano asked.

"Not great," she said.

"Did you buy a few bottles at the duty-free store in Mexico City like I suggested?"

"Yes," said Sofia.

"I have an idea," said Serrano. "But first things first. I need your team to head over to the nearest bar and order two shots of tequila each."

"You trying to kill me?" said Sofia.

"Trying to keep us all from getting killed," said Serrano. "Here's the plan."

About a minute later, she ended the call, not entirely sure how this gambit would play out or if it was really necessary. Couldn't hurt to try.

CHAPTER 27

Eva Kingston knew they would be trouble the moment they boarded the plane and passed her in the flight attendant galley. The smell of tequila was unmistakable. She quietly passed the word to her colleagues and greeted the rest of the passengers while keeping a close eye on the group—who were seated together on the starboard side of the aircraft. Two rows of two, plus one in the aisle across from the group's first row. They were boisterous but not obnoxious. Dressed nicely enough. If Eva hadn't smelled tequila on their breath, she wouldn't have given the group a second thought.

While welcoming a young family on board, she saw a bottle in her peripheral vision. It vanished just as quickly. Were they drinking on the plane? Shit. The absolute last thing she needed. The thought of refereeing a bunch of drunks for the three-hour flight to DC didn't sit well. She had a long day ahead of her.

She kept an eye on the group while the rest of the passengers boarded, never seeing the bottle again. Maybe she'd imagined it. Maybe the group had grabbed a few shots to ease their fear of flying just before the flight. The gate agent appeared in the doorway, holding the passenger manifest. As the senior flight attendant, it was Eva's responsibility to review it for any passenger issues like allergies, medical conditions, and possible tight flight connections at the next airport.

Kingston sifted through the manifest and identified the five. Their journey had originated in Mexico City. She followed the gate agent into the jet bridge.

"Did you see that one group that boarded? Hispanic. Four women and one guy?" said Kingston.

"Yeah. They smelled a little boozy, but they weren't acting up too much."

"Too much?" said Kingston.

"I think they're celebrating a wedding or a baby?" said the gate agent. "I saw them discreetly pass around a bottle a few times. But they seemed fine when they boarded."

"You saw a bottle?" said Kingston.

"Sorry. They were very polite when they boarded. Swiped their boarding passes without any issues," said the gate agent. "I guess I should have said something. Sorry again. Are they causing a problem?"

"Not yet," said Kingston. "Just—if you see people drinking booze at the gate, you need to report that."

"I know. They just didn't look like trouble. And they were clearly celebrating something."

"All right. Thank you," said Kingston, before stepping back inside the aircraft.

The pilot met her in the galley. "Everything okay?"

"Uh. I don't know," said Kingston. "I have five passengers traveling together who are not belligerent but are very likely drunk. Point of origin: Mexico City. Strong smell of tequila. It seems like they're celebrating something. I thought I saw them passing a bottle around inside the cabin. Rows ten and eleven. Starboard side. One of them is in the row eleven aisle seat—portside."

The captain casually glanced beyond her, his eyes widening a little.

"They just passed a tequila bottle to the guy on the portside," said the pilot. "And he just took a swig and passed it back. Let's get them off the plane."

"I'll take care of it," said Kingston, before turning to Stewart, her counterpart in the forward galley. "Do you mind backing me up? Just follow me down the aisle, staying about five feet behind me. Pleasant face as always."

"I got your back," he said.

She picked up the phone in the galley and dialed the back of the plane, explaining the situation. Thankfully, she had identified this issue before they closed the boarding door. If they'd secured the door, this would've immediately escalated to a TSA issue, likely involving US Customs and Border Protection agents—because all five of the individuals were Mexican nationals. A minimum one-to-two-hour delay.

If she could get them off the plane without a problem, TSA would temporarily take them into custody. If their papers checked out, they would be released after a brief hold and would have to seek alternate transportation to their ultimate destination. She reached row ten, where she witnessed a petite woman in the window seat, maybe in her late twenties, take a quick swig from a bottle of tequila. The woman didn't try to hide it. She buried it in her lap, between her legs.

"Birth or wedding?" asked Kingston.

"Wedding," said the woman seated in the aisle seat. "My sister. And an upcoming birth, if you know what I mean. Sorry if we're causing a problem. We're just very excited, and this is our first flight to the US."

Shotgun wedding, so to speak. She understood that well. Her daughter had been born six months after she had gotten married.

"I see. And I understand," said Kingston. "But the pilot would like you to deboard. Exit the plane."

The woman, who Kingston had just noticed had a scar across the right side of her neck, grabbed the bottle out of her friend's lap and offered it to her.

"We won't be any trouble."

"I don't know. I'll have to talk to the pilot," said Kingston.

"Fuck this!" said the guy across the aisle. "We're here to fucking celebrate!"

"Ma'am," said Kingston, "I need your group to deplane immediately. Before Customs and Border Protection gets involved."

The woman leaned across the aisle and poked the man in the shoulder. "I told you bringing booze on board was a stupid idea."

"What's the big deal?" he said.

"Let's just do what they ask," said the woman. "We can get another flight on a different airline. The wedding is three days from now. No reason to miss it by causing a scene."

"Seriously?" he said.

Kingston grabbed the moment. "Seriously. It's the pilot's call. He wants you off the plane. That's it."

The man stumbled to his feet and addressed the passengers behind him in an accent that sounded strangely Cuban. "Say good night to the bad guy! The last time you're gonna see a bad guy like this again."

The group left the plane with their carry-on luggage, several TSA agents taking them into custody inside the jet bridge. A few minutes later, the plane backed out on time. No delay. Another situation defused. Thankfully without much trouble.

CHAPTER 28

Serrano took Sofia's call just as they'd located their rental car at the Dallas-Fort Worth International Airport's massive rental-car farm—after having been tossed from their flight.

"Qué pasó?" said Serrano.

"Nada," said Sofia. "TSA just let us go. The gate was clear when we were escorted off the plane. If anyone was watching you board, I think it's fair to assume the same."

"I'm still not entirely convinced," said Serrano. "Your stalker could have been hiding somewhere in the terminal. The regional jet gates are jam-packed all the time."

"No. I left Neva behind. Figured she could grab a flight to DC later tonight," said Sofia. "The woman who was taking pictures of us left after everyone else boarded. Headed right out of the baggage claim doors and was picked up by an SUV."

"Did she get the license plate?"

"No."

"Jesus. Seriously?"

"She was too busy crawling along the curb to place a GPS tracker on the vehicle without being noticed by the occupants," said Sofia. "Everyone else noticed her, apparently. She thinks they thought it was a movie production."

"Well. Neva for the win, then," said Serrano. "Mann's crew has not been able to shed any light on the car service that whisked away the two persons of interest who flew from Bozeman to Tampa. Could be the same service."

"Maybe we should stay here instead of trying to make our way north?" asked Sofia.

"Not a bad idea," said Serrano. "We're looking at a twenty-hour drive, which I think we'll cut in half by grabbing a flight in the Midwest—depending on what your GPS device says. Maybe everything points to Florida like they thought?"

"We need to run it by Mann," said Sofia.

"Yeah. But for a different reason," said Serrano. "Someone bought tickets they didn't use—to verify that we boarded both legs of our flights."

"The Juárez Cartel," said Sofia.

"Yes, but I'm not sure they're acting alone," Serrano said. "The woman Neva identified doesn't sound like a cartel professional. They have people all over Florida. This feels like something different. A handoff."

"The cartel giving someone our itinerary and verifying that we boarded the first leg?" said Sofia. "Makes sense."

"That's kind of what I'm thinking, but the big question is, who did they hand us off to?" said Serrano. "Or are we looking at another inside job?"

"Inside ARTEMIS?" said Sofia.

"Happened before with the bus ambush," said Serrano. "Mann knew our itinerary."

"Mann wouldn't fuck us over," said Sofia.

"I know," said Serrano. "But something is clearly off. I'll let Mann know. My guess is that whoever is on the receiving end of the intelligence provided by our stalkers planned on attacking Mann and our crew in baggage claim, which is outside TSA security—or inside the parking garage."

"They really want him dead," said Sofia.

"They want us all dead," said Serrano. "But yeah, it's fair for them to assume that he'd show up to greet us. Kill two birds with one stone. Not guaranteed he'll be there, but a damn-solid guess. Or maybe they planned on trying to follow us back to wherever ARTEMIS is holed up right now."

"Except we won't be there," Sofia said.

"No. And neither will Mann after I chat with him. Hopefully," said Serrano. "He might have other ideas. How is the GPS tracker looking?"

"Headed west on Interstate 75," said Sofia. "We'll keep you posted. If it stays on 75 after Fort Myers, it's headed toward Tampa."

"All roads seem to lead to Tampa right now," said Serrano. "The two unidentified surveillance operatives Mann's team followed after the ranch fiasco. And now the woman who somehow had advance notice that Sofia's team would be on the Miami-to-DC flight is headed in that direction. If the woman heads south after reaching Fort Myers or stays in the city, I'll reconsider that assessment."

"We'll know soon enough," said Sofia. "Josephine might fuck the place up. The hurricane is building steam in the eastern Caribbean. Tropical depression right now, but they're predicting a Gulf of Mexico route."

"A Tampa hit?" said Serrano. "Most predictions have it hitting the north coast of Florida. Possibly New Orleans."

"It'll still create one hell of a weather event," said Serrano. "Might work to our advantage if your tracker gets us somewhere."

CHAPTER 29

Mann stepped out of the operations center and approached the three groups assigned to pick up Cata's crew at Dulles International Airport. The plan had been to assign one Special Surveillance Group investigator and one SWAT agent to each of the two SUVs that would transport Serrano's people to the warehouse complex—after executing a lengthy surveillance detection route. Mann would have joined the security detail assigned to link up with Cata and Sofia as soon as they exited the TSA secure zone and escort them to the awaiting vehicles. Both missions had just been scrubbed.

"The pickups are off," said Mann. "I just got a call from Serrano. Neither team got on the second leg of their flights. Cata's team detected cartel surveillance at the boarding gate in Mexico City, and Sofia's team identified surveillance at the gate in Miami. The Miami surveillance looks to have been outsourced by the cartel, or it could have been True America. Either way, someone wanted to confirm that they boarded both legs of their flights."

"Kind of odd," said Jessica Mayer.

"Why is that odd?" asked Turner. "She made a deal with the cartel. They were just making sure she kept up her end. Or at least took it as far as they could. I'm sure their boss requires a fairly high level of due diligence."

"That's what I suggested," said Mann. "But they all agreed that the cartel wouldn't bother. Except maybe confirming that they boarded the first leg of the flight. But even that's overkill, from what they've seen before. The cartels are purely transactional. You make a deal, and you either deliver or you don't. How you go about delivering is not their problem. Unless it's something they really want delivered, which isn't what they conveyed to Cata."

"What makes her think True America was involved?" said Kerri Wallace.

"Sloppiness," said Mann. "Neva sat down behind the woman pretending to take selfies and watched her snapping pictures and taking video of Sofia's crew boarding the plane. Neva got up and relocated. The woman never glanced in her direction."

"They probably had someone else watching over the woman," said Turner.

"Not likely," Mann said. "Neva sat down at another gate after that and waited. The woman got up and left about five minutes after the last passenger swiped their boarding pass and walked into the jet bridge. Neva followed her out of the airport. She was whisked away outside of baggage claim like the two that Brooklyn followed to Tampa."

"So, wait. I'm confused," said Turner. "You said they didn't board the planes."

"Two things. First. They pulled a little bit of a prank and got kicked off both flights. Pretended to be drunk and disorderly. Not enough to get arrested, but enough to draw attention and get escorted off before the flight crew closed the doors. That way they avoided Customs and Border Protection detention. TSA grilled them for about an hour and let them go—with the tequila."

"Tequila? How the hell did they get tequila on the flight?"

"They bought a few bottles of tequila at the duty-free shop in Mexico City, which they are permitted to bring on board the plane as long as they are sealed in the original duty-free bags with the duty-free paperwork. The tequila was intended to be shared with us when they finally arrived here," said Mann. "Each group headed over to the bar and ordered shots right before boarding was called. One shot down the hatch. Half of the second down the hatch, the other half on their clothes. They started discreetly passing the bottle around after they boarded, and let's just be thankful that we have some very observant flight crews out there. They were asked to deplane and complied."

"Without being observed by surveillance," said Mayer.

"Sofia's group was definitely not observed. Neva confirmed this," said Mann. "We're making an assumption about Cata's group, but it's fair to say that the two surveillance teams used the same method. Or close enough. Wait five minutes after the last passenger enters the jet bridge and leave."

"Big assumption," said Turner.

"Yes, it is," said Mann. "But here's why we think the assumption is fair under the circumstances. Neva placed a GPS tracker on the SUV. The vehicle is headed west on Interstate 75."

"How long since the tracker was attached?" asked Frank Vincenzo.

"Over an hour," Mann said.

"Discreet placement?" said Vincenzo.

"Instant epoxy well past the rear bumper," said Mann.

"No such thing as instant epoxy," said Vincenzo. "Ten to twenty minutes at best. But if it's still attached and traveling at eighty miles an hour down the interstate—it ain't comin' off. I remember talking to Neva about trackers. Magnetic is easier, but plastic vehicles these days don't give you many discreet opportunities. Trailer hitch–attachment points are your best bet, but you can spot those from across the street."

"That's good news," said Mann. "And our assumption is that if they witnessed Cata's group deplane about fifty minutes earlier, the operative watching Sofia's crew would have stuck around to see if they did the same."

"Fair enough," said Turner. "So. Sofia's crew is following the tracker?"

"Yes. They just got out of the airport. TSA kept them for a while."

"Not a bad play," Kerri Wallace said.

"If it truly worked," said Mann. "Turner's skepticism isn't unfounded. If either group was seen deplaning, we could be looking at anything. They could be driving that tracker into an ambush site, whether it's the Juárez Cartel or True America—or both, working together."

"Now that's a scary thought," said Rico Melendez, who had appeared out of nowhere. "But not unimaginable."

"Not another can of worms," said Turner.

"Gotta keep cracking those cans open until you get to the bottom of it all," said Melendez. "The cartel is extremely practical."

Karl Berg stood next to him. He didn't look well. Maybe it was the accommodations? Rumor had it that he lived on the water in the Caribbean. A far cry from a warehouse in Maryland. That said, the fact that he had agreed to bunk among the task force at this mercenary enclave and share his advice while they sorted out this mess spoke very highly of him.

"You think they'd shop her deal around?" Mann asked.

"Without a doubt," said Berg. "Sorry to interrupt."

"No. Go for it," said Melendez. "You have more experience with this stuff than all of us combined."

"I don't know about that, but patterns are patterns. And patterns are very hard to break, which is the only reason I think Mann and anyone on his task force is still alive. ARTEMIS doesn't follow any discernible patterns because they do whatever they want—and that's been throwing everyone for a loop ever since they started," said Berg.

"Well. I'll take that as a compliment, even though I hadn't put any thought into that strategy," said Mann.

"Which is why it's worked," Berg said. "I wish I hadn't brought it up, to be honest. Because now I'm afraid you'll be trying to game the system to ignore the patterns."

"I wouldn't know where to start," said Mann. "Back to True America and the Juárez Cartel. How would they even link up?"

Berg continued.

"There's no way the cartel didn't identify a problem a few years ago. Their people disappearing again after SINKHOLE. The CIA's absolute failure of an attempt to infiltrate the cartels. Maybe they never fully got to the bottom of why hundreds of their people vanished over the past couple of years, but I could see them putting the feelers out. Actually, more than that: real money and real effort. They're paranoid as fuck, as you can only imagine. The US is their lifeline. If that goes away, they go away. I could see them shopping Cata's deal around discreetly to every contact they've made over the past years.

"I'd be shocked if they didn't land on True America sooner than later in their search. Maybe True America strung them along until the time was right to form some kind of limited partnership. The dismantling of LABYRINTH and imminent possible discovery of DOMINION sounds like that kind of trigger to me. They probably struck a similar deal, just a few tweaks to the terms. The cartel gives up Serrano's crew and whoever you had planned to send to the airport to pick them up to True America, striking a major blow to ARTEMIS, in exchange for the list of DOMINION sicarios and some preferential treatment if True America's horse wins the race for the White House."

"Maybe the Juárez Cartel doesn't terminate the list like Serrano had originally bargained," said Mann. "They could 'recall' the sicarios, who still think they're working for the cartel, and repurpose them for their own needs. I'm sure they could find a suitable business use for a few hundred operatives who have been specially trained to assimilate into American society."

"That's what I would do," said Berg. "Why waste good talent."

"I wonder what they sent to the airport," said Turner.

"I'm guessing they would have tried to hit you right as you loaded up the SUVs," said Melendez. "Something high explosive."

"Like an AT4?" Turner asked.

"Yeah," said Melendez. "Or a couple multiple-grenade launchers, light machine guns. Something definitive in a location like that. Kind of nowhere to hide."

"Do you really think they'd be crazy enough to conduct an attack like that at an airport? Especially a DC airport?" asked Vincenzo.

"True America is capable of anything," said Berg. "And the kind of people they hire for these kinds of jobs are the 'high risk for high payout' types."

"Like the mercenaries in Montana," said Mann. "We found text messages on all their phones, informing them that the payout had been doubled. Timed almost exactly with the departure of the FBI convoy. Another text arrived less than a minute after the first, tripling the payout. Sounds like Sokolov was negotiating at the last minute, and whoever had their hand on the money spigot knew that the Russians' window of opportunity was closing fast."

"Did we ever determine the payout amount?" said Wallace.

"No," said Mann. "But it must have been high. From what forensics could determine from the Russians' positions situated around the house, none of them backed down from what could only be described as a suicide mission."

"Which they came frighteningly close to pulling off," said Turner.

"Too close," said Mann. "So. The answer to Frank's question is yes, and I'm glad you asked it. Because we have to assume they'll go to any lengths to secure whatever they've been promised in exchange for the upcoming election."

"Where do we go from here?" Jackson asked.

"Let's head inside and start thinking this through," said Mann. "Brooklyn tracked the two lookouts in Montana to Tampa International Airport, where they promptly vanished. And now we have a second possible Tampa hit. The operative who confirmed that Sofia's crew boarded their Miami flight is driving west on Interstate 75, approaching Naples, where the interstate veers north. If her vehicle follows 75 past Fort Myers, it's fair to assume they're headed to the Tampa area."

"I might start planning a trip to Tampa. Unless you have a better lead here," said Berg. "And the sooner the better, given the hurricane building steam in the Caribbean."

"Josephine," said Mann.

"Doesn't look like it'll hit Tampa, but it'll wreak havoc on travel, house rentals, and hotel arrangements in the area. Especially once they narrow down the track," said Berg. "Not to mention it might provide the perfect cover for your teams to operate. If the storm continues on its predicted path, Tampa will be hit by mid-grade tropical storm winds and a crazy amount of rain."

"How far out is the storm?" asked Mann.

Anish Gupta yelled the answer from a window on the second level of the container operations center. "Three days until it passes due west of Tampa!"

Mann gave it some thought. "How long of a drive is it for us?"

"About thirteen hours," said Gupta.

"How long for Cata's group in Dallas?"

"Sixteen hours."

"Why do I feel like you're a few steps ahead of me?" said Mann. "And always listening over my shoulder!"

"Because I am!"

Mann was about to say something, but Berg shook his head.

"I've been doing this for a long time," said Berg. "Anish has this rare, but very annoying, ability to put things together faster than anyone I've ever met. It's why he's been working with this group for so long."

"He can be a little annoying himself," said Mann. "But unquestionably helpful."

"Better to focus on the helpful part," said Berg. "Because 'a little annoying' might be an understatement."

"You talking shit about me, Karl?" yelled Gupta.

"Never!" Berg said.

Mann patted him on the shoulder before addressing the team. Other than the groups who were about to head out, everyone else was either lying on an air mattress or seated at one of the folding picnic tables next to the air mattress grid.

"Things are moving fast, and we need to strategize. It's entirely possible that we'll be headed to Florida first thing in the morning. Maybe sooner."

CHAPTER 30

While the task force game-planned the logistics of transporting the gear they'd most likely need from the DC warehouse complex to Tampa, along with finding as-discreet-as-possible accommodations to house nearly thirty people and their gear, Mann internally counted down the minutes until the teams sent to kill them at or near the airport discovered that neither group of Mexicans had gotten off their respective aircraft. Both planes landed at nearly the same time, just ten minutes apart, only five gates away from each other in the terminal, unless the airline changed gates.

He assumed that the team sent to attack them at the airport would have spotters stationed near the gates to confirm their arrival and follow from a distance, providing updates to the assault teams. Gupta suggested they'd have people somehow watching the tarmac below the plane, looking for a discreet handoff to a runway maintenance truck. They had to assume Mann had a few tricks up his sleeve, and the federal authority to make them happen.

When the passengers failed to emerge and a clandestine runway transfer was ruled out, worry would start to set in. They'd either assume the Mexicans had effectively disguised themselves and slipped by or that Mann had arranged for them to wait on board the aircraft until the flight crew absolutely had to start the flight-turnaround process. Probably the latter. Once they crossed that off the list, the panic would hit.

They'd be forced to accept one of two outcomes, neither of which would get them paid: Their targets had given them the slip, or they'd never gotten on the plane in the first place. The first would be their fault, and they'd go about retooling the kill-zone part of the operation. All the mercenaries outside the TSA security zone would be scrambling to locate Serrano's people as quickly as possible. The sooner they found them, the quicker they could modify the attack or possibly stick with the same plan. The longer it took them, the lower their chances of any degree of success. He wished he could be there to see it.

"The tracker is still on Interstate 75, almost at Sarasota Springs. Just an hour out of Tampa," said Berg.

"Even if Tampa isn't where we find DOMINION, we'll find something. We always do."

"That's how this business works. I once sent a team to the old nuclear testing ground in Kazakhstan to track down the slimmest of leads," said Berg.

"Did it pan out?" asked Mann.

"Got a third of them killed—just to collect another piece of the puzzle," said Berg. "But in the end, we wouldn't have solved the puzzle without that piece. So I guess it was worth it."

"That's how I've felt ever since we showed up at the roadside body dump in Minnesota," said Mann. "Every lead we've pursued has gotten someone killed or hospitalized."

"That's why I used the example. It's the price of threatening the darkest plots and secrets of the power hungry. They make you pay for it dearly—or at least, they try," said Berg. "This might be a heavy time for a pep talk, but your team is good at this. I see why O'Reilly has your back and the rest of your chain of command supports you—even if they can't come right out and say it."

Mann considered Berg's words, deciding they meant a lot coming from him. O'Reilly wouldn't—or more likely couldn't—share any details about his work with the CIA, but she made it clear that Berg was one of their silent legends. Rarely in the spotlight but always shining a light on the nation's enemies, foreign and domestic. Plus, she obviously trusted him, which wasn't easy with O'Reilly. It had taken Mann close to a year to get more than feigned smiles and grunts out of her during debriefings. Not the easiest person to warm up to.

"Will you be joining us in Tampa?" said Mann.

"I'm headed in that direction," said Berg, "if you could use someone to keep Gupta from getting out of hand."

"I heard that," said Gupta from a small makeshift office in the back corner of the container.

The office had a doorframe but no actual door. And a large window frame with no window. It served as more of a separate space for Gupta to arrange all his computer gear, radio receivers, and server equipment.

"You were supposed to," said Berg.

Gupta flashed him the middle finger over his shoulder.

"I assume you've seen his van," said Berg.

"He only lets two of us in it. Chad Lianez, one of our surveillance techs, who is now Gupta's protégé. I'm sure to lose him to Gupta's organization when we're finished with this True American business. And Kerri Wallace, one of our SWAT-trained agents. He likes the way she drives."

Berg glanced at Agent Wallace.

"I'm sure that's the only reason."

Gupta shot up from his desk, then sat back down—furiously typing and scrolling through news feeds on the three wide-screen monitors arranged at his workstation. Mann could have sworn he saw a burning aircraft.

"Anish! What's going on?" he asked.

"Hold on. I'm transferring news feeds to the main screen behind you," said Gupta. "They've had at least one plane crash at Dulles International Airport!"

At least one?

"Jesus," said Berg.

A split screen showing CNN and ABC broadcasts appeared on the 120-inch TV at the front of the room. Both broadcasts displayed the flame-consumed wreckage of what looked like a Boeing 737. Except Mann could immediately tell that they weren't the same plane. One looked to be located far from the terminals, either still on one of the landing runways or on a taxiway. The camera view of the other burning aircraft showed a nearby terminal, its wide glass windows partly blown out. Everyone in the room stood up and muttered in disbelief, all of them thinking the same thing.

"Any flight numbers?" said Mann.

"I can't find anything yet," said Gupta.

"When did this happen?" said Mann.

"Just a few minutes ago," said Gupta. "I'm working on those flight numbers. I'll need to do a little digging."

Mann scrambled toward Gupta's office. "Stop! Do not hack any government system to seek this information. I know you're the best in the business, but they will turn over every stone imaginable trying to get to the bottom of this. You don't want to be the FAA's or Dulles airport traffic control tower's first hack after these explosions. And it doesn't matter from our standpoint; Serrano's people were not on either of those planes."

His next thought was not one he was prepared to share yet. This might actually help the task force in the short run, but they'd have to move fast to take advantage of it. True America thought they had just cut the task force in half, but that wouldn't last long. His phone buzzed. Cata. He answered it instantly.

"Did you hear?" asked Serrano.

"We just saw it," said Mann. "I don't know what to say, other than I'm glad that you got off those flights. We all owe Neva a drink."

"That's all we're worth?"

"Sorry. We're still in shock. We just learned about it—"

"I'm fucking with you, Garrett. Seriously," said Serrano. "But yeah, we owe Neva more than a few drinks. I'm thinking more like a new car."

"I can't imagine anyone would be opposed to that," said Mann. "I'm so relieved you weren't on one of those planes. I know it sounds selfish—"

"Have you gone soft on me while I was gone?" said Serrano. "I'm happier than hell I wasn't on that plane. Assuming this isn't an unrelated disaster. Can't see how it is, though. Two 737s landing when our planes were supposed to land?"

"We haven't identified the flight numbers, but I'm certain they'll match up with your flights," said Mann. "Based on their surveillance in Miami and most likely Dallas, we expected them to attack your crew and whoever we sent to pick you up. But nobody here floated the possibility that they'd take out two 737s. They probably killed close to three hundred people."

"Which means they are more desperate to stop us than we thought," said Serrano. "All the more reason to make sure we kill every last one of them."

"Speaking of killing," said Mann, "you might want to warn anyone at risk down south. The Juárez Cartel obviously gave you up to True America. You have to assume all agreements with them are null and void."

"We're way ahead of you," said Serrano. "Immediate and closer family members who opted to take the precautions we recommended have been transported across the border using their B-2 visas and passports. Please thank your people again for calling in a favor at our Ministry of Foreign Affairs. It normally takes an eternity from start to finish to get a passport down there these days. Dozens of passports in two weeks is unheard of."

"I'm just glad you started the process right away, or those visas would be useless," said Mann.

"We have ways of getting across without paperwork," she said.

"It's a lot harder these days," said Mann. "Where will everyone go while we take care of business up here?"

"As far away from the border as possible. I don't think they expect to return to Mexico. Maybe even Canada, depending on the election," said Serrano. "The cartel has a long reach and even longer memory."

"Well. We might be able to help with that. And I'm not talking about passports or paperwork. Something a lot more permanent. I can't really talk about it right now," said Mann.

"You don't think someone on the task force might be—"

He lowered his voice.

"No. You probably wouldn't be talking to me right now if we had a leak," said Mann. "And they certainly wouldn't have blown up those planes. I can list more than a dozen reasons."

"True," said Serrano.

"You might want to stop on the way and buy some rain gear. Looks like we're heading into a hurricane. We're bringing plenty of staples, like food and water—not that I think we'll need it. And of course, we'll supply all the specialty equipment your team will need."

"We'll gear up," said Serrano. "We have about another fourteen and a half hours of driving ahead of us. I'm thinking we'll probably drive straight through. The hurricane is still a few days out, but I figured we'd better beat the traffic."

"I'll send you information on where we'll be staying once we figure it out. You'll get there well ahead of us," said Mann. "Get some sleep. I have a feeling we're going to need it. I want to move fast and furious once we get a little rest. True America might think you're out of the picture, but it won't be long before the TSA and the airline put two and two together and link the two planes to the two groups of deplaned Mexicans."

"I hadn't thought of that," said Serrano.

"I'm embarrassed to say I did," said Mann. "I have to let you go. We need to get this train rolling. Keep me posted."

"Will do," said Serrano, before ending the call.

Mann closed his eyes for a few moments, the gravity of the situation weighing him down. He hadn't killed those people, but if he'd somehow wrangled a government jet to pick up Serrano's team, more than three hundred people would have landed safely at Dulles ten minutes ago.

"I know that look," said Berg, putting a hand on his shoulder. "Not your fault. And for what it's worth, I happened to overhear some of your conversation. I hadn't thought of TSA linking the two together yet. You're better at this than you think. You have a rare instinct for the work."

"I'm not sure if that's a good or bad thing," said Mann.

"It's both. Or neither. Just depends on how you use it."

Mann let that sink in for a moment before replying.

"I plan to use it to take down True America."

"I'm at your service," said Berg. "Just don't expect me to do any shooting. I'm a terrible shot. I spent most of my thirtysomething-year career behind a desk or standing in front of an operations-center screen."

"Any way you could convince Audra to join us in Tampa? I could use the experience—and the help. If we find what we're looking for down there, I suspect we're going to need every one of our shooters or surveillance techs in the field to pull this off."

"I'll see what I can do," said Berg. "What about O'Reilly?"

"Better she doesn't get too close to this."

"Afraid she'll disapprove?" said Berg. "If that's your concern, I'd consider giving her a ring. I'm sure she's due for some vacation. Has she taken a day off since she was released from the hospital?"

"No. She rolled right into the office in a wheelchair and nearly passed out from overdoing it."

Berg laughed. "Sounds like she could use a vacation to Florida."

"During a hurricane," stated Mann.

"Not everyone has the best luck with the weather in Florida."

CHAPTER 31

Clara Furst stormed down the hallway, ready to sucker punch or kick Hendrick in the groin if he didn't yield. Nothing was going to stop her from tearing off Greely's head—figuratively, of course. Unless that weaselly little fuck pissed her off even more, which she was pretty sure wasn't possible. Hendrick either knew why she was here or sensed her rage. Maybe both. Because his usual stoic face looked justifiably alarmed.

"Ms. Furst," he said, definitely sounding concerned.

"Out of the way, Hendrick," said Furst.

"He's not taking any meetings at the moment," said Hendrick.

"This isn't a meeting," she said. "It's an ass-kicking. Out of the way, please."

The closer she got to him, the less confident he looked.

"I really can't let—"

"Move," she said, right in his face.

"No."

The intercom next to the door came to life.

"Let her in, Hendrick," said Greely.

He opened the door and she stormed inside. Greely sat in his wheelchair at his desk, facing two wide-screen computer monitors. He turned his chair to face her.

"Shall I keep the door ajar?" asked Hendrick.

"Shut it," said Furst.

"I guess we're shutting the door," said Greely.

When the door closed, Greely started to speak, but she cut him off.

"Are you out of your fucking mind?" she said. "Do you even have the remotest clue what you've done? The entire country is at DEFCON One. Homeland Security just invented a new color to address the shit you pulled this afternoon. Two hundred and sixty-three dead. Burned alive. Twenty-three survivors."

"Twenty-three?" said Greely.

"Oh. Don't worry. None of them have been identified as Mexican nationals—yet. Some of them were burned so badly, it was impossible to make any immediate determination. But even if anyone from Mann's Mexican crew miraculously survived, they won't be much of a threat to us while they spend the next six to nine months recovering at a burn center. What the hell were you thinking?"

"That we had to be sure," said Greely.

"Well, congratulations. Mission accomplished," said Furst. "Oh. And thanks for giving me a heads-up. Asshole. Our new mercenary team barely got out of the airport before they locked the whole place down. Heavy weapons and all, somehow."

"Their plan—your plan—would have attracted just as much attention, and there was no guarantee of success," said Greely. "Mann's people have this way—"

"Of getting under your skin? Leading you to make rash decisions?" said Furst. "We had a chance to take out Mann, and you scared him away."

"He didn't show?"

"Of course he didn't show. Explosions and fireballs in the distance tend to make you think twice about things," said Furst. "Serrano was probably sending him live updates so he could time her crew's pickup perfectly to minimize exposure. Then explosions. Then nothing. Doesn't take a genius to figure out something went terribly wrong. Shit. If we'd just managed to kill Mann, it would have been a hundred times more impactful than this."

"We just neutralized almost half of his task force," Greely said.

"I don't see how this doesn't bite us in the ass," said Furst.

"It won't," said Greely. "We just gave our friends some serious political capital. The current administration has been weak on immigration. Weak on defending the country. Now terrorists blow up two commercial airliners? This could be the final nail in their coffin."

"Or it could rally the country like 9/11," said Furst.

"Rally them against immigrants," said Greely. "I already have that worked out."

"Who?"

"Take your pick from any of a hundred Arab militant groups with an axe to grind," said Greely. "Some of which may have slipped inside the US through our porous borders."

She shook her head. It didn't take a wild stretch of the imagination to see how that could resonate with Americans against the administration.

"Dare I ask how we managed to blow up two planes leaving from separate airports?" she said.

"A new breed of drones," said Greely. "A project I commissioned a while back."

"Kamikaze drones?"

"No. Way more sophisticated. They can be programmed for nearly any kind of target, if you have the target schematics, imagery, three-dimensional digital modeling. A few other parameters. In this case, we identified the precise locations of the wing and centerline fuel tanks and programmed the drones to seek out those locations and attach themselves magnetically. The drones look like quadcopters but are technically tilt-rotor aircraft like the V-22 Osprey, which means they can fly faster than a typical quadcopter but can also hover. We timed the attachment of the drones with the start of each aircraft's taxi off the runway, to avoid any potential issues with excessive jet engine turbulence during the landing. No operators necessary once the drones are launched."

"Someone had to have seen a few of them approach the planes," said Furst.

"I haven't seen any reports, but I'm sure you're right," said Greely. "Those pesky jihadists sure do hate America. Good thing True America has been warning everyone about our country's security weaknesses for years."

"No trace back to us?"

"There's no such thing as one hundred percent," said Greely. "But we feel confident that investigators won't catch a whiff of this possibly being an inside job."

"I hope you're right," said Furst, heading for the door and stopping just before opening it. "One more thing. Hurricane Josephine is still projected to hit the middle of the Panhandle. It'll get a little rough here, but there's been no suggestion of relocating. And local authorities have not issued any evacuation warnings."

"Then we'll ride it out," said Greely. "Sorry for keeping you in the dark about this afternoon. And for the spectacle. We just can't take any chances with ARTEMIS at this point."

"I need to be kept in the loop," said Furst. "I need to be able to always trust you one hundred percent. This kind of thing does not help with that trust."

"I understand. Sorry again," said Greely.

He didn't sound very convincing.

"Last thing. Fiedrick is almost back from Miami. She met with the Russians and secured some more funding before she went to the airport to confirm that one of Serrano's teams boarded their plane. What should we tell her? The Russians will have questions."

"Whatever keeps the Russians paying," said Greely.

She shut the door behind her, having decided that Greely would not be continuing the True America journey very long after the new administration took power and Furst got her hands on this new drone program. She could see some extremely useful and persuasive applications of that system.

CHAPTER 32

O'Reilly caught a glimpse of Kevin fast-walking toward her office. She couldn't see his feet double-timing across the tile, but his head, visible above the top of the cubicle walls, moved like it was on an out-of-control factory conveyor belt. This couldn't be good. Then again, everything had changed in the blink of an eye about—she checked her watch—ninety-three minutes ago. She was surprised it had taken this long.

Kevin reached her office out of breath. "James is on her way."

"You could have just called," said O'Reilly, grabbing a water off the top row of filing cabinets behind her and offering him one.

He shook his head. "I overheard her tell Becky not to call and not to log the visit."

"You heard her say that?"

"I was just inside the entry, out of sight," said Kevin.

"You just happened to be there the moment James arrived."

"A little birdie may have given me a heads-up," said Kevin. "I prefer the division doesn't get caught off guard."

"And I appreciate the effort," said O'Reilly. "Especially on a day like today."

"Let me know if you need anything," said Kevin. "The tactical operations center is up and running, if you'd prefer to meet James there."

"It's up to her," said O'Reilly. "She obviously has something up her sleeve."

"I'll leave you to it," said Kevin, stepping out of her office moments before James entered CIRG Division's workspace.

O'Reilly stood up, using the desk for leverage. James signaled from across the office for her to sit down, but she stayed upright. It took more effort for her to sit down than stand up. James shut the door behind her after entering and took a seat across from O'Reilly.

"Seriously. You should sit down," said James. "It's going to be a long few days."

"Weeks," said O'Reilly, taking a seat. "Huntsville has been mobilized. They'll be on the ground in just under two hours. Headquarters and nearby field office bomb technician teams are already at the airport."

The FBI's Hazardous Device Operations Center was in Huntsville, Alabama, housing the Hazardous Device School, which trains FBI and other federal agency bomb technicians. It's also home to the FBI's Terrorist Explosive Device Analytical Center (TEDAC), which inspects and analyzes explosive devices from around the world to maintain an unmatched level of expertise on the subject. TEDAC investigators are sent far and wide to support US and allied bombing scene investigations.

"Anything stand out so far?" said James.

"A few unverified witness reports of a possible drone sighting in the vicinity of the aircraft closest to the terminal," said O'Reilly, scribbling on her notepad, then flashing it to James.

Planes were supposed to be carrying our Mexican friends

James shook her head before responding. "Like a quadcopter FPV drone?"

"That's what was reported," said O'Reilly.

They got off their flights due to suspected TA surveillance at gate

"We've all seen the videos out of Ukraine," said James. "I didn't think they could pack enough explosives on one to blow up an airliner."

"I guess we'll find out soon enough," said O'Reilly. "But whatever was used must have either set off all the fuel tanks simultaneously, or it could have been some kind of massive explosive device stowed on board. It's not enough to detonate one of the tanks."

"What do you mean?" said James.

"This isn't off the top of my head. I did some quick research into suspected fuel tank explosions. Particularly incidents that occurred on the ground," said O'Reilly. "So. A Thai 737 exploded near its terminal in 2001, with the crew on board preparing for the next flight. And a similar incident occurred in 1990, while a Philippine Air 737 was taxiing just prior to takeoff from Manila, with 120 people on board. Here's the thing: Only one out of the eight crew members on the Thai aircraft was killed. And only eight died in the Philippine Air disaster—and that plane burned down to the runway in four minutes. And now we have two explosions and no survivors."

"This is something entirely different—and new," said James. "Which is disturbing."

"I couldn't agree more," said O'Reilly. "Possibly a new technology."

And it's likely in True America's hands

"Even scarier," said James.

TF tracked Miami gate surveillance to marina in Tampa

Jesus, mouthed James. "So. What can we do about this right now?"

"Nothing. It's going to take a while to figure out what happened—and then get to where we can point a finger at someone. Who knows what'll happen between now and then."

Mann asked me and Audra Bauer to fly to Florida to oversee an operation—Hard to see going anywhere right now

James took the pad and pen from O'Reilly.

I can run the show from here for a few days—I assume it won't take longer than that

O'Reilly:

Probably not. Unless it's a dead end. The director will lose her shit if I leave

James:

Not if you pull this off—she's very concerned about the TA connection.

O'Reilly:

You told her?

James:

No. She's good friends with the former director—who idolized you BTW

O'Reilly:

He's the best. Sharpe knows everything there is to know about True America. I'll brief the department heads and arrange to meet up with the TF in Tampa. Drag Bauer down with me. Berg is headed down too.

"Sounds like we have the A-Team on it," said James. "So I'm not worried. Is it fair to assume that Kevin is your de facto deputy assistant?"

O'Reilly self-admittedly had trust issues, so she had resisted having the CIRG deputy assistant position filled until James had finally given up trying. And because CIRG had such a diversity of sections and specialties, nobody outside of James's branch pushed the issue. Each section within CIRG had pretty much always run itself.

"He is," said O'Reilly. "Ran the show while I was in the hospital."

"Good. We're going to need all the help we can get," said James.

"And some," said O'Reilly.

I need to talk to the two of you in director's executive conference room in twenty minutes

O'Reilly gave her a thumbs-up. The moment James left the main CIRG office space, Kevin emerged from one of the side offices and made his way to her.

"How did it go?" he said, peeking his head in her door.

"Fine. Get in here," she said, pushing the notepad toward him. "I have a little light reading for you. Bring you up to speed."

"Certainly," he said, reluctantly accepting the pad.

He perused the page, turning paler by the line. She took the pad away when he'd finished and added a final line.

You are effectively running CIRG until I get back. James is your official mouthpiece. Don't fuck it up.

"I won't," he said. "Can I have one of those waters now?"

"Take as many as you want," said O'Reilly. "See you in twenty."

CHAPTER 33

Gupta had thought she looked familiar. The two pictures of the woman Neva had managed to snap at the Miami airport had consumed him. While the rest of the task force scrambled to pack the vehicles, he scoured the digital files—taking short breaks to prepare his gear for the trip. Neva had snapped her pictures cautiously, which translated to sloppily. Not her fault. She wasn't an intelligence professional, and if she'd drawn attention to herself, she could have blown the entire deal.

Unfortunately, none of the images she'd forwarded fully synced with the facial recognition software embedded in his database. One of the images cut his workload significantly but still left him with hours of manual image sifting. Two hours and eighteen minutes, to be precise, her image buried deep in the True America files. But why would they have used her for this job? She wasn't a field operative. No wonder she'd fucked it up spectacularly.

"I found her!" said Gupta.

Berg appeared immediately, glancing around the office. "Have you even started packing? We're leaving in about thirty minutes."

"Been a little preoccupied," said Gupta. "Where's Mann. Melendez. Anyone?"

"They're busy sorting and packing the gear," said Berg. "Does this require an audience, or can you share it with everyone on the road?"

"Yeah, yeah. I'm a little behind."

"A little?"

Mann stepped inside the office a few seconds later, appearing to take a similar inventory. "Jesus. Are you leaving this all behind?"

"No. Ten minutes and I'm good to go," said Gupta.

"Thank God," said Mann. "What's the hubbub? Who did you find?"

"The woman Neva tracked," said Gupta.

Suddenly, Mann seemed to have forgotten about his precious departure timeline. He made his way over to Gupta's workstation.

"Who is she?"

"Anya Fiedrick," said Gupta. "She was part of the True America administration in 2008 and 2009. Low level, if you consider the chief assistant to President Alan Crane's chief of staff, Beverly Stark, as low level."

"Stark and her staff passed every investigation with flying colors. And the DOJ didn't pull any punches," said Berg. "Even the CIA scoured the cracks. We didn't find anything. She had been purposefully kept out of the loop because she would have warned Crane. Stark was True America crazy, but not crazy enough to kill tens of millions of Americans to keep True America in power."

"Looks like Ms. Fiedrick found her crazy footing at some point between now and then," said Mann.

"Apparently so," said Berg.

"What do we have on the marina?" asked Mann.

"Nada," said Gupta. "I don't think there's a more Mexican cartel–Russian Mafia–Sicilian Mob–True America–friendly marina in the US. I hacked their system and got—"

"Nada?" said Mann.

"Exactly," said Gupta. "I found twenty-three slip contracts out of a possible 212. The latest Google Maps image shows over forty boats in the open. The rest of the eighty slips are covered. This is the marina you go to if you want to keep prying eyes off your boat."

"Do you think DOMINION is on one of those boats?" said Mann.

"It would have to be a big boat," said Gupta.

"Which would have to be in the open, I assume," said Mann. "I've worked this angle before in Mexico. The bosses owned a hundred-plus footers, minimum. No way to put those under cover."

"I've been raking the US registration system back and forth looking for anything with the name Montana," said Gupta. "Plus, several of the usual countries used to register vessels you'd prefer the authorities to avoid or ignore. I came up with—"

"Nada," said Mann.

"Sí."

"And the GPS signal stopped in front of the marina for about a minute, then continued onward to a strip mall several miles away. It's still transmitting, right?"

"Yes," said Gupta. "The tracker was obviously never discovered."

"Then we'll have to get down to that marina and use our *ojos*," said Mann. "It's a decent-size marina, but it's not that big. I'm sure once we get down there, the answer will jump out at us."

"During a hurricane?"

"The hurricane is still a few days out."

"It'll be raining by the time we reach Tampa," said Gupta.

"Then you better pack up," said Mann. "The way I see it, we'll have the hurricane on our side."

"On our side?" said Gupta.

"Bad conditions," said Mann.

"I'm not tracking," said Gupta. "Karl?"

"I need to pick up Audra and O'Reilly. So I leave the two of you to argue for the next hour," said Berg. "See you in Tampa."

"O'Reilly?" said Mann.

"Last-minute decision," said Berg. "I was sworn to secrecy, but I'm terrible at keeping secrets."

"Probably better that I didn't know. I won't say a word," said Mann. "But it sounds like we have our operations center staffed with the best in the business."

"I don't know if I'd go that far," said Berg. "But it does feel like we're getting the band back together. Hopefully, there's a venue to play."

"I'd be very surprised if the marina or one of the boats at the marina wasn't our DOMINION target," said Gupta. "Gut feeling."

"You're rarely wrong," said Berg. "But when you are—oh boy."

"Nice," said Gupta.

"We'll be in touch on the way down," said Mann. "We're still working on accommodations."

"Should be fun," said Berg, before leaving.

"I think he's living in the past," Gupta said. "Nothing about this will be fun."

"I couldn't agree more," said Mann, before glancing around the office. "Ten minutes?"

"Maybe twenty," said Gupta.

"We leave in thirty," said Mann. "I want to get down there before the weather turns to shit. Before everyone starts to hunker down. The more people we can see coming and going from the marina, or at the marina, the better. Never know who we'll spot. Plus, we'll be able to read boat names and registration numbers on the hulls. Run them through the system. Worst case scenario, we just storm the entire marina and see what happens."

"You're joking, right?" asked Gupta.

"Sort of," said Mann.

"I was hoping you wouldn't say that."

PART IV

CHAPTER 34

Studying the stern of the superyacht through a pair of powerful binoculars, Mann couldn't help but marvel at the arrogance on display. Not to mention the sloppy workmanship. The two combined seriously made him wonder whether they were walking into yet another trap. But this didn't feel like a trap.

Men and women carrying compact, partially concealed assault rifles patrolled the decks and the main dock jutting out from the marina's onshore office building. Security details were swapped out on a regular rotation, vans arriving at the marina every six hours and heading to the four-story apartment complex to the southwest.

A similarly timed trickle of ruffians moved back and forth between the marina and a run-down motel east of the apartment building used by ARTEMIS to observe the marina and yacht. They'd have to take that trickle into account later. The motel group could respond quicker than the van-shuttled crews. It all added up to more than a trap, but he was still just slightly suspicious. Not because they'd been burned before, but because someone had renamed the boat *True American.*

It had taken Mann all of about ten seconds to put this together when he first looked through the binoculars about twenty hours ago. He'd expected to spend a day or more watching and waiting for the right set of patterns that would give away True America's elusive hideaway. Nope. He started and finished with the largest yacht at the marina. Motor vessel *True American*, recently registered to the Marshall Islands.

Recently being right around the time Gerald McCall ate a bullet on a Georgetown rooftop.

The Marshall Islands had long ago become a flag of convenience for shipping companies looking to dodge higher taxes imposed by their owners' nations and avoid onerous safety regulations. International law only requires a merchant ship to be registered *somewhere*, and a few less-than-scrupulous nations had stepped up to create tax and regulation havens for fleets of ships.

Yacht owners sought out these flags of convenience for similar reasons, but with one additional twist: privacy. With lax business standards, yachts could be purchased through multiple shell companies, making them nearly untraceable to their true owners, thereby shielding them from taxes and, in this case, enemies.

Motor vessel *Montana*, wherever it had been registered, ceased to exist upon *True American*'s new registration with the Marshall Islands, but the raised letters on the stern hadn't been erased. High-resolution imagery taken from the apartment balcony showed that the new owners hadn't bothered to scrape away the marine-grade acrylic decal letters; they'd just painted over them. Taking down this yacht wasn't going to be easy, and good people would likely die. That much he could tell by what he could see. But it wasn't a trap. He wouldn't be sending agents and friends to their deaths for no reason. It didn't make him feel better about it, but like Berg had implied—it kept him focused on the mission.

A gust of warm wind swept over him, filling the apartment. A distinct bank of dark clouds filled the southern and western horizons, advancing on the light-gray clouds that had blanketed the sky since they arrived.

"When is the rain supposed to start?" asked Mann. "The winds are already kicking up."

"Tonight. Midnight or so," said Gupta. "Building through tomorrow night, until the eye passes east of us around one in the morning."

"Looks like they plan to stick around. Dock lines have been doubled, and they've added extra bumpers," said Mann.

"There's no reason for them to leave," Gupta said. "Unless something drastically changes with the hurricane's path, we're looking at consistent thirty- to forty-mile-per-hour winds, with occasional gusts in the fifties. That won't be fun for them, but the marina is well sheltered. It'll really suck for us, though. Have you given any thought to how we'll get on board? It's not like they'll have the gangplank down. They'll be buttoned up."

"Ripley and Patillo are in charge of that," said Mann. "US and Mexico Navy SEAL powers unite!"

"That wasn't funny," said Gupta.

"It really wasn't," said Serrano.

"Agreed," said Brooklyn from the kitchen.

"It's Navy SEAL shit," said Mann. "Is that better?"

"Barely," Gupta said.

"Anyway," said Mann, "boarding boats is their business. They'll figure it out."

"Wish we had someone from the Coast Guard on the team," said Gupta, getting a few laughs. "See? That was funny."

"Yep," said Mann. "Brooklyn. Garza. I assume you're good to go here? I don't pretend to know the first thing about long-distance shooting, but I thought I'd ask."

Garza soft-limped into the main room from the kitchen. The limp was barely noticeable, but he wasn't going to break any speed records anytime soon. Same with Brooklyn, who looked like she'd taken a much harsher beating than Garza. Mann had been given a little background on the two. They'd both been severely injured on the job working for a private security firm based out of Los Angeles. The pair sat down at the table next to the balcony slider. Serrano joined them, while Gupta remained at the dining room table with his portable rig.

"It's your show," said Garza, nodding at Brooklyn.

"Really?" said Brooklyn.

"You're a slightly better shot than I am," Garza said. "The stakes are too high here for us to flip a coin. I'm spotting for you on this one."

"You flip coins to decide who shoots?" Serrano asked.

"We provide surveillance and armed overwatch for high-risk rescue operations conducted by our firm," said Brooklyn. "We're both very good at what we do. But yes, I'm a little better."

"How many shots have you taken during these operations?" asked Serrano.

An awkward pause answered the question.

"Zero," said Brooklyn.

"Okay. Perhaps we need to rethink the sniper situation?" said Serrano. "Melendez is supposed to be one of the best in the business."

"I discussed this with Melendez. Not because I doubt your skills, but for the reason Cata just stated. But Rico is too valuable on the ground," said Mann. "He assured me they could more than handle this."

"We're only talking five hundred feet to the stern of the boat," said Brooklyn. "Six hundred to the bridge. I can repeatedly shoot sub-MOA at that range. My primary rifle will be a suppressed FN SCAR 20S. 7.26mm. Semiautomatic. Equipped with a 10X thermal sight. The civilian version of the military's MK20 Sniper Support System."

"Will the sight work in the rain?" asked Mann.

"Not great, but it's the best option for the conditions," said Brooklyn. "Night vision will be essentially useless in the rain we're expecting. Something you need to consider for your assault teams. If things get really ugly down there, Garza will use our backup rifle, a civilian version of the M110 Semi-Automatic Sniper System. Same caliber. Just a little less range. But at five hundred to six hundred feet, Garza is shooting sub-MOA as well."

"What is this *sub-MOA*?" Serrano asked.

"Long story short," said Garza, "for a hundred-yard shot, roughly a hundred meters, MOA is one inch. Which means, if Brooklyn were to take several shots at that range, she would hit inside one inch of her intended target most of the time. MOA increases by one inch every hundred yards. So, at the maximum range we anticipate shooting, six hundred feet or two hundred meters, she would hit inside of two inches of her intended point of aim. I'm considered a sub-MOA shooter, but she hits sub-MOA more often than I do."

"Essentially. We can very easily handle a straightforward sniper mission or a more complicated countersniper situation," said Brooklyn. "If anyone starts shooting back accurately, Garza can engage them while I keep my focus on protecting the assault teams."

"So. We're in good hands," said Serrano. "That's impressive, by the way. I don't tend to shoot at anything more than twenty meters away from me, even with a rifle. Mann can attest to that."

"I wouldn't dare," said Mann.

They all shared a quick laugh before Mann moved them along to one of the many harsh realities they faced.

"The wind will be an issue for you. Same with the rain."

"Yes," said Brooklyn. "I will likely not be shooting sub-MOA in the winds Gupta described. But at two hundred yards or under, I'll be hitting my targets squarely every time I pull the trigger. I won't be going for headshots under these conditions. I'll aim for the upper thorax. Even if I catch an armor chest or backplate, they'll be knocked flat for several minutes. Same with Garza."

"Anish. Back to timing," said Mann. "Is there any advantage to waiting for the winds to die down a little? Maybe let the eye pass to the east?"

Gupta finally looked up from his screen. "Honestly, I think we hit them when the storm is the worst. Even securely tied to the dock, at least half of the people on board will be experiencing some level of seasickness. It won't be optimal for anyone, but I think we should take advantage of the conditions."

"What if we can't effectively board the yacht?" asked Mann. "Even given Ripley and Patillo's best efforts?"

"Then I say we hit it with the two remaining AT4s. Both aimed at the bridge. Toss every grenade we have on board. Swiss cheese it with every gun we have," said Gupta.

"Maybe we should just go with that from the start," said Serrano.

"And give up DOMINION?" said Mann.

"Destroy DOMINION," said Serrano.

"What if the sicario network has standing orders, stacked up and triggered over time—if they lose contact with whoever is controlling them? A fail-safe system," said Mann.

"That's what I'd do," Gupta said.

"That's where I got the idea," said Mann. "We need to seize that yacht and take control of DOMINION. At the very least, we need to acquire the SATCHEL data so we can identify every LABYRINTH graduate still at large in the United States."

"I suspect the two are one and the same now," said Gupta. "AXIOM kept the SATCHEL, in the unlikely event that some lunatic FBI task force agent somehow took down their headquarters so they could migrate the data to an alternate DOMINION software–enabled location."

"Sounds familiar," said Mann.

"But it seems very clear that they either don't have the capability to migrate the DOMINION control software to another location, or they think they don't need to. That nobody will find this place. Or maybe they like the luxury and prestige of operating from a superyacht and can't let it go. Bottom line is that they clearly see the *True American* as important, regardless of whether they've migrated the whole DOMINION system elsewhere—so we need to take it down. Hard. No matter what we find on board, this will send them a message that will haunt them until we finish them off."

"Damn, Anish," said Mann. "You went full—"

"Please tell me the next word out of your mouth was not going to be *gangster*," said Gupta.

"I was thinking more like *full throttle*," said Mann. "But maybe *gangsta* would have been more appropriate."

"Don't you have somewhere else to be right now other than here?" said Gupta.

"I suppose I do," said Mann. "Should I send everyone that will operate out of this apartment over tonight? Just in case our True Americans decide to head out?"

Gupta cracked his knuckles and stared at the ceiling for a moment before nodding.

"That's not a bad idea. If they start untying lines and revving their engines, or whatever a yacht does, we'll need everyone in place here if this is going to serve as our tactical operations center. The assault teams, assuming their gear is properly staged at the rental houses, can kit up and be here in fifteen to twenty minutes, which is plenty of time to hit the yacht once we detect that our friends may be leaving the dock. That, and we'll want Maria and Gloria in place to head out immediately to stop the Diamond Motel reinforcements cold. Same with Mayer's team."

"Sounds like a plan," said Mann. "I'll brief everyone as soon as I get back and put the assault teams on ten-minute standby. Everyone else will head here within a few hours. Discreetly."

"Don't forget the air mattresses," said Gupta. "We have two bedrooms with one bed each, a sectional couch that can sleep two, and a recliner. That's five out of the eleven covered. I know everyone will say that they'll be up all night . . . blah, blah, blah . . . but come three in the morning, only the two assigned to watch the dock and yacht will be awake."

"Four air mattresses," said Serrano. "Got it."

"Quick math," said Gupta. "She's a keeper."

"No doubt about that," said Mann, hoping that didn't sound weird.

"Also. And I apologize for not thinking of this earlier. But we'll need to install blackout curtains on all the windows. We'll also need to build a small blackout vestibule inside the apartment, next to all the balcony glass. Kind of like an air lock for light. So you can go back and forth to the balcony from inside without any light escaping."

"Excellent idea," said Brooklyn.

"I wish I could say it was my idea," said Gupta. "I recommend buying the largest and thickest tarps available. Brown. Not black, silver, or blue. We'll have all the shades drawn to small cracks for viewing, but better to have a neutral color in case anyone takes a close look. Also, buy an electric-powered, heavy-duty stapler. We're going to cut the tarps and staple them in place over the windows. We'll staple the vestibule tarp pieces to the ceiling."

Everyone looked up at the smooth drywall.

"Are you sure it'll hold with staples? Even the heavy-duty kind?" asked Garza. "Maybe we should measure out the ceiling height and buy some two-by-fours to create posts to reduce some of the pull. Thick tarps like that can be surprisingly heavy."

"I have a tape measure in my van," said Gupta. "I'll head down and grab it. Last thing. Buy a few dozen full-spectrum dimmable smart light bulbs. I can sync them up to my phone and change them to dark red. We'll still be able to see and read, but if we have a slipup with the blackout situation, the red light will be far less noticeable to night vision. Especially in the rain. Do you need to write that down?"

"I have no idea what he's talking about," said Serrano.

"I got it," said Mann, pulling out his phone and making a note anyway.

He had a lot swirling through his head right now.

"All right. We'll hit a hardware store first, before we head back to the rental house. Just in case they close shop early because of the storm," said Mann. "Anything else?"

"A lot of snacks and drinks," said Gupta. "Plus, microwaveable meals for eleven. It's just easier that way. Anyone can eat whenever they want."

"I'll let them know," said Mann. "Why don't you text all your meal requests or dislikes over to Lianez so you have some input in what you'll be eating for the next twenty-four hours."

Gupta gave him a thumbs-up. He turned his attention back to Brooklyn and Garza.

"Good luck, and don't be shy if you think of anything or need anything," said Mann. "We probably won't meet up again."

"Are you not planning on making it out of this alive?" Garza asked.

"No. I just assumed once we took the yacht, you might want to make yourselves scarce," said Mann. "Head back to the rental houses and wait out the hurricane before returning to Los Angeles. None of the FBI people will be returning to those houses. My task force's mission is sort of on the books. That'll probably depend on the outcome, to be honest. Everyone else's status is essentially a wild card situation."

"Depending on the outcome of the mission," said Serrano.

"More or less," said Mann. "There's only so much Deputy Director O'Reilly and I can do to guarantee your—I hate to even say it."

"Immunity from prosecution," said Gupta.

"It's better that you get as far from here as possible once we secure the yacht," Mann said. "O'Reilly and I can flash our credentials, which will satisfy local, state, and even the federal agencies we never notified—for a while. It'll become pretty evident once the storm dies down that my band of misfit toys didn't pull this off by themselves. Best if you're off the radar at that point."

"Make sure your team brings a few 7.62mm sniper rifles to leave up here or bring along," said Gupta. "Unless Brooklyn and Garza are willing to leave theirs behind."

"We'd rather not," said Brooklyn.

"We have two M39 EMRs and a few good shooters," said Mann. "Good catch, Anish. Keep that kind of stuff coming. The more normal this entire scene looks, the better for everyone."

"We should get going if we're going to hit a hardware store," said Serrano.

"See you on the other side," said Gupta, not looking up from his computer.

Everyone rolled their eyes, even though they knew he was probably right.

CHAPTER 35

After the Concept of Operations briefing, which loosely tied all the teams and pieces together, Mann met with each of the specialized teams headed to the apartment overlooking the marina. He'd work with the two assault teams, who would remain at the rental houses until the raid, to develop a detailed plan for the yacht takedown. They had the Custom Line 180's general schematics, taken directly from the yacht-builder's website, along with dozens of pictures scoured from the internet to give them a general idea of what to expect inside.

He grabbed Lianez and Mills first.

"Stay with O'Reilly and the others in the apartment until we secure the yacht," said Mann. "Gupta will board the yacht with the assault teams, so he can take whatever measures are necessary to keep True America from destroying digital evidence or sending DOMINION elsewhere. And if they send it elsewhere, he'll start the forensic trail. Once the yacht is secure, you'll link up with Mayer's team. You can work out the details with them at the apartment. If the assault teams get wiped out tomorrow night, just do whatever O'Reilly tells you to do. Good?"

"That's your final pep talk?" said Mills.

He put a hand on Mills's shoulder. "Sorry. If things go sideways tomorrow, thank you for believing in ARTEMIS from the beginning. You've been a great asset to the team and a good friend."

"Okay. Now you're pushing it. See you when the deed is done," said Mills. "Chad. Do not engage this fool."

Lianez laughed. "See you on the dock."

Serrano walked up with Maria and Gloria.

"I told them I could translate," said Serrano.

"Did they suddenly forget how to *hablan inglés*?" said Mann. "I'm not falling for that."

"Whatever," said Maria, one of her muscled arms helping an oversize nylon duffel bag defy gravity.

"The tactical ladder in Gupta's van will get you to the rooftop. I know I don't have to say this—" said Mann.

"But he's gonna anyway," said Serrano.

The two women finally broke a grin.

"First. Don't forget to bring the ladder onto the rooftop with you. In the winds we expect tomorrow night, it won't be there if you leave it in place," said Mann. "Second. If you find yourself in trouble, for whatever reason, contact Gupta sooner than later. We'll have another team on the ground by the apartment building that can respond very quickly. Plus, our sniper team has a line of sight to your position and the parking lot between you and the Diamond Motel."

"We'll be fine," said Gloria. "They won't know what hit them."

"How did I know one of you would say that?" said Mann. "When you determine that your business is done at the Diamond Motel and the yacht is secured, someone will pick you up and bring you back here." He looked at Serrano. "They don't have to do this. We can swap them out."

He was essentially asking them to gun down about two dozen people, who may not even know what they were guarding when they reported for their shifts at the dock or on board *True American*. It didn't feel right.

"They're good. Just don't leave them hanging," said Serrano.

"I won't," Mann said.

Serrano had a quick chat with them before they headed to the garage.

"Seriously. They signed up for this. Nothing is more important to them at the moment," she said. "Success tonight means more to them and their families than you can imagine."

"I can't imagine," said Mann, before nodding at Mayer, who brought Neva and Bella over.

"We don't need the speech," said Mayer. "We got this."

"Never had a doubt in my mind, but when we're talking AT4 rocket launchers, I feel the need to check in," said Mann.

"We'll only use them if absolutely necessary," said Mayer. "We also have one of the heavy-barrel HKs at our disposal. My guess is that'll be all the punch we need to handle any vans that show up, along with rifles."

"I hope so, but your number-one priority is getting the rest of the tech team onto the yacht, unscathed. After you deal with whatever shows after the fireworks start," said Mann. "So don't hesitate to use the AT4s if that helps expedite the process."

"Oh, I won't!" said Bella, a former Mexican State SWAT officer.

"She seems way too excited about the AT4s," said Mann.

"She didn't get to fire one last time," Serrano told him. "Kind of a letdown."

"Yeah, well, there are only two AT4s and there are three of you. Might want to play a little rock, paper, scissors before the hostiles show up," said Mann.

"Funny," said Mayer.

"Godspeed, Jess. You have the shopping list, right?"

"Had to make the women do the shopping, huh?" said Mayer.

"The women outnumber the men two to one at the apartment, but I could give the list to Lianez and Mills," said Mann.

"Fuck no," said Mayer. "They'll toss the list and we'll be eating pork rinds and Salisbury steak microwave dinners and drinking Diet Pepsi for the next twenty-four hours."

"That's what I thought," said Mann. "And please do your best to accommodate Gupta's vegetarian requests. He's hard enough to work with as it is."

"Can't make any promises," said Mayer.

"Hey. You're the one who has to spend the next twenty-four hours with him. Not many places to hide in a 1,200-square-foot apartment," said Mann.

Karl Berg appeared out of nowhere, as usual. "Buy Gupta twice as much as Mann put on your list. Trust me. He's like a small child when he's working these jobs. Keep him fed. Let him do his thing. And he won't bother you."

"Sound advice," said Mayer, before turning to Mann and Serrano. "See you on the dock."

"Yep. Hopefully in a little over twenty-four hours, this will all be finished," said Mann. "And don't skimp on Gupta's snacks."

"Seriously?" said Mayer. "That's all you're worried about?"

"Less talking, more shopping," said Mann.

"I swear," started Mayer, "when this is over—"

"Make sure you have a pen to cross off the items as you put them in the cart," said Mann.

Mayer's middle finger ended the exchange.

"She's punchy," said Berg. "Always like that?"

"Always," said Serrano. "That seems to be a task force requirement."

"Reminds me of some people I used to work with," Berg said.

"Do you want to grab Audra and Dana? I don't really have anything for you. I think between the three of you, we're in very capable hands. I'll send over our first detailed plan later tonight."

"That's not why I invited myself over," Berg said, before lowering his voice. "Things will not go as planned tomorrow. I'm sure both of you know that. Not everyone here will have vital signs when this is done."

"I hope this isn't—what do you call it—a pep talk?" said Serrano.

"More like advice, but the kind you get whether you want it or not," said Berg. "The bottom line is, the two of you will see this through. The mission will succeed. I'm certain of it. No matter what goes down."

Mann was surprised. He'd expected Berg to continue with his doomsday prophecy. Of course, Berg wasn't one to land soft blows—which meant he wasn't finished.

"Here's the advice, and you're probably not going to like it. Keep yourselves alive. It sounds terrible to say that, given what you'll direct everyone to do tomorrow, but lead from the front, just don't be reckless about it," said Berg. "If either one of you is taken down hard, the people you've brought this far will falter—and that will most likely kill the entire show. I've been around long enough to see these operations play out a hundred times. Trust me when I say it's imperative that you keep yourselves in the mission, no matter how distasteful or difficult the decisions. You're both indispensable leaders."

Cata shook her head. "I'm not in charge of—"

"Stop right there," said Berg. "The only reason they're here is you. They trust you implicitly. They look up to you. They rely on you. I can see that. It's incredible. Yes, they all have their own reasons, but ultimately they're here because of you. You made this happen. Sorry to be the bearer of this heavy news."

Serrano looked oddly relieved. "Thank you, Señor Berg. I actually needed to hear that."

"Please call me Karl. And don't hold it against Señor Mann for not having been this blunt with you. Despite what the task force has accomplished and suffered, he is relatively new to this kind of work—and the harsh realities that come with it—even though I feel like he's kind of an old soul in business somehow," said Berg. "Same with you."

"I'm nothing," said Serrano.

"Oh. I don't think so," said Berg. "To be completely honest, I'm far more impressed with your accomplishments than Garrett's. No offense."

"None taken," said Mann.

"But we don't have time to get into that right now," said Berg. "We have to get down to business. Do you want to chat with Dana and Audra before we head out?"

"No. You know what to do," said Mann. "Don't forget. The apartment will turn radioactive for anyone not in the FBI once the shooting starts."

"Yeah. Audra and I will head back here—or keep driving if it turns into a complete shit show," Berg said.

"Better fill your tank on the way to the apartment," said Mann. "Whatever happens tomorrow night won't be pretty."

Berg grinned. "I have to admit, I kind of miss this. Thank you for inviting me to what I can only hope is my last shit show."

"Thank Audra and Dana," said Mann. "You came highly recommended."

"They just want some plausible deniability if things go sideways," said Berg.

"Like I said. You came highly recommended," Mann said.

Serrano laughed and said, *"La piñata."*

"I can guess what that means," said Berg.

Mann extended his hand. "No matter how this goes down, I don't expect to see you again. Thank you."

"My pleasure," said Berg. "And yeah. After this goes down, I'll probably lay low for a long time. But never say never. If you stay off O'Reilly's naughty list, our paths might cross again."

"I hope so," said Mann, shaking his hand.

Serrano accepted Berg's hand with both of hers and just nodded. When Berg left to find Audra and Dana, Serrano turned to Mann.

"He seems like a very sad man," she said.

"I think he's seen more of this kind of work than we can imagine," said Mann. "And that's saying something. We've been put through hell over the past few months."

Serrano discreetly grasped his hand. "I hope Karl is right. I can't live like this anymore."

Mann squeezed her hand gently. "Same here. I may be an old soul in this business, like Karl suggested, but I have no interest in continuing it beyond tomorrow."

"Unless we fuck it up and have to do it again," said Serrano.

"Good point," said Mann, laughing under his breath. "I'm going to have food delivered. Then we get to work."

CHAPTER 36

The entire house rattled, and the lights flickered. Not good. Hurricane Josephine had edged her way a little farther east than predicted, the winds registering about five to ten miles per hour higher than initially predicted, which made a bigger difference than Mann would have expected. He meandered over to the dining room table, where Lianez had arranged four side-by-side wide-screen monitors that he could control remotely from the apartment. The two on the left displayed high-resolution feeds from Gupta's latest-generation, zoomable night vision, and thermal-imaging-capable cameras. One focused on the yacht. The other on the dock and marina office.

The middle screens were administrative, in a sense. One constantly displayed a map, focused on the route to the marina. Mann could interact with that one. The other gave them the kind of internet access one might normally expect from a home computer setup. Except Gupta and Lianez controlled the system and could jump in at any time. Which Mann welcomed. He could type a question, and the answer arrived within seconds. Same with the map screen. If anyone started interacting with it, Lianez or Gupta would pop up on the screen asking if they could help. Gupta had become synonymous with Alexa or Siri, the assault teams resolving any difficult-to-answer questions with "Ask Gupta."

Another powerful gust buffeted the house, prompting Ripley to get up from the couch and make his way over. Patillo, who had been teaching Wallace and Cook solitaire in the kitchen, joined him.

"The ladders are a no go, I assume?" said Mann when they reached him.

"You tell me," said Ripley, nodding at the live feeds. "And I'm not being a dick. I just need you to give me your honest opinion. This wind is more than we anticipated."

The yacht held steady against the dock. Sort of. It clearly wasn't going anywhere, but it heaved up and down, the gap between the hull and concrete pier expanding and contracting with each gust.

"I don't see it happening," said Mann.

"I agree," said Patillo, studying the feed. "The aft sea deck is our best option."

"I think it's our only option," said Ripley. "We can time the rise and fall of the yacht to make the jump a little easier on the body, but that'll definitely slow down the boarding process."

"Maybe we'll have to go lighter," said Mann. "Ditch the backplates and secondary weapons. Carry less ammo. I don't know. But we're definitely wearing the self-inflating vests if we're not using the ladders."

"I don't recommend shedding any gear. We just need to adjust. If we plan to board the yacht at a significantly slower pace, we might want to consider holding part of the second assault team behind to provide overwhelming fire superiority against any threat to the first team," said Ripley. "Our snipers should be enough, but I prefer to be overcautious in situations like this."

"Estás de acuerdo?" said Mann.

"Yes," said Patillo.

"I swear you guys do this to mess with me," said Mann.

"Sí," said Patillo. "But out of respect."

"Gracias," said Mann.

"You're welcome."

"Nice," said Mann. "So. We're about an hour out. We didn't see much of a shift changeover due to the weather. Nobody trickling back and forth from the motel. Only one van showed up. What are you seeing in the RF spectrum?"

"RF surveillance suggests that at least four guards took shelter inside the marina office."

Gupta had installed a radio frequency receiver-pinger on the balcony and attached a stand-alone pinger relay to an electric pole several hundred yards to the south, which he used to identify, catalog, and track hostile threats carrying radios. Using a software program he'd designed, Gupta could analyze all RF transmissions within line of sight of the receiver and eliminate the background layer—based on frequency range and movement—leaving him with the hostile network. The separate pingers allowed his software to triangulate the signals, giving him a five-to-ten-meter accuracy.

The radios carried by *True American*'s security entourage utilized the latest generation of encryption, so Gupta couldn't hack them and listen. But he could identify their unique user codes and communicate with them with a quick ping. The radios responded to the undetectable pings, essentially nailing down the yacht's network of security and crew members.

Most of the security radios remained on the yacht or dock and were turned over with the changing of the guard. A few sat scattered around the local area, two at the Diamond Motel and three at the apartment complex across the marina canal.

"We'll have to figure out how to deal with them without raising the alarm prematurely," said Mann. "Looks like everything else is clear."

"No guards in the open on the dock or topside decks," said Gupta. "Roughly fifteen of the rotating security guards are either inside the yacht or the marina office. Plus, the in-house security."

The in-house security posed a problem. They'd identified at least six security officers who never left the yacht. Only two of them had come topside long enough to be accurately photographed. A facial recognition database "accessed" by Gupta only identified one of them—Paul Kraus, a former member of Germany's elite GSG9 counterterrorism unit. A significant step above the former GRU and Russian army Spetsnaz commandos used in Montana. They had to assume the other three, and possibly more, would live up to the same standard of mercenary quality.

"I'm a little concerned about the in-house crew," said Ripley. "I know we've discussed it, but we're talking extremely tight-quarters combat with at least one mercenary who spent close to fifteen years training to do one thing: shoot in close-quarters combat situations. I know Turner is kind of against the idea because it will slow us down even more, but even with the whole jumping on the stern platform thing—we should bring all six of the ballistic shields. They'll be lifesavers on the yacht."

"That wind could yank one of those out your hands and toss it at the rest of the team like Captain America's shield," said Turner.

"We'd have to be very careful," said Ripley. "But we're already going to be slow as fuck getting on board. Our snipers and the assault teams will make quick work of anyone who ventures topside on the yacht, but inside is a different story. Even if we can toss a few on board to use, that'll make a big difference."

Melendez and Murray McDonald, the newest of Bauer and Berg's associates to join the festivities, jumped into the conversation.

"Couldn't help but overhear," said Rico. "I think it's worth the hassle to try and get a few shields on board."

"Agree," said McDonald. "Between ARTEMIS, our crew, and Serrano's contingent, we have enough SWAT or close-quarters battle-trained operators to make really good use of those shields inside and outside of the yacht."

"I'm one hundred percent on board with that," said Turner. "I think they'll be problematic to get down the dock with the wind, but I'm sure we'll manage."

Mann checked his watch. Twelve twenty.

"Itching to go?" asked Turner.

"If the security detail is turned over and nothing has changed," said Mann, "I don't see how waiting for a specific time helps or hurts us."

"The only variable we'll experience is the wind," said Turner. "The hurricane nudged east, but it also picked up speed. If we wait an hour, the winds might die down a little. But not that much. We won't perceive a significant decline in wind speed until at least four in the morning."

"Is there any advantage to waiting for the winds to die down?" Mann asked.

"Honestly, it might make things worse," said Turner. "Things will be dicey enough jumping over. When the winds die down, the storm surge will subside. We've seen them adjust the dock lines a few times to account for the rising water. The surge isn't bad, but when it heads back out of the bay, the boat will drop back to its normal position."

"But the wind will still be rocking it," said Mann.

"Exactly," said Turner. "We still won't be able to use the ladders, and even a well-timed jump will drop you twice the current distance."

"All right. Let's check in with the apartment," said Mann, clicking the call button on the desktop's virtual meeting app.

Gupta appeared immediately.

"Had a feeling you might give us a call," he said, moving his chair over.

Bauer and O'Reilly slid into view next to Gupta. Berg just waved a hand in front of the camera.

"Or you were eavesdropping," said Mann.

"I have the capability," Gupta said. "But we were just going over the wind speed and storm surge predictions—and were about to call you. This is about as bad as it's going to get for the winds and rain. We don't anticipate any security or personnel changes happening until the storm dies down. Brooklyn and Garza have been on the balcony for about thirty minutes. They're not seeing anything topside or detecting anyone peeping out of the windows. They have cameras pointed toward the marina office and the approaches to the dock alongside each side of the building, but they haven't moved since we started watching them yesterday. I found the camera type. Standard night vision, constant feed—as expected."

"Motion sensitive?" said Mann.

"Yes. But I dug into a few marine forums, and the consensus is that they're basically useless on a dock in weather like this. Even their website says performance will be degraded unless the boat is essentially stationary. The boat movement relative to the dock sets off the motion-detection feature nearly nonstop, so my guess is they have disabled that function for now."

"What's your gut feel?" asked Mann.

"Mine?" said Gupta.

"All of yours," said Mann.

"It's your show," said O'Reilly.

"Aren't you my boss?"

"Think of this as an in-the-field performance evaluation," said O'Reilly.

"But without the pressure," said Berg, from off camera.

They all laughed for a moment.

"Let's do it," said Mann. "We'll be kitted up and on the road in fifteen minutes. Get everyone on your end in position."

"We'll get them rolling," Gupta said. "I am activating our radio frequency repeater—right now. Hopefully, that doesn't pop up on some kind of receiver on the yacht. Everything looks good. I can now monitor and respond to all of our radio nets. We'll be listening in on all police and emergency radio traffic. Once everyone is geared up, we'll do a full radio check."

Gupta had installed the RF repeater on the balcony, where it had unhindered lines of sight to all their key mission areas.

"How are Brooklyn and Garza doing out there?" Mann asked. "Could they use a fifteen-minute break?"

"Probably," said Gupta. "It's brutal out. The lights have been flickering, which isn't a bad thing. I'm running a UPS system. Uninterruptable Power—"

"I know what it means," said Mann. "What about the *True American*?"

"Interesting question," said Gupta. "I'm guessing that the yacht is probably running on shore power right now, but its critical equipment is hooked up to their battery bank—which is basically one giant-ass UPS. They could keep the lights on and the air-conditioning running for several hours."

"Is there any benefit to trying to cut off their shore power?" said Mann.

"No. *Uninterruptable* means exactly that," said Gupta. "Plus, if they looked outside and saw lights anywhere near the marina, they would get suspicious. The last thing we want them to do is cast off their lines and get underway. That yacht is more than capable of weathering these conditions."

"Did I miss that in one of the briefings?" said Mann.

Turner piped in. "I don't remember us discussing it."

"Same," said Ripley.

Did this change things?

"How long would it take the yacht to get underway under emergency conditions?" Mann asked.

"Five to ten minutes," said Gupta. "Assuming everyone on board reacted immediately and could do their jobs efficiently. The biggest problem they face is the crew casting off the dock lines. It will be no small feat doing that in this weather. Under gunfire? Impossible. They're not going anywhere."

"Our snipers can't see that side of the yacht," said Mann.

"But all of you can," said Gupta. "The assault teams can keep the deck crew under fire until they board. Maybe keep two from Turner's team on the dock or in the marina office to make sure they can't cast off the lines?"

Mann turned to Luke. "I'll keep Cook or Tianna on the dock. They're the least tactical on my assault team, but they can shoot. How about you leave Jax behind until we secure the bridge? That way we only take one away from each team."

"I can live with that," said Jax from the couch.

"Same with me," said Cook from the kitchen.

"No hard feelings?" said Mann.

"None," they both said at almost the same time.

"All right. Let's saddle up," said Mann. "With any luck, this whole thing will be done within an hour."

CHAPTER 37

The four SUVs carrying the two assault teams came to a slow stop a block away from the marina. They'd approach on foot from here. Even in the near-blinding rain, with the vehicle lights off, the yacht's cameras would catch them if they drove up to the marina office. The big risk being that someone on board would be watching the security feed at that precise moment. A risk Mann wasn't willing to take. They had enough obstacles to overcome without tipping their hand before off-loading.

The office presented their first critical challenge. They understood that it was essentially impossible to hit the office and not alert the yacht. Someone inside would sound the alarm. The assault group had no choice but to accept this reality. They just couldn't afford to get stuck inside the office. Mann needed everyone focused on the yacht as quickly as possible.

Turner's job, leading one of two assault teams, was to tear through the office quickly, not quietly, and link up with Mann's team on the dock, ready to suppress any efforts by the crew or security team to cast off the dock lines, while Mann's boarded the yacht. Each team consisted of eight shooters, with skill levels ranging from "the best" to "pretty good."

Once both teams had boarded, they'd split up, with Turner's team moving down the starboard side and Mann's taking port—and then the two teams meeting up at the bridge to take control of the yacht. Once they had shut down the engines, the mission turned into a mop-up operation. A potentially costly one. As much as Mann wanted to take the DOMINION system intact, both to capture the sicario network and provide it as evidence of True America's betrayal of the United States, the task force had agreed that acquiring DOMINION itself wasn't worth excessive losses. Every group involved had lost enough at this point.

That was where things got a little blurry. Everybody wanted to see this to the end, but nobody was willing to concretely define what *excessive losses* meant. It would be up to Mann to decide at what point they would just scuttle the ship and send it to the bottom of the canal, instead of taking more losses. *More* losses being the operative term, because losses were inevitable. The only question was how many casualties were acceptable to take possession of DOMINION—and he honestly didn't know the answer.

He contacted Gupta. "This is Mann. We just pulled up."

"I see you," said Gupta.

"How are things looking?"

"Same. Same. Nothing has changed," said Gupta. "Maria's team is in position across from the motel. Mayer's team is on the ground floor, waiting at the door closest to the south parking lot. All is quiet. Except for the sideways rain and gale-force winds outside."

"Yeah. Our vehicles are rocking on their suspension."

"Wait until you step outside," Gupta said.

"How is the sniper team doing?"

"Not good. They're getting hit with direct winds," said Gupta. "The sooner we wrap this up, the better. No pressure or anything."

"We're about to step off. Five minutes until we hit the marina," Mann said.

"I'll let them know."

Mann glanced at Serrano, who was in the front passenger seat. "Ready?"

"No. But let's get this over with," she said.

Mann triggered his radio. "All support units are in place. Let's go. Keep the ballistic shields angled down, end pointing into the wind. They might drag along the ground, slowing us down a little, but any other position will be a showstopper."

"We'll see," said Turner. "Heading out now."

Mann tried to open his door, the SUV facing into the wind. It took every bit of strength he had to open it far enough to slip a leg through and plant his foot on the ground. He leveraged his body against the door to open it far enough to slide outside. The door slammed shut the moment he cleared it. There was no way they'd be able to bring the shields; they'd be ripped from their hands within seconds.

"Leave the shields behind," said Mann, pushing against the gale-force winds.

"Yeah. We just lost one," said Turner.

Mann turned around in time to see one of Turner's ballistic shields a block away, toppling end over end down the street. He backed up and took cover between the lead vehicle and the second in the convoy, where everyone in his vehicle had taken refuge. He assumed that the second vehicle's occupants had done the same. And on and on down the line.

Serrano grabbed his arm. "What took you so long?"

"Just taking in the beautiful weather," said Mann.

"It's not that bad," said Serrano.

"Unless you're trying to carry one of the shields."

"It was worth a try," said Serrano. "We still have body armor."

"Yeah," said Mann, before transmitting over the net. "A1 and A2. Move into pre-assault position ALPHA."

The pre-assault positions kept them out of sight of the yacht's cameras, essentially putting them on the edge of the northern marina entrance. One step beyond that exposed them to the cameras. Once A2 dashed across the area exposed to the cameras to breach the marina office, the clock started ticking.

Mann had never experienced anything like this before. The wind nearly stopped him in his tracks.

"This is unbelievable," he said. "Maybe we wait until this all dies down. We can't bring the ballistic shields on board."

"I think we can," said Serrano.

"How?"

"We have six shields."

"Five," said Mann. "One of them is on its way to Disney World."

"Five shields," said Serrano. "There are sixteen of us. We form a tight human shield around the five carrying the shields. Once we get to the marina office, we'll be totally blocked from the wind. The team breaching the office can use all of them. We can move to the yacht using the same concept. Turner's team forms a human wind block while our team tosses them on board. It's worth a try. They'll save lives once we get on board."

Wallace grabbed his shoulder. "She's right. There's no downside to trying. But a ton of upside if we get them on board. We'll bring them along the starboard side, which is out of the wind. If we can get two or three of them to the bridge, that would be a game changer once we start clearing the yacht."

Mann nodded. "Let's go for it."

He passed instructions along, and the teams formed up next to his SUV. From what he could tell, the plan would work. The shields barely moved behind the human wall assembled behind him.

"Moving out," said Mann, stepping off.

Pushing against a constant fifty- to sixty-mile-per-hour wind felt like walking through Jell-O, with the occasional gust simply stopping them in their tracks. They should have parked closer. By the time they reached the alarm trigger point, Mann was exhausted.

"Overwatch. Any changes?" he said.

"Negative," said Gupta. "According to every weather source, you are hitting the yacht under the worst conditions we'll see tonight."

"It's brutal out here," said Mann.

"They won't see this coming," Gupta said.

"That's the plan," said Mann. "I'm about to push Turner's team into the marina office. Once he's inside, we're going to stack up along the northern side of the building, out of the wind. We'll link up on the dock and start the boarding process after he clears the building. We still have five of the six shields. I'd like to get the rest on board."

O'Reilly jumped into the conversation. "Garrett. This is Dana. Focus on getting the team on board. You have them at a serious disadvantage. They're tired, seasick, and not expecting to be hit. Especially not in the middle of a hurricane. Keep it simple."

"Copy that. Thank you," said Mann, before addressing both teams over the tactical net.

"Turner. Take all five shields with you to clear the office," said Mann. "But leave them behind when you emerge to cover our boarding. We can't afford the time or effort it will take to get them on board."

"I'll try to get one or two through to the yacht," said Turner. "If the wind starts tossing them around, I'll let them go."

"Sounds good," said Mann. "Ready when you are."

"Moving out," said Turner, his team breaking cover and pushing against the wind until the building provided a wind block.

Turner's team manually breached the front door using a sledgehammer and disappeared inside. No gunfire erupted, which normally would be a relief. But Gupta had said that four of the rotating security officers had taken refuge inside the office.

"Turner. This is Mann. What's your status?"

"Do you mean why is it so quiet in here?" asked Turner.

"Yes."

"We've made our way to the door opening to the dock," said Turner. "There's nobody here. And there's no second floor."

Gupta broke into the conversation. "I'm still pinging four radios within ten meters of the west end of the building."

"Is there any way they could be on the yacht?" said Mann. "Maybe inside the sea deck on the stern?"

"That's too far—hold on. Fuck. I'm getting a lot of RF chatter coming from the boat. Same with the apartment building and the motel," said Gupta.

"They know we're here," Mann said.

"And I'm still showing four encrypted radios nearly on top of you, Turner," said Gupta. "You have four hostiles in proximity to your team."

"I'm telling you. There's nobody inside this building," said Turner. "What are the snipers seeing?"

"The snipers still have nothing," said Gupta. "The radios must be close. What else is close?"

"I have no fucking idea. There's no second floor," said Turner.

"I'm moving my team up to take a look at the dock," Mann said. "Maybe they have a guard shack set up that we can't see from the apartment or street."

"Maybe we should just jam the two AT4s down their throats and call it a day," said Turner.

"I vote for sinking the yacht," said Serrano.

"We're not sinking the yacht until we've given this a try," said Mann. "I'm moving up. If things get ridiculous, we'll sink the yacht."

"This is already completely ridiculous," said Turner.

"More ridiculous," said Mann. "You know what I mean."

Automatic gunfire erupted in the distance.

"The Diamond Motel massacre is in progress," said Gupta.

"Wonderful," Mann mumbled to himself. "Heading out."

They hadn't even made it to the dock before the shit show took on a life of its own.

CHAPTER 38

Maria pressed the trigger again, holding it longer this time, until the heavy-barrel automatic rifle ran dry—the barrel smoking and slightly glowing from the 120 rounds she'd put through it in the last two minutes. The rain sizzling against the overheated barrel created a layer of steam that had admittedly hindered her from hitting everyone in the motel parking lot.

"Reloading," she said, taking cover behind the rooftop's raised wall.

Gloria shifted her focus from the few stragglers who had made it out of the initial kill zone to the motel parking lot—the actual kill zone. Bullets chipped away at the top of the wall around her as Maria slammed a new sixty-round drum into the rifle.

"Head to the west side and make sure nobody slipped into the marina parking lot. The last thing Mayer's team needs is any kind of distraction or surprise," said Maria, before sliding the rifle's bolt home and moving about fifteen feet to her right.

She popped up in what she hoped was an unexpected location. They'd moved twice already since the shooting started, the first two moves throwing off the handful of security officers who survived the initial half minute of gunfire. The gambit worked. Five security officers stood exposed, two of them firing in Gloria's direction. The others aimed close to where she'd originally ducked. They adjusted their aim quickly, but not fast enough to save themselves. Maria drilled all three with a short burst before shifting her sight to the two tracking Gloria.

One of them swung his rifle in her direction, but that was the extent of his progress. She centered the rifle's sight reticle on his head and pressed the trigger, dropping him like a sack of rocks behind the SUV that had kept him alive thus far. The last security officer ducked between two cars, moments before she unleashed a hastily aimed volley. Her bullets peppered the hoods and windshields of both sedans, possibly nailing the shooter if he hadn't taken cover fast enough. The man popped up and squeezed off a few shots at her, all going so wide that she didn't hear their sonic snaps. His head jerked sideways before she could press the trigger again.

"Thank you," said Maria. "Any stragglers headed toward the marina?"

"Two," said Gloria.

Two shots later, she came back on the net.

"Zero."

They never knew what had hit them. A good half dozen men and women had piled out of their rooms moments before and assembled in plain sight, two men handing them rifles and ammunition magazines from the back of an SUV.

Maria scanned the parking lot. She didn't sense any movement at the moment. A few of them had undoubtedly survived, but they seemed to have the better sense to stay down at this point and tend to their injuries.

"TOC. This is Maria. Mission accomplished. The Diamond Motel is as quiet as it's going to get. We're heading out," she said over the support net.

"Copy. We heard the fireworks," said Gupta. "Make your way to the northwest corner of the Dollar Tree store across Thirty-Fourth Street. Set up facing east toward the motel to deny that approach. That'll let Mayer's group focus on the street in front of the marina."

"Understood," said Maria. "I'll let you know when we're in position. How are things going at the dock?"

"Still unknown. Out," said Gupta.

She glanced at Gloria, who shook her head. Exactly. Not good. They should have hit the yacht by now. Something was holding them back.

CHAPTER 39

Harrison Greely had been moments away from requesting to be moved from the yacht to one of the apartments when the first alert went out over the security radios, one of which sat in a charger in his stateroom.

"All stations. Stern security cameras caught a group of about ten heavily armed and armored personnel crossing north to south on the sidewalk leading to the front of the marina office."

Furst's voice answered immediately.

"This is Furst. Any sign of forced entry into the office?"

"Stand by," said the security officer.

"Harrison. I'm headed down to your stateroom," said Furst over the net.

Greely swiped the radio from the charger. "Switch to the executive frequency."

"Yep," she said.

The handheld radio in the cupholder attached to his left wheelchair arm squawked.

"Harrison. This is Clara."

He dropped the security radio in his lap before grabbing the other radio. He didn't bother with any pleasantries.

"Before you head down, have the captain prepare to get underway. Everything but the dock lines," said Greely. "Put all security on high alert and recall everyone from the motel and apartment. Shoot first and ask questions later."

"We don't have room for everyone on the boat," said Furst.

"They won't be coming with us," said Greely. "We'll use them to slow down whatever we're facing. Give us time to get out of here and into open water."

"Could this be Mann?"

"Has to be," said Greely. "But it doesn't matter. We just need to get the fuck out to sea. This boat is designed to deal with this kind of weather."

"Copy. See you in a few."

How the hell had Mann's people found them again? They'd taken every precaution. All digital devices used anywhere near any of Mann's task force or Mexican colleagues ditched. Professional surveillance detection routes executed. The yacht registry changed and untraceable to McCall. Every possible box checked. And they still did it somehow—assuming it was Mann. But who the hell else could it be?

"All stations. We have a confirmed breach in the marina office," said the security officer in charge of the yacht's security hub. "Eight hostiles making their way to the doors leading to the dock."

Furst's voice broke through again. "Boat and sniper teams. You are cleared to engage anyone who steps out of that building or approaches from the street."

The muted thumping of automatic fire somehow penetrated deep into the yacht. Greely grabbed the radio in his lap.

"Are they trying to rush the boat?" he asked.

"Negative," said the security officer. "That's coming from the motel. The off-duty shift is under heavy gunfire. They were distributing weapons in the parking lot when all hell broke loose."

If Mann's people knew about the motel, that meant they'd been watching the yacht for at least twenty-four hours. Maybe longer. They'd also know about the security officers who arrived by van from the apartment complex. This wouldn't be a hastily assembled raid. Mann had more than enough time to come up with a plan—picking the apex of the hurricane to execute it. The timing wasn't a coincidence. Furst entered his stateroom a moment later, looking like she'd just run the fifty-meter dash.

"We need to get underway immediately," said Greely. "This is far too organized to be—"

More gunfire boomed, this time a lot closer. The diesel engines rumbled to life just after the gunfire started. That was it. Time to go.

"Dock teams have engaged," said the security officer over the radio. "Two groups of eight hostiles on the dock."

Greely grabbed the radio in his lap. "This is Harrison Greely. Blow the dock lines!"

"Are you sure, sir?" said the security officer. "Is the captain aware?"

"Make him aware! Then blow the fucking lines!" said Greely before turning to Furst, who seemed to be on the same page as him for the first time in years.

"I'm headed to the bridge," she said. "The captain won't take orders from the security hub babysitter."

"Agreed," said Greely. "And don't forget what they did in DC. For all we know, they have more of those rockets at their disposal. We need to get underway now!"

"I heard you the first time!" said Furst, bolting out of his cabin.

Hendrick popped in right after her.

"Sir. I think it might be time to get you in your bed or figure out a way to secure you and your chair," said his bodyguard. "We're looking at five to ten times the instability we've already experienced. I recommend the bed."

"I'll trust your judgment," said Greely. "Just don't tie me down like a criminal."

Hendrick entered the stateroom and pointed to a series of metal loops above Greely's bed, then down to more loops along the frame holding up the bed.

"That's not how it's done anymore," said Hendrick, kneeling down to access the lowest drawer under his bed. "We'll use something called a lee cloth, which is basically a fabric shield that connects to the overhead loops and secures to the edge of your bed—to keep you from rolling out. One on each side."

Hendrick pulled a dark-blue contraption from the drawer and went to work trying to figure it out.

"Sorry. First time rigging one of these," he said. "The first mate showed me where to find it."

"No worries," Greely said. "Hendrick?"

The man answered but kept working. "Yeah?"

"Keep a close eye on Furst. Both you and Rafe," said Greely. "I trust her, but I don't trust her. And we're about to enter uncharted waters. Pardon the pun."

"Pun appreciated," said Hendrick.

"I'm doubling your salary. Same with Rafe," said Greely. "And when we dock safely somewhere friendlier, I'll transfer a one-time bonus of three hundred thousand dollars to your account. One hundred to Rafe's."

"You don't have to do that, sir."

"I do," said Greely. "I've put you at odds with Furst, who controls Dragos's team."

"I see," said Hendrick. "I'll pull Rafe in close. Let him know the deal."

"Actually. He might be more useful interacting with the rest of the crew and security detail," said Greely. "Discreetly."

Hendrick nodded. "All right. I'll bring him up to speed."

"Thank you."

"You still have the MP5K?" asked Hendrick.

Greely patted the bulge in the blanket next to his right hip.

"We need to make sure you have quick access to that after I get you situated," said Hendrick. "If I'm not present, when anyone enters, assume they've either sold you out or come to kill you. If I am present, don't forget the distress code."

"Room service," said Greely.

"Exactly. You will never hear me utter those words unless you are in danger."

"Hopefully, it will be smooth sailing from here," said Greely. "Poor choice of words."

"Very poor, if you don't mind me saying," Hendrick said. "Once we get out of the bay, things are going to get shitty on board. Like nothing we've experienced before."

"Where will you be once we get out of the bay?" asked Greely.

"Sitting on my ass outside the door to your stateroom, with my feet planted against the deck."

The nearby gunfire continued, but it didn't sound any closer to the yacht.

CHAPTER 40

Someone had dragged Turner deep into the office and removed his tactical vest. He didn't really remember anything after stepping out of the office. His eyes came back into focus—on Jax, who was seriously invading his personal space. What the fuck had just happened? His vision was blurry, and his hearing wasn't right. The gunfire sounded more like a snare drum than sharp cracks.

"Jax," he said, barely able to hear his own words.

"Just stay down," she said, her voice muffled. "You got hit hard."

"What?" he yelled, his voice coming through a little more.

She put her head next to his and yelled in his ear. "You stepped outside and got fucking hammered by machine gun fire!"

"What happened to the shield?"

"The shield is the only reason you're still alive," said Jax. "But the wind took it."

Another familiar face appeared. Melendez. He was starting to come around.

"Is he okay?" asked Melendez.

"A bullet sliced through the side of his shin. Another grazed his left shoulder. Nothing critical."

Turner tracked all this. He lifted his left arm, the pain a seven on a one-to-ten scale but doable. There was nothing physically wrong with his shoulder.

"I'm good," he managed to say. "What the fuck happened?"

"They had a team on one of the smaller yachts tied up on the left side of the dock," said Melendez. "Lit us up—correction, lit *you* up the moment you stepped through the door. We managed to pull you back before they could finish you off. We've shredded that team, but there's another yacht across the canal that's keeping us pinned down. Another light machine gun. Mann's team is hunkered down along the northern side of this building, focused on the yacht and the dock lines. Our snipers can't see the shooters on the second yacht, so we're kind of stuck."

Turner was still having trouble focusing. Melendez leaned closer.

"You took two bullets to your helmet," he said.

Turner touched the top of his head. "Where's my helmet?"

"One of the bullets cracked. We tossed it. So don't stick your head out if you can help it," said Melendez. "Do you understand any of what I just said?"

"Yeah. I took a pounding. Probably have a concussion," said Turner. "No gunfire from *True American*?"

"He sounds good to—"

Jax never finished her sentence. She dropped on top of him, groaning. Melendez dragged them even deeper into the office, yelling "Sniper!" When they stopped, Melendez passed more details over the tactical net, which Turner could hear better over the gunfire.

"This is Melendez. Jax is down. Countersniper support requested," said Melendez. "Taking fire inside the marina office, suspected direction of incoming sniper fire estimated to be two-five-five-zero to two-eight-five-zero degrees from the back of the office. Range unknown, but I'm guessing it came from an elevated position, possibly a concealed topside location on *True American*. There are no other clear lines of sight."

Garza responded, "It didn't come from the yacht. We've been watching it closely. No heat blooms or indications of gunfire."

"This is Mann. Same. We've been keeping a close eye on the yacht."

"Then it has to be one of the apartment buildings to the west," said Melendez, pulling Jax off him, before frantically inspecting her for a gunshot wound.

Time wouldn't be on their side if she'd taken a midsection hit.

"We're looking," said Garza.

"Jax?" said Turner, grabbing her hand.

She mumbled something before Melendez flipped her on her stomach.

"She's good. Just got the wind knocked out of her," said Melendez. "Straight hit to her backplate. Good thing we didn't ditch them. Might need to see a chiropractor in a few days, though."

"Melendez. This is Mann. Do you need to get anyone medical attention?"

"Negative," said Turner, jumping onto the net. "I got my bell rung and Jax needs a chiropractor. Just don't stick your head out around the corner of the building until Brooklyn and Garza take out the sniper."

"And the yacht across the canal is still active," said Melendez. "They have some kind of light machine gun rocking the dock. I don't recommend breaking cover."

"The yacht engines have fired up," said Mann. "We don't have much time."

"We don't have many options with a light machine gun and sniper team goal-keeping the dock," said Turner. "Especially if we can't use the shields, which are definitely not an option in the open with this wind."

A sharp clang echoed through the office, lingering over the howling wind.

"Sofia is down," said Emily Miralles over the net. "Not down hard. Ricochet off the corner of one of the shields. Bullet fragments nailed her right forearm. She's going to need medical attention at some point relatively soon."

"Pull everyone well out of sight until the sniper is neutralized," said Mann.

"Shouldn't be long," replied Garza. "We caught a flash on thermal from the corner of the closest apartment building."

"I was supposed to say that," said Turner to Melendez.

"Say what?"

"The part about staying out of sight."

"You're still operating on two-bullets-to-the-helmet time," said Melendez.

"Maybe you should take over for now," said Turner. "Until I shake this off."

Melendez nodded, helping him to his feet. He stood for a few moments, feeling wobbly.

"Assault two, this is Turner. Melendez is in tactical control of the team until I say otherwise."

A bullet punched through the west-facing wall of the office, snapping by his unprotected head. A few inches to the left of his cranium, if he had to guess by the crack. Melendez yanked him down.

"Everyone hug the floor for now," said Melendez over the radio. "Mann. You might want to back your team up from the corner. They just put one right through the wall."

"Shouldn't be long now," said Garza. "The sniper is deep inside the room. Hard to see."

"I'd say take your time," said Mann, "but we're about to lose the yacht."

"AT4 time," said Turner. "One for the machine gun. One for *True American.*"

"Not a bad idea," said Mann.

"Hold off on that idea," said Gupta over the net. "I have two vans headed to the marina from the apartment complex."

CHAPTER 41

"What are you thinking?" asked Garza.

Brooklyn could barely hear him over the wailing wind and driving rain slapping against the tarp shelter they'd hastily assembled on the balcony. They'd created it the night before, by securing a heavy-duty tan canvas tarp to the bottom of the balcony railing and drilling thick anchors into the stucco about a foot and a half above the patio base to attach the tarp to the building. The hope was to create something that looked like hurricane preparation if someone ran a pair of binoculars over the apartment building.

Raised on the building side, it allowed them to crawl inside from the apartment and nestle under blankets made from materials designed to minimize their heat signature. They also wore full-body camouflage suits made from the same fabric. Before heading outside, they each took a quick shower in their suits at the same temperature as the rain, to further reduce any contrast between their body heat and the ambient environment.

The tarp contraption was far from waterproof, so they remained constantly soaked with air-temperature rain on the balcony, maintaining the heat differential long term. Still. Hurricanes brought in cooler air. Mid to high seventies. A full twenty-degree difference. As long as they concealed or contained most of that difference, the poor visibility would do the rest.

"I'm thinking that the shooter is lying flat on a bed or table about fifteen feet back from the slider. That's the only way the angle to the marina office works. They could be seated at a table or kneeling behind a chair, but they'd have to be draped with a thermal blanket, which would be a little awkward. But the flash definitely came from that height inside. I simply can't see the shooter, and we're almost forty-five degrees off angle. I'd have to shoot through the wall next to the slider."

"Nothing easy about this one," said Garza.

She ran the angles repeatedly in her head and kept coming to the same conclusion. The shooter was too far back in the room for a direct shot. The only way Mann was getting on that boat was for them to shoot through the wall to the right of the slider and try to force the sniper into moving or giving up on the position.

The sniper should know the shots came from a position high and to the left, unless the building material drastically altered the bullets' trajectories. Would the shooter take the bait? And if they did, would she be able to see them reposition, or would they stay concealed inside the apartment—taking their time to scope out every possible shooting position? She might never know until she saw the flash that ended her life, or Garza's.

"Would you be opposed to me trying to flush out the shooter with a few well-placed shots?" said Brooklyn. "Might get lucky and take one of them out. Assuming there are two of them."

"We might not know until—"

"They'll get one shot," said Brooklyn. "Get behind your rifle, just in case they get lucky. Let Mann know what we're doing and evacuate the apartment until this is settled."

"Mann. This is Garza. We're going to engage the sniper. We do not have a visual, but we have a plan. May or may not work. We'll keep the shooting to a minimum to avoid civilian casualties in the building."

"Copy. Happy hunting," said Mann.

"Gupta. Evacuate the apartment. Never know what they'll throw at us once we take a shot," Garza said.

"Give us ten seconds," said Gupta.

"I'm taking my earpiece out," said Brooklyn, removing the earbud from her right ear. "Keep yours in for updates."

"Yep," said Garza, before putting down the spotter scope and settling in behind his rifle.

"Range 960 feet," said Brooklyn. "Wind speed steady around thirty-six, coming from two-zero-zero degrees. A few gusts have come close to forty."

"Input applied," said Garza.

The digital thermal sights did all the elevation and windage calculations for them and adjusted the sight reticle. Other factors could come into play at longer ranges, but at roughly one thousand feet, it was a straightforward shot for the two of them. Even under these conditions. The bullets would take about a third of a second to reach the apartment building. With the sights exhaustively zeroed and the calculations made for them, she didn't anticipate being too far out of MOA.

"What's your aim point?" said Garza.

"About four feet up from the balcony deck and three feet to the right of the edge of the open slider," said Brooklyn. "First shot coordinated. Two more at your own pace."

She started to take steady, deep breaths.

"I'll go five feet up and four over," said Garza. "Ready."

Neither of them made another sound until Brooklyn started the countdown. They'd rehearsed this countless times.

"On three. Two . . ."

They counted in silence until both rifles barked simultaneously. Her bullet hit four inches left of where she aimed. The wind sweeping across the open water of the marina was stronger than what the gauge installed on the balcony indicated. She aligned her sight picture, accounting for the four inches and pressed the trigger again. Dead on. She repeated the process. Another sub-MOA shot. Garza fired the last shot, but only by about a half second. He was a little slower in general.

Neither one of them moved. Brooklyn put every bit of her focus on the thermal image in front of her. Ten times magnification was the best she could expect from even the most high-end thermal rifle sights. Anything higher than that, and the resolution went to shit. She caught temperature differential inside the apartment.

"Did you see that?" asked Brooklyn.

"Yeah. Looks like the shooter just repositioned," said Garza.

"Engage at will," said Brooklyn, a moment before the apartment across from the marina bloomed white.

She pressed the trigger—her reticle centered on the bloom. A second bloom lit up the apartment, but the shot shattered the far-left side of the balcony slider. A trigger twitch after the barrel shifted. They'd taken out the shooter. Hopefully, it was a one-person show.

"I hope that did it," she said, keeping focused on the apartment.

When Garza didn't answer, she took her eye off the scope for a moment. His head was face down in the thermal blanket under them, and a small red hole had replaced the ball cap that had been there moments ago. A dark basketball-size stain on the tarp above and slightly behind him dripped onto his back—but not from the rain.

Brooklyn replaced her earpiece and went back to the scope. Nothing else moved inside the apartment. But the shooter couldn't have been working alone. They'd identified Brooklyn and Garza's shooting position too quickly.

"Brooklyn. This is Mann. What are we looking at? We have vans inbound, and the yacht sounds like it's about to get underway."

"Garza is KIA," she said over the net. "Hostile sniper is down, but there's something else out there that I'm missing. Something doesn't add up."

She slowly scanned the other balconies and windows, looking for—son of a bitch, three apartments down. A barely cracked open slider and just enough of a heat signature to justify a shot. Probably not a trained spotter, but another machine gunner waiting for the dock assault. Saw their shots and reported them to the sniper. Dozens of blooms erupted from the opening. Bullets initially flew overhead, shattering the glass slider next to her, then they started to walk left—the gunner focused on the apartment. He had no idea there had been two snipers shooting from the balcony.

Brooklyn sighted in just above the flashes and pressed the trigger, the thermal fireworks exploding from the apartment coming to an abrupt stop.

"Mann. This is Brooklyn. They have people all over the place. I just took out a machine gunner on the second floor of the apartment building across from the marina," she said. "I'd rocket the fucking yacht and call it good. Still on overwatch."

"Copy that," said Mann, his voice sounding deflated.

"Gupta. I'm not sure how safe the apartment is right now," she reported.

"We're headed back in to help with Garza's body," said Gupta.

"Negative. I can't afford any distractions right now. We have people exposed on the ground," she said, fully aware how strange that must sound to everyone on the radio net.

But Brooklyn had blocked Garza out of her mind for now. Lives still depended on her.

CHAPTER 42

Mann cleared his mind. They could mourn the loss later.

"Gupta. Send Jess up the AT4s," he said. "This ends now. We'll hit the yacht with the machine gun and put one as close to the yacht's bridge as possible. Then try to board the boat."

"The vans just cut through the roundabout to the south," said Gupta. "They're headed right for the marina office. ETA one minute."

Mayer cut in. "We're set up across the street. If I send Bella with the AT4s, the vans will spot us here. Could complicate the situation."

"The situation is already complicated," said Mann. "Send her across and cover her."

He continued. "Gupta. Move Maria and Gloria into position to help with the vans and keep an eye on the approach from the motel, just in case we get a straggler or two. That should be more than enough firepower to keep the van reinforcements away, if not wipe them out completely. I need those AT4s now."

"Copy," said Gupta. "We're moving back into the apartment. I have better control from there."

Machine gun fire erupted from the third deck of *True American*'s stern, the bullets splintering the wood in front of and above Mann. The shooting stopped just as fast as it started.

"Machine gunner down," said Brooklyn. "But the back slider just opened. They could be crawling all over the third deck. I don't have any shots."

Bella arrived with the AT4s a few moments later, heavy automatic fire from the street behind them echoing off the trees and building. Mayer's and Maria's teams hopefully made short work of the security crew in the vans. He turned to Serrano, who crouched behind him along the wall. Javier and Wallace knelt next to her.

"Do you think there's any chance we can board that yacht?" said Mann.

Miles and Bilyk, whose rifles had been pointed at the stern of the yacht since they'd stopped along the wall, started firing short bursts—sparks exploding off *True American*'s railings at three or four points along the deck. Javier and the rest of the team joined them, shattering the stern's tinted-glass windows and sliders and punching holes in the fiberglass hull.

"This is a very exposed position," said Bilyk. "We're trying to keep their heads down, but it's just a matter of time before we take a beating."

"Mann. You need to pull back," said Brooklyn. "They're all over the stern. Every level now. Just popping up here and there. But not long enough for me to take an effective shot."

Serrano grabbed his arm. "This isn't going to work. We need to take cover and blow this yacht sky high."

"Start moving back to the street, but keep firing at the yacht," said Mann, snapping off shots as they backtracked along the side of the marina office. He slid by Bilyk, Miles, and Patillo, who had formed a human shield close to the corner of the building and were pumping burst after burst into the boat's stern. Miles dropped to a knee just as Mann was about to order the group to seek cover.

"Miles is hit," said Mann. "Get to cover. Now!"

Javier and Bilyk grabbed Miles and pulled him behind the corner of the building just as a torrent of automatic gunfire blazed from *True American*'s stern. The bullets skipped off the sidewalk and smacked into the corner board, pulverizing it. Bullets started to pass through the wall, forcing them even farther back.

"Mayer. This is Mann. We're pulling back. What's the situation with the vans?"

The two vans sat in the middle of the street, turned at angles, but the driving rain made it impossible to assess the situation. The last thing he wanted was to take fire from another direction.

"Handled," she said. "Maybe a few wounded to mop up."

"We're going to scuttle the yacht," said Mann. "Or at least fuck it up so bad, they can't get out of the canal."

"Sounds good to me," said Mayer.

A series of several explosions rattled the ground underneath his feet and shook the wall he leaned against. He scrambled to the corner of the building and risked a look; *True American*'s stern—consumed by billowing clouds of smoke—was no longer visible. At first, he thought Bella had somehow snuck away from him and fired the AT4s, but a quick look over his shoulder confirmed that she hadn't moved. And the smoke appeared to originate from the dock, pushed north by the winds to conceal the yacht.

"Brooklyn. What just happened?" asked Mann, peeking around the corner of the building.

"I think they blew the dock lines!" she said. "I saw several small explosions along the dock."

"What about the smoke?"

"I can't say for sure, but I think they threw a dozen or more smoke grenades onto the dock," said Brooklyn. "I can't see that side of the yacht."

"Is the yacht underway?" said Mann.

"It's definitely not where I saw it before the smoke screen started," she replied.

"Unload everything you have at the yacht," he said, raising his rifle and emptying his magazine into the fading shadow. "Everyone. Light that thing up!"

Tianna, Cook, and Wallace knelt next to the corner and started firing while gunfire erupted inside the marina office—Turner's team pounding the yacht with a combination of automatic and semiautomatic fire. Javier grabbed Mann's shoulder while he was reloading.

"Señor Mann!" said the former Mexican National Guard SWAT officer. "People live here! Every bullet that misses hits something else. We can barely see the boat anymore."

He was right. "Check fire! Check fire! All units check your fire and take cover!"

The dock went silent. Mann took it all in for a moment. The hull was barely visible through the smoke, which had started to dissipate.

"Bella! AT4! Now!" he said.

She appeared at his side like she'd been there the entire time.

"I'll do it," said Mann. "If I miss, it's on me."

Serrano spun him around and got so close, he could smell the cigarettes on her breath. "What's the effective range of an AT4 against a point target?"

"It's within range," said Mann.

He extended the shoulder stop, yanked himself out of her grip, and took a knee, placing the tube on his right shoulder. Next, he pulled the safety pin.

"Bella?" said Serrano. "Effective range against a point target?"

"Three hundred meters," said Bella. "Around one thousand feet."

Mann slid the cocking lever forward until it caught. All he had to do now was press the safety lever and the trigger button at the same time. He aimed at the rapidly disappearing silhouette down the ridiculously simplistic and presumably highly inaccurate iron sights. How hadn't this thing evolved to incorporate something better?

"Bella. How far away is the yacht?" asked Serrano.

"I can't tell."

"Mann. How far?" said Serrano.

"Don't give a shit," said Mann, depressing the safety lever.

"Bella. How many times have you fired one of these?"

"Three times. In training."

"Have you ever hit anything with it?" said Serrano.

"Negative."

"How close were the targets?"

"Two hundred meters," Bella said.

"What were the weather conditions?" said Serrano.

Dammit, Cata. Don't do this. The AT4 was their last chance. Even if he didn't disable the yacht with the rocket, he'd fuck it up enough that *True American* would probably hit the docks on the side of the pier and lose control.

"Desert conditions. Light wind."

"Garrett. The end of the pier is four hundred feet from here," said Serrano. "The yacht has been underway for nearly a minute now. The wind is almost forty miles per hour! It's out of effective range. You pull that trigger and the rocket will more than likely hit one of the condo buildings beyond the end of the canal. Kill a family hunkered down for the hurricane."

Mann activated his radio. "Brooklyn. What's your best guess of the range between me and the superyacht?"

"Seven hundred feet and picking up speed," she said.

"Thank you," said Mann, lowering the rocket launcher. "Where's Miles?"

"Bilyk and Cook are stabilizing him. A bullet punched through his right clavicle. No exit wound, so it deflected and went deeper into his chest. Bleeding is bad, but not arterial. He'll need medical attention very soon."

"Gupta. This is Mann. We need a medevac for Sofia and Miles. What are we looking at for trauma centers?"

"Already ahead of you on that," said Gupta. "The closest level one is in Tampa General, but it's across the bridges from St. Pete. I wouldn't risk that transit; plus, it's forty minutes away in normal conditions. Orlando Bayfront is a level-two trauma center. Ten minutes away."

"Contact Bayfront and let them know what's coming their way," said Mann. "One patient with a non-life-threatening bullet wound to the right forearm. One patient with a bullet wound to the right clavicle. Heavy bleeding. Bullet probably deflected into chest."

"Copy," said Gupta. "I just checked my police and emergency bands. Saint Petersburg is still sending out EMS. Nearest ambulance is three minutes away. Do you want me to place a 911 call?"

The last thing they needed was a police presence, but he wasn't willing to risk anyone's life to delay that.

"Yes. Call 911."

"I'll have O'Reilly make the call," said Gupta.

"Not a bad idea," said Mann, before turning to his team. "Now what? Steal one of these yachts and ram it?"

"I'm on board with that, if we can get one started," said Serrano.

"We can't," said Mann. "It's not that easy to get one of these things underway."

That got him thinking. "Smaller boats. Something that just takes a key to start—or someone who knows how to hot-wire a boat."

"I know how to hot-wire a boat," said Patillo, the former Mexican Navy SEAL. "We did it all the time."

That would work.

"Gupta. What's the nearest municipal marina? Nothing like this one. Nothing with yachts. We need Boston Whalers or smaller."

"You're not thinking about chasing them down in a hurricane . . ." said Gupta.

"That boat's next stop could be Cuba, for all we know," said Mann. "We'll either board it if possible or hit it with the AT4s and sink it."

"Board it?" said Gupta. "In this weather?"

"Not impossible," said Mann. "But I promise I'll sink it if we can't get on board."

"Checking on marinas—even if this is the stupidest idea I've ever heard," said Gupta.

"It's impossible in this weather," said Serrano.

"You coming or not?" said Mann. "We just need to get close enough to sink the boat."

"Of course I'm coming," said Serrano. "I can't fucking swim, but I'm still coming."

"That's why we brought the self-inflating life vests," said Mann.

"Somehow that doesn't make me feel better."

Gupta's voice came over the net. "O'Reilly's Marina. About one-point-two miles south of here. Google Maps shows some sailboats. But mostly speedboats and rigid-hull inflatables."

"That's perfect. We can board with the RHIBs and bring everyone else on board when we take the bridge and slow the boat down," said Mann.

An optimistic plan, to say the least.

"Assuming anyone else is up for your borderline-suicide mission," said Wallace.

"This is strictly voluntary," said Mann.

"Like any of us has a choice," said Wallace. "I'm in."

"Gupta. Can you put me on with everyone?" said Mann.

"Done," said Gupta.

"All stations. We have one last shot at the yacht," said Mann. "There's a marina about a mile from here with boats we can try to hot-wire. Being out there on a small boat won't be safe. In fact, it'll probably be the dumbest thing I've ever attempted in my life. But this is probably the last shot we'll have at either capturing or destroying DOMINION. I intend to board the yacht if we can steal the right kind of boats and have enough people to pull it off.

"If not, we'll take whatever we can out there and catch up to the yacht. Hit it with the two AT4s, toss every grenade we have on deck, and machine gun the shit out of it. If you're up for giving this a go, we'll meet on the road along the north side of the Marina Walk apartment building. Give us a little shelter from the wind. Time is critical. So make your choice and make your way over. Bring all vehicles to that rendezvous point. And I'm serious when I say this: If you don't want to continue with this insanity, I completely understand.

"Is anyone not in?" he said to Assault One, which was huddled around him. "You absolutely do not have to do this."

"DOMINION at the bottom of the bay is nice," said Wallace. "DOMINION in our hands and True America fucked for good sounds even nicer."

Everyone indicated they were still on board.

"Turner. What's the verdict in there?" said Mann over the net.

"The only question I got so far is—where are the life jackets?" said Turner.

"They're in the back of our SUVs," said Mann.

Maria and Gloria dashed across the street to meet up with him, arriving at the same time as Mayer and Neva.

"We're in," said Maria.

Mayer gave him a thumbs-up. "I'm good. But Neva is terrified of drowning. We all are, but I think this is something different."

Mann approached Neva and put a hand on her shoulder. "That's totally fine. I need someone to look after Sofia and make sure she gets the medical help she needs. I'm going to bring someone down from the apartment to help make those arrangements."

"I'm sorry," said Neva. "I've never been on a boat before in my life. I can't."

"No need to explain. You did more than what was asked of you," said Mann, before triggering his radio. "Turner. I'm sending Neva in to watch over Sofia and Miles until the ambulance arrives."

"We're at the streetside door," said Turner, before stepping onto the sidewalk.

Miralles followed, guiding Sofia out. Neva and Serrano made their way over, talking faster than he could understand.

"Mann. This is O'Reilly. I'm headed down to the marina. I'll run interference when the ambulance and police arrive. Brooklyn is headed down."

"I'll keep you posted. Sorry for the mess," said Mann.

"Wouldn't be ARTEMIS without one," said O'Reilly.

"All right. Let's move out," said Mann. "A boat that big will have to proceed slowly in the bay to avoid navigation hazards. We might have a chance to hit them before they reach open water."

Doubtful. But if he told them they were more than likely headed into the Gulf of Mexico, they'd undoubtedly have second thoughts.

CHAPTER 43

Clara Furst steadied herself, moments before the yacht slammed into the northern wall of the canal. The near-forty-mile-per-hour winds out of the southwest were just too much for the captain to effectively compensate for in the 110-foot-wide canal. The yacht spanned nearly a third of that width, its tall superstructure acting like a sail. The captain had been realistic about the situation. He'd spent about ten seconds bitching about how a yacht this large was oversize for that marina, before just getting down to the bottom line. If they made it out of the canal without sustaining significant waterline damage, they should be fine.

But transiting the four-thousand-foot canal would take more than just skill—it would take luck. The fewer heavy gusts, the better, and there was no predicting how many of those they'd experience. The captain kept them on a mostly steady course down the middle of the canal—until a heavy wind gust hit and the yacht suddenly veered to starboard. The captain seemed unable to slow the inevitable crash into the northern wall.

The result of each gust was different. Most just brushed them against the small docks extended into the canal, sweeping them away. Some felt far more serious, like this one. The yacht eased back into the center of the canal, the gust having died down.

"How much longer can we sustain this?" asked Furst.

"We're two-thirds of the way to open water," said the captain. "I have the entire crew on the starboard-side lower decks, looking for water intrusion. Nobody has reported any leakage or damage."

"Fingers crossed," said Furst. "And we'll be fine in the Gulf?"

"Yes. Unless we sustain unusual structural damage leaving the canal," said the captain. "We'll be headed directly into the waves and wind at first, which is actually ideal for this boat. We then have a choice: Sail down the coast of Florida, which will get us out of the wind and waves quicker—the hurricane has already passed Tampa. Or continue on a more southwesterly course. The advantage of the southwesterly course is that we'll keep sailing into the seas. If we turn south along the coast, we'll experience quartering seas, which is the most uncomfortable ride possible."

Maybe that would keep Greely and his bodyguards under the weather long enough for her to swipe this whole thing out from under him. The last report from belowdecks had Hendrick, Rafe, and Greely emptying their stomachs into bags for the past two hours.

"I say we turn south outside of the bay," said Furst. "Key West. Then somewhere outside of the US. The people hunting us have very limited reach overseas."

"The seas are going to get miserable."

"I don't get seasick," she said. "I feel tired but not nauseous."

"Same. That's a rare trait. One in about three hundred people," he said. "My first mate would be doubled over by now."

"I haven't seen her," said Furst. "Is she below with the others?"

"No. She's on the starboard bridgewing," said the captain. "Took a bullet in the right temple when she went out to make sure we were clear on that side when we decided to get underway."

The snipers. There had been two of them up there on the balcony. Kali Chandra, the mercenary sniper Greely had hired, had reported only one. They were lucky to have escaped the dock. Mann had been watching them for a while, waiting for the right moment. Except this time, she had been in charge of the overall security posture, which had made all the difference. What she couldn't control was the weather, which appeared to be the only factor that could prevent their escape.

"Another gust," said the captain.

She saw it before it hit the yacht, the water ahead of them spraying from the force of the squall. The yacht heeled to starboard, once again headed for the canal's concrete seawall. This time, they barely scraped the wall, only taking out the protruding docks.

"Getting the hang of this," said the captain. "We're almost there. I can see the end of the canal. The last challenge will be shooting through the Delgado Memorial Bridge pass. It's about seventy-five feet wide, flanked by concrete bumpers. But we'll mostly be facing into the wind, so it shouldn't be so bad. We'll keep the bumpers attached to the port-side. If we get nudged by the wind while transiting under the bridge, they should be enough to soften the blow. After that, we're clear."

CHAPTER 44

Anish Gupta wasn't sure what to do at this point. He sat in an apartment he'd rented using an untraceable bank account, with Garza's body, which was wrapped loosely in a tarp. A shattered balcony slider let gallons of water pour in by the minute—the tarps stapled to the ceiling and 2x4s flapping like Saran Wrap. A few dozen bullet holes in the west-facing wall, at least three of them punched through the widescreen TV in front of the sectional couch. Two of his four screens had also been perforated by a bullet or two.

Not to mention the damage to the rest of the apartment. Overall, not exactly what he had been hoping for. Mann passed along a report, which he acknowledged. Sirens cut through the wind and driving rain. The marina was about to become radioactive for anyone not carrying an FBI badge.

"Mann's on the road to the marina. So what now?" said Gupta. "Do we stay, or do we go?"

Berg shrugged. "Now that the police are all over the place, I'm not sure it's a good idea to get on the road."

"You think?"

"No need to get nasty," said Berg. "We've taken everything in from the balcony."

"You mean the dead body," said Gupta.

"Anish. Please. We've been here before. This isn't my first rodeo," Berg said. "The shattered slider will look like normal hurricane damage.

The bullet holes on the outside won't attract any attention until the storm has completely passed and the rain stops, which could be twelve to twenty-four hours from now. I say we lay low and keep the lights dim. Help Mann however we can. O'Reilly is on the ground. You know her better than I do. She knows the stakes here for all of us."

"Maybe I should head down there to lend her a hand," said Audra Bauer. "I still have government credentials."

"CIA credentials?" asked Berg. "That'll complicate things."

"Fucking right about that," muttered Bauer.

"And what about Garza?" said Gupta.

"Garza is gone," said Bauer.

"No. How do we get his body out of here?" said Gupta. "We're not the only people staying here. Once the storm dies down, people will start moving around."

"We can take the body down right now and put it in one of the trunks."

Nobody said a word.

"I'm just being realistic. We obviously can't report this. The official removal of his body by the city or county coroner will generate unanswerable questions, which I won't be around to answer," said Berg. "He's licensed as a private detective and armed security bodyguard in California. We can't say we were all just sitting here on vacation watching TV when bullets ripped through the walls."

"All right. Let's get him down to one of our vehicles," said Gupta. "Audra? Any input?"

"I agree with Karl. We also need to take everything that was on the balcony with us. The rain and wind will clean up whatever is left," said Bauer, before glancing around the apartment. "Is there any reason for us to stay?"

"Ideal radio communications capability with the task force," said Gupta. "The higher the antennas, the better. Then again, we could just switch the whole thing over to satellite comms and head over to the rental houses."

"In this weather?" said Bauer. "It'll work, but maybe not as well as the radios."

Gupta knew she was right. Satellite communications worked in cloudy conditions, just not as well as clear skies. Normally not a big issue, since radios had their limitations, too. But the hurricane had brought more than just an overcast day. It had dragged in cloud layers thirty to forty thousand feet thick, along with dense rain, which caused "rain fade," where the water droplets absorbed the radio waves.

"We should stay here for now," said Gupta. "There's no telling what kind of support Mann might need."

CHAPTER 45

Garrett Mann squeezed the stainless-steel roll bar above his head with both hands to keep himself upright while he did the grim math. Wind gusting to forty miles per hour, sideways rain, punishing seas, and near-zero visibility. Not exactly a recipe for success. But what choice did they have? If the superyacht escaped and somehow survived the hurricane, it would unleash a far more dangerous storm across the nation. A storm unlike anything America had seen before.

The combined speed of the boats and gale-force wind drove the raindrops into their faces. Fortunately, their skin exposure was minimal. But the few areas of unprotected skin under the goggles and just above the tactical-vest neck sleeve took a beating. Like hundreds of tiny pebbles stinging their skin.

They'd considered wearing a Gore-Tex outer layer, but Patillo and Ripley, the task force's former Navy SEALs, had told them that the gear would be rendered useless within minutes on the water in these conditions—just an extra layer of clothing hindering their movement. Good advice, given that Mann felt about thirty pounds heavier from the water, which had soaked him to the skin at this point.

He glanced to his left and right, only able to see the closest boat on each side. To his left, a rigid-hull inflatable and, on the right, an open-cabin speedboat. Two more boats, one an inflatable and the other a speedboat, were out there somewhere—hopefully close by. They'd commandeered five vessels from a nearby marina, all of them now speeding recklessly in what he hoped was some semblance of a line toward the yacht's stern light, which appeared as a dim green orb through his night vision. Barely. The driving rain rendered his night vision goggles nearly useless, blurring his view of the light they desperately needed to follow.

He wasn't sure how this plan would work. The superyacht sped due south at cruising speed, which was around eighteen knots, or twenty miles per hour, trying to muscle through the dirty side of the hurricane headed for the Florida Panhandle. With their primary plan stopped cold at the top of the pier by the yacht's security detachment, they'd scrambled to launch a Hail Mary plan. Chasing the 160-foot yacht into a rapidly strengthening hurricane, on five boats "borrowed" from a nearby marina. All five boats having no business being out in this kind of weather. Mann triggered his radio.

"All teams. We're about a hundred meters out. Maintain formation until we've almost reached the back of the boat. We'll shift to a column formation at that point, with Alpha One, Two, and Three in the lead."

Alpha meaning "assault." The three four-operator teams would do the dirty work on board. He still wasn't sure exactly how they would board the yacht. Jump from the bows of each small boat onto the aft deck, leaving the drivers behind? Run the boats onto the aft deck and debark everyone? The yacht's generously wide, sea-level aft deck was designed to allow wave runners to drive right onto the stern platform. That way, they wouldn't leave anyone behind. He presumed they'd need everyone to pull this off.

"Sierra One and Two will then flank the vessel and clear the decks ahead of the assault teams," said Mann.

The "Sierra" designation identified the support boats filled with light machine gunners and sharpshooters, who would do their best to take down any threats trying to prevent the assault teams from reaching the yacht's bridge. The key was to take the bridge as fast as possible. With the bridge under their control, they could slow down the boat and bring necessary team members from the two support vessels on board. The rest would be a cleanup job. A potentially bloody one—but at least the yacht would be under his task force's control. Along with the DOMINION command center, the crown jewel of their operation. With DOMINION shut down, the nation had a chance to return to some semblance of normalcy.

"We have a problem!" said Javier, who was driving Mann's boat.

"What's up?" said Mann, moments before seeing the problem for himself.

The rightmost boat in their line had sped ahead and crossed in front of the formation. *What the fuck?* The inflatable boat appeared as a dark blob on the water, the two infrared chem-lights attached to its stern giving Mann his only orientation. They'd tied the chem-lights to the back of each vessel, unobservable to the yacht, in case the boat's security detachment was using night vision gear.

"Alpha Three. Get back in formation. We're still—"

The boat hit a wave, its bow rising dramatically upward—a sudden wind gust catching it at the worst possible moment and flipping the boat over, dumping its crew of five before the craft landed open-side down in the water.

"Slow down!" said Mann to Javier, before ordering the entire formation to slow to bare steerageway—just enough to maintain control of their boats.

"We don't have time for this!" said Serrano from the bow as the boat decelerated.

"We don't have a choice! Ten people are not enough to take the yacht!"

A few seconds later, his boat glided past the upended RHIB. No survivors bobbed on the surface. *Jesus.* Had they just lost a third of their assault team—including Turner, who was irreplaceable? Or was it simply too dark to see them in the rough water? His night vision didn't pick any of the life vest strobes, and he didn't dare activate a flashlight, which could alert the lookouts on the yacht. Had they miscalculated how much weight the vests could float?

"Turn us around!" said Mann, and the boat turned hard to port a few moments later.

As Javier slowly approached the capsized boat, the survivors popped up one by one—their water-activated life vests finally dragging them to the surface. He counted three flashing strobe lights. There should have been four.

"Let's start fishing them out of the water!" said Mann.

Javier nodded, easing the boat alongside the closest survivor. Mann and Serrano pulled Patillo on board, followed by Bella, before they motored about thirty feet to drag Bilyk onto the boat. Mann searched the turbulent water. Still no Turner. Shit. They really needed him. Or did they? Miralles and Melendez, plus some of the former Mexican SWAT and Special Forces operatives, had worked miracles before.

"What happened to Turner?" he asked after they dragged Bilyk on board.

"I'm fine. Thanks for asking!" said Bilyk. "He sank like a brick. Insisted on carrying twice the necessary ammunition."

"Fuck!" said Mann. "He has to be here somewhere."

Someone grabbed his vest and spun him around. Serrano. She held him by two hands, the wind buffeting the two of them.

"We need to move—now!" she said.

Wallace protested, "We can't just leave him. He could still be out here."

"Look around!" said Serrano. "He's gone."

She was right. And Turner wasn't mission critical. They had the talent necessary to execute the mission without him. Maybe. Perhaps this was less about Turner's skills . . . and more about the fact that he was one of the last original members of ARTEMIS who had survived to this point. Not a small accomplishment, given what they'd faced over the past year. That, and the fact that Turner had exceeded Mann's expectations. Turner's career had been marred by one misstep after another, despite performing far above his peers. Mann had been skeptical of him at first, but Turner had proven himself beyond any doubt. It killed Mann to move on without him, but the mission came first.

"Let's go!" said Mann, slapping Javier's shoulder.

Before he could contact the other boats, a familiar gravelly voice cut through the wind.

"Are you fucking serious? You were going to leave me behind?"

Turner pulled himself halfway up the starboard-side tube as the boat picked up speed. He coughed and gagged while Mann and Serrano grabbed him before he could slip back into the water. They hauled him on board, Mann noting that Turner had ditched all his vest-mounted ammunition magazines, his rifle, and a spare bag that had contained additional magazines—along with a mix of fragmentation and flash-bang grenades.

"How long were you under?" asked Mann.

Turner hacked up some seawater before answering.

"Too long. Fucking ammo kept me about ten feet below. Had to ditch most of it. The vest kept me from sinking to the bottom."

"At least you kept your pistol," said Mann, patting his shoulder.

"Funny. A lot of good that'll do me," said Turner.

"We have plenty of spare rifles," Mann said. "What happened out there?"

"Bottom line? My Spanish is shit," said Turner. "I said something and pointed toward the stern. The rest is history. Watch your speed. The faster you go, the higher the waves lift the bow. We took a gust and—end of story."

"I don't think we have a choice at this point. They've pulled too far away," said Mann, turning to Serrano. "Tell Javier to max out our speed."

"Is that a good idea?" asked Serrano.

"No. It's not. But conditions are getting worse by the minute, and the less time we spend on the water, the better," said Mann. "I've already added at least another five minutes to our pursuit, and now we're carrying twice the cargo."

"You should have kept going," said Turner.

"I know," said Mann. "Let's just hope I didn't make too big of a mistake rescuing your ass."

PART V

CHAPTER 46

Brooklyn steadied her rifle as best she could. No easy task under the circumstances. Almost impossible, to be honest, but she'd try her best. She'd rigged latex surgical tubing between the folded Bimini stanchions above the driver to support her rifle, the flexibility somewhat minimizing the constant up-and-down beating taken by the Boston Whaler. If she'd placed the rifle against one of the stanchions or the hull, she'd be completely at the whim of the boat's wild movements.

The elevated position also helped. It kept her on two legs, which also served to slightly dampen the boat's movement. Between the tubing rig and flexing her knees, she was able to keep the stern of the boat in her thermal sight as their flotilla of four boats rapidly closed the distance. She identified one heat signature on the sea deck and had seen a few on the third deck, portside, earlier in the approach.

"This is Brooklyn. I have one target on the sea deck," she said. "No sign we've been detected, but it won't be long."

"This is Mann. I can barely see the yacht through night vision, so we probably have a little more wiggle room if you need us to close the distance for the shot."

"It's not going to be a shot," said Brooklyn. "I'll be lucky to hit the target using a full magazine."

"Whatever it takes," said Mann. "Let me know the moment the target is down. We're gonna go full throttle and try to board. If boarding is not possible for whatever reason, your boat is going to speed along the starboard side and hit it with machine guns and both AT4s. Frank's boat will head down the portside tossing grenades. One way or the other, the *True American* is done."

"Copy that," she said, before patting their driver, Callie Jackson, on the shoulder. "Bring us up a bit!"

"You got it!" said Jax, the boat pushing forward a little faster.

Brooklyn didn't bother with any breathing exercises. Even inside the yacht's relatively smoother wake, the constant fifteen- to twenty-foot swells made this more of a dexterity-and-luck game than anything else. Distance didn't matter at a few hundred feet. The bullet drop would be nearly nonexistent. Windage was anyone's guess, so she'd zeroed it out. All she hoped to do was put one or two bullets center mass in the target. Enough to take them down and keep them down. Ideally preventing them from raising the alarm.

Most of the rotating dock and yacht security wore stripped-down plate carriers, outfitted with a half dozen rifle magazines, over civilian clothes. No helmets. They'd been trying to maintain a low profile in a densely populated area. The plate carriers were specifically designed to protect against center-mass shots.

But they protected the chest only, plus a little bit of the lower midsection. She just needed to slip one under or above the plate. Even a direct hit to the plate with one of her armor-piercing rounds would suffice. If the plate was latest generation, it would prevent the round from passing through, but it would knock the target flat.

She took as much pressure off the trigger as she dared, given the boat's erratic movement, and waited for the crosshairs to glide across the human-shaped signature. The rifle bucked once. Nothing. The target barely reacted. She readjusted her aim and pressed the trigger again. Definitely got their attention that time. *Need to speed this up.* Six more shots in rapid succession did the trick. The target stumbled forward and fell into the water. *That one was for you, Garza. More to come.*

"Target neutralized," said Brooklyn. "Sea deck is clear!"

"Nice job!" said Mann. "Support boats, slow down and let the assault boats pass. Once we're clear, start moving up along your assigned side. Frank to port. Jax to starboard. Hang back until I give the order. Then hit the throttle and start clearing targets on the decks."

Two smaller boats raced forward, forming a column, as Jax slowed the Boston Whaler. Brooklyn didn't care which option played out, just as long as they killed everyone involved with True America on board.

CHAPTER 47

Serrano muttered a quick prayer as the distance between their small boat and the yacht's aft sea deck closed. Mann had briefly explained the process to Javier, who quickly crossed himself before nudging the throttle forward. They'd needed to time the swells. The yacht's wake cut down on the rough chop, and its sleek design seemed to plow through the rolling seas, but the stern still slightly rose and fell with each swell.

They wanted to slide the boat onto the sea deck when it dropped slightly below the waterline. If they timed it wrong, the front of their boat would hit the side of the deck, when it lifted a few feet above the sea. They wouldn't be moving fast enough to significantly damage the boat, but the situation out here had proven to be anything but predictable. Mann said they'd try twice before giving up and disabling the ship with the rocket launchers.

He'd somewhat come to his senses when it came to using the rocket launchers. Gupta had examined the yacht's schematics and identified a way to disable it without sinking it and possibly killing everyone on board. The crew members likely had nothing to do with True America. Greely had probably inherited them from McCall when AXIOM owned the yacht.

With the yacht disabled, *True American*'s captain would have no choice but to call the Coast Guard—according to Gupta. If they didn't, the yacht would eventually be pushed back to the coast by the winds, where a wide range of fates awaited it. Anything from a simple grounding to a very messy capsizing in shallow water. And the Coast Guard would respond regardless. They were probably tracking the yacht right now, hoping they wouldn't have to send one of their cutters out in this mess to rescue some clueless billionaire. If the yacht started sailing erratically or heading straight, they'd more than likely respond even without a distress call.

The downside to disabling and not seizing the vessel hadn't been lost on any of them. Months of grueling work and dozens of tragic sacrifices—measured in body bags—would be diminished by an anticlimactic end. The overall mission would still succeed. DOMINION, for the most part, would be stopped. The sicarios would still be out there with some version of running orders that would undoubtedly terrorize the nation, but True America would no longer be directly pulling those strings and fraudulently guiding the American electorate. Maybe that would be enough.

Maybe US federal law enforcement agencies and their Department of Justice could collect enough evidence from LABYRINTH, AXIOM, and the True America–directed killings of over two dozen FBI agents, to expose the links between them all before the election. She got the feeling Mann wasn't too confident in that outcome, or they wouldn't be trying to board the yacht in a hurricane.

Mann turned to her, the two of them at the bow of the RHIB. "You don't jump until I slap you on the back. We go together. Got it?"

"I'm not going anywhere without you!" she said, the sea deck rapidly approaching.

"Slow down!" yelled Mann over his shoulder, giving Javier a frantic hand signal.

Everyone else crouched. Turner and Patillo were right behind them. The other three were behind Javier. Mann warned them they might have to do this twice to get everyone on board, unless they got lucky. He shifted slightly to address everyone packed into the bow.

"As soon as we get on board, our number-one priority is to take out all the slack on the ropes and tie them to the nearest cleat. If the boat starts to slip back before we tie the lines—let go of the line. You will not win a tug-of-war contest with the water. They'll just have to make another approach."

Everyone nodded, and Serrano tightened her grip on the thick line in her hand, the rest of the line neatly coiled in a nylon bag attached to the inflated rubber tube next to her. The other end was attached to a D ring located along the starboard exterior of the inflatable tube. The yacht's stern rose for a few seconds, before beginning to drop.

"Now! Now!" yelled Mann.

The RHIB lurched forward, the distance between the sea deck and bow decreasing at an alarming pace. Just when she had become certain that Mann had miscalculated the burst of speed, the sea deck dropped out of sight and the boat hard-skidded onto the sea deck and tipped to starboard—its V-shaped hull more than halfway on the yacht's deck.

The sudden and unexpected tilting thoroughly disrupted the boarding plan. Serrano and Patillo, crouched along the starboard-side tubes, hopped effortlessly onto the skid-free deck. Mann and Turner tumbled off-balance, crawling off instead of trying to regain their footing. The boat started to slip back into the water, gaining momentum as the seawater rushing along the aft section of the RHIB tugged along the hull. Javier stayed at the helm console as the other three rushed forward, trying to beat the clock.

Time wasn't in their favor. They got into the bow section just as the stern rose and the boat slipped back into the Gulf of Mexico. Mann wasted no time contacting Javier over the radio.

"Javier. Nice job. I'll guide you in for another run," said Mann. "If you can't safely make it off, just fall in line behind one of the support boats. We'll get you on board once we take the bridge."

"Copy," said Javier. "Lining up for another run."

"I'll guide you in," said Mann, before turning to Serrano and the others. "Cata. Turner. Watch the stairways leading down to this deck. It looks like we took out their camera during the firefight on the dock, but there's no reason to take any risks."

"I'll take the starboard side," said Serrano, unslinging her rifle.

The yacht pitched and rolled uncomfortably, but she'd never been more relieved in her life. Even the upcoming fight through the yacht was preferable to spending another minute on that boat on the open ocean, in the middle of a hurricane.

CHAPTER 48

Mann grew more nervous by the moment, and not because of the boardings. Javier had shrewdly backed off from his second attempt, Mann's timing of the sea deck's rise and fall off just enough to prevent the RHIB from sliding onto the yacht. His next attempt was flawless, the boat tipping like before, but everyone was ready for it. The first three off grabbed Javier as the RHIB slid into the Gulf of Mexico, uncrewed.

His real fear was the onboard security detail. The guard assigned to the sea deck had tumbled into the sea, taking his radio with him. For all Mann knew, the yacht's security force had already assembled on both sides of the ship and inside the engine room, the only other way to access the sea deck from the inside. He'd considered sending a small team through the engine room and up into the yacht, but they would have to navigate tight passages to get anywhere in the boat.

He'd rather rally his assault teams on the bridge and move in a coordinated way from there, keeping Gupta and Lianez down here with a protective detail—mostly out of harm's way until the entire yacht was taken. His assault teams would have to split up at some point. One heading to the bow, where the largest stateroom was located. Presumably Greely's. The other heading aft to locate the DOMINION operations center.

Further complicating matters, he'd have to leave at least four members of the task force on the bridge. One to guard each exterior door to the bridge. One to control the captain. And another to watch the hatch leading from the bridge to the interior of the ship, in case any of Greely's people slipped by the teams Mann had sent below.

Ripley drove his RHIB right onto the sea deck, all four on board his boat requiring no assistance to hop onto the yacht before their boat slipped back into the water. He sent Ripley to watch the hatch leading to the engine room beyond the wave runner and rubber dinghy secured in the sea deck hangar.

"Any movement near the stairways?" he asked over the radio.

Both Serrano and Turner reported *all clear*. Now the harder part, if that were possible. He'd thought it through as best he could while being tossed and turned for thirty minutes as they caught up to the yacht. Based on the yacht schematics, the layout was fairly simple. They'd all studied it prior to heading to the dock. But things tended to go sideways or skew in your head when your life was on the line. He reoriented them very quickly and split them into the groups they had discussed previously.

Two teams. One moving forward and up to the bridge on each side of the yacht. Unfortunately, he'd have to leave Mayer by herself on the stern. Once they took control of the bridge and slowed *True American*, the support boats could pull alongside the side of the sea deck and offload. Mayer would remain on the stern, but she'd have company.

"You good?" he said to Mayer.

"I'm a big girl now. I can take care of myself," said Mayer, mocking him. "I'll stay by the engine room door. If anyone comes down the exterior stairs, they're headed for the dinghy. If they come through the door, they're either going for a dinghy or trying to flank you. I got this."

"That's what I thought," said Mann, before handing her a rough canvas satchel the size of a high schooler's backpack. "You use this only if I, Turner, or Serrano tell you to. It's a fail-safe option."

He activated his flashlight, momentarily blinding them.

"Sorry," said Mann. "But I really need you to see this."

When her eyes adjusted, she recognized what she was holding.

"A satchel charge?" said Mayer.

"Modified for the modern battlefield," said Mann. "Pull the safety pin here. Open this patch and check the bright-orange digital display. It should say *Armed.* Yank the fuse handle here and the display should say *Get Clear of Device.* It's crude, but field-tested. Ten-second fuse, so just jump off the back of the boat and the support boat will pick you up."

"Who's staying out there?" asked Mayer.

"Brooklyn and Maria," said Mann. "If the charge doesn't stop the yacht, they will."

"Jesus," she said.

"If I ask you to use this, we've exhausted all other options," said Mann.

"What about the rockets?"

"We need to be sure," Mann said. "It took one of the best snipers I've ever seen several shots to hit a human-size target in these swells. Firing rockets? Sounded good in the briefing. Not so sure now that we're out here in the thick of this. If I pass the order after the support boats off-load, do your best to convince everyone to jump off the back and blow the engine room."

"Got it," said Mayer, before unslinging her rifle and giving it a quick once-over. "Better get moving."

He patted her on the shoulder before giving the order to move out. His team formed up on the starboard side, moving up to Serrano, who joined the stack when they reached her. Mann led them slowly up the stairs, the starboard side mercifully shielded from the winds. Turner's team would have one hell of a time pushing up the portside. The exterior walkway along the main deck appeared clear to the next stairway. The only real concern was the completely blacked-out windows running along the walkway.

Gupta had done some research. If the lights were on inside, they would not be visible due to the fishbowl effect. If the lights were out, an observant sentry might notice them, but it was unlikely. Visibility across the water was extremely limited due to the hurricane, the lights of Tampa barely detectable at this point. It was nearly pitch black out.

"Stay as low as possible," said Mann over the net, leading them about forty feet to the next stairway.

Time for a little insurance policy. "Support One and Two. Move into position alongside. All assault team members, snap your IR glow sticks."

The glow sticks would identify them as friendlies to the machine gunners using night vision sights.

CHAPTER 49

Seth Payne was ready to call it a night. He'd already puked twice in the trash bag he kept nearby, his legs barely able to support him. He sat slumped in the captain's chair, resentful that the man didn't appear the least bit bothered by the rolling and pitching sea.

"This doesn't bother you at all?" he asked.

The captain glanced at him. "The storm?"

"No. The smell of my vomit," said Payne.

"Neither bothers me," said the captain.

"Is that why you chose to be a boat captain?"

"No. Actually, I found that out later," he said. "I used to crew cargo ships. Big and small. Container ships. Worked my way up to captain. I'm not saying this doesn't bother me. I would love nothing more than to lay down and pass out. But I just don't get sick. As in—"

"Let me demonstrate," said Payne, before launching what little was left in his stomach into the trash bag.

"As in that," said the captain.

"Well. Lucky you," said Payne. He checked his watch.

Time to check in with the rest of the security shift. The contract group had turned out to be less than competent. Rogues with guns. Contemptible shits overall.

"Sea deck. This is the bridge," said Payne. "How are we looking back there?"

No reply. Fucker was probably fast asleep. He hated working with contract security. That said, their job back at the dock hadn't been half bad, despite the fact that the other half of them got bushwacked at the motel. Not a single one of them had made it to the dock. He wasn't sure if that was a testament to the competency of the crew that took them down or an indication of their uselessness. It didn't matter now. They'd cleared the bay. It was nothing but smooth sailing from here on out. Well. Not exactly *smooth*.

"Sea deck. Come in," said Payne.

No response.

"Son of a bitch," said Payne.

The security officer standing on the starboard side of the bridge took his mouth off his puke bag for moment.

"Want me to head back to check on Stan?" he asked, his words sounding slurred.

Payne couldn't remember all the contract security officers' names. He assumed Stan was the lookout assigned to the back of the yacht.

He nodded. "If he's asleep, take over his post and send his ass up here."

"Got it, boss," said the man, before opening the door and disappearing into the night.

Several seconds later, as he started to doze off, Payne thought he heard gunfire. Or was it thunder? He was no expert on storms, but this one hadn't produced the kind of thunderstorms he expected from a hurricane. Not that he knew much about hurricanes. Knowing what he knew now, he'd have passed on this job if he'd known this was the start of hurricane season—and the job involved being permanently stationed on a yacht.

"Is the storm picking up?" mumbled Payne.

"What do you mean?" asked the captain.

"I just heard thunder."

"We're inside the thunderstorm band," said the captain. "Just wind and nasty sea conditions for now. I think maybe something came loose and slapped against the side of the yacht. No point in worrying about it now. We'll make repairs in port."

"No thunder?" said Payne.

"None."

What was the name of the security guy he'd sent aft to check on Stan? Chris. Yes. Chris. And how long had it been since he'd left? No idea, but it felt too long.

"Chris. This is Payne. Any update on Stan?" he said over the radio.

No response.

"Intraship communications are still up, right?"

The captain examined the sweeping digital screen in front of him. "Affirmative. No issues at all, from what I can tell."

"Chris. Stan. This is Payne. On the bridge. Report your status."

Again, nothing. Something was off. And even if everything was fine—fuck these contractors. He'd teach them a lesson. Mind your own, or everyone suffers.

"All Helon security personnel," he said over the net. "Head aft along the exterior walkways to the stern. Wake up Stan. If you run across Chris along the way, send him to the bridge."

Warm and toasty days were over for that group.

CHAPTER 50

Maria sat in the stern of the Boston Whaler, the most stable position on the most unstable platform she'd ever operated from. She'd identified Mann's team on the main deck, their IR glow sticks poking through the driving rain. They waited at the bottom of the stairwell leading to the upper deck and the bridge for clearance to proceed. She's just gunned down a single sentry headed aft, with Brooklyn's help.

"How are we looking?" said Mann.

"Brooklyn?" said Jax, who drove the boat.

Brooklyn's thermal sight had proven to be the most useful item on board their boat. Maria could only identify friendlies using night vision. Brooklyn could see everyone.

A bright light appeared one deck above them, about ten feet forward of the stairwell. A few figures emerged from what she assumed to be a doorway. Number unknown. The door shut and complete darkness enveloped the deck again. An IR laser reached out from the boat, clearly visible through the night vision sight attached to her light machine gun.

"Maria. This is Brooklyn. Same deal. Short bursts where I point the laser."

"Sí, señorita," she said, sighting in on the laser's end point and pressing the trigger.

"Target down. Shifting," said Brooklyn.

Another burst.

"Second target down. One more out there!" said Brooklyn. "They took cover behind the bulwark. Your bullets will punch right through that fiberglass, so we just need to give this a second or two. They'll poke their head up soon enough—there!"

She fired two long bursts where the IR laser was aimed.

"Third target down," said Brooklyn. "Caught a quick thermal bloom indicating blood spray!"

The bridge door opened; a figure was barely silhouetted in the dim light cast from inside the bridge. Whoever oversaw the bridge understood light discipline better than the three who had piled out of the yacht a few moments ago, but it wasn't enough to conceal someone standing in the middle of the doorway. Maria shifted the heavy-barrel HK416 to the bridge and fired a long burst.

"Target down," said Brooklyn.

Five or six flashes lit up the bridge from inside.

"Did you catch that?" asked Maria.

"Yeah. Maybe gunfire going out the portside door?" said Brooklyn. "Jax. Can you check with Support Two?"

"On it," said Jax.

A few seconds later she came back on the net. "They nailed three heading aft. But nobody opened the port bridgewing door. Both assault teams have been apprised of the situation."

"Interesting," said Maria. "Someone inside the bridge shot someone inside the bridge, and none of us were involved. Pass that along. The bridge might already be secure."

"Copy. Just passed it on," said Jax. "Teams are moving up. Watch for threats."

Maria reloaded, never taking her eye off the starboard side of the yacht.

CHAPTER 51

Mann inched toward the open bridgewing door, a motionless body lying a third of the way out of the door's threshold. He fired a single bullet from his suppressed rifle into the head, the body remaining still, and no noise or motion detected from inside the bridge.

"Assault Two. This is One. What's the status of the port bridgewing hatch?" said Mann.

"Still closed."

"Nobody exited that hatch at any point?" said Mann.

"Negative."

"Copy. I have a wide-open hatch on my side, and I don't think any of this is random," said Mann. "We're heading in."

"Assault Two is ready if you need help," said Turner. "We're attaching a small breaching charge to the port door."

"Stand by," said Mann, before moving the last foot to the door—and taking a quick peek inside.

Very interesting. "Move on me. Hold your fire."

Mann rushed into the bridge, finding a man wearing a uniform seated in the only chair on the bridge. A figure lay slumped against the portside door, a rifle lying under him, the door's window splattered with something. Vomit? Blood? Impossible to say in the bridge's dark-red light. The rest of Mann's team filled the bridge. A pistol lay on the deck below the chair.

"Kick that over here," said Mann, nodding at the pistol.

The man in uniform complied, and Mann removed the magazine from the pistol before ejecting the round still in the chamber. He tossed the pistol to Serrano.

"Over the side," he said.

She threw it into the Gulf of Mexico.

"And you are?" said Mann.

"My name is Andres Janssen. Captain of *True American*, formerly the motor vessel *Montana*. I surrender," said the man. "I shot the security guard at the portside hatch with the pistol I just kicked over to you. I understand that you're probably skeptical of my involvement in whatever the hell my client is up to. Same with my crew. But I assure you that, as distasteful as it sounds, we have no idea what's going on and we don't care. We get paid very well to run this yacht like any other luxury yacht. I have nothing to do with security. I just keep the yacht in tip-top shape and safe underway, catering to my client's every need. Gourmet meals. The works."

"But you know something is fucked up," said Mann, his rifle aimed at the captain's head.

"Of course," said Janssen. "The previous owner paid too well to babysit a yacht. But my crew is not complicit in whatever is happening down below."

"And what exactly is happening down below?" asked Mann.

"I have no idea," said the captain. "But whatever is going on? It's happening in the dining room. I assume you have the yacht's schematics?"

"Yes. What's happening in the dining room?"

"It's closed off from the rest of the main deck," Janssen said. "I've served as captain for two Custom Line 160s previously. On both vessels, the dining area was open to the interior main deck salon. This boat's interior configuration raised questions—which I didn't ask."

"Because of the pay?" said Mann.

"You don't ask questions if you want to keep working in this business," said Janssen. "Unless you witness something egregiously wrong.

An enhanced security presence, plus a strange interior modification, did not warrant—pardon the pun—the torpedoing of my career."

Mann understood, but he didn't have time to get into a discussion about hard decisions and tough career choices right now.

"I need you to slow the yacht to bare steerageway," said Mann, pulling his FBI wallet from a pouch on his vest and showing it to the captain. "I intend to bring more associates on board."

Janssen studied the badge and ID card, nodding in approval.

"Slowing the yacht will alarm my client, and their more capable security officers. Mercenaries," said Janssen. "If they haven't already figured out something is wrong."

"Bare steerageway," said Mann, putting away his badge.

"My crew is gathered in their quarters behind that door," said Janssen, pointing behind Serrano, who stood near the starboard bridgewing hatch. "Six of them. I want assurances that they will not be harmed."

"I plan to leave four agents on the bridge while we take care of business down below," said Mann. "As long as your crew stays put, and you're not fucking with me somehow—I promise to keep them safe."

"You have my word," said the captain. "We're doing eighteen knots. I can bring us to six, for a few minutes. Any slower than that, and the hurricane will entirely decide our fate. Any longer than that, and the hurricane will have a big say in it. Meaning, things will get very unstable. Is that enough time?"

"It'll have to be," said Mann, his earpiece cracking a moment later.

"Mann. This is Turner. What are we doing?"

"The bridge is clear," said Mann.

Patillo headed to the portside door.

"It's unlocked," said the captain. "This hasn't been the swiftest security team I've worked with."

Turner's team poured into the bridge, the space now dangerously overcrowded. One grenade and . . . game over.

"How many are left?" asked Mann. "We've neutralized the sea-deck guard, five on the starboard side and three on the port."

Turner glanced at the security guard on the deck by the door, clearly doing the math in his head.

"Did this guy commit suicide?"

"I shot him," said the captain. "Which makes ten. The man you killed in the starboard doorway was one of the mercenaries. Not the quietest or neatest of shootings, by the way. Nearly killed me."

The captain nodded at various areas on the bridge, drawing their attention to the bullet damage on the starboard-side window and interior portside, plus the two bullet holes punched through the side of his chair.

"But not bad, if the shots were taken from one of the boats flanking the yacht," said the captain. "And they must have been suppressed weapons, or the bridge would have been swarmed by now."

"You knew about the boats?" said Mann.

"Of course. The bridge windows are tinted differently than the rest of the yacht, for obvious reasons," said Janssen. "I took cover the moment that idiot opened the starboard hatch."

"So how many does that leave?" asked Turner.

"We were going over that," said Mann.

"Sorry if I'm late to the party."

"That's it for the contract security," said Janssen. "That leaves three of Ms. Furst's mercenaries. Plus Mr. Greely's two bodyguards."

"Easy peasy," said Turner. "Do we really need to bring everyone else on board?"

"Where would they go otherwise?" Janssen asked.

"Back to Tampa," said Turner.

"What kind of boats?" said the captain.

"Boston Whaler types," said Mann.

"If you can bring them on board, they'll be safer," said Janssen. "You were running into the seas during your pursuit. Uncomfortable for sure, but stable. Those boats are built for cutting through waves. If you send them back, they'll be dealing with following seas and trying to navigate safely back to a marina. Aft-quartering seas, to be precise. The least stable situation for any boat."

"You said Ms. Furst. As in Clara Furst?" said Mann.

"Yes," said Janssen. "She's running the show."

"Furst is running the show?" said Mann.

She was in the True America background files informally shared with the task force by Bauer and O'Reilly, but her name had never jumped out at them enough to warrant further investigation. She'd vanished into the murky depths of DC's think tank world, never to surface again. Until now.

"What about Greely? We assume he's on board?" said Mann.

"He is," said Janssen. "He's in a wheelchair. Paralyzed from the waist down. But Furst is in charge. Greely just thinks he is because he's paying for this. I can see it in their interactions and the way she acts when she's not around him."

"What do you know about the remaining mercenaries and their most likely locations?" asked Mann.

"One of Furst's people is always stationed in the converted dining room, which is on the main deck, as you already know," said Janssen, before pointing at the door Bilyk stood guard over. "Through that door, you'll find yourselves in the electronics room. All back-end interfaces for the yacht's radar, consoles, and radios. The stairway from that room leads down to a landing that can take you forward or aft. Forward takes you to the kitchen and galley storage. Aft takes you into the dining room. The door leading to the dining room has never been opened since AXIOM hired me to captain the yacht. A few of my crew have accidentally tried to open it and found it locked."

"And the remaining mercenaries?"

"Since the dock attack, two follow Furst everywhere," said Janssen. "The other two rotate standing watch outside of Greely's stateroom, which is located on the main deck—all the way forward. The only access to that stateroom is via a passageway along the starboard side of the yacht. Since the attack, both bodyguards have taken up posts outside of his stateroom."

"Who else is on board?" said Mann.

"Three VIPs. I don't know their names. They're berthed on the lower deck, which is only accessible from the salon aft of the dining room," said Janssen. "And two men who spend most of their time in the converted dining room. They eat and sleep in the main deck, aft salon. I see Furst speaking with them frequently when they're not in the dining room. Whatever they're up to in there, she keeps close tabs on them."

"What are the chances of drawing them up here when we slow down?" asked Emily Miralles.

"High. They'll try to reach Payne first," said the captain, nodding at the dead mercenary on the starboard side of the bridge. "Then me. If I ignore them, they'll send someone up. Maybe more than one."

"What if you slowed down and turned the yacht around?" said Serrano. "Then answered Furst's call and told them you didn't want to have anything to do with this anymore. That you were thinking about calling the Coast Guard."

"Checkmate, I think," said Mann.

"We wouldn't have to slow down. The change in course would be enough to panic them," said Janssen. "Of course, they'd wonder about Payne and the other security guards."

"They can wonder all they want," said Serrano. "If they can't reach them, they'll have to investigate. Right?"

"Furst would probably send everyone to the bridge," said the captain. "She might even show up herself."

"Using that door?" said Mann, nodding at the door Janssen had recently identified as leading directly to the dining room—DOMINION.

"She's never gone topside since we left the marina," said Janssen.

Mann weighed all the options available to the task force. He'd rather flush out the rats and kill them than hunt them down.

"Captain Janssen. Turn the yacht around and slow to whatever speed you deem safe for navigation," said Mann, before triggering his radio. "Support One and Two. We've had a slight change of plans. We're turning the yacht around to draw out any remaining resistance. We'll bring you all on board once we've neutralized all armed threats. Stay on our flanks and continue to provide covering fire. We can't see the exterior walkways along the main deck."

Jax and Vincenzo, the two Boston Whaler drivers, acknowledged the change to the plan while Bilyk opened the door to the electronics room. Turner's team slid inside, leaving Mann to pick members of his team for overwatch duty. Captain Janssen had been very accommodating, but he'd had little choice, with several guns pointed at his head. Mann would have to leave three people on the bridge unless he wanted to pull a few from Turner's team.

And they didn't have time to move people around. The captain had already slowed the yacht and input a new course. The ship heeled gently to port, indicating a starboard turn.

"Patillo. Take the portside. Javier. Starboard. The gunners on the support boats should keep anyone from reaching the bridge, but just in case," said Mann. "Kerri. You're going to keep an eye on the captain and the door to his crew quarters—which will remain shut. Correct, Captain?"

"Absolutely. They've locked it from inside," said Janssen. "We're halfway through our turn. Do you want me to pick up speed when we reach our reciprocal heading?"

"Will that help with the seas?" said Mann, already noticing a significant degradation to the yacht's stability.

"Somewhat," said Janssen, shrugging.

"Do it," said Mann. "We can steady up when this is over."

CHAPTER 52

Furst grabbed the edge of Greely's bed and steadied herself. Something had changed. She'd more or less adjusted to the yacht's fairly predictable up-and-down pitch, occasionally being thrown off-balance by a yaw to port. Not a big deal, overall. For her. But she was in the minority, as the captain had pointed out. A small club that didn't simply give up the will to live under harsh sea conditions—or vacate the contents of their stomachs every half hour or so. She hadn't once felt nauseous. Tired, for sure. But not sick.

Which only heightened her disdain for the already pathetic excuse for a human being lying before her. She wanted to put a pillow over his face and put him and their entire movement out of its misery, but now that she knew that most of their funding stemmed from his banks and investments, she was forced to put up with him. For now.

"Look," he said, barely raising a hand to point at the screen behind her. "We've slowed to ten knots and we're coming around."

Coming around? What the hell did that mean? She looked over her shoulder at the bulkhead-mounted screen, which displayed a live GPS track of their transit and a dozen or more data points. Speed. Course. Wind speed and direction. Depth. Temperature. Distance to next destination. Estimated time of arrival. *Wait.* Why was their estimated time of arrival fifty-three minutes? They were headed to Key West, which she had been told would take at least twenty hours.

"Can you zoom in on the navigation screen?" said Furst.

He handed her the remote. "I have no idea how to work this thing. Hendrick can help you."

"I don't need help," she said.

In fact, she didn't need to see any more. She understood compass headings. Zero degrees being north. Ninety: east. One-eighty: south. And their current course was zero-two-six. It had been one-six-five, almost due south, just a few minutes ago. They were headed back to the Tampa Bay area or somewhere in that vicinity. She grabbed the radio from her belt.

"Captain Janssen. This is Clara Furst. Why did we reverse course?"

Static.

"Payne. This is Furst. Report your status."

Nothing.

"Fuck!" she said, before trying the captain again. "Captain Janssen. Wake up Payne. We appear to have slowed down and changed course."

"Payne is no longer with us," said a voice she recognized to be Janssen's. "Same with the other security guards on the bridge. I killed them, and my crew has taken their weapons. We are heading back to Tampa Bay, where a US Coast Guard cutter will meet us. This has all gone too far."

"Are you fucking crazy?" said Furst. "This is a death sentence for you and your crew."

"Executed by who?" said Janssen.

"By me," she said. "I'll see you in a minute. For any of your crew who are listening, anyone caught outside the crew quarters section will be shot on sight."

The yacht veered to port for a few moments before swerving to starboard, nearly throwing her off her feet.

"Good luck with that," said the captain. "Out."

"Shit," said Furst.

"What is he thinking?" said Greely.

"No idea. But he's the only person on board that can operate this boat, so I can't exactly send the goon squad after him," said Furst. "One hasty trigger pull and we'll have no choice but to call the Coast Guard."

"Much later. After we've cleaned up," said Greely. "How hard can it be to operate this thing? It's all digital. Dominguez and Stern can figure it out. Set the autopilot for the Keys and we go to work sanitizing the boat. Start making calls to marinas and yacht-charter companies in Key West. I'm sure we can find another crew if we dangle enough money in front of them."

"And the current crew?"

"We throw the captain and his crew into the Gulf, like we did with the dock casualties."

"Maybe we should just set a course for Cuba," said Furst. "The gunfight at the dock is going to flag us anywhere in the US. We'll need Janssen for that."

"Whatever you need to do," said Greely. "Just get us pointing south again. We can figure all that out later."

"I'll be right back," she said.

"Clara?" said Greely.

She paused for a moment.

"What?"

"Why are you still wearing a suit?"

"Because I was on a video conference with some potential investors in Asia when Mann hit us at the dock," she said. "Some of us actually work."

She brushed past Hendrick and Rafe, completely ignoring them. Dragos headed down the passageway ahead of her, Emma following closely behind. Neither had left her side since the dock attack. Damon Sykes, the third remaining member of the team, guarded the DOMINION operations center. She switched to a secondary frequency, which transmitted to all the security officers on board. Normally, she just passed orders through Dragos's people, who had authority over the rotating contract team.

"All security officers, this is Clara Furst. Report your status."

Nothing. She repeated the call. Same result. Furst reached the end of the passageway before it opened into the salon—and entered the eight-digit code that granted her immediate access to the DOMINION operations center. Everyone else entered a six-digit code, which notified the mercenary on duty inside, who visually confirmed their identity. The door clicked and buzzed for a few seconds, before the keypad flashed a green light. She pushed the heavy door open and stepped inside, summoning Dragos and Emma to enter, before she shut it behind her.

"We have a problem," said Furst.

Hector Dominguez, who had taken over field communications with the sicarios after Oscar Marino's untimely but planned death in Georgetown, rose from his seat in front of the bank of screens covering the far wall of the room.

"It sounds like our captain has gone rogue," said Dominguez.

"Or something else," said Furst. "None of the Helon security officers are responding."

"Maybe they took the dinghy and bailed," said Kyle Stull. "The stern camera is out. And the sea deck sentry didn't respond to Payne's radio check. They could be gone for all we know, along with Janssen. He could have killed the bridge crew and programmed this maneuver. We might be carrying on a conversation with someone who is well on his way to the closest marina or beach."

She hadn't thought of that. More reason to get to the bridge immediately.

"Stull," she said, producing a small waterproof bag from one of her cargo pockets. "There's a flash drive in this bag containing a program named FAILSAFE. If I don't contact you in five minutes, or anyone tries to breach this room from either door, upload the program. Get it prepped while we head out."

He took the bag and unzipped it. "What does it do?"

"It gives a series of progressive orders to our DOMINION operatives leading up to the election, before releasing a virus that will wipe the DOMINION software from the system."

"Shit," said Stull, holding the flash drive in front of him. "This is like a doomsday key."

"Don't overthink it. Just make it happen—if worse comes to worse," said Furst. "Once that program is run, this is just a yacht with no connection to anything the FBI can prove. You'll be free and clear."

"What about SATCHEL?" said Dominguez. "I know it's essentially useless without the DOMINION software, but in competent hands, the data could be exploited. Identities revealed. It represents a liability to the movement."

"You make a very good point," said Furst. "If we had the time, we could probably create another DOMINION hub and migrate the SATCHEL data. But we don't have that kind of time. Hector. Toss it overboard. Immediately. DOMINION will live on no matter what happens."

"What about our VIPs?" said Dominguez.

"If we deliver DOMINION, True America is guaranteed positions in the new administration's cabinet," said Furst. "If we're wiped out, there's a secondary group standing by to ensure the new administration keeps that promise."

"How?" said Dominguez.

"Don't you have something to throw over the side?" said Furst.

"Yes, ma'am," said Dominguez. "Port, starboard, or aft?"

"Why don't you head to the stern and toss it off the back of the yacht," said Furst. "Check on the RHIB while you're there. If it's gone, we'll know what happened to the crew."

"On my way," said Dominguez, punching in his code on the keypad.

He was out the door and on his way a moment later, the secure door locking behind him. A personal code was required to enter or leave the room, mostly for administrative purposes. To track access.

"Kyle?" she said.

"The program is uploaded," he said. "Just a mouse click away."

"And a password," she said.

"TRUEAMERICA?" said Kyle. "No space between the two words?"

"How did you guess?" said Furst.

"Years in the business."

"Funny," said Furst, heading over to the door that opened to a stairway that led to the electronics room and ultimately the bridge. She entered her code and pulled the door open, the light from the DOMINION operations center revealing a team crouched in the tight confines of the stairway access room, their rifle barrels pointed at her head. *Fuck me.* Her last thought.

CHAPTER 53

Bilyk and Bella, his two breachers, quit their work affixing explosive charges to the door and dropped to the deck the moment the hatch's door handle turned. With nowhere to go in the tight space, lying flat got them out of the way. Turner didn't hesitate. He started pressing his trigger the moment the door opened into the DOMINION operations center, revealing four figures pointing weapons into the stairway chamber.

Two rounds through the first hostile's head—a woman dressed in a business suit, carrying a submachine gun. The same for the two standing behind her. Melendez and Miralles did the same. A third hostile dashed out of view before they could get off a shot. Everyone else held their fire as agreed. The last thing they needed was a barrage of bullets ricocheting around the room, potentially destroying DOMINION.

"Bangers!" said Turner.

Ripley and Serrano surged forward, each tossing two flash-bang grenades inside the room. Turner, Melendez, and Miralles moved up to the door, stepping on Bella and Bilyk—the space too tight to avoid it. A moment later, the four flash-bangs detonated in rapid succession. Turner burst into the room after the fourth and immediately turned left. A figure semiobscured by the flash-bang smoke held a hand to one of his ears, the other hand still holding a compact rifle. Turner pressed the trigger three times, flipping the man off like a light switch. He dropped to the deck with a thud.

"Clear!" said Turner, everyone else pouring into the room.

"Not clear!" said a voice he recognized as Serrano's.

He shifted his aim to the portside of the room, where the rest of his team converged on someone lying flat on the deck. Turner made his way over to the man lying prone, with his hands clasped over his head. Mann knelt next to the man, his rifle touching the back of the guy's head. The man pleaded for his life. His words barely intelligible. Serrano crouched down and grabbed a flash drive from the man's hands before placing her rifle against his head.

"Everyone shut the fuck up!" said Turner, silencing the group for a few moments. "Is he armed?"

Mann and Serrano probed the guy, turning him over and searching him.

"Nada," said Serrano.

"Who are you?" said Mann.

"Kyle Stull. I worked at AXIOM on the DOMINION operation as a programmer and coder. I was home recovering from gall bladder surgery when you guys took it all down. I assume it was you?"

"Why are you here?" said Turner.

"Because of my wife and baby," he said. "I didn't feel like I had much choice, if you know what I mean."

"Yeah," said Mann. "What's on the flash drive?"

"Marching orders for DOMINION, and a virus that will destroy this system," said Stull.

"Did you upload it?" said Mann.

"No," said Stull.

"Where's the SATCHEL?" said Turner.

"Are you going to kill me?" said Stull.

Turner aimed his rifle at Stull. This fucker was playing games at zero hour? Mann got his attention and shook his head.

"Not if you cooperate," said Mann. "Is the SATCHEL on board?"

"Hector Dominguez took it aft, to throw it overboard," said Stull.

Mann immediately transmitted over the radio net. "Jess. They're trying to throw SATCHEL over the side. Assault One, move to the stern to support Mayer. All friendlies except Mayer are clear of the stern."

"Copy," said Jax. "Moving into position."

Mayer transmitted. "I'll head up the stairway on the starboard side. If he opens one of the main deck hatches on that side, I'll be in position to hit him. Jax's boat can cover the stern. Frank. You got the starboard side."

Jax and Vincenzo acknowledged. They had the yacht covered. More or less. Dominguez could probably burst out of one of the doors and toss SATCHEL into the water before the bullets reached him.

"Dominguez isn't that bad," said Stull. "His heart isn't in this like the others."

"If he tries to throw that bag over the side, his heart is going to explode from several bullets," said Turner.

CHAPTER 54

Hector Dominguez felt oddly at ease, despite the hollow thumping of gunfire that had just taken place inside the DOMINION operations center. He lay on the couch in the salon that had served as his bed for the past few weeks, the SATCHEL on the deck by his side. He'd had every intention of heading aft and tossing it into the sea, until he saw a cluster of bullet holes in one of the windows a few feet aft of the DOMINION operations center. Unsure whether they had been fired from inside the yacht by the security team or from outside in, he searched the salon with his flashlight until he discovered the truth. A similarly tight cluster of three bullet holes in the portside of the salon's overhead.

He did the math. Ran the angles. The gunfire had come from the outside, at sea level, the bullets punching through the glass at a high angle. That was all he needed to see. They weren't alone out here, and he had no intention of presenting himself as a target on the stern sea deck. So he took a seat, which led to him lying down.

The SATCHEL wouldn't save his life. They could shoot him and take it. But his knowledge of the DOMINION network was priceless. Or so he hoped. As a show of faith, he'd share another piece of information with whoever found him. He'd seen one of Greely's bodyguards in the library just forward of the DOMINION operations center. Another guard, presumably Hendrick, knelt at the far end of the passageway leading to Greely's stateroom. That fuck wasn't even letting his bodyguard inside to seek cover. What a miserable existence they'd all tolerated for these people. For money. He was done with that. Whatever came his way, he'd lie here and take it.

CHAPTER 55

Mann rushed to the door, slapping his hand away from the keypad.

"Slow the fuck down, Luke," he said, trying to keep his voice down. "We need a plan. Just storming through the rest of the boat shooting at shit isn't a plan."

Turner nodded. "Yeah. Yeah. I'll take my team forward and secure Greely. You and Serrano head aft."

"Don't kill Greely," said Mann.

"I won't," said Turner.

"Promise?"

"Pinkie promise," said Turner, holding up his hand.

"I'm not doing that," said Mann, before punching in the code Stull had given them.

Turner pulled the door inward and peeked down the passageway toward the front of the yacht. His inquisitiveness was met with gunfire.

"Am I allowed to use grenades?" said Turner facetiously.

"Funny," Mann said. "Go for it. It's not like we'll sink the yacht."

"I need grenades!" said Turner.

Mann took a quick look down the passageway, witnessing a pathetic sight. One of Greely's bodyguards stood in front of the door to his suite, pounding at the door. Mann raised his rifle, a moment before the bodyguard looked over his shoulder. The two of them locked eyes, the man at the door no longer in the fight.

"Drop your rifle!" said Mann. "And get on your knees!"

Turner leaned out of the doorway and fired three short bursts down the passageway, knocking the man off his feet.

"What the fuck was that?" said Mann. "We need witnesses."

"Not witnesses armed with assault rifles," said Turner. "They're hired guns. This guy Stull and Dominguez are who we need."

He was right. "Cata?"

"Right here," she said.

He'd lost track of everyone in the mayhem.

"Jax. Any business on the stern?" he transmitted over the radio.

"Negative. We're about thirty feet behind the yacht. Nothing so far," said Jax. "We came down the starboard side before moving into position. No thermal hits."

"Copy," said Mann. "Frank. Anything on the portside?"

"Nothing on thermal or night vision."

"Copy. Jax. I'm moving aft with Serrano to investigate," said Mann. "We'll head down the starboard side."

"Wave your IR chem-lights when you go topside," said Jax. "So we don't light you up."

"Got it," said Mann, before turning to Serrano. "Ready?"

She nodded and Mann slapped Turner on the shoulder. "Cover us."

"Go," he said, leaning out of the doorway with his rifle.

Mann bolted out of the room and hugged the interior of the passageway, Serrano holding on to his vest until they spilled into the salon a few seconds later.

"Stairway is on the portside," said Mann.

"I'm right behind you," said Serrano.

"Wait! Wait!" cried a voice from the darkness of the salon.

Mann crouched. Serrano settled in next to him, their rifles sweeping the space.

"Identify yourself!" said Mann.

"Hector Dominguez. I'm lying on a couch about fifteen feet in front of you, if you're facing aft. I have a glow stick I can crack, if that would help."

"Crack it," said Mann.

A few seconds later, a green light radiated from a couch in the middle of the salon, illuminating the aft half of the space. The couch faced aft, so they couldn't see Dominguez.

"I'm not armed," said Dominguez. "I have the SATCHEL. It's yours. All I ask is that you don't kill me."

"Why would we kill you?" said Serrano.

"Because I've been running DOMINION since Greely killed Marino," said Dominguez. "And I've been working with the sicario teams in the field. Meeting with them. Fine-tuning them. Weaponizing them. I can help you dismantle the whole operation."

Mann glanced at Serrano, who nodded.

"Hold your glow stick up with both hands," said Mann. "Do not let go of the glow stick for any reason. We will shoot through the couch if we can't see both hands at any point while we approach. Understood?"

"Understood," said Dominguez, raising the glow stick with both hands. "One of Greely's bodyguards is hiding in the library located halfway down the passageway leading to his stateroom. The other guard—"

"Is dead," said Mann, before transmitting over the radio. "Turner. You have a hostile in the library located on the left side of the passageway."

"Good timing. We were about to head out," said Turner.

"We found Dominguez. He surrendered," said Mann.

Unless he'd wired himself up with a suicide vest. The guy didn't sound right.

"Good news. The SATCHEL?" said Turner.

"We're approaching Dominguez now," said Mann.

"Careful, my friend," said Turner.

"Yeah. I know," said Mann. "Don't kill Greely, by the way. Just a friendly reminder."

"We won't," said Turner. "But he doesn't leave this boat alive. Right? Are we in agreement on that?"

"Very much so," said Mann. "He has too much money at his disposal. And we haven't exactly followed the rules. Not a great combination for a successful prosecution. Don't kill the bodyguard if you don't have to. They're hired guns. If we had the money, we could have hired them."

"It's up to them," said Turner.

Mann nodded at Serrano, and the two of them moved forward. The glow stick remained upright, both hands in sight, as they flanked the couch. A solid-looking rectangular nylon briefcase sat on the floor below Dominguez. He nodded at Serrano, who moved in with a thick zip tie, pulling his wrists tightly together. Mann examined the SATCHEL, while she finished the job by taking the chem-light out of his hands and looping a cuff-lock cable tie over each hand and taking out all the slack. They could cut it open later and make it more comfortable if he didn't give them any trouble.

"Here's what we're going to do," said Mann. "We're going to take cover. Then you're going to get up, keeping your hands high. You'll kick the SATCHEL in any direction you'd like."

"I swear I haven't rigged a grenade or any kind of IED."

"You have five seconds," said Mann, quickly taking cover with Serrano behind the marble bar.

He figured the marble would serve as a nice shield against fragments. He watched as Dominguez got up and kicked the bag several feet away from the couch.

"Take ten steps forward," said Mann.

Dominguez complied.

"Let's go," said Mann, the two of them moving quickly to secure their star witness.

A thorough search revealed no explosive devices. Not even a wallet. The SATCHEL appeared to be safe as well.

"No explosives inside the SATCHEL? Like some kind of fail-safe system?"

"Not that I'm aware of," said Dominguez. "But you don't need SATCHEL if the DOMINION operations center is still operational. I assume you stopped Stull from uploading the flash drive?"

"Yes. He was very cooperative," said Mann.

"They forced him into this," said Dominguez. "I was Marino's second, so I can't exactly say the same. But I didn't know about True America until that Greely guy and Furst swooped in after McCall's death."

"Greely killed McCall, Marino, and Conway on the rooftop in Georgetown. Knifed Marino and Conway in the neck from behind and shot McCall in the head," said Mann. "Stole the SATCHEL and the yacht from AXIOM. Stole DOMINION, basically. They were the original client."

"Sounds about right for them," said Dominguez.

Yelling erupted from the passageway leading out of the salon.

"Turner?" said Mann.

"We're good," said Turner. "Greely's last bodyguard surrendered."

"Hold on, we'll be right there," said Mann. "We have Dominguez and the SATCHEL."

"Copy. We'll secure the bodyguard," said Turner.

"Bring them back into the salon. I don't want them near DOMINION until we've dealt with Greely."

"Bringing them back right now," Turner said.

"How many survivors?" asked Dominguez.

"You. Stull. One of the bodyguards. The captain and his crew," said Mann.

"The captain and his crew were around during McCall's time," said Dominguez. "I'd keep a close eye on them."

Turner appeared, pushing the mercenary into the salon, with Melendez and Miralles close behind him pushing Stull. When they reached the couch, Mann contacted Wallace on the bridge.

"Tell the captain to set the best course and speed to take on the support teams," said Mann. "We'll head south to Key West or Miami once we get everyone on board. We just have one loose end to tie up."

"Copy," said Wallace.

"Jax. Frank. This is Mann. We're maneuvering into the best position to take you on board. Mayer is aft. She'll help with the transfer."

CHAPTER 56

Harrison Greely lay in his own filth. He could neither find the trash bag nor lean over the side in time to prevent the mess he sprayed over his stomach. Fortunately, he had already ejected most of his stomach into the trash bag over the past few hours. Unfortunately, his latest bout of uncontrollable vomiting had triggered other eruptions.

Just when he had accepted the likelihood that he'd die in this dirtied state, the yacht came around. He felt the turn first, the yacht heeling slightly to port. Then the screen showed that they were changing course, eventually settling on a southwesterly heading at eight knots. Not as fast as he expected, but at least they were headed in the right direction. Furst had quelled whatever mutiny the captain had initiated. He grabbed the radio on the shelf next to him.

"Hendrick. Rafe," said Greely for the tenth time.

He was pretty sure Hendrick was dead. Two bullet holes in the door after a quick exchange of gunfire felt definitive to him. But Rafe never stood by the door. He preferred to sit in the library. Smart move on his part. Maybe Rafe had been killed storming the bridge. Not exactly ideal for Greely, given that Furst clearly despised him. She came across as the type who would toss him overboard if she weren't beholden to his financial support. And he'd made it clear that most of the support to this point had come from him.

He was a little disturbed to hear that she was meeting with Asian investors, so he called his financial provost the moment she left the stateroom, pleasantly surprised to find that he still had satellite phone access through the yacht's integrated communications system, and triggered SPOILSPORT. Which not only immediately stopped all support to True America but also activated wide, sweeping clawback provisions that launched everything from liens to lawsuits in order to recover any money sent to the accounts overseen by Furst. He'd cancel SPOILSPORT only after he felt safe, which would probably require a complete changeover of leadership and a heavily guarded villa in Greece.

The door opened without any announcement, and a head barely peeked inside. Garrett Mann. Shit. The jig was up.

"Are you armed?" said Mann.

"No," said Greely, slowly pointing the MP5K submachine gun he was concealing under the sheet toward the door.

The submachine gun lay across his chest, his left hand on the trigger. His other tightly wrapped around the weapon's foregrip. Not optimal since he was right-handed, but on full auto—the MP5K would shred anyone who stepped through the door. The problem was that Mann wasn't giving him much of a target. He'd have to lure him inside.

"Improvised explosive devices? Suicide vest?" said Mann. "Or any reason I can't walk in here and walk out alive?"

"Are they all dead?" said Greely.

"Dominguez, Stull, and Rafe are alive," said Mann. "DOMINION and the SATCHEL are intact and in our hands."

"Then what are you waiting for?" said Greely. "Just get it over with. We all know where this is headed."

"I can toss you a pistol loaded with one bullet and close the door," said Mann. "Open it when I hear the shot."

"I'm not letting you off that easy, Mr. FBI guy," said Greely. "If you want to get rid of me, you'll have to do it yourself."

CHAPTER 57

Mann leaned into the stateroom, his rifle aimed at the bed. Most of Greely's body was concealed by the blue nylon lee cloth that kept him from rolling out of the bed. Only his head and bare feet were visible. He flipped the selector switch on his rifle to automatic and considered emptying the thirty-round magazine into the bed from the cover of the doorway, but something prevented him from carrying out the long-overdue execution.

Maybe it was the temptation to arrest him and bring the horrors of True America back into the national spotlight—with a face to go with it. Or maybe he wanted to let Melendez and Miralles work Greely over for more information on the aft deck of the yacht before tossing him into the dark, turbulent waters to drown. Whatever the motivation, he stepped into the cabin, his rifle pointed at the center of the lee cloth.

Automatic gunfire erupted the moment his body crossed the cabin door's threshold, Mann knocked backward by what felt like sledgehammer strikes against his body armor. He reflexively tried to press the trigger of his rifle, but it was no longer in his hands. It clattered to the deck next to him as he slammed against the wall.

Serrano leaned through the doorway and fired her rifle into the tattered lee cloth, Greely's feet and head convulsing until her magazine ran dry. As Mann slumped to the deck, Serrano entered the room and drew her pistol. She fired twice, and Mann saw two holes punch through Greely's forehead.

"I got you this time!" she said.

Turner, Rico, and Miralles rushed into the stateroom, covering all the corners before searching the closets, bathroom, and any cabinets large enough to conceal a person.

"All clear," said Turner.

Mann tried to stand up, but he could barely breathe. Serrano eased him back down into a seated position before checking for injuries. She opened the first aid pouch attached to her vest and went to work wrapping a thick layer of hemostatic gauze around his wound.

"Is he okay?" said Turner.

"One bullet through the upper-right bicep. Not that bad," said Serrano. "Everything else absorbed by his body armor."

He finally felt like he could talk.

"Clear the rest of the yacht. We still have three VIPs below. Apparently, they're all seasick, snug in their beds like Greely," said Mann, his voice gravelly but audible.

"Same treatment?" said Turner.

"I don't think we can dispose of them without facing some tough questions," said Mann. "Dominguez, Stull, the bodyguard, and the crew. They know they're on board."

"I suppose you're right," said Turner.

"Let's get the rest of the task force on board, before we head below to grab the VIPs," said Mann. "Once everything is settled on board, we'll figure out where we're headed and how to explain this mess."

"Let O'Reilly worry about the mess," said Turner. "That's why she gets paid the big bucks."

"You can tell her that," said Mann.

Turner patted him on the shoulder. "I'll let you handle it. I think you get paid more than me."

"Don't be so sure of that. I've seen your paystub," said Mann.

"I vote for over the side," said Melendez. "Wipe every living connection to True America off the map. These people are a clear and present danger to the United States."

"And whoever is getting the VIP treatment on this yacht must be important to the True America movement," said Miralles. "I vote for over the side without a life jacket."

"I can't say I disagree," said Serrano.

"Restrain them and bring them up to the salon—for now. We're going to need some witness testimony from the inside. Plus, I'm starting to get the distinct impression that Greely and Furst were running the show. That said, we don't know who's down below. Could be investors. Could be key members of the coup they were planning," said Mann. "I'm not crossing the option off the list, but we're not going to outright execute them until we know more about them."

He couldn't believe he even suggested the murder of unarmed civilians. But were they really unarmed if their money financed the purchase and use of DOMINION against the American people? If they were part of whatever True America had more than likely negotiated with traitors within a political party trying to steal the election? Unarmed was unarmed. He shouldn't have shot Greely, but the man had been too dangerous to live. Greely had unleashed hundreds of terrorists on the American people to inflict a sick version of his father's warped political philosophy on the nation.

Part of him hoped the VIPs tried to put up a fight. Made the decision a no-brainer. Somehow, he doubted he'd get off that easy—like Greely had said. And perhaps he didn't want to. Maybe there was more truth to what Berg had said than Mann cared to admit. That he now had more in common with Melendez and Miralles, mercenaries Berg had worked with for decades.

"All right. I'll split my team up. Half on guard duty in the salon. The other half helping the rest of the task force get on board. At least one to watch the staircase leading belowdecks to the VIP staterooms."

"I'll head to the bridge. Then make that call to O'Reilly once we shed some light on the identities of the VIPs," said Mann. "The second Gupta and Lianez step on board, I want them in the DOMINION operations center. Have someone bring Stull in too but keep Stull under close watch. Do not remove his restraints. I get the feeling he won't try to pull any tricks on us, but we can't take any risks. DOMINION is our key piece of evidence. We can't afford to lose it."

Turner gave him a thumbs-up and took off. Serrano dropped onto one of the couches in the stateroom. She looked like he felt. Worn out.

"It stinks in here," said Mann. "Let's head to the salon."

She didn't move. "I can't believe this might be over. The whole thing wrapped up."

"We've come a long way," said Mann. "A year ago, we were chasing a serial killer. Two, apparently, but we didn't know it. You did. But there was no way to know that both of them were in the US."

"I'm sorry I didn't come clean with you about that from the start."

"Raul never killed anyone in the US," said Mann. "We were never after him. Alejandro was our killer."

"I know," she said. "But I regret not being entirely honest with you from the beginning. I wasn't sure I could trust you."

"And now?"

"I think you know the answer," said Cata.

"I do, and I'd like nothing more than to sit next to you right now and continue this conversation," said Mann. "But I'm about to throw up from the smell in here. I think Greely shit his pants."

"So. Where do we go from here?" said Serrano.

"You and I, or this whole mess?" said Mann.

"Both."

"Let me give O'Reilly a call and get this sort of under control," said Mann. "We'll have plenty of time to discuss the rest on the way to the Keys or wherever she sends us."

"But there's a me and you? Right?" said Serrano.

"Yes," he said. "There's definitely a you and me. Unless you get sick of me."

"Or the other way around."

"Not much chance of that," said Mann, pulling her up from the couch. "Maybe if you don't bail on my next try at vacation plans, we can sort it out."

CHAPTER 58

Dana O'Reilly ended the call. She sat in a chair outside the surgery suite working on Special Agent Jeff Miles. The bullet that hit his collarbone had indeed gone deep into his chest. The surgical team had been working on him for close to an hour. The prognosis was still touch and go.

Mann's call, which included the last-minute addition of Anish Gupta, had put her at ease. DOMINION and SATCHEL had been secured without any apparent damage or degradation. Gupta had only spent a few minutes with the system before jumping on the call, but he felt like they'd captured everything intact.

Incredible, under the circumstances. Mann deflected any credit, as usual, but it was clear that his persistence had paid off. He could have let the yacht go. O'Reilly could have called the Coast Guard to intercept. And the flash drive recovered from one of the DOMINION operations center techs would have scrubbed the evidence, after sending a series of progressively more horrific orders to the hundreds of sicarios hidden throughout the country.

Without that evidence, they'd face a hard, uphill slog to prove that the yacht was involved in anything nefarious other than protecting its passengers. It wasn't like Mann had stood on the dock with his FBI badge and announced himself. Or had a warrant to hold in the other hand. ARTEMIS had essentially attacked the yacht unprovoked.

The same set of facts still existed, but the gravity of what they'd seized on the yacht, and its nexus to the events of the last few months, carried a weight that tended to transcend warrants. Her boss agreed, which meant the director of the FBI had given her some leeway. So they created a story—over burner phones, of course. A rough story, with many details to manufacture. The hazier, the better, in this situation, since they'd never actually required a warrant. Watching someone through binoculars didn't require a judge's approval. Boarding the yacht required a warrant, and they never boarded or appeared to have attempted to board the yacht. Dozens of security cameras in the area would back up that narrative.

The marina dock was private property, but that would be lost in the bigger story. Mann's team simply attempted to walk down the dock and engage in a conversation with the yacht's owner. They were taken under machine gun and sniper fire without provocation, resulting in an FBI casualty—along with a few innocent bystanders. O'Reilly accompanied Miles and Sofia to the hospital, while Neva, Bauer, and Berg worked frantically to sanitize the scene.

The apartment was their primary concern. When the hurricane conditions eased up and the sun rose, the police and local FBI would eventually notice the damage to the apartment's windows and facade.

They removed Gupta's equipment, leaving nothing but a bank of radio chargers and O'Reilly's laptop behind. Wiped down the surfaces as best as could be expected in a short period of time. One of the task force's registered 7.62mm semiautomatic sniper rifles leaned up against the wall inside the apartment next to the slider, along with a few spare magazines mixed in with the used magazines. Brooklyn had been present enough to grab the FBI rifle and fire two magazines into the water beyond the pier, dirtying the weapon. All traces of Garza and Brooklyn being on the balcony had been removed, with Berg and Bauer handling Garza's body.

They left the tarp structure inside the apartment. Mann's team was unique and talented. Going above and beyond procedure to remain undetected would reinforce their claim that surveillance had been their primary mission. Until they started to notice a proliferation of illegal weapons on the dock.

If a serious forensics team took a fine-tooth comb to the apartment, it probably wouldn't pass muster. Fingerprints would be an issue, despite their best efforts to remove them. That said, she was a deputy FBI director, which carried weight. Technically, it wasn't a crime scene. The only interest investigators should have would be in the balcony, where one of the SWAT-trained agents had fired in support of the task force. They could decide on who that would be later. The focus right now was on the big stuff. The kind of things that would appear out of place to an FBI agent walking through the apartment.

Then there was the story behind how they found the yacht. Without throwing the Mexican task force under the bus, they'd have to come up with something inventive. The answer would have to revolve around Brooklyn, the story being that they'd hired her as a private investigator to watch for irregular activity near the Montana ranch since they needed every agent available for the raid. She identified and tracked two operatives from Bozeman International Airport to Tampa—then the marina, where she watched them board *True American*. The tickets were in her name. She was a licensed private investigator. Nothing illegal there. Mann had outsourced the job due to resource scarcity. Hard to argue with that.

That still left whatever mess they had created on board *True American*, which sounded like a big one. They all still had several hours to figure that out, before the yacht reached the Coast Guard station in Key West. Plenty of time to "clean up," as Mann had put it. She wasn't sure what that meant, and didn't want to know—even though she had a pretty good idea what Mann had been talking about.

They'd found Trent Summers, a partner at a prestigious law firm in Memphis, who'd served as head of the Department of Justice's Office of Professional Responsibility after True America's 2008 presidential win. He'd kept a low political profile since then—until today. Gary Smith turned up in one of the staterooms. Colonel Smith, retired, had suddenly become a staunch isolationist once he started working for the Hauter Institute, a beltway think tank funded by shell companies formed in all the usual suspect countries used by transnational crime syndicates and the Russians. Then there was Kara Hill, who had been appointed as the US ambassador to Belarus in 2008, where she served for four years. A nice way to make Russian contacts without making it too obvious.

The yacht's captain suggested that the trio had been sequestered on board after the Montana raid, which suggested Greely wanted to keep them out of sight until the dust settled, underscoring their importance to Greely's power play. Possible cabinet positions in exchange for DOMINION's influence on the election? The dots weren't that difficult to connect. O'Reilly assumed that the sharks would get fed at some point tonight.

She had a tough call ahead of her with James, but at least she'd go into it knowing that no matter who won the upcoming election, True America would have no part in any of it. She'd been fighting this fight for close to two decades. They could fire or force her into retirement tomorrow and she'd walk out of here with her head held high.

PART VI

CHAPTER 59

Enrique Mendoza wasn't in the best mood. Not only had he somehow bet on the wrong horse despite careful analysis—he'd also rigged the race. Yet he still lost, and now there was no deal. Not a disaster by any stretch of the imagination when it came to getting business done. He didn't need the network in the US. He had thousands of people working for him, stretched from the south of Mexico well into Canada. It just bothered him that he'd so significantly underestimated Serrano and her associates and overestimated Harrison Greely.

Mendoza promised himself that he'd tear that decision apart piece by piece looking for the flaw. The one or two warning signs that should have told him to either stay neutral or pick Serrano. That was how he had made it this far. Confidence was essential in this business. Overconfidence got you in trouble. Walking a fine line between the two was how he had controlled a seven-billion-dollar-a-year criminal enterprise in plain sight for so long.

Errors like this tended to snowball. He hoped this hadn't been one of those mistakes. His vast intelligence and surveillance network had reported an uptick in police, National Guard, and military activity in the state. Nothing to suggest he had a problem on his hands. Probably just a show of force to appease the Americans, who had undoubtedly figured out by now that he'd betrayed Cata Serrano's team to Harrison Greely's associates.

He expected a couple of raids tonight at a few of his sacrificial distribution or manufacturing sites. Mendoza always operated a few higher-visibility, lower-volume sites to give Mexico's drug enforcement units—and more importantly, government leadership—just enough wins to keep everyone happy. Including the Americans trying to pull their strings.

His chef opened the access door to the kitchen, pushing an oversize stainless-steel cart to their table under the pergola in the middle of the courtyard. He loved eating al fresco in the summer with his family, when night had descended and the desert had cooled to a comfortable temperature. Mid-seventies with a light breeze. Perfection.

A few minutes later, they dined on custom-cut Wagyu beef medallions accompanied by an exquisite chimichurri sauce, along with several choices of perfectly prepared sides. The chef always included a few kid-friendly options, his children more often opting for panko-encrusted chicken nuggets or fish sticks instead of the three-hundred-dollar-per-pound beef.

The chef topped off their wine before asking if he could bring anything else.

"This looks fantastic. Thank you," said Mendoza.

"Shall I post an attendant to take care of any other requests?" said the chef.

"I think we're fine."

The meal felt a little awkward. Forced, perhaps. All his fault. He couldn't relax and just enjoy the food. The True America debacle still weighed heavy on him. His wife tried her best to put on a *nothing is wrong* face, but she still looked stiff, her feigned smile not passing muster. The kids sensed it, barely picking at their food.

"Do you want calamari?" he said to the kids. "They can fire up calamari in five minutes."

"I'm fine, Papa," said his youngest.

"Me, too," said his daughter.

The phone he'd placed on the table buzzed. Everyone froze like he'd just slammed his fist down into his food. The phone had never buzzed during a meal. Maybe that was why they looked so fearful. It had always sat there like a bomb waiting to go off, and now it buzzed to life. They weren't stupid. They knew something was wrong. He couldn't blame them for being afraid.

"Sorry. I need to take this," he said, getting up—knowing that wouldn't ease their worries.

Or his. Only three people had the number to this phone. His second-in-command, who knew he was having dinner with his family and would never interrupt him unless it was an emergency. His mother, who went to bed at eight. Two hours ago. And his accountant. Strangely, the number on the phone didn't match up with any of the three. Once he got out of earshot of his family, he took the call.

"Who is this?"

"Cata Serrano."

She was looking to re-up their deal! Perfect. He knew she was practical. He could kill everyone near and dear to her with a phone call.

"Señorita Serrano. It's good to hear your voice," he said. "Look. I'm not going to pretend that I didn't side with your adversary. And I'm not going to apologize. I did my analysis and admittedly underestimated you and your associates."

"Yes. You did."

"But from a very practical standpoint, I still see us doing business," said Mendoza. "Same deal. Immunity for all your associates and their families. And I get rid of your problem in the US. I'll let you know how and when so you can verify that I've taken the DOMINION network down."

"Now you know the name of the network?" said Serrano.

"What can I say. Greely overshared," said Mendoza. "How did you get this number, by the way?"

"Carlos Fuentes. He's dead."

His second-in-command.

"How did you find him?" asked Mendoza.

"Same way we found you," said Serrano.

"What?"

"A virus that infected every phone that spent any time outside of my apartment in Juárez," said Serrano.

"I never got near your apartment," said Mendoza.

"But your people did," she said. "And a friend of mine across the street infected every one of their phones, which daisy-chained across your entire network. Right now, the Mexican government, with a lot of clandestine aerial support from the north, is seconds away from hitting hundreds of your labs, storage facilities, safe houses . . . the list goes on."

"Bullshit," said Mendoza.

"Do you hear that buzzing?"

He took the phone away from his ear for a few moments. A distant buzz cut through the night.

"Yes."

"That's the sound of six Switchback drones circling overhead."

"What do you want?"

"I want you to turn to your left and walk to the wooden bench in front of the fountain."

"Why?" said Mendoza.

"Because if you don't, we'll crash a nineteen-pound high-explosive antitank warhead on top of your head right now," said Serrano. "Do you know the kill radius of a Switchblade 600?"

"You'd kill my family?"

"Like you killed my mother? And hundreds of mothers, daughters, and sisters by letting La Triada run wild?" said Serrano. "Not if I don't have to. The fountain is outside the kill radius and is deeply shielded from the dinner table by the house."

He looked at his family and waved as enthusiastically as a dead man could. They barely waved back.

"And where are you right now, Señorita Serrano? Watching this from the hills?"

"No. I'm sitting in a warehouse complex somewhere in El Paso, watching the drone operator's screen," said Serrano. "Three warehouses filled with hundreds of screens. It's quite the setup."

One mistake. That was all it had taken.

"You promise not to kill them?"

"I do," said Serrano.

"Then I guess I'm taking a walk," said Mendoza.

He waved again. "I have to take this inside! Love you!"

A minute later, he sat down on the bench in front of the illuminated three-tiered Italian marble fountain. A buzzing sound started to compete with the splashing of the water. A few moments later, it all went silent.

CHAPTER 60

Miguel Ochoa pushed his grocery cart through the produce section of "El Supermercado." His next stop was the butcher's counter. Yes, his training had told him to shop at Kroger or Meijer like the rest of his Detroit neighbors, but he was craving the kind of authentic food he'd grown up with. Lengua. Pancita. Tongue and tripe to grill and put on corn tortillas made here daily. You could only get these cuts of meat at real Mexican markets, and El Supermercado had become a staple for them. The place was massive, selling everything he would have had to spend an entire day trying to find across half of Ciudad Juárez.

He grabbed a few bunches of cilantro. A bag of avocados. Green chiles. Tomatoes. The choices were overwhelming here. Everywhere in the United States. He'd never seen this level of abundance before in his life. Why would he risk throwing this all away? There had to be a way out. He'd thought about disappearing and approaching the authorities. His story had to be worth something. But his "wife" rarely let him out of her sight longer than a trip to the grocery store. Even then, he'd spotted her following him on occasion. She was a true believer. A cartel disciple.

Like all of them, she came from nothing, and they gave her everything she had no hope of ever acquiring in Mexico. Purpose. Money. Family. The promise of making a difference—and a life. But there was no life ahead of them. Their first mission was simple enough: a string of home invasions. No lethal violence permitted, unless threatened. They'd robbed seven homes or apartments, beating the adult occupants if they were home. Stuffing their kids and pets into dryers without turning them on. Pure fear tactics.

But none of the targets seemed connected to the cartel's business. That much had been obvious from the start. It all felt very random. He felt like they were being used for a different purpose. His phone rang. Carmen—his "wife."

"I'm hustling," said Miguel. "Be back in fifteen minutes."

"Ditch the shopping cart," she said. "We've been recalled to Mexico."

"Seriously?"

"It came through the proper channels," said Carmen. "Probably because you fucked up or something."

They had never gotten along.

"When do we leave?"

"On the first flight we can book to El Paso," said Carmen. "Then we rent a car and cross into Mexico at the Ysleta-Zaragoza Port of Entry. There's an Oxxo a few blocks from the Mexican immigration checkpoint, where they'll have a car that we'll follow. They'll take care of the rental later."

"Sounds like we've been made," said Miguel.

"Something's up," said Carmen. "But orders are orders. They can always use us somewhere else."

"I'm walking to the door," said Miguel. "Be back in a few minutes."

He didn't like the sound of this at all, but it sure as hell beat spending a long stretch of time, possibly the rest of his life, in a US prison. He wasn't sure how US authorities would treat them. Like espionage agents? Miguel had no intention of finding out. He let go of the cart and made his way to the parking lot.

Miguel steered their compact rental car toward one of the two lanes open at the US side of the Ysleta-Zaragoza crossing. Only three vehicles in front of them. This was it. He never imagined it would happen so fast. Ten thirty in the morning, he was shopping at El Supermercado in Detroit. Three thirty in the afternoon, they were on a plane. Nine in the evening, after a one-hour stop in Dallas, they sat in a car a few hundred meters from Mexico under bright stadium-level lighting.

The US Customs and Border Patrol booth on the way into Mexico was a formality—or so they had been told. Maybe a few questions. If you traveled with young children, they might request the child's passport. Human trafficking was big business these days.

When they reached the CBP booth, he lowered the window and smiled politely at the agent, who nodded but didn't really show an interest in them one way or the other.

"Just need to scan your passports," said the agent.

They had been told that, due to a perceived heightened safety threat to Americans along the border, CBP would scan their passports to keep a record of US citizens in Mexico. He handed over both of their passports, which had been stashed in one of the cupholders. The agent scanned both quickly and handed them back.

"How long do you anticipate staying in Mexico?" asked the agent.

"We're visiting my aunt and uncle. One week, at most. They might come back with us to spend a few months in Detroit. They've never been to the US."

The agent typed a quick line before nodding at them like he'd been listening. "Careful down there. It's been a little active. Not against visitors. But there's something shaking up with the cartel. Listen to your aunt and uncle. I'm sure they know the deal."

I guess he was *listening.*

"Will do. I think that's why they finally decided to maybe visit us," said Miguel.

"Not a bad time to get out of Ciudad Juárez," said the agent. "Not that Detroit's any better."

"Good point," said Miguel.

They drove the few hundred meters to the Mexican immigration plaza, where they pulled right up to one of the immigration officers.

"Passports, please," said officer.

He handed them over. The officer took a quick look at each before stamping them.

"Do you have your digital tourist card or a printed copy?" said the officer.

"Yes. They're on our phones," said Miguel, Carmen reaching over to hand them to him.

The officer waved them off. "Just as long as you have them," he said, returning their passports. "How long will you be staying?"

"Hopefully not longer than a week," said Miguel. "My tío and tía are thinking of coming back with us to spend a few months visiting. We have a lot of family in the Detroit area."

"Very nice," said the officer. "Do they live inside the city here?"

"Mascareñas. Close to the Home Depot."

"That's a quiet area. It's been a little hectic down here lately."

"We heard," said Miguel.

"I recommend you stay on Avenida Ejercito Nacional as far as you can before you have to turn north. Just follow this road. It turns into la Avenida a few kilometers west," said the officer.

"Gracias," said Miguel.

A moment later, they were on their way, the brightly lit border fading behind them. The distinctive red-and-orange **Oxxo** sign appeared ahead of them. Carmen called their cartel contact and had a quick conversation.

"Pull up behind the SUV parked next to OXXO," she said. "We're going to follow them inside a small warehouse, where they'll provide further instructions."

"I'm relieved to be back home," said Miguel.

She didn't bother to reply. Their business relationship had ended after she passed along the instructions. He followed the black SUV several blocks to a fenced-in lot lit by a single light pole at its entrance. The SUV rolled up to the middle of three warehouses, the bulb in the light above the open bay door barely illuminating the vehicle. They followed it inside the dark bay, the door rolling shut behind them. Once the door slammed closed, someone turned on the lights. Nothing but broken crates and rusty equipment. A nice front.

Four men got out of the SUV, one of them waving Miguel and Carmen over to the brightly lit office, where they were told to take a seat at a desk facing a man wearing a suit. Not a cheap one, either. Crisply pressed. Nice gold watch on his left wrist.

"Welcome back," said the man.

"I'm relieved to be back," said Miguel.

"We'll see."

"Qué?"

The door behind the man opened; three heavily armed men dressed in body armor burst in. Their vests displayed the words Guardia Nacional. The four men from the SUV had pistols drawn, badges now displayed on their belts.

"Miguel Gonzales Lopez and Carmen Lucia Rodriguez. You are under arrest. The details will be provided at a central federal processing station in Mexico City," said the man, before nodding at the officers behind the two of them. "Let's reset for the next batch. Another couple just passed through the US side. It's going to be a busy few days."

The whole thing had been a setup. Hundreds would pass through the Ysleta-Zaragoza crossing and be taken into custody. The entire network had been compromised. He glanced at Carmen.

"Don't look at me," she said.

His eyes darted to her lap, where she held a knife. *Don't do it.* Too late. She lurched across the desk, the knife slashing inches from the National Guard detective's face. A single gunshot knocked her sideways, spraying half of her head across the wall next to the desk. Every rifle turned to Miguel.

"We're not going to have any problems with you, are we?"

He shook his head. The detective, or whoever he was, nodded at the men behind Miguel.

"Send the next batch to warehouse two. It's going to take us some time to clean this up."

CHAPTER 61

Anya Fiedrick took her cappuccino and sat toward the back of her local neighborhood coffee shop—a quiet, unassuming place she'd frequented for as long as she'd kept an apartment in Miami. Annoyingly, her preferred table at the back was currently occupied by a middle-aged Latino couple. Maybe Cuban. She couldn't say, but it was as good a guess as any. It *was* Miami, after all. They looked very comfortable together. Probably out for the afternoon while their kids sat in day care or school. One less direction to worry about.

She checked her phone. The flight out of Miami to Buenos Aires was on schedule. Still not time to head to the airport. The nonstop flight left around nine tonight and landed around six in the morning. She hated airports, even though they did provide a level of security she couldn't guarantee anywhere else in the US, outside of a True America safe house. And, given the events of the past three days, she couldn't rely on any level of safety or security.

The yacht had vanished. Video footage retrieved from several businesses and the marina suggested that Garrett Mann's task force had tried but failed to board the boat. They'd clearly made it out of the marina and into the bay. Recordings of Saint Petersburg police and Coast Guard transmissions didn't indicate that the boat had crashed or been recovered; they'd made it out of the bay into the Gulf of Mexico. But nobody seemed to be able to cast any light on what had happened once the yacht escaped the bay. And that was the problem.

Fiedrick and her small team in Miami had been Furst's backup plan if things went south in Tampa. And things had most definitely gone to shit at the marina. But she had no information beyond their hasty departure during Hurricane Josephine. Did they capsize and sink during the storm? She doubted it. Josephine's power was aimed at the Florida Panhandle. The yacht's captain was a seasoned mariner. If pressed to depart during the storm, he would have slipped due south and dealt with some very brutal, but survivable, weather.

She couldn't envision any scenario in which Mann's team boarded the yacht under those conditions once the boat had left the dock. Fiedrick checked a specialized app on her phone. Nothing. True America was either finished or in hiding for now. She'd wait this out in Argentina at an apartment she'd arranged a few years ago. A safe house. If True America came back online, she'd fly back to the US. If not, she'd vanish.

A couple walked into the coffee shop, the woman turning to lock the door behind her. Shit. Fiedrick glanced over her left shoulder at the counter, which was now empty. No baristas. No manager. She slid her hand into the purse at her side and gripped the compact Glock hidden in a customized holster inside.

"Not a good idea," said a voice from behind her.

She glanced over her shoulder; the couple at her usual table were pointing pistols at her head. Not even keeping them concealed. Just aiming them straight at her head. She recognized them from a briefing years ago. Leftovers from the last True America struggle.

Fiedrick scanned the rest of the coffee shop. Nobody was alarmed. Nobody seemed to care. The couple who'd entered the shop approached her, the woman aiming a pistol at her head. Fiedrick placed both of her hands on the table. Everyone else just kept drinking their coffee. Shit. They were all part of the task force!

"Anya Fiedrick?" said the man walking toward her.

She nodded slowly.

"I'm Special Agent Garrett Mann," he said, before the two of them moved chairs to her table and sat down.

"And I assume I'm under arrest?" said Fiedrick.

"Do you want to be?" said Mann.

Interesting. They needed her.

The rest of the shop patrons got up and moved their chairs around her table—removing their hats, wigs, and various disguises. She now recognized more than a few of them. Luke Turner. Jessica Mayer. Shit. ARTEMIS. They'd identified her apartment and watched her for a few days while she waited on word from the yacht and meticulously planned her departure from the United States.

"We don't really need you," said Mann. "We have DOMINION. That network is being dismantled as we speak. Greely and everyone on the yacht is dead. You're the only link to the airliner bombings. I mean, we have video of you in Miami, watching the boarding of a flight that never made it to the terminal. We even have footage of you taking video of people boarding the flight. There's nobody left to take the blame. Except you."

"What do you want?" asked Fiedrick.

"Everything," said the woman seated next to him. "From start to finish."

Fiedrick considered a smart-ass response, but the woman placed a small serrated blade on the table before she spoke.

"It's either everything, or I work you over with this for a few hours out back," said the woman.

"What's in it for me?"

"I don't work you over for a few hours out back," she said.

"Immunity?" said Fiedrick.

"Depends on what you can offer," said Mann.

"The Russians," said Fiedrick. "But I'll need some serious protection if I screw them over."

Mann placed his badge on the table. "Best I can do in writing is US federal witness protection. But if you crack the Russian angle open for us, we'll keep you safe. You have my word on that."

"What about them?" said Fiedrick, nodding at his team.

Mann turned to the woman next to him. Fiedrick assumed she was Cata Serrano.

"She's the only one I'm worried about," said Mann. "You good?"

Serrano shrugged. "I say we kill her in the alley, cut her into pieces, and drop her parts in dumpsters all around Miami—but if you're willing to give her a chance, I can roll with that for now."

"Deal?" said Mann.

Fiedrick nodded. "Deal."

Mann pulled out his phone and sent a quick text. Sirens wailed in the distance a few seconds later, getting closer. A lot of sirens.

"The Russians are watching the coffee shop," said Mann.

"They're watching everything," said Fiedrick.

"Which is why we're going to put a hundred or so police officers and federal agents in the neighborhood," said Mann. "And we're hitting a few dozen of their clubs and hangouts throughout the city."

"Sounds like I'm important," said Fiedrick.

"Don't oversell yourself," said Mann. "If you fuck with us, we'll drop you off in Sunny Isles Beach with your ankles broken."

Sunny Isles Beach was known as "Russian Miami" for a reason. She wouldn't last ten minutes there after this debacle, even with two good ankles.

Fiedrick was at their mercy. For now.

CHAPTER 62

Serrano stared out at the Mediterranean from their seaside table. Not as beautiful as Mexico's beaches, but much more relaxing. The waves lapped along the beach instead of crashing against the surf. Or maybe it was just the fact that she wasn't in Mexico, where she'd known nothing but struggle and pain from her earliest memories. She'd never told anyone about her dad, who'd been a cop. A traffic cop who pulled over the wrong car. Killed by the cartel before she could even learn to say the word *papá*. She hadn't known why her mom had lived alone with her until she was in elementary school. She sipped her orange juice. Fresh squeezed.

"You look like you're a thousand miles away," said Mann.

She nodded, still staring at the glistening water. "Probably more like six thousand. Sorry."

"No. You just take it all in. Pretend I'm not here."

"Hard to pretend you're not here," she said.

For more reasons than the fact that he attended to her like a doting concierge. Five days into their vacation in Nice, and she was about to read him the riot act. Not that she didn't appreciate the attention. He was just playing it too safe. Which she appreciated. But didn't. A tough balance to negotiate. He'd made it plain enough lately that he had feelings for her. And she'd done the same. But they'd spent the past couple of years in a purely business relationship. Neither one of them seemed to want to break through that barrier.

Their breakfast arrived, delivered by no fewer than six waiters—drawing attention from the rest of the well-dressed seaside crowd. Rich people who probably did this several times a year thinking she and Mann must be Russian oligarchs. Or worse. She wasn't sure what *worse* meant. What was worse in public than a rich Russian? A rich Mexican?

"We definitely overordered," said Mann. "But you only live once."

"That's so cliché," said Serrano.

"And stupid," said Mann.

"Kind of the same thing," she said. "But it would be a shame to waste this . . . abundance."

"It would," said Mann. "You've earned it."

There he went again. Didn't he see what he'd accomplished? What they'd accomplished?

"We've earned it," said Serrano. "Not another word. Just eat and enjoy."

Mann took the hint, even if it sounded more like a threat. He dived into the croissant plate, the butter already melting into the tiny openings in the bread. Several fruit preserves in small glass containers awaited him, each identified by a small folded piece of thick paper in front of it. Serrano went for the seafood tray. Thin salmon slices, lemon aioli, and capers—rolled into dill-infused crepes. She hadn't varied from this breakfast since she'd first tried it. He'd move on to those next. This was their morning ritual. And he loved it.

Cata tensed, placing her silverware on her plate. He scanned the seaside tables and the beach. Son of a bitch. Berg and Bauer strolled hand in hand along the waterline. *Seriously?*

"Sorry," he said. "I have no idea what they're doing here."

"Following us—apparently," she said.

"Should we just get it over with?"

"Probably," said Serrano.

Mann got up and approached them. "Fancy meeting you here. Staying nearby?"

"Funny," said Berg. "Unfortunately, our budget doesn't include five-star hotels on the Mediterranean. Five-stars a few blocks back."

"Glad to hear you're not suffering," said Mann, his eyes glancing at their hands, which were still locked together.

"She's not exactly sure this is a good idea," said Berg.

Mann laughed. "Sounds familiar. Care to join us? We've ordered too much. As usual. My fault entirely. I'm still navigating this."

"Briefly," said Bauer. "We're still navigating this as well."

Berg and Bauer joined them for breakfast, which seemed to put Cata at ease. When the next round of coffee arrived, Berg raised his espresso cup.

"To a narrow victory and those who made it possible—whoever they may be."

"Victory?" said Serrano.

"Did you see the news?" said Berg.

"We've been avoiding it," said Mann.

"Tight election," said Bauer. "But the late-October surprise sealed it. Someone leaked everything to the press about LABYRINTH, DOMINION, and True America's ties to the opposition party a few weeks before the election. The swing states just barely nudged the needle, but it was enough. Unfortunately, Trent Summers, Gary Smith, and Kara Hill weren't available for comment."

"A real shame," said Mann.

"And the Juárez Cartel?" said Serrano.

"The Juárez Cartel, as we knew it a few months ago, has been entirely wiped out," said Berg. "Somehow, their entire communications network was compromised. They can't seem to hide from our drones or the Mexican government counter-narcotics teams. Unfortunately, the Sinaloa Cartel and Zetas have moved in—but they're killing each other at a record pace. And rumor has it that their phones might be infected with the same virus that gave us—I mean, someone—the Juárez Cartel's locations."

"What's O'Reilly up to?" asked Mann.

"The same," said Berg. "Won't take credit for anything. Plans to retire in three months, like she did six years ago. Tap-dancing so you can enjoy yourselves."

"She's a piece of work," said Mann.

"A piece of work that won't be appreciated for a long time," said Berg. "Like all the greats."

"We should get going," said Bauer.

Berg drained the rest of his espresso. "Thank you for the hospitality. Don't hesitate to reach out. I think you're both in the clear, but in this business . . . you can never tell."

"And what business is that?" Serrano asked.

"The kind of business where you don't always follow the rules," said Berg. "Where you stretch the limits as far as you can to win."

When they were finally alone again, she grabbed his hand. "That was a job offer, right?"

"I suspect so," said Mann.

"I'm done for now," she said.

"For now?" he said, squeezing her hand.

"There's a lot more work to be done," said Serrano. "Just not now."

"Where? When?"

"Out there?" said Serrano. "Always."

"Did Berg or Bauer get to you somehow?"

"No. But people like Emily and Rico never rest. There's always another threat brewing. They're the only thing standing between—"

"Good and evil?" said Mann.

"It's not that simple."

"No. It isn't."

"You sound deflated," said Serrano. "Sorry."

"For what?"

"For not being what you were looking for?" said Serrano.

Mann stifled a laugh. She had no idea.

"This is funny?" said Serrano.

"No. You're exactly what I've been looking for," said Mann. "I'd just like a few months off. I'm tired."

"Me, too."

"Then let's just relax for a while. There's no rush to save the world."

ABOUT THE AUTHOR

Steven Konkoly is a *Wall Street Journal* and *USA Today* bestselling author, a graduate of the US Naval Academy, and a veteran of several regular and elite US Navy and Marine Corps units. He has brought his in-depth military experience to bear in his fiction, which includes *A Clean Kill* and *A Hired Kill* in the Garrett Mann series; *Wide Awake*, *Coming Dawn*, and *Deep Sleep* in the Devin Gray series; *The Rescue*, *The Raid*, *The Mountain*, and *Skystorm* in the Ryan Decker series; the speculative postapocalyptic thrillers *The Jakarta Pandemic* and *The Perseid Collapse*; the Fractured State series; the Black Flagged series; and the Zulu Virus Chronicles. Konkoly lives in central Indiana with his family. For more information, visit www.stevenkonkoly.com.